THE
SLEEP
OF
REASON

**David Derbyshire
and Mark Rowley**

Legend Press Ltd, 51 Gower Street, London, WC1E 6HJ
info@legendpress.co.uk | www.legendpress.co.uk

Contents © David Derbyshire and Mark Rowley 2022
The right of the above authors to be identified as the authors of this work
has been asserted in accordance with the Copyright, Designs and Patents
Act 1988. British Library Cataloguing in Publication Data available.

Print ISBN 978-1-80031-0-124
Ebook ISBN 978-1-80031-0-131
Set in Times. Printing managed by Jellyfish Solutions Ltd
Cover design by Rose Cooper | www.rosecooper.com

Printed and bound by CPI Group (UK) Ltd, Croydon CR0 4YY

Sir Mark Rowley's highly successful 31-year career in policing included posts as Chief Constable of Surrey; Assistant Commissioner at the Metropolitan Police; and lastly, head of UK Counter Terrorism Policing. Globally recognised for his leadership expertise in national security and policing, after retiring in 2018 Sir Mark was knighted in the Queen's Birthday Honours for his 'exceptional contribution to national security at a time of unprecedented threat and personally providing reassuring national leadership through the attacks of 2017'.

David Derbyshire is an award-winning national newspaper journalist and has written features for *The Sunday Times*, *The Times*, the *Guardian*, *Daily Mail*, *Daily Telegraph* and the *Observer*. He was the 2004 Medical Journalist of the Year, and was joint winner of the 2008 Press Gazette Environmental Press Awards campaign of the year.

Visit David at
www.davidderbyshire.co.uk
or on Twitter
@dderbyshire
or Instagram
@dgderbyshire

To Helena and Alison

'The sleep of reason produces monsters.'

Francisco Goya

DAY 1

Wednesday Morning

Chilton Park, Kent

The queue had paused, so Zahra took the opportunity to close her eyes and listen. It was a game she had played as a young girl, and one she turned to regularly during the moments of tedium that occupied so much of her sixteen-year-old life. She slipped her hands into the pockets of her donkey jacket and focused. The clanking of the ride machinery, as if an iron bar was being dragged along kerbstones, dominated her soundscape, but not enough to drown out the barbs of the gobby group of girls behind her taking turns to damn each of their absent friends. She listened harder and caught the burble of a blackbird staking out its territory from the clump of young silver birches and evergreen shrubs planted alongside the queue.

They'd queued under the scruffy winter skies for more than an hour now, far longer than her brother Jawad had predicted, lurching forward, spreading out and then bunching up again like an immense concertina. Around them were miserable attempts to decorate the ride in fibreglass and concrete. An upturned telephone kiosk, now pink rather than poppy red, lay alongside a bored sabre-toothed tiger while, nearby, a blonde Viking stood proudly with one boot on the neck of a tentacled alien. For a theme park ride, the theme was a complete mystery, thought Zahra.

Her initial excitement at joining the queue for Notorious had quickly given way to boredom and then frustration as the skies had begun to unleash a fine but persistent drizzle. But now, finally near the front of this interminable line, the listlessness in Zahra's stomach was being pushed aside by the blossoming of nervous anticipation.

Jawad, dressed in a lumberjack jacket and black jeans, was at the front of their group with her mother and Jawad's friend Imran. Zahra was at the back, next to her closest friend Maryam.

'You nervous?' Maryam asked softly.

'Nah.' That was a lie, of course. The bravado with which she'd agreed to come to the park on her school's inset day was wearing thin, but she did not want to lose face in front of her brother and particularly not in front of his friend. She sneaked a glance at Imran laughing effortlessly with her brother, with his immaculate hair and black leather jacket. And those eyes, those scintillating eyes, that always seemed to ignite when she approached.

The roller coaster screeched to a stop. A man in an emerald sweatshirt kicked at a pedal at the back of the train, releasing the restraints which flipped over the passengers' heads, letting them clamber out on the opposite side from the queue. As the line surged again, Imran, Jawad and her mother walked into the stalls, ready to get on the next train. Zahra's cousins and Jawad's friends filled the rest of the stalls, leaving no space for her or Maryam.

Zahra's mother turned to face her. An effervescent woman, always quick to laugh, she seemed somehow even more radiant surrounded by her family and their friends.

'Sorry, love,' she mouthed, 'you get the next ride, we'll wait at the exit.'

Zahra nodded. That was fine. She didn't want her mum – or Imran – on the same ride anyway. She wasn't convinced her language would be appropriate for her mother, and she was terrified that Imran would see her being sick.

#

On the platform, Gareth Fletcher flattened his oily hair and gave a thumbs up to the woman in the control cabin. At her command, the eight cars rolled out of the platform to be yanked up the slope to the first drop. Fletcher slipped his left hand into his trouser pocket to rest his fingers around the metal that lay invitingly inside.

Notorious had two trains running at once and Fletcher had ten seconds before the other rolled into the station. A gust of pine disinfectant filled his nostrils and his gaze fell upon a splatter of vomit next to the rail which the cleaners had overlooked. It wasn't worth reporting, but it irritated him. Why couldn't people do their jobs properly? Lazy bastards. *Lazy black bastards*, he added to himself, like a reflex.

He glanced down the track as the other train began to creep into the station and he slid his hand into his pocket again. The train was seven seconds away. Maybe this was the time. Then, as he surveyed the queue, he spotted a middle-aged Asian woman with a group of seven or eight young men and teenage girls. His heart leapt. The men were full of bravado, laughing and pushing each other, showing off in front of the girls. He kept watching. *Indian? Maybe Pakistani or Bangladeshi?* From the head coverings on the woman and two girls, they were probably Muslims, he thought. Fletcher watched for a few moments, then glanced around the other passengers waiting to board. No little kiddies. That was good. No coppers. No squaddies. No heroes.

And then the fire raged again, erupting from the pit of his stomach, ripping through his chest and into his head. He could feel his brain pushing out against the inside of his skull. Too

11

many thoughts, and so much disgust. And this fire, that made him alive and sterilised his doubts and fears, it would soon start to purify the world.

The coaster rolled alongside the platform and juddered to a rest. Once the passengers were out of the carriage and through the exit gate, he pressed the button on the wall to open the stalls, allowing the next passengers to get into their seats. The Asian group were laughing as they settled down. The middle-aged woman couldn't reach her restraint, so Fletcher tugged it into place for her. She thanked him and smiled. He smiled back. *Nice eyes*, he thought.

The fire was burning still, not as rampant as a moment ago, but still streaming through his arms and fingers. He'd never felt so vital. He had ultimate control over these people, over who would live and who would die. And after it was all over, he would take his place in history, one of the growing army of warriors who had stood up and fought to secure an existence for his people and a future for white children.

He watched the woman settle into the seat. Not now. Not until they'd been round one time. One last time.

#

The ride was so much worse than Zahra had imagined. The restraint was too tight, her back hurt and now it was pelting down.

As the car began the steep ascent, she screwed her eyes tight and was aware of nothing but the blast of bitter, wet air on her cheeks. The clanking stopped and Zahra knew she was at the top but resisted the urge to peek. Then her body was slammed into the seat and her stomach entered her head as she plummeted. She battled to hold her head still as the train looped and twisted and rolled, and then panicked as she realised she was momentarily upside down and only the restraint was stopping her from popping out of the car like a cork from a bottle.

And then it slowed and stopped with a jolt, and it was over.

She swore quietly. And again loudly. Maryam laughed.

'Your face. Brilliant. Wish I had my phone.'

Zahra wiped away the beads of perspiration on her forehead and self-consciously adjusted her hijab. The coaster had come to a rest ten metres before the station on a flat section of track. The train in front – the one with her mother and brother and his mates – appeared to have stopped in the station, but passengers were still in their seats. Zahra's eyes darted along the train to find Imran, but its headrests made it impossible to see the occupants clearly.

The guy in the emerald shirt was ambling up the platform alongside the train in front, bending over every few seconds. It looked like he was fiddling with something, Zahra thought. She squinted. The man had something in his hand.

And then someone screamed. It could have been Maryam. It could have been Zahra. Now that her senses had begun to gather, she could see clearly that the object in the man's hand was a knife. At that moment, he lunged towards one of the passengers. An arc of something sloppy and dark flew up in the air and someone screamed again.

For a moment there was just the rushing of blood pumping around Zahra's skull. She experienced a floating sensation, as if she was looking down on herself, clawing at the buckle and restraint. And then the true horror of what was happening in the carriages ahead of her crashed into her mind with a force that robbed her of breath. Her mum, her brothers, her friends, they were in the train in front, and they were trapped by the ride's safety restraints. And that man was attacking them where they sat, unable to free themselves.

She cried out, breaking the silence and yanking her mind back into her body. Nausea welled in her guts. She tore at the buckle and opened it. But still the restraint wouldn't budge.

The attendant leant forward again. Zahra couldn't see who

he was attacking, just the backs of their headrests and the very tops of their heads. A pair of hands flew upwards from the seat to push him away, and then, instinctively, their owner held them over their face in a futile gesture of defence. The man slashed the blade at the exposed part of their body under their arms. An animal howl filled Zahra's ears.

Maryam's eyes were wide open with terror. 'Stop him,' she yelled. Zahra wished she'd had the sense to call out too. The queue of passengers didn't seem to have moved and the woman in the cabin was still in her seat. Couldn't they see what was going on?

The man in the emerald shirt continued to move in slow motion. He stooped in front of the next car and again a hand reached out, fingers splayed, clearly the desperate attempt to stop him. But the hand met the knife and there was another jet of blood and, with it, a chunk of something fleshy.

Zahra's heart pounded. Sweat was trickling down her back and her head was hot. And still the man kept moving down the train in front. Was that her mum? The train was too far away for her to see clearly, and her vision was blurred with the sweat she kept desperately trying to blink away. But it was a woman's arm that had shot up and, for a second, she caught a chilling glimpse of her mother's hijab.

Zahra cried out again, and then, finally, there was movement in the queue of people waiting in the stalls. A bald, middle-aged man yelled at his family to stand back, then dodged under the wooden barrier and picked up the pole the attendant had been using minutes before to check the height of the children on the ride.

'Get back,' the father shouted over the train. The attendant looked up and stopped, his hands by his side, his blade still gripped tightly. For a second, no one moved. Then he dropped the blade, which landed with a metallic clatter, and sprinted along the platform and through the exit gate that led to the rest of the park.

#

Fletcher felt only a crushing urge to run. He wasn't supposed to run, that hadn't been the plan. He was supposed to have stayed at the ride, singling out the Muslims first, but also targeting other Asians and blacks if he could, taking them out one by one until he was stopped by the police or the army or some have-a-go-hero, until he could fulfil his destiny as a martyr. For weeks he had thought of nothing apart from the moment when his suffering would finally be over, not in an empty gesture, but a statement so bold it would trigger an earthquake around the world. But surrounded by the gore and the blood, all those carefully drawn-out plans had evaporated. It was not that he wanted to live, he simply did not want to die, not there, not then.

No one was following as he sprinted, head down, through the rain. He pulled the sweatshirt over his head, noticing as he did that his hands were smeared crimson. He wiped them on the material before throwing it into a hedge. Free from his uniform, wearing a long-sleeved grey T-shirt, he pushed through the crowd, who were unaware of the raw, desperate scenes two hundred metres away, and made his way to the staff entrance.

The winter sun had finally emerged from the curtains of cloud and was casting honeyed beams of light on the theme park and the distant North Downs. It was beautiful. It was England at its most glorious and it was worth fighting for. Fletcher pulled out his key ring, fumbled with the padlock and then yanked his bike free from the rack. Raising a hand to the security guard as he passed, he cycled on, propelled by adrenaline and wild giddiness, around the barrier and out of the park.

DAY 1

Wednesday Afternoon

Chilton Park, Kent

Detective Superintendent Sophie Gabriel spotted the staff entrance to Chilton Park a fraction of a second after her driver passed it.

'Bugger, it's there – back there,' she said. Her driver, Detective Sergeant Jorell Campbell, braked hard and swerved into a lay-by, using it to do an imprudent U-turn across four lanes before heading back up the road. Ten seconds later, he threw the Volvo around the corner into the narrow track, sending a water bottle tumbling across the back seat.

Campbell opened his window and waved his ID card at the rat-faced security man on the barrier and was ushered through, past two cars and a TV news van parked on the verge. Two journalists clutching notepads shouted out as they drove under the lifted barrier, but Gabriel didn't catch the questions.

A high-profile murder like this came with a wave of adrenaline for Gabriel – usually followed by an even bigger backwash of guilt that the excitement came at the expense of other people's misery. Three years earlier, a colleague had returned from a trip to Chicago with a T-shirt for Gabriel depicting a corpse and the slogan: *When your life ends, our work begins.* It was crass, but lurking beneath the joke was an irrefutable truth.

As their journey from London had progressed, Gabriel had been conscious of a growing thrill; a sensation she had missed during these last few weeks trapped behind her desk. Crime scene visits were rare now for Gabriel and she had grabbed the opportunity to travel to Chilton Park with almost indecent relish.

Being at the park would make it easier for her to visualise the crime scene as she directed the investigation in the days to follow. She had googled Chilton Park as she waited for Campbell to pick her up. It had emerged thirty years ago on a former gasworks in the shadow of the Dartford Crossing thanks to a healthy sprinkling of European regeneration cash and was the UK's fourth most popular theme park. It was handy for the M25 and good for the day trippers from East London and Kent, but, as Gabriel had discovered that morning, a pain to reach from the centre of the city. Even with a blue light, the drive had taken a frustrating fifty minutes. She had used the journey to make calls – getting updates from Kent Police control room and the duty detective inspector at the scene, discussing lines to take for the ravenous press and ensuring that the manhunt for this Fletcher was underway.

#

Campbell pulled up in the staff car park in a gap between a dirt-streaked van and an oversized SUV. Gabriel clambered out, twisting her body to negotiate the gap between the vehicles and stepping in a puddle, which seeped ooze over her left shoe.

Thirty to forty cars were squeezed into a scrappy patch of ground hidden from visitors. Behind her was the security barrier and hut, next to that a pole concreted into the ground and topped with a CCTV camera. Behind the barrier, another TV van had pulled up, the driver arguing with the security man who was still refusing to let the press through. The journalists shouted again to Gabriel, but she chose to ignore them. There was nothing to say yet that had not been in the press release issued half an hour earlier by Kent. She recognised a bulbous reporter as the crime specialist for the local news agency, probably sent down by one of the nationals, who had doorstepped her repeatedly during the Abu Mujahid business two years earlier. He was the last person she wanted to speak to now.

Their destination was at the end of a roughly asphalted path, bounded by a metal wire fence decorated with faded bindweed, a cruel echo of the summer on this stinging January day. Gabriel placed a hand against the rusting wires while she pulled off her shoe and rubbed at the grit clinging to her sodden tights. The fence had stained her hand and she carelessly brushed it clean against her jacket, realising too late that it had left a mark. One shoe down. One jacket down. At least the trousers were still in one piece, she thought.

To the left was a fir hedge littered with faded cans. Ahead, where the path swept to the left, a greyish animal scurried out from the hedge, sauntered across the path, turned to stare and then slowly squeezed itself through the fence and out of sight.

'Tell me that was a squirrel, Campbell,' said Gabriel.

'It was a squirrel, ma'am,' lied Campbell.

'Bollocks it was. That was a rat, wasn't it?'

'Yes, ma'am. But more spooked by us than we are of it.'

'Don't believe a word of it,' said Gabriel. 'That little shit wasn't scared of anyone. Did you see the look he gave you? That was the look of someone eyeing up dinner.'

They continued down the path. She led the way, taking easy big strides over the puddles while he scurried along in her wake.

Some people grow into their features as they age. Some try to cling to their youth. Gabriel had simply stopped caring quite so much. She was aware that her face was angular, her nose on the beaky side and her complexion pasty. Her hair, cut in a sharp bob, had been intended to soften her features, but it merely accentuated them, and she was stuck with it for now. At almost five foot nine inches, her height had advantages when challenging suspects and male colleagues, but she considered herself too gangly, more like a freshly sprouted adolescent than a woman in the grip of middle age. She wore a simple charcoal suit, which looked like Marks & Spencer but was actually something more expensive from a designer store in Chelsea.

She and Campbell made a contrasting pair. With his thickset features, he looked every inch – or rather every five foot seven inches – of reliability. People looked at Campbell and the word that sprang to their minds was 'safe'. That was a useful attribute in a sergeant, thought Gabriel. It meant people opened up to him.

From the waft of rancid cooking fat, it was clear they were approaching the park kitchens. They had a couple of minutes before they would be at the crime scene, so she ran through the facts with Campbell. She planned to talk to the victims' families later and needed to be on top of the details.

'Gareth Fletcher, white, twenty-one, lives alone,' she said. 'One previous for minor assault. No known political affiliations. And – surprise, surprise – a bit of a loner. His colleagues said, and I quote, "He kept himself to himself".'

Campbell grinned. It was a running joke in SO15 that every serial killer and terrorist was described by neighbours and work colleagues as a loner who kept themselves to themselves.

Gabriel continued. 'In addition to this startling insight, according to his nearest and dearest – or his boss at least – Fletcher had never expressed a particular urge to murder anyone. Until today when he took it upon himself to stab a dozen fee-paying passengers, mostly Asian, before fleeing via the staff car park.'

She looked around, trying to visualise the scene two hours earlier as Fletcher sprinted down this path. What was his plan?

Or maybe he had no plan. Maybe this was a spontaneous act of barbaric cruelty fuelled by God knows what petty grievances.

Her phone rang. It was DI Eva Bose from the office, who had been updating her all morning. As ever, she had proved capable and succinct, passing on what was vital, and shielding Gabriel from the irrelevant. Nothing was more irritating for Gabriel at the initial stages of an investigation than being deluged with trivia.

'Eva. We've just arrived. There's a CCTV camera at the staff entrance,' said Gabriel. 'Have Kent Police got the video yet?'

'Yes, ma'am,' said Bose. 'Fletcher came past the security barrier three minutes after the attack ended. He grabbed his bike from the rack and cycled north. The closest council CCTV is half a mile down the road. We've got a team pulling it from the local authority.'

'What about his phone? Anything from GPS or cell data?'

'Sadly not, ma'am,' said Bose. 'We've got his number, but the phone's been switched off since the attack. We're pulling historic phone records, of course, and ploughing through his regular contacts.'

Bugger, thought Gabriel. Phones had transformed investigations more than anything else since she had joined the force twenty years ago. The GPS running constantly in the background of smartphones meant it was possible to locate the owner to within a few hundred feet, either in real time or at any time during the last few weeks or months as long as the phone was on.

Bose continued: 'We've also got his bank details and an alert's in place, so we'll know the moment he uses a card or withdraws cash. We're pulling social media contacts as you've requested and fishing out any interesting sites he might have used.'

'Latest casualties?' Gabriel asked.

'Six now confirmed dead at the scene, one dead in the ambulance, three more serious at Thameside Hospital. The comms team have been deluged with media requests and there's a horde gathered outside the Yard following on from the three-line statement Kent Police put out earlier, so we've put out a holding statement. It says... hang on...' she rustled for a piece of paper, '...it says, "Terrorism is one motive being considered and the Met's counter terrorism detectives are working closely with colleagues from Kent on the initial investigation." That's it.'

'If that doesn't bore the pants off them, nothing will,' said Gabriel. She ended the call. She could see the trajectory of the coming media storm clearly in her head – with all its speculation, blame games and half-truths – and the thought of being thrust back in the spotlight again left her cold. But that was for later.

#

The scene-of-crime officers were at work in their white paper over-suits, inching like beetles over the ride's platform as a local uniformed constable waved Gabriel and Campbell through. Gabriel unzipped her go-bag – the pre-packed holdall that contained everything she might need at a crime scene – and yanked out a paper suit and rubber gloves.

The Notorious roller coaster train was still in the station, its yellow seats streaked with crimson. The anonymous lumps of six bodies lay on the platform, covered with plastic sheets. Empty body bags had been piled to one side. The air hung with the smell of new death – not the rotten meat odour that Gabriel knew from decomposing bodies, a smell that haunted your nose and clothes for hours, but the faintest tang of iron and faeces. The stench of the slaughterhouse.

Obscene trails of blood on the platform showed where victims had been pulled from their seats by the paramedics. There had clearly been some miserable work here as the ambulance crews battled to preserve flutters of life. As a younger officer, Gabriel had watched paramedics cut open chests of road accident victims still strapped in their seats in order to massage their hearts directly with gloved fingers, and she knew the reckless desperation of those last few moments.

One of the local PCs put down his roll of tape and came over.

'Morning, ma'am,' he said. He looked like he was going to throw up.

Gabriel directed her most amicable smile at him. *Poor kid. Looks about twelve. Probably got homework when he gets home tonight.*

'Where will I find the duty inspector?' Gabriel asked.

'She's with victim liaison and the key witness in the staff canteen, ma'am.' He waved towards the concrete buildings that Gabriel and Campbell had passed on their way to the ride.

'Thank you. This is a tough day for everyone, keep up the good work.' The constable smiled thinly as she walked off.

#

The smell of vinegar and stale cooking fat assaulted Gabriel as she walked into the canteen and began a silent headcount.

After meeting the duty inspector, Gabriel's initial reaction was positive. The first 999 calls had gone through to Kent Police, who had shut down the park and carried out the initial witness triage. The Kent DI running the show had the nous to keep the victims' families out of the public cafes, which appeared to be decorated with jolly pirates and woodland animals, and herd them into the less offensive staff canteen. Witnesses at the front of the queue who were unrelated to victims had been taken to another public cafe where their details and statements were taken down, while local police had sent home the rest after getting their details.

There were sixteen people slumped around the canteen tables, mostly nursing or ignoring cups of coffee. A couple of young women in their twenties were crying, another couple sat holding hands. Just like the victims on the ride, most seemed to be South Asian, Gabriel noted.

There was no obligation for Gabriel to talk to the victims' families but, from past experience, she knew a few moments of compassion now could pay dividends later. The last thing she needed was a victim's uncle going rogue on day four and whining to the press about the police.

Her voice, clear and penetrating with remnants of her native Mancunian vowels, silenced the murmurs almost immediately. She'd done a couple of these talks before, but never to so many people. The trick was to stay distant while looking sympathetic, to be thoughtful, but not to think too much. And to remember this was a performance.

'I'm Detective Superintendent Gabriel, from Scotland Yard's counter terrorism unit, and I am heading up the investigation into what's happened here today.' She paused, more for effect than anything.

'Please, let me start by saying I'm truly sorry for your losses and what you've all gone through. I can't begin to understand how you must be feeling. I appreciate this will be tough, but my colleagues will need to ask you questions about what happened here. We'll try to keep it as brief as possible.'

She paused again. Stay on autopilot, she told herself. Stay professional.

'What happened today was an act of evil. We know who has committed this crime and we are doing everything in our powers to find him and bring him to justice. It's looking like this was racially motivated and we're treating this as a potential terrorist attack.'

She paused to let them absorb what she was saying. The silence was dense and uncomfortable. 'I'm afraid I won't have time to speak to each of you in person, but each family here will be given their own family liaison officer. They'll be your point of contact with us and they'll help keep you informed with what's happening over the next few days and in the next few months. They're here to help you – please use them and speak to them about anything linked to what has happened here.

'I'll pass you over to the victim liaison team in a moment, who'll explain what we'd like to do next. But first, do any of you have any questions?'

A teenage girl with pretty brown eyes raised her left hand. She was sat with another girl of a similar age.

'Please,' said Gabriel.

The girl hesitated. 'I just wanted to know something about when we go home from here, when we go back to our families…' she said in a numbed voice.

'Yes?'

'Will we be safe?' Again, the silence. Gabriel waited for a few seconds.

'What is your name?'

'Zahra.' Gabriel sensed the girl had been about to add 'Miss' but had stopped herself in time. 'My mother and brother…' She couldn't finish.

Gabriel studied the girl. Her coat was neatly folded on the table and she was dressed in a pink and black patterned jumper. Her large eyes were rimmed with red. She wore an elegant grey and silver hijab. How old was she? Fifteen? Sixteen?

Gabriel's heart felt like it had been stifled. There was something about this girl. For a second, the invisible shield she'd erected before her, the shield that let her stay detached and distant, a shield created not from cynicism but from Gabriel's fear of unleashing everything she'd tried to bury, finally fell.

She breathed deeply. Why did the dead have the unerring knack of popping up when least wanted? She couldn't afford to be dwelling on this now. Save the past for later. Her palms were sweaty. Her chest was getting tight. This was rubbish. Come on.

She took a third deep breath. 'Zahra, I'm so sorry for your loss. We don't know why that man did what he did. We may never know. But what we do know is that he represents a sickness, but it's a rare sickness, and a sickness that we will do everything in our powers to wipe out from society. These people want to create fear, discord and distrust. And we'll do everything we can to stand up to them. And to get you home safely. Our liaison team will be there to support you – and look out for you. And we will get justice for your mother and brother.'

The girl said nothing.

#

Life hangs on such a narrow thread, thought Gabriel as she walked out of the ladies. Trivial decisions in a fairground queue or in an ops room have life-changing and life-ending implications. But why had that been so tough? She'd done plenty of death speeches before. Why had she needed to steady herself in the loo?

'That was good, ma'am,' said Campbell. There was a hint of multicultural London English in there, thought Gabriel, but it was still mostly old-school Estuary.

'You're right. Best pee I've ever had, Campbell, but not really any of your concern,' said Gabriel.

Campbell looked flummoxed for a second. 'I meant the words. What you said.'

Gabriel half-smiled grimly but said nothing. They were walking along a concrete path scoured with lines to create the illusion of paving. Waste bins on either side were overflowing with burger boxes.

What had just happened? A panic attack? No. She didn't have those. So, what was it? A wobble? A tug on memories that she'd dealt with long ago?

She'd spent the first half hour of the day, before getting the call to Chilton Park, on her weekly review into the whereabouts of Abu Mujahid, so perhaps she had unwittingly dredged up something from her subconscious. But that was ridiculous. She looked at Campbell – he hadn't spotted anything out of place.

'I can't imagine a more miserable way to spend a day than at a place like this,' said Gabriel, looking round at the silent rides. 'You got kids?'

'Two boys, ma'am. Seven and nine. They love these places.'

'I get why kids like it; they don't know any better. But grown-ups? Surely there's a better way to spend a wet Wednesday than queuing an hour for thirty seconds of vomit inducement? When did adults stop growing up?'

The question was rhetorical.

'What's your take on Fletcher? A lone actor?' Gabriel asked.

'Think so, ma'am.'

'And you're one hundred per cent sure this was a racist attack?' she said.

'Ninety-nine per cent,' said Campbell. 'Thirty people were on that coaster and Fletcher singled out ten. All were Asian or black, almost all were Muslim. He's walked past ten white people, maybe more, and ignored them.'

Gabriel said nothing. Racially motivated, yes. But working alone?

She looked back at the top of the ride, poking out from the tangled fingers of winter trees over her left shoulder. For a moment she allowed herself a glimmer of imagination and she put herself in its seats less than three hours ago. Trapped, unable to lift the restraint and with Fletcher approaching them. A vivid sense of fear, of powerlessness and panic engulfed her. This was truly the stuff of horror movies. It was too much, and Gabriel hurriedly bolted the doors of her imagination. The luxury of empathy would have to come later when she had the time to process these events.

She walked towards the park manager, a pallid man in his early fifties wearing a shabby suit who restlessly tapped his fingers against his thigh as he spoke. It was an irritating tic that drew Gabriel's eyes every few minutes.

'How long before I can let the families go home?' he

wittered. 'I've got head office coming up in thirty minutes and we need to know whether we can reopen tomorrow and what we can say to the press.'

Gabriel gave him a withering look.

'Tell you what, Mr…' She leaned forward deliberately to read his name badge, allowing her nose to get uncomfortably close to his sweaty face. 'Mr Foster, you can let them go when I say you can let them go. In the meantime, make sure they get food and some space. I noticed the families have yet to be offered any proper hospitality. Not much to ask given that one of your employees has just wiped out a significant number of their nearest and dearest, is it?'

The manager fell silent. Campbell looked uncomfortable. *Oh, Campbell. You're too nice for this job*, thought Gabriel.

'Let's focus on what's important, shall we? What can you tell me about Fletcher?' said Gabriel.

'Of course,' said the manager, flicking through a folder. 'Been with us for two months, good references, no absences and punctual. Bit of a loner.'

'Kept himself to himself, did he?' asked Gabriel.

'Exactly. But no complaints from staff or customers. He didn't have any particular friends, but Lisa, the girl he worked with, said—'

'Woman,' interrupted Gabriel.

'I'm sorry?'

'I assume that she was over eighteen, so she wasn't a girl, was she?'

'Er, no,' said the manager, flustered. 'Lisa, the *woman* he worked with, said he was pleasant enough.'

'Any signs of extreme or odd views?' asked Campbell. 'Any complaints of anti-Semitism? Islamophobia? Racism?'

'Of course not,' said the manager with indignation. 'We take our responsibilities seriously. We're an inclusive company.'

'I'm sure you are,' said Gabriel. The word inclusive was her current pet hate. It was a meaningless buzzword, like sustainable or diversity, trotted out as a virtue-signalling exercise.

'Did he have a locker?' asked Campbell.

'Of course, I'll take you to it now.'

The locker, in a corridor alongside the staff canteen, was empty aside from a copy of last week's *Daily Herald* and a half-drunk litre bottle of Coke. Gabriel lifted up the newspaper with a cautious finger, letting it drop with a slap.

She let the manager go and watched with detached amusement as he scuttled away, ear clamped to his mobile as he took orders from head office.

'Patronising tosser,' said Gabriel to Campbell. 'Let's go and talk to the SOCO boys.'

'Think you mean men, ma'am,' said Campbell, but under his breath and out of earshot.

#

New Scotland Yard, Victoria Embankment, London

Assistant Commissioner Steven Tennant ended the call to the National Security Adviser and swivelled his chair to face the Thames. He had read recently that the river was as clean as it had been since the Industrial Revolution and that otters and fish and porpoises were now splashing through the water like a scene from a Disney cartoon. But from the tenth floor, it looked the same dirty brown torrent, washing the secrets and filth away from London and out to the North Sea. He recalled a grim summer night, early on in his career, when he fished the body of a drunk out of the festering water, and even today the thought of the corruption and sewerage below the river surface left him uneasy.

He rubbed at his stubble with the back of his hand. Chris always told him off for doing that at home, insisting it made him look indecisive. He prodded the flesh under his jaw, conscious that it was too prolific, as were the bags around his grey eyes. He stared at the reflection in the window. His hair was thinning, in contrast to his waist which seemed to thicken every year, and his body moved too easily in the places where

28

it shouldn't and refused to move in the places it should. He was flabby and grey, he thought, like one of the plump pigeons perched on the ledge in front of him.

Tennant rose from the chair to stretch his legs and get a better view. The Met had moved to this refurbished office block on the Victoria Embankment in 2016 and installed the Counter Terrorism Policing Headquarters on the tenth floor. From here, eighty senior and support staff co-ordinated the work of thousands of counter terrorism officers in eleven regional units around the country. The biggest single part of this network was the London Counter Terrorism Command, also known as SO15 and based at the shiny, new Counter Terrorism Operation Centres twenty minutes' drive away in St Pancras. Working here at the Yard away from the action at CTOC was frustrating for Tennant at times, but the proximity to Whitehall, and having the rest of the Met's senior leadership team in the same building, outweighed the disadvantages.

New Scotland Yard was the Met's fourth HQ and, as Tennant's boss, the Met Commissioner, had pointed out more than once, technically should have been named New, New, New Scotland Yard. The interior had been decorated in corporate white and could have belonged to a bank. One of the few concessions to its new occupiers – aside from the rotating New Scotland Yard sign by the front doors – was in the toilets, where architects had displayed a rare sense of humour and decorated each cubicle with a historical police car livery.

The downside of the open office was lack of privacy. The lavatory cubicles were too small to change in, and more than once, Tennant had to ask his staff to stand guard while he slipped out of his suit in an empty meeting room before a press conference or public meeting. More than once, a DC had done a quick about-turn at the sight of the boss in his underpants.

The call to the National Security Adviser – the Prime Minister's adviser on terrorism – had gone well. Downing Street had called a COBRA crisis meeting for 3pm, but it would be brief, as it always was in the aftermath of an attack like this. There wasn't going to be much to report, particularly if this was the work of a lone actor, and brief was good in the current political climate.

COBRAs had been challenging enough before the general election. But over the last nine months, with the influx of People's Party members into the new coalition government, the point scoring had escalated to new heights of inanity. He threw his mind back to his last encounter with politicians: the National Security Council a couple of weeks earlier. These were supposed to be routine meetings, a chance for cabinet ministers to chew the fat with the heads of the security agencies – MI5, GCHQ, the Chief of the Defence Staff and SO15. But the agenda had been hijacked by Lesley Hogarth, the new deputy prime minister and leader of the People's Party, who had rounded on the director general of GCHQ over some spurious Russian cyberwarfare story in the Sunday papers. It had been frivolous and embarrassing.

Tennant glanced at his watch, a present from Chris last birthday. The PM would want an early briefing before COBRA within the hour. But before that, he needed his own update. The discovery that Sophie Gabriel was on the case was welcome news. He had not spoken directly to Gabriel for six months, but she always impressed him, and he kept one eye on her career. He pulled out his phone and pulled up WhatsApp. *Sophie*, he messaged. *Appreciate you're snowed under – anything you've got would be helpful before COBRA*. Technically, he shouldn't be speaking to Gabriel directly. There were three ranks between them, and Gabriel's commander would be livid if he found out he was arcing the chain of command. But what he didn't know wouldn't hurt him.

Ten minutes later, his phone buzzed.

'Sophie, good to hear from you,' he said. 'It's been a while. Ray well?'

'He's fine, sir,' said Gabriel. 'Still determined to sneak The Clash into the year seven music curriculum. So far the head of music doesn't seem to have noticed.' Tennant smiled. He'd met Gabriel's husband at a Christmas party a couple of years earlier and had instantly liked him. They'd spent ten minutes arguing over the merits of The Ramones.

'Sorry to arc like this, but I'm in Downing Street shortly,' said Tennant. 'What's your take? One for us?'

'Without a doubt, boss,' said Gabriel. 'Fletcher was clearly racially motivated.'

'And a lone actor?' There was more earnestness in his voice now. Tennant was generally a good sleeper, who rarely struggled to catch a decent seven hours a night, no matter how stressful the work. But the one issue that could play on his mind at 3am, when the house was still and Chris was gently wheezing in bed beside him, was the rise of a new, violent and organised extreme right.

Gabriel paused before answering. 'On the surface, yes,' she said. 'No live video stream, no social media, and from the early look into his background, no links to extreme right groups.'

Tennant sensed her doubt. 'But…?'

'But there's lots that doesn't fit the normal pattern. Lone actors usually like to go out with a bang – suicide by cop, or holed up with a hostage. They don't usually go to ground. And there's no note.'

'But nothing to suggest an accomplice, or that he was part of something bigger?'

'No.' She hesitated again. 'But he's not acting like your normal loner.'

'Not sure there's such a thing, Sophie,' said Tennant. 'Look – keep me posted and if there's any developments, anything to suggest this is more than a man with a grudge and a knife, let me know as soon as. And I'm happy to use unofficial channels if you are.'

He hung up. She was a bright officer. Her instincts were good and they'd saved him from humiliation in the past. He returned to his workstation and prepared for COBRA.

Eltham, South East London

Rod Houghton sat in the passenger seat of his car and clicked the refresh icon on the laptop. He pressed command and tab and the video-editing app came up, with Fletcher's face frozen in a grimace. This should have gone online two hours ago, but there was no way he could put it up in its current state.

He slipped the headphones on and reviewed his latest edit.

'In 1939, our country faced a threat from foreign invaders, determined to destroy the British people and the values that we hold dear – democracy, decency, fairness, pride.' Fletcher had done this bit well, thought Houghton. 'Today we face another threat just as great, but unlike 1939, this threat doesn't come from one country – it comes from one religion. A death cult that would subjugate our women and daughters, and wipe out a millennium of our laws with the laws based on a cruel, medieval faith…'

It went on. Every word carefully chosen by the boss. Every reference to the Muslims and every line vilifying the Jews, the blacks, the gays. Right up until the killer last line. 'And I've done this, I've made this ultimate sacrifice, I've given my life, in the name of the National Resistance Force.' A great line but now utterly useless thanks to Fletcher's cowardice. Houghton felt a stab of frustration.

He went back, playing the video at half-speed, then deleted the line 'I have given my life' before playing it again at full speed. Now the jump in picture was obvious and clumsy. Maybe he could use an image to hide the cut? He went to the *BBC News* coverage of the attack, screen-grabbed a still of the roller coaster and inserted it over the edit. That was better. Not perfect, but enough to go up. The laptop was connected to a burner phone he'd bought for this occasion.

The phone rang. The number was withheld. Houghton disconnected the headphones from the laptop and plugged them into his phone. 'It's me,' came the voice from the headphones. 'What the fuck happened?'

'He bottled it,' said Houghton.

'I thought you said he was under control.'

'It's not a fucking science,' he snapped. 'You can't predict what anyone will do under those circumstances.'

Silence. 'Has he made contact?'

'No, and he can't. He's on his own.'

Another pause. 'Are you compromised?'

'No,' said Houghton.

'And the video? Can you salvage it?'

'I'm recutting it now. Most of it is useable. I'm taking out the lines about martyrdom. What about phase two?' Even on this secure burner phone, Houghton was instinctively cautious.

'We're going ahead as planned. Still waiting for the organisers to confirm the date, but I'm hearing it's likely to be this weekend, possibly Saturday. And make sure they follow the script this time. Is Dougie ready?'

'Spoke to him earlier. He's okay. But…' Houghton paused. 'Go on?'

'Given what happened today, I'm going to go with him. Just to be on the safe side.'

There was silence. 'No fuck-ups. Understood?'

The line went dead.

#

Chilton Park, Kent
Gabriel slipped her phone into her jacket pocket and returned to the fairy-grotto themed cafe where the SOCO team had made a temporary home. Tennant was one of the decent ones. She'd first met him at a Met leadership training day where he was introducing the latest initiative on diversity. She, new and mouthy and working for the Directorate of Professional Standards, the body that investigates complaints about officers, had stood at the back of the conference room and

challenged him publicly. At lunch, Tennant had sought her out and, over a plate of weary ham and cheese sandwiches, they had continued the discussion. She didn't think she had told him he was talking batshit, but she had said something pretty close.

But she had immediately liked Tennant, and had respected his candour and humility, enough for her to stick her neck out for him a few months later. He subsequently claimed she had saved his skin and she did not disagree. Their paths had crossed a handful of times since then as she'd moved away from investigating corrupt officers into investigating terrorists at SO15. And two years ago, he had repaid the debt during the media whirlwind that followed the Abu Mujahid affair. The inquiry had hung over her for eighteen months as she had trodden water, unable to step away from the prying press, unable to shake the suspicion that colleagues and superiors viewed her as a lame duck. Tennant had covered her back, ensuring that she was not cast aside by a commissioner who was renowned for blowing with the wind to appease the media.

'Jesus Christ, Campbell,' muttered Gabriel as they took their seats at a table overshadowed by a mural of a five-foot-tall rabbit. A teenage boy handed them a polystyrene cup containing a warm brown liquid. Gabriel took the boy's word that it was coffee, took a sip and put it down quickly.

The lead SOCO joined them, ripping off his purple gloves as he sat.

'Fletcher dropped the knife when he fled the scene,' he said, putting his stubby nose into the coffee and rejecting it. 'It's spring-assisted with a four-inch stainless steel blade. Could have bought it legally online for under twenty quid.'

'No phone? No electronics?' asked Campbell.

'Not a thing.'

'And no note?' said Gabriel. 'No helpful video to let us know why he jumped out of bed this morning and decided to murder seven people?'

'Nothing, ma'am.' The lead SOCO lifted his black case onto the table and gathered his papers.

'Damned inconsiderate of him.' Gabriel's phone buzzed again. The Leeds accent told Gabriel it was DI Neville Skeffington, a man whose rise up the ranks astonished Gabriel. He was, in Gabriel's view, full of bluster and bullshit.

'I'm at Fletcher's flat in South Croydon,' said Skeffington. 'SOCO have completed the initial search and there's not much to go on. A lot of pamphlets, Nazi fanboy magazines and printouts from the internet about Islam. They've gutted his room, but no sign of a phone, no SIM card, and no laptop, tablet, PC – nothing.'

'I'm not buying that,' said Gabriel. 'People like Fletcher are addicted to the internet. Take the flat apart – get a PolSA team in.'

In Gabriel's experience, Police Search Adviser teams worked miracles. Last month, an Islamist cell based in a semi in West Ham had been sent down on the evidence from a SIM card the PolSA team discovered in a toy train at the bottom of a crate in a loft.

'You sure it's worth it, ma'am?' said Skeffington.

That was so bloody typical of the man, thought Gabriel. The path of least resistance every time.

'Not a debate, Skeffington.'

She ended the call and sat in silence. She stared at the wall opposite – a painting of a rabbit in a pinafore dress, dancing with a goose in red trousers while a band of beetles played instruments. How had they managed to make the goose look so creepy? He resembled an avian sex pest. Maybe it was the mood of the day, but she couldn't imagine anything better designed to terrify toddlers.

There was something deeply wrong here, thought Gabriel, and not just with the paintings. Lone actors like Fletcher were usually predictable. On the whole, they were heavy internet users who wanted to go out in a hail of bullets with their final moments live-streamed online. Fletcher seemed different.

Campbell was on his phone, getting another update from the office. The video team would be scouring CCTV for Fletcher by now and pulling his financial records. But Gabriel was not optimistic. In this weather, on a bike, wearing an anonymous grey top, Fletcher could take days to identify. His photo had gone out to docks and ports and police across the south-east, but he could be anywhere in London by now. And surely Britain's most wanted man – no matter how panicky or disturbed – would have the common sense not to use a bank card.

Her thoughts returned to Fletcher's missing technology. He must have a phone, or a laptop, or a tablet, and he had taken care to hide it. The flat was the obvious hiding place, but maybe there was something here at the theme park that forensics had overlooked.

#

Back at the Notorious ride, SOCOs were still at work, swabbing victims, fingerprinting the carriages and photographing every square inch of the platform, stalls and track. It could be hours before they finished and the victims finally taken away for post-mortems in Central London. Gabriel pulled on her sterile forensic suit and gloves, crossed the scene-of-crime tape and strolled briskly to the cabin on the station where Fletcher's colleague Lisa had been working.

The cabin was little more than a fibreglass box with two windows, a wall-mounted electric heater, a desk and chair, and lingering body odour. The floor appeared solid and was covered with stained yellow linoleum. Gabriel put down her bag and gave the corner of the flooring a tug, but it stayed put.

What about the ceiling? She pressed gently upwards on a polystyrene tile and it moved. She pushed again and slid it to one side, wincing at the squeak of polystyrene against polystyrene.

'Pass me the chair, Jorell.' Campbell yanked the plastic

chair from behind the table, allowing Gabriel to step onto the seat and gingerly poke her head through the gap in the ceiling.

'Jorell – turn on the torch on your phone and hand it over.' Her voice was muffled inside the cavity.

She felt the phone being pushed into the palm of her hand. She squeezed it through the gap alongside her head and held it out. The glare of the blue-white light made her blink as it revealed a shallow space of dust, cobwebs and there, just out of reach, a biscuit tin.

'Got something,' Gabriel said, reaching further in, her heart beating faster. She flicked the tin carefully towards her and stepped off the chair, placing the metal box on the table. She prised off the lid with a fingernail, breaking it on the way, and exposed a stash of papers. She recognised most of the sources. There were printouts from *Flashlight*, a neo-Nazi Danish site beloved by British fascists. At the bottom was a piece of ancient history – a grubby copy of *Spearhead*, a far-right magazine from the 1980s.

Gabriel clambered back onto the chair and poked her head through the gap once more, this time facing the other direction. Half an inch from her probing fingertips was a small plastic bag. She raised herself on her tiptoes, gripped a corner and pulled it towards her face. She dropped it on the table alongside the biscuit tin and stepped down.

Gabriel could feel Campbell's breath on her cheek as he leant forward to watch her slide a mobile phone from the bag. Gabriel stared. It was an expensive model, from the last year, and not the sort usually used as a burner – the pay-as-you-go phones bought over the counter, hard to trace and popular with drug dealers, organised criminals and terrorists.

The cabin seemed suddenly claustrophobic and Gabriel felt the urge for fresh air. She stood outside on the platform, deep in thought.

'Ma'am.' Campbell interrupted her. He was holding out his own phone. 'Think you need to see this.'

He handed it over. The screen was playing a YouTube

video, posted online minutes earlier, and she immediately recognised the puffy face and greasy hair of Gareth Fletcher. He was stood in a shabby sitting room, in front of a Union Jack, a swastika and a poster of what looked like a trident symbol. A line of letters was scrawled on a sheet of paper above his head – Gabriel could make out the first two, RA, but the rest were unclear. Over them, someone had scribbled the numbers 14 and 18. Fletcher's white vest revealed a tangle of tattoos on both arms. On his left shoulder, Gabriel could make out 88 in a gothic font. Gabriel was well aware of the obsession on the extreme right wing with numbers and codes, but this seemed excessive, even for a neo-Nazi.

He spoke quickly, too quickly for Gabriel to catch all the words on her phone's speaker. It was rambling, nervous stuff, blaming the Muslims, blaming the Jews, blaming the blacks, blaming the gays. The editing was rough too – there were obvious cuts and missing words. She watched with a professional's detached interest until the last line, when she nearly dropped the phone.

'…and I do this today in the name of the National Resistance Force, in the name of history. Fourteen words. We must secure the existence of our people and a future for white children.'

The NRF? Gabriel's immediate instinct was disbelief. The NRF was a crackpot group, outlawed a year or two earlier, but not regarded as a serious threat. She was suddenly aware that Campbell was staring, waiting for her reaction. If this was right – and the phone hidden in the ceiling above them and Fletcher's furtive preparations for this attack suggested it was right – then Fletcher's claim he was making history was no exaggeration. This bloody mess was the first attack of its kind by an organised extreme right-wing group on British soil.

But there was something more.

'Campbell, does anything strike you about this video?'

Campbell shook his head. 'Usual XRW stuff, ma'am.'

'Look again.' She handed over the phone. 'Look at the

flags, the posters, the way he's stood. Doesn't it remind you of anything?'

Again, Campbell shook his head.

Gabriel looked at her watch. Tennant would be heading to Downing Street by now for the pre-COBRA meet. Technically, she should be contacting her direct boss, the commander. But sod it. And again, she felt the glow of an errant schoolchild as Tennant answered.

'Of course, just because Fletcher claims he was with the NRF, doesn't mean he was,' Gabriel said, almost hopefully, after she filled him in. He had seen the video just moments before.

'No, but what you've found is hugely indicative. And no electronics at his home?'

'No,' said Gabriel. 'Which again suggests he was taking care not to reveal links with someone or some organisation.'

Gabriel was leaning against a wooden fence near the ride exit. The park's staff were scrubbing at the concrete on the other side of the tracks with industrial-strength disinfectant and the astringent smell of hydrogen peroxide irritated her nose.

'One more thing, boss. The video. There's something not right. I don't mean the content – that's par for the course for these people. But the way it was filmed, the language. I was racking my brains for why it rang a bell. But it's shot for shot, prop for prop, like a pastiche of an ISIS suicide video.'

There was stunned silence.

'You're kidding?'

'I'm not. Look at it objectively. All that's missing is Fletcher holding up an AK47. And his tone, his language, it's like he's announcing his martyrdom.'

'But he ran off,' said Tennant. 'He was a pretty shit martyr.'

'I know, but maybe he simply bottled it? I think there's enough here to warrant a change in tack. This isn't just a manhunt for Fletcher, we've got to assume that the NRF is a serious threat, and that they could be planning further attacks.'

Downing Street, London

It took Tennant three minutes to walk from New Scotland Yard to the black fortress gates of Downing Street where a cheery constable waved him through. For each step of that journey along the secure, gated shortcut that ran between the Met's HQ and the neighbouring Ministry of Defence, the implications of Gabriel's words filled his head. If she was right, they had to assume more was to come, maybe tomorrow, next week. There was now a desperate urgency to get to the bottom of this group.

Half a dozen TV political correspondents were lounging on the pavement opposite Number Ten. The pack was conferring – making sure their lines were consistent before speaking to their news desks – and they barely registered Tennant's presence. He lifted the black knocker and let it fall, disturbing the Downing Street cat, a self-contained creature which had outlasted the four previous PMs and which had been licking its bottom contemptuously on the doorstep, its rear end facing the journalists. *A media critic*, thought Tennant.

The door was opened by a security guard who ushered Tennant onto a red carpet that crossed the foyer of Number Ten and extended down the corridor leading to the PM's office. He made his way briskly down the passage and into the anteroom with its funereal oil paintings, past the staircase adorned with pictures of ancient prime ministers and finally into the lobby outside the PM's office where a huddle of civil servants and the head of MI5, or Thames as the agency was known in Whitehall, was waiting restlessly for the pre-COBRA briefing with the PM and Home Secretary. Tennant preferred these small, informal meetings to the full COBRA. He could be more open about operational matters away from the leak-prone junior ministers.

Downing Street's aura of urgency blended with sedateness never grew stale for Tennant. There was something tangible about the echoes of the past in these rooms. Was that a chair where Clement Attlee liked to sit? Was this a carpet that Lloyd George trod on? The PM's chief political adviser, a towering man with a close-shaved head, beckoned the waiting group into the office. Tennant pulled out his mobile, switched it off and left it in a cubbyhole by the door, then walked into the brightly lit room with white-panelled walls and surprisingly pungent vanilla air freshener.

The PM, grey-haired and grey-faced, rose from his antique desk to shake hands. On television, he came across as a slight man. Tennant had been surprised to discover on his first meeting that he was six foot three and filled rooms. And not just with his physical size.

'Apologies for the stench – Rupert had an accident in here earlier,' he said as he waved them to the mahogany conference table. For a second, Tennant was flummoxed. The PM didn't do jokes. Surely, he didn't mean Rupert Sealy, the Education Minister?

The Home Secretary Ben Thomas, a big Geordie whose warm smile lay below cautious, watchful eyes, was already sat at the table. He nodded at Tennant as they settled down.

'Same problem with my Labradoodle Edward – good as gold normally, then eats some crap and, bang, new carpet time,' said Thomas.

Ah, thought Tennant with some relief. Rupert was the PM's Cocker Spaniel, an animal who had become a minor celebrity in the last few weeks after the Downing Street cat had taken a swipe at him on the doorstep.

The PM nodded to Tennant. *No jokes*, he told himself, *no smart asides, just a massive dump of content. Not unlike Rupert.*

He summarised the casualty figures and gave an update on the hunt for Gareth Fletcher.

'This Fletcher,' said the Home Secretary. 'Are you taking seriously his claim that he's with the NRF?'

Tennant shrugged. 'Nothing's ruled out, Home Secretary. For now, we have to chase every line. When the NRF were proscribed by your predecessor, we had intel they had the intent to commit attacks and were trying to build capacity. It's possible they've achieved that.'

The Prime Minister turned to the head of MI5. 'How good is your infiltration of the NRF?'

'Could be better, Prime Minister,' she said. 'They're relatively new, we've got agents only at low levels and we don't have much on the new leadership. It's a priority for us, of course. Along with all the other priorities,' she added more quietly.

Tennant paused, sucked on his front teeth, and decided to take a gamble. 'There is also concern by some senior officers about the NRF video. It could be interpreted as the opening salvo in a new sustained campaign of terror by this group. We have been warning about the rise of the extreme far right for some considerable time.'

The Home Secretary tutted and fidgeted in his seat. 'I'm sorry, Steven, but what worries me more right now is the backlash from the Muslim community, not the imagined response of the far right.' He leant across the table towards the Prime Minister and jabbed a finger on its surface. 'There will be reprisals. Ishmail Sherif has already been on Twitter whipping things up.'

Sherif's apparent opportunism came as no surprise to Tennant. The man usually wasted no time at throwing petrol on the fire. A self-proclaimed cleric with a dubious history in Syria and a conviction for fraud, he now seemed to spend his life, in Tennant's view, touring TV studios denouncing the police.

There was a trace of irritation in the PM's expression. 'We're pushed for time, Ben, so I'd rather keep focusing on the facts right now, if that's okay. COBRA in fifteen minutes. Ben, can I grab five minutes?'

The meeting dispersed. As the door closed behind him, Tennant could hear raised voices. The head of MI5 raised an eyebrow in Tennant's direction.

'Was that my imagination or was our beloved Home Secretary a little testy just then?' she said quietly.

'Probably just stress,' said Tennant tactfully. But privately he agreed. The fault lines between these two most senior figures in the government had come to the surface since the election. Thomas had been the architect of the coalition deal and it was public knowledge that the Home Secretary had fought hard to persuade the PM to get into bed with Lesley Hogarth.

And that wasn't the only thing that had changed. Thomas had increasingly become sceptical about the threat of the extreme far right, presumably, Tennant thought, as a gesture to his coalition partners. But that was the first time he'd challenged Tennant directly. *Worth watching the old fox*, he thought as he followed the civil servants towards the Cabinet Office.

#

Behind Downing Street's public facade of charcoal bricks and chalk-white windows lies a labyrinth of rambling passages, cramped offices and handsome state rooms that stretch from Number Twelve at the Horse Guards Road end to the Cabinet Office on Whitehall. It was through this maze that Tennant scurried, a few steps behind the civil servants as they twisted their way past sombre Georgian anterooms, along 1960s corridors floored with nylon carpets, and up and down tatty stairs originally built for the servants of eighteenth-century aristocrats. The route, Tennant mused, resembled so much of the UK's political system – cobbled together from old and new, ramshackle in places, utterly long-winded, and yet usually managing to get there in the end.

COBRA crisis meetings were a frustrating mixed blessing for Tennant. The principle of getting security services and decision-making ministers around the table during a crisis was sound, but they were also called by prime ministers for public show – to tell the public that their political masters were in control, even if facts suggested otherwise. Twenty years ago, the public was unaware of COBRA, now they were a hybrid of a national crisis management meeting and PR event.

The meetings took place in a suite of windowless offices below street level in the Cabinet Office, far from prying electronic ears. Civil servants love a good acronym and so early in the 1970s, soon after the first gathering took place to discuss the miners' strike, the location of the suite – Cabinet Office Briefing Room A – became COBRA. The first time Tennant attended, he was struck by how much the venue resembled a Hollywood director's vision of what a top-secret room should look like with its beech-panelled walls, black leather chairs and a wall of TV screens.

Tennant was sweating from the exertion of the walk from Downing Street by the time he signed in at the entrance of the suite and locked his phone in a pigeonhole. He stepped into the clear plastic security pod which scanned him before letting him into the lobby. His staff officer and two sergeants had arrived twenty minutes earlier and were monitoring a computer screen in a small bunker off the lobby.

'Any more on the manhunt?' said Tennant.

'CCTV search has yielded nothing so far,' said the staff officer. 'Social media contacts still being chased down, as is his internet and phone data. We've had angry statements from the usual suspects on the left and there's a call for a peace protest in London for Saturday, organised by anti-fascist groups and which has already been supported by the leader of the opposition on Twitter.'

'It didn't take her long to jump on the bandwagon,' muttered Tennant.

#

In the COBRA meeting room, Tennant looked for his name card and glanced at the single-sided agenda on the table as he took his seat. His was one of the few spaces with a computer screen and keyboard, which allowed him to communicate with his officers in their bunker off the lobby. He sat, suddenly conscious of a white stain on his tie. Where the hell had that come from? He attempted to scrape off the mark with a bitten thumbnail.

Seconds before 3pm, the Prime Minister took his place at the head of the table, facing the TV screens. 'Let's keep this brief, please. First over to JTAC.'

JTAC, the Joint Terrorism Analysis Centre, was an arm's-length body that worked closely with MI5's counter terrorism branch to assess the threat to the UK. The director of JTAC, a quietly spoken dark-haired man who resembled a librarian, cleared his throat. 'Thank you, Prime Minister. In light of the nature of today's attack, we are leaving the threat level at severe.' Tennant fought to control his frustration. That was ridiculous. He had briefed JTAC half an hour earlier that there was a real threat of a follow-up attack.

The director continued: 'This decision is on the basis that today's attack involved only one known individual, although of course he may have had an accomplice, no sophisticated weaponry or explosives, and the wider intel picture that the National Resistance Force is unlikely to have the resources or capability of organising sophisticated, or multiple, attacks.'

Tennant felt himself reddening. He could not challenge the director in COBRA, but equally, he could not hold his tongue.

'Prime Minister, I do think there are some facts beginning to point to this being part of a more sophisticated plan that leads me to be concerned about further attacks,' he said. 'The context of the rise of the extreme right wing, which I've expressed concerns about on many occasions, also needs to be considered carefully. But I accept these are fine judgements and JTAC has a tricky job with a limited intelligence picture.' The director of JTAC shot a glance at him. He hadn't meant to use the phrase limited intelligence, but too late now.

A gentle cough broke the uncomfortable silence. 'Mr Tennant,' said the Deputy PM Lesley Hogarth in her flat north Lincolnshire accent, with a deliberate emphasis on his honorific. Hogarth was a short woman with blow-dried blonde hair sat over a stony face. She had a penchant for brightly coloured jackets, but today had opted for a more restrained burgundy. 'With all due respect, your views on the extremists from the right are well known. Where's the evidence that this was anything more than the violence of a sick man living out some fantasy? Surely our priority remains ISIS and the proven threat from organised Muslim extremism?'

Tennant winced. Was using an inflammatory phrase like 'Muslim extremism' rather than Islamist terrorist a deliberate slip of the tongue? He wouldn't put it past her. Surely, he thought, this was an act. She couldn't be that crass and that dim all at once.

'I think you meant to say Islamist extremism, Deputy Prime Minister,' he said, forcing a smile. 'And apologies if I didn't explain myself clearly. I'm not saying that Islamists pose no threat. There are currently,' he looked at his notes, 'twenty-three groups under surveillance thought to be planning attacks in the UK right now, which I think is a record. So please, let me reassure the Deputy Prime Minister that our eye is very much on the ball. However, there's also very good evidence of increased terrorist intent on the extreme right wing. Chilton Park may only be the start. We could very well be seeing more of the sort of attacks we've seen on the continent here in the UK over the next twelve months.'

The Home Secretary butted in.

'Thank you, Steven. I share some of Lesley's concerns that we're in danger of overstating the threat of the extreme right at the expense of the severe threat from the jihadists. I don't see much organisation at Chilton Park – a loner with a knife and a grudge does not make a paramilitary threat.'

Around the table, junior ministers were sitting up in their seats, paying slightly more attention, sensing something was up. Was Thomas attempting to redefine the threat to suit his political ambitions?

Thomas continued: 'I also share Steven's concerns about the risk of an escalation, which is why I think we need to send a strong signal, both to the Muslim community but also to the terrorists, and the potential terrorists, that we will have law and order on our streets. We know that the police are stretched, we know that they don't have the spare manpower because we hear it often enough from Steven and his colleagues, and so I believe it is time we supported the bobbies on the street with an armed military presence.'

Hogarth muttered 'Hear, hear' as if she was in a university debating society. The PM's expression remained inert, but he looked to Tennant, who took the cue.

'Prime Minister, at this stage, we are putting more armed officers on patrol, but we are not asking for you to approve military support at this time,' said Tennant. 'I will, of course, keep this under review.'

'Thank you, Steven,' said the PM. 'Ben, you've made this request before. I fully support Steven's operational judgement and I don't believe our citizens are made safer by filling the streets with soldiers. I think it's vital that we send a message that it is business as normal.' A couple of junior ministers muttered agreement.

'With all due respect, Prime Minister,' said Thomas deliberately, displaying anything but respect, 'I'm afraid I cannot disagree more fully. I can see why Steven is squeamish about tightening up armed security on the street – after all, the Isobel Harris inquiry wounds are still very deep.' He smiled patronisingly. 'But I'm not sure why you…'

'Your views are noted, Home Secretary.' The PM cut him off.

The Deputy Prime Minister interjected. 'Back to the job in hand, if I may? Are you speaking to his family? And are you looking for his computer equipment?'

Well, thought Tennant, *that wins the 'No Shit Sherlock' prize for the most inane question of the meeting*.

'We are doing everything we can, Deputy Prime Minister,' he said politely.

#

Cabinet Office, Whitehall

As COBRA ended and the civil servants, security experts and politicians filed out, Ben Thomas sidled up to Lesley Hogarth.

'Time for that coffee now, Lesley? Upstairs in the cafe?'

Hogarth smiled. 'Perfect, Ben. I'll need to pick up my spad on the way.'

The pair walked through the security pod into the lobby. Nina O'Brien, her special political adviser, or spad as the job was known, was sat in the lobby outside the COBRA suite dressed in a beige jacket which, with her red-dyed hair, made her stand out among the throng of black suits scuttling past her, like a jay among blackbirds.

The three walked through four double doors and into a coffee bar in the basement of the Cabinet Office. Hogarth and O'Brien sat next to a window, bathed in the rays dragged down into the depths of the building by the skylight above, while Thomas fetched the coffees.

O'Brien was one of those women who exude invisible beams of reassurance. Hogarth had noticed this the first day they'd met at the People's Party fundraiser four years ago. Even then she'd been impressed not just by O'Brien's intelligence but by the way she handled people. Within four days Hogarth joined the People's Party and within four months O'Brien had persuaded her to stand for leader. Her nickname in the party HQ was O'Brains. But never to her face.

The People's Party had been in existence less than five years and for most of that time, its influence had been minuscule. But in the last two years, since Hogarth had become leader, it had seen extraordinary growth in popularity and it had transformed the political landscape. Hogarth knew much of that surge was down to her easy charm. She had risen to prominence as an iconoclast newspaper columnist and occasional chat show guest, who spoke for the ordinary folk. She liked a pub and a pint. She came from Immingham. She rode a motorbike. And she had a public disdain for the Westminster elite, despite the fact that she was now part of it. The contradiction didn't lose her sleep.

She'd been happy to stay on the sidelines of power – nudging and pushing and causing trouble. But that had changed after the shock general election which had robbed the government of its majority and sent eighteen People's Party MPs to Westminster. Despite grumbles from the backbenches, and protests from the liberal mainstream media, the PM had swallowed his pride and struck a deal with Hogarth.

'Sorry about the delay.' Ben Thomas came bounding over, hands filled with three cups. 'And hello again, Ms O'Brien.' He emphasised the 'Ms'. As the Home Secretary bustled around depositing the drinks, Hogarth studied him. His 'people skills' (a ghastly phrase which Hogarth mentally drew the speech marks around in her mind) were superb.

Hogarth was partly convinced he put on the Geordie accent for show. A good regional accent was regarded as pretty much essential for anyone in his party keen to present themselves as the champion of the squeezed middle. It was ironic really, Hogarth thought. She'd spent most of her life stifling her north Lincolnshire roots to appeal to the same voters. 'Thanks for this, Lesley, and Ms O'Brien, of course. The thing is I'm keen – and this is a purely personal perspective here – and completely off the record,' he glanced at O'Brien, 'but I'm keen to build some bridges.' He leant back in the chair and crossed his ankles. 'What did you make of COBRA?'

'Bloody shambles,' said Hogarth. 'Between you and me, I'm not convinced Steven Tennant is the right man for this.

The man's so bloody woke. He has a bee in his bonnet about the far right, yet seems immune to the dangers from more proven threats. What did the *Herald* call him? The PC PC?'

Thomas smiled thinly. 'I think you got it spot on back there. One nutter does not make a far-right threat.' He sipped from his coffee. 'You know, Lesley, I've always felt far more unites us than separates us. Yet I'm not sure that's always properly acknowledged by our leadership.'

Hogarth eyed him. He was impossible to read. She wondered if the PM knew he was meeting her.

'A good marriage isn't just about shared interests, Ben, is it?' she said. 'It's also about ensuring neither partner takes the other for granted. One of the benefits of leading a smaller party is that one is always at the coalface of opinion. And I have to say, there's considerable anxiety we're not seeing all the benefits of coalition that we were promised.'

Thomas's face was neutral. Hogarth had practised these lines with O'Brien that morning and her adviser's gaze was fixed on the Home Secretary. Hogarth continued, 'I mean, take the Hate Crime Bill. We haven't seen hide nor hair of it. The Migration Bill, that's another one. Seems to have been kicked into the long grass.

'What concerns people out there, Ben, is the breakdown of normal decency. Knife crime, illegal immigration, drugs – in our schools and prisons and streets.' She remembered a phrase O'Brien had given to her for her last column. 'We're close to a national emergency, Ben. Rather than pushing through bits of legislation here and there and risking it all getting frittered away in committees and then softened in the Lords, surely there's an argument for one bill pulling all these issues under one roof. Immigration. Hate crime. Anti-extremism. Segregated communities. More powers for the police. All together in one place. A Freedom Bill.'

Thomas put down the cup and looked at Hogarth.

'I'm not sure I can see the PM agreeing to that,' he said.

'It would soothe the anxieties of many of my members.

And it would be an appropriate response to the inevitable Muslim backlash we're going to see in the coming days.'

'Let me consider your suggestion carefully,' said the Home Secretary. 'As I say, we do need to be working more closely. And sometimes country comes first, Lesley. I'm not sure that everyone in the government appreciates the existential threat Britain is facing.'

#

Hogarth and O'Brien walked away. Thomas watched them briefly, before turning and heading for the gents. *Ghastly woman*, he thought, although that O'Brien was a bit of a looker. Shame about the piercing, but still, shows a bit of spirit. But Hogarth? Beneath the friend-of-the-people facade, she was clearly bright. A phoney, yes, but an intelligent phoney. And a useful one. He washed his hands carefully and set off back to his office.

DAY 1

Wednesday Evening

University of Islington sports ground, North London
The shriek of the whistle brought the game to an end and Omar Asad said a silent prayer of thanks. His breathing was painful in the acidic night air and the stitch in his right side was like a jabbing needle. Asad grabbed his backpack, pulled out a black hoodie and said goodbye to the brothers.

He had left the university sports complex and was passing through the gate into the residential road leading to his hall of residence when he sensed someone running towards him. Tanvir Mirza was a couple of hundred metres behind, still on the pitch, waving.

Asad was surprised. Normally, in public, Mirza barely acknowledged Asad's presence. He waited as Mirza jogged up and rested his hand on Asad's damp shoulder as he caught his breath.

'Omar, man, you got to see this.' His deep-set eyes were fiery as he roughly shoved the phone in Asad's hands.

Asad wiped a drop of sweat from the screen and read the headline: *Six dead in theme park terror attack.* He skimmed through the report with disbelief, struggling to absorb the enormity of what had happened. Mirza snatched the phone back. 'It's unbelievable, man. This kafir, he's singled out the Muslims on this ride. A mother out with her family and their friends. Some were still kids. And no one held him back or pulled him off.'

Asad could feel the muddle of anger rising inside him. That rage was always with him, it was part of him, like an arm or foot. He couldn't remember when he hadn't felt rage, just out of reach, constantly fuelled by the injustices that filled his waking moments. Sometimes the rage was quiet, a background hum to his existence. Other times, like now, it rolled and steamed like the home-made jam on his parents' stove at home, ready to rise up, to spit and to scald.

Mirza carried on. 'The media's making out like he's a nutter. It's double standards, man. If a brother hurts a kafir, then it's Muslims this and Muslims that, but if it's a white guy killing us, then he's just a sicko, just a bit unstable. I'm so sick of it. Now look at this.'

He fiddled with the screen and handed it over.

It was a video of a white, pasty-faced man in front of a Union Jack and symbols that meant nothing to Asad. '…it comes from one religion,' the man on the screen said. 'A death cult that would subjugate our women and daughters, and wipe out a millennium of our laws with the laws based on a cruel, medieval faith…'

Mirza snatched the phone back. He was shouting now. 'This sick bastard does this – then he calls us a death cult?'

Asad, still dazed, still unable to process his emotions, nodded dumbly.

Mirza turned around as he walked off. 'This is it, man. This is the moment. See you at the Group on Friday, yeah?'

Again, Asad nodded and walked away, lost in thought.

He knew Chilton Park. He'd been there when he was fourteen or fifteen when he was shipped off from Cardiff at the start of the summer holidays to spend three weeks with his cousins in Ealing. He could see the roller coaster train in his head, the restraints coming down, his own flailing arms desperately pushing the attacker away. What would he have done if he'd been stuck in the seat? An echo of his dad's stern voice came into his head. 'It's not always about you, Omar, don't take everything personally.' It was his dad's favourite phrase, dragged out whenever his father thought Asad was being 'oversensitive', as he called it.

But so often it was about him. Asad couldn't see why other people – people like his parents – allowed insults, barbs and digs to pass without any comment. His parents seemed blind to the experiences they faced every day. They turned their cheeks to the bullies who tormented Asad at primary school, to the far-right leaders in Europe who declared war on Muslims, to the bigots in their own street who hadn't spoken to them in decades because they were Somali. But why should he feel inferior? Why wasn't he an equal even though he was born and raised in the UK?

And this latest attack at Chilton was personal for Asad. How could it not be? What if his own sister had been lying on the platform of that theme park, her body sliced up by this Nazi? What if he had been there – and had a chance to stop him? Would he have stepped up to defend his family, his brothers, his sisters? Of course he would. He needed to talk it over to sort out the chaos in his head, he needed some company, and he wished the Group was meeting tonight, not Friday. They would help him sift through his emotions and make sense of this.

He felt inadequate, he felt cold, and he felt tired.

He walked back to his room, but instead of heading for a shower, he flicked on the TV and sat in front of the rolling news, flicking between the BBC and Al Jazeera, and catching up on Ishmail Sherif's speeches online, until long past midnight.

#

Bexleyheath, South East London
It was going to be a long night. The car was snarled up on the A2 in Eltham and the journey back to her office in CTOC

at St Pancras, which had taken less than fifty minutes that morning, would take at least ninety. Gabriel could not justify asking Campbell to use the blue lights, so she was stuck. When she was a child, London used to have two rush hours a day – morning and evening. Now rush hour started at 8am and ended around 10pm.

Campbell was drumming his fingers on the steering wheel, a habit which irritated Gabriel. She left a message with Ray to warn him she would be late home and then checked in with DI Bose at St Pancras.

'Just heard from the digital team, ma'am,' said Bose. 'They've tracked Fletcher on CCTV to Crayford about thirty-five minutes after he left the park. But then he's disappeared. He's either ditched the bike or taken a route to avoid cameras.'

'What about friends and social media? Anyone in that neck of London?' she said.

'Very little close family – a dozen or so known associates,' said Bose. 'House visits have started on those and will continue first thing tomorrow. Nothing from his financial records yet, but we'll get an alert the second he uses a card.'

'Thanks, Eva. Any more on Abu Mujahid?'

There was a slight, awkward pause. Gabriel had asked Bose to do the weekly check with the intelligence agencies on the whereabouts of the jihadist before she had left that morning. 'Sorry, ma'am, we've been focused on Fletcher. I'm afraid Abu Mujahid's on the back-burner today.'

Gabriel sensed Bose's discomfort, which in turn irked her.

'I'm aware of that, DI Bose, but we can't afford to let him slip away just because of what's happened today. Put in the calls, please.'

She was bloody good was Eva, thought Gabriel as she leant back in her seat and stared at the crawling car headlights around her, and she shouldn't have snapped. But Bose knew how important Abu Mujahid was to her.

She had another hour in the car and had already planned the briefing that would take place on her return, so made a conscious decision to rerun the day in her head. She retraced her movements and thoughts from her arrival at Chilton Park. But when she reached the briefing in the canteen, and the moment she was shaken by the penetrating, dark eyes of the teenage girl Zahra, the girl who reminded her so much of Isobel Harris, her train of thought was derailed. She banished the day's events and delved deeper into memories which were now uncertain and confused. This was a place she usually avoided going. She hated the weakness, the vulnerability, the guilt, but this evening these memories were too easy to slip into.

Her thoughts shifted back two years, to the moment she was sat in the ops room, tuna sandwich in hand, and she heard that Jack Pearce – this was before he took on the kunya, or adopted name, of Abu Mujahid al-Britani – had fled. His name had faded from public consciousness, but for a few days he had been, like Fletcher, Britain's most wanted man. Pearce, a recent convert to Islam, had been the leader of a terror cell based in the West Midlands and had been on trial for conspiracy to murder, and the evidence against them was robust. Yet while the accomplices had gone down, Jack Pearce had been acquitted.

His smirk as he walked down the red-brick steps outside Birmingham Crown Court had made the front page of every paper the following day. Within hours, the Home Secretary had slapped a TPIM – a Terrorism Prevention and Investigation Measures notice – on Pearce, forcing him to move to Basingstoke in Hampshire, wear a tag and accept close police, and less visible MI5, monitoring.

And that was when Gabriel got involved. Pearce seemed to accept his new fate as a prisoner-and-yet-not-prisoner of the state and for five months he was followed, tagged and monitored during his trips outside the house in daylight hours. He did nothing wrong, met with no one he should not have met and lived an apparently blameless life. And then, on an otherwise unremarkable Friday, he vanished. Gabriel had been on duty that day and two hours before he slipped away she had made the call to redeploy the surveillance team to an apparently more urgent case, a supposed cell holed up next to a primary school in Camberley. The decision handed Pearce a ninety-minute window to get out of sight. He had used a borrowed car on his convoluted journey to Portsmouth, where he was pulled over by a patrol officer on the outskirts of the city. Pearce stopped, and as the officer approached, Pearce pulled a handgun and fired three times. One shot injured the officer in the leg, the second grazed the arm of a woman passing by, the third hit a schoolgirl, Isobel Harris, in the chest. Isobel was on the way home from football. She died a week later.

Isobel Harris. Gabriel had never met her, but her face was engrained in her head. In the days that followed, the press dug out a family snapshot, a thirteen-year-old girl in school uniform stood by her front door with a goofy grin and piercing brown eyes. The picture was used in every paper, on every news bulletin. *She'd be fifteen by now*, thought Gabriel.

Pearce fled amid the chaos and was last heard to be in Syria under his new name Abu Mujahid. Gabriel had blamed herself for Isobel's death, and so had the tabloids, who leapt upon the tragedy as an example of incompetent policing. Gabriel's name had emerged quickly as the figure to blame and she had endured a week of late-night calls and doorstepping. Columnists and bloggers she had never heard of called for her resignation, and there were even questions at Parliament. The story lasted ten days before running out of steam, only to resurface briefly when the inquiry cleared her of wrongdoing.

Tennant had saved her in the end, stepping in when it looked like she was about to be thrown to the wolves, persuading her to stay in SO15 and insisting to her superiors that she remain in post. She'd been unsure at first and had wondered about a move from London to another force, but she'd stayed put and was glad she had. The last year had been the busiest in counter terrorism since the IRA rampage of the late 1980s.

Ray called. She squashed the memories back.

'All right, kiddo? Saw the news. Terrible business. Close to finding the killer?' She loved his Valleys accent and she never tired of it.

'No. He's vanished. And it's going to be a long, crap day.'

'Cheer up. At least it's not tomorrow. That'll be even worse.'

He was right too, she thought as the car made its sluggish way to CTOC. Tomorrow would be worse.

#

Bexleyheath, South East London

Time had passed, but how much time? The woods had darkened hours ago, and it must have been thirty minutes since Fletcher had seen the girl picking her way through the trees, her yappy little terrier scampering around, scratching at the fallen litter of leaves and getting too close. He had no wristwatch and hadn't dared turn on his phone, so could only guess the time from the sky.

His hands were numb, his thighs ached and the jagged peaks of the tree bark pressed hard into his back. And with only a thin cotton top on, he was bitterly cold. The stench of stale piss filled his nostrils as he shifted his weight. He hadn't remembered pissing himself, but the evidence was there in the dampness around his crotch. He guessed he was hungry, probably thirsty too, but he felt nothing but the desperate urge to get shelter from the cold and the rain.

There was no sound now. Peter's house couldn't be far. Propping his hand against the tree behind him, Fletcher pushed himself onto creaking joints and raised himself up fully. Jesus, that hurt.

His only thought as he sprinted through the theme park had been to get to these woods. He knew Pete would be away this week, working in Bradford, or Bolton, or somewhere northern. He couldn't think of the name, but he knew it was one of those shit cities where white people were being driven out. He didn't dare take public transport, so he cycled along back roads, head down, avoiding CCTV cameras and using the Thames and the railways as a guide. He barely saw where he was cycling, his eyes just saw his hand stretch out again and again, blade slashing, red spurting. Where was the knife? He must have dropped it. It would have his fingerprints on. But so fucking what? They knew who he was. It made no difference.

It had taken a couple of hours before he found the edge of Abbey Wood, where he hid his bike in the dense overgrowth and waited in the cold and damp.

He let his mind drift back to his childhood, when he had played in these woods with Peter and the gang. They'd made dens in the undergrowth, smoked fags and got pissed on cider they'd nicked from the corner shop. They'd lit fires and talked rubbish and made plans. Pete had sliced his arm here, just for a dare, with his dad's Stanley knife. It had bled for ages and taken a lot of bottle. Pete's house backed on to the southern boundary of the woods. Fletcher had last been here a month ago for their Friday beer and takeaway. It had been a curry last time. Next time it was going to be a kebab. But there wouldn't be a next time.

It took ten minutes to find the edge of the woods in the dark. It had stopped raining and the skies were clouded over, but the steady stream of aircraft heading west to Heathrow was more helpful than any compass and within twenty minutes he'd walked to the trees at the back of Pete's garden.

With trembling hands, Fletcher reached up to grab the top of the fence and pulled himself with flailing legs up and over, into a heap on the flower beds and shrubs. His leg caught the fence panels as he fell, and the bang seemed to thunder through the gardens. Fletcher lay in a heap on the ground, not daring, not able to move. Was that fox shit on the lawn? Disgusting. He hated foxes. He'd shoot them all.

There were no lights on in the house. Panting and catching

his breath, he moved to the French doors at the back of the house. Locked and double-glazed. The kitchen door was firmly secured too, but it had a cat flap. When Fletcher pushed his hand in, he couldn't reach the lock. Maybe the kitchen window would be easier to force?

The padlock on Peter's shed door came apart with just one blow of a brick that Fletcher found in the rockery. And inside the shed was a heavy screwdriver, strong enough to jemmy open the kitchen window. Inside the house, Fletcher pulled the curtains and lit the gas fire. Then he sat on the floor, holding his knees to his chin with his arms, and the screwdriver in his hands, as the warmth slowly soaked into his clothes and skin. And he sobbed in the darkness, not for his victims or their families, but for himself.

#

Newhaven Ferry Port, East Sussex
Vicki Braithwaite nudged the gears into first and eased the lorry forward. She had timed her arrival to ensure the dockside would be busy and she had been waiting in the lorry queue for forty minutes. 'Travel when it's busy,' Dave had told her, 'and it helps that you're a girl and a white girl at that. They don't stop girls as much.' Braithwaite had no idea if that was true, but this was her seventh job for him, and she had yet to have a problem with customs.

The articulated lorry in front pulled away, and she found herself at the front of the queue. She pulled level with the window and leaned out, handing her passport and paperwork to a weary customs officer in a fluorescent tabard.

'What's in the back?' the woman asked.

'Chilled food,' she answered, concentrating hard to look relaxed.

The customs officer looked through the paperwork and Braithwaite focused on breathing. She had done the same at Dieppe. 'Go through Dieppe,' Dave had said, 'cos they've got no heartbeat monitors there. And they don't look in the back of fridges if they're sealed.'

'Okay. Off you go.' Braithwaite realised she had stopped breathing and slowly exhaled, wound up the window and slipped the lorry into first.

At the Welcome To Britain sign, she flicked on the radio.

'Police continue to hunt tonight for the man who killed eight people in a major terror attack at Chilton Park,' said a slightly too jolly voice. 'Police say the victims were stabbed as they sat in a stationary roller coaster at the Dartford theme park. The killer, who is believed to have worked at the ride, fled the scene.

'All the victims were black or Asian and Metropolitan Police counter terrorism officers leading the investigation say the attack appears racially motivated.

'The incident happened shortly after 11.30 this morning on the Notorious roller coaster. Julie Reynolds reports…'

Braithwaite stopped listening and drove on into the gloom of the night. Her rendezvous was an industrial park on the outskirts of Brighton, far enough away from Newhaven to reduce the risks. Dave had told her not to use satnav, so instead she had directions on a scrap of paper on the seat next to her.

It took thirty-five minutes to reach the park, which had been built alongside an embankment climbing up to a busy dual carriageway on the road out to Lewes. She pulled up and switched off the engine and lights, but kept the fridge motor on.

She was fifteen minutes early. She wondered about opening up and letting the cargo out but thought better of it.

The cargo were a funny lot. She'd seen them briefly in Waterloo, Belgium, as they got in the back. Five Asian or Arabic men, she couldn't be sure which, and a balding white guy with an outsized, straggly ginger beard. There was something rat-like about his face. He'd not said a word, but she didn't like the look of him. His eyes were dull and he didn't hide his disdain for her. *Probably doesn't approve of women working. Well, sod him*, Braithwaite had thought.

At 6.31pm, the glare of headlights briefly swept across her cab. She checked the mirror to see a vehicle had pulled up. The lights went out. There was no flash of blue lights or sudden movement, so Braithwaite clambered out. It was a white Ford Transit and an Asian man stood by the open driver's door.

'You Dave's driver?' He spoke in a northern accent.

'This way,' and she led him to the back of the lorry, which she unlocked. The handle was stiff, and the door was a nightmare to open. The evening was cold, but as the door opened, a blast of even cooler air hit them in the faces. *They must be freezing in there*, thought Braithwaite.

The man flashed a torch on half a dozen pairs of anxious, blinking eyes peering out from behind the cellophane-wrapped pallets.

'Out, and quick. Chop-chop.' Braithwaite wanted this over quickly. The cargo crept out and dropped to the ground. They were wrapped in blankets and hats but were shivering and sluggish after their twelve hours in the fridge. The last to emerge was the white man with the ginger beard.

The van driver looked at him in surprise. 'Who the fuck are you?'

'Me?' The man's voice was high-pitched, cold and soft. 'I'm no one.' There was quiet, confident menace in his voice and the van driver was unsettled.

'I'm not taking him.' The van driver turned to Braithwaite. 'I'm not paid to take him.'

'Don't worry yourself. I've made my own arrangements.' And with that, he began to walk away from the lorry in the direction of the dual carriageway.

Braithwaite watched him go. She was happy to have got rid of the first part of her cargo and she needed to get off. She was due in Luton by ten and then was off on holiday to Florida for three weeks. By the time the white man had reached the top of the dual carriageway embankment, her lorry was already out of the park and he was out of her mind.

Abu Mujahid al-Britani waited until the lorry was out of sight before getting out a mobile phone from his pocket. He felt filthy and stiff, but at least the warmth was returning to his body. He brushed dust from his beard while waiting for his call to be picked up.

'I'm here,' he barked into the mobile, and listened for directions above the drone of cars. Without saying another word, he put away the phone, hitched his rucksack over one shoulder, briskly strode into the night.

DAY 2

Thursday

Bexleyheath, South East London
Fletcher woke just after 5am. He lifted his head and peeled his cheek off the leather sofa where he'd crawled to sleep just a few hours earlier. He blinked, puzzled at the gas fire, still on and framed by fake marble blocks.

Why had he woken? Had he heard a noise or had he been dreaming of the clanking of the roller coaster? Fletcher's throat burned and his gut ached. He rubbed his eyes and found his way to the kitchen. The back door was locked, the window still shut. It was still dark, so he listened. Perhaps it was just his imagination, or maybe it had been a cat outside.

And now what? Pete would be back tomorrow night. Pete was sound enough, thought Fletcher, he hated the Muslims and the Jews and the gays. But would he turn in his mate for doing what they all secretly wanted to do? He knew he couldn't risk it. *Need to get out of London*, he told himself, *away from the cameras everywhere*.

If he was going a long way, then he needed cash. He went up to Pete's bedroom, wrenched open drawers and checked in the jackets in the wardrobes. He found a spare set of house keys, but no money. And none in the kitchen, or the cupboard under the stairs.

Back in the kitchen, he pulled down the blinds and turned on the portable TV. And there he was – his face, pale, surprised and fat, staring out of the screen. It was the picture from his ID card at Chilton. The TV picture moved to the roller coaster, then to a floodlit reporter at the gates of the park.

His head was still in a mess, and everything hurt. If he was going out, he needed to change his clothes. What had he seen in the bedside table upstairs? He went back up and yanked open the drawer. Yes. Clippers. They would do.

Thirty minutes later, a clean-shaven white man with a fresh crew cut and grey beanie walked out of the front door of the semi-detached house in Abbey Wood. His eyes traced the lines on the pavement and the feet of the few passers-by as he made his way down the quiet avenues into Heron Hill.

Don't look up, don't be seen. Don't look up, don't be seen. He walked in time with the mantra. The words were a dam that kept the memories back and let him focus on what was happening now.

'Watch it, mate. Look where you're going.' The voice was indignant. Fletcher glanced up. He'd walked in front of a man in a suit and overcoat, forcing him to step into the gutter. The man glared angrily at him. Fletcher mewed a weak 'sorry' at him, then scurried on. The man stopped and stared, before shaking his head and continuing on his way.

Don't look up, don't be seen. Don't look up, don't be seen.

He turned left into another tree-lined street, then right. Ahead he could hear the engines and splashing of tyres through the puddles from yesterday's rain in the high street.

He knew there was a garage with a cashpoint close to the Indian takeaway. He reached the high street and kept close to the shops and offices, his collar up against his neck and his beanie pulled down.

The four minutes to the garage were the longest of Fletcher's life. His thoughts were racing back to yesterday.

Eight dead, they'd said on the news. They fucking deserved it. It wasn't killing people. It was clearing out vermin. He was a hero and others would follow him.

At the ATM, he fumbled for his bank card in his back pocket. A woman appeared, standing too close behind him. He stepped back a little, forcing her to move out of the way. He should have been paid the day before – maybe they'd held it back. But no, his account had had £478.90. What was his limit? £300 a day or £500? He sensed the woman's impatience behind him. He tapped in £470, stuffing the notes into his coat pocket.

Five minutes later, he was back at the house, breathing heavily and with blood thumping through his splitting head. Had he been seen? Fuck knows. But he decided there and then to lay low for a day or two. Then he could move. That gave him some time to plan his next move. Pete kept his computer in the spare bedroom, and Fletcher knew the password from their post-pub sessions playing games until the early hours. He fired up the machine and started to search the web.

#

CTOC, St Pancras, London
Gabriel reread the report from digital forensics with growing frustration. Fletcher's phone was a recent model and while forensics were confident they could hack it, it would take up to twenty-four hours. Her concerns about a follow-up NRF attack were as strong as ever and a day's delay could make all the difference.

Gabriel dropped her bag and coat on the floor of her desk and sat down rather too heavily, dislodging the mechanism that kept the chair back upright and sending her coffee over the desk. She fiddled around with the levers, conscious that her failure to work a chair was being watched from outside her glass office.

'Ma'am.' Bose stood at the door, her round face and brown eyes creased with mild amusement. 'Ready to go through?'

Gabriel nodded and followed her into one of the conference rooms overlooking the tower of St Pancras station.

Gabriel had worked with Bose for two years. She had never believed in first impressions – and Bose was an example why. On their first meeting, Gabriel had barely noticed the short, slightly overweight woman in her forties in the corner. Bose tended to get overlooked – not helped by her conservative dark suits and subdued voice. But within weeks, Gabriel had singled her out as one of the stars of her team.

Every SO15 team needed a broad palette of skills and specialisms and while someone like Neville Skeffington was happiest getting his hands dirty on the doorstep, Bose thrived behind a desk. Not only was she a formidable expert on returners – the British Islamists who had set off to the Middle East to fight for ISIS and were now slinking back to the UK – she had a good grasp of the extreme right.

Around one hundred officers were packed into the room, some on chairs, others standing around the edges. Skeffington, long and lanky, was leaning against the back wall, scratching the moustache under his aquiline nose with the end of a long finger as he whispered to a bored DC next to him.

'First, the NRF,' said Bose, from the central chair. 'They broke away four years ago from England For The English, purported to be about peaceful protest, then moved to hate propaganda, generally against immigrants and Muslims. They graduated to advocating violence, were proscribed by the Home Secretary eighteen months ago. Their leader got sent to prison and the forty to fifty known members, a ragbag collection of oddballs and a significant number of ex-squaddies, seemed to fragment.

'On to Fletcher. A record for petty violence. Held a job as a clerk in an insurance firm, colleagues say he was shy around women, resented being overlooked for promotion and was disciplined for offensive comments about a black footballer. No military connection. No known girlfriend or boyfriend. On to the video.'

The NRF video, downloaded from the internet, appeared on the screen behind her. She froze the image.

'The trident symbol here,' she pointed to the drawing behind Fletcher, 'is a runic symbol – the life rune – appropriated by the Nazis in the thirties. Fletcher's had the numbers eight eight tattooed on his left shoulder. It's code for HH – or Heil Hitler – H being the eighth letter of the alphabet. Again, we see it used by white supremacists globally. Similarly, the one eight here stands for AH, Adolf Hitler. The one four isn't a code – it's a reference to the fourteen words in the rallying slogan for white supremacists, which Fletcher repeats at the end of his speech: "we must secure the existence of our people and a future for white children". Finally, the blurred letters on the wall appear to be RAHOWA, which stands for racial holy war.

'These codes and symbols may seem childish, but you must be familiar with them – you may see them on tattoos, graffiti, T-shirts, football shirts, email addresses, letters. I've got a full list here – I warn you, there are dozens. These people are obsessed.'

She handed a wad of papers around the room.

Gabriel was staring at the screen. Bose had closed down the video file, and its title was on display.

'DI Bose, is that the original title of the video file?' she asked.

'Yes, ma'am. We got it from the internet streaming company. Forensics have looked at the file, it was uploaded at an internet cafe in Central London, the video was probably shot in the last few days.'

'Enlarge it, please.' Gabriel scribbled down the filename. '420chiA_C. Anything in that?'

Skeffington interjected from the back.

'Looks pretty random, ma'am,' he said.

'I disagree,' said Gabriel, scribbling away. '420, according to DI Bose's list, is Adolf Hitler's birthday. Chi could be Chilton. But what's A_C?'

'Maybe Fletcher was a fan of Alice Cooper?' said Skeffington.

Gabriel ignored him. 'Something combat? Or it could be one underscore three if you use the alphabet code in reverse?' she said.

'But they don't tend to do that, ma'am,' said Skeffington.

She shot him a withering glance. 'They don't tend to kill people on roller coasters either, DI Skeffington, and yet here we all are.'

#

Back at her desk, Gabriel looked through Bose's briefing notes. The lack of intel on the NRF and the extreme far right was frustrating. There must have been a similar problem in the late 1990s when the threat from the Northern Irish paramilitaries was ebbing in the wake of the Good Friday agreement, just as the seeds of a new type of Islamist terror were being sown around the world. Then there must have been some urgent adjustments, some re-juggling of old thinking and a desperate shortage of intel about these new jihadists.

It was hard to imagine a time when the IRA was the biggest threat on the mainland. Gabriel wondered if her dad had been involved in counter terrorism. The skills of surveillance riders were easily transferrable from serious crime to organised crime to counter terrorism. She'd never thought to ask him when he was alive. Another wasted opportunity.

She had been asked in her interviews for SO15 whether her father's career in the Met had influenced her own job choices. It was an obvious question, but one she had never actively considered until then. She had just known since she was ten that she wanted to join the police and the fact that her dad was in the service was simply part of the furniture of her life, like the green wardrobe in her bedroom.

Gabriel had enjoyed a speedy rise through the ranks. She'd graduated from Nottingham University and been one of the few women to get on the police's High Potential

Development Scheme, a fast-track career path for graduates. She worked for four years as a beat bobby in Surrey and then quickly moved up the ranks, getting an early promotion to DI aged just thirty-three. She married Ray a couple of years later and moved to the Met to work in the Directorate of Professional Standards. She had been happy enough there and had risen to rank of detective superintendent, but it was not until the summer of 2017 – the summer of Westminster Bridge, London Bridge and Manchester – that she had felt her first real calling and had requested a transfer to counter terrorism. A vacancy came up six months later.

The last few years had seen the highest highs and the lowest lows. Her team had prevented a potential catastrophe at Luton Airport, pulled in a cell planning an attack on a school in Brighton and broken up a network organising a simultaneous bomb attack on two of London's most prominent skyscrapers. Yet the lows had been intense, Abu Mujahid and Isobel among them.

Banish these thoughts, she told herself. She returned to Bose's notes. These people were obsessed with codes. It was the mentality of a primary school child, not a terrorist. She was doodling on a pad, playing with the letters, when Campbell came to her door.

'Some positive news, ma'am. We've had an alert from Fletcher's bank. His card has been used in an ATM on a garage forecourt in Bexleyheath, not far from Chilton Park. Had a notification about a minute ago.'

'Bexleyheath? Rings a bell.' Gabriel scrambled for the notes on her desk. 'Yep – he lived there as a kid, moved out aged fourteen.'

'He'll know the area well – makes sense for him to hide out there, ma'am,' said Campbell.

'Okay. Get down there – contact the digital forensic team. And a surveillance unit too. And pull the local council CCTV. And get a team sifting through footage of far-right demos from the last three years. Let's see if Fletcher has any pals in the NRF.'

Finally, a break, thought Gabriel. If Fletcher had been stupid enough to use a cash machine, he would have made other mistakes. Surely, they were just a few hours behind him now.

#

Stonebridge, North West London

A short woman in her thirties with a tight-fitting blue trouser suit and straight strawberry-blonde hair was waiting outside the block of flats, swinging a fob of keys in one hand and clasping a folder in the other.

'Mr Jenkins?' she asked as Abu Mujahid approached the door.

'Correct,' said Abu Mujahid, proffering a grin.

The woman eyed him up for a few seconds. 'Right on time. So you've booked for a week, but want to look at an extended stay?'

'That's right – I need somewhere for the next three weeks.'

'Well, I think you'll like it and we've no bookings till February half-term, so that's all super. Would you like to follow me in?'

The flat was on the top floor of the five-storey block, built in the 1980s or 1990s. Abu Mujahid followed the woman into the lift and across the landing's diamond-patterned red carpet.

The pair stepped through the front door into a corridor lit only by the pools of daylight creeping through the glass panes above each of the five interior doors.

'Two bedrooms, a large bathroom with spa bath – room for you and a friend – the kitchen and here's the sitting room.' The woman opened the last door with a flourish. 'Wooden flooring throughout and newly decorated.'

'It's lovely. My girlfriend will adore it.' Abu Mujahid scrutinised the room. 'The details on the website said there was outdoor space?'

'Indeedy.' She walked over to a pair of French windows, fiddled with the lock and pushed them open. They led out to a balcony.

'Take care with the edge cos the fence isn't that high. Great views too. On a clear day, you can see IKEA.' She laughed at her own joke. Her phone trilled. 'Excuse me, I need to take this. Close the door behind you and I'll see you downstairs.' She disappeared down the hallway.

Abu Mujahid's body language and manner changed in an instant as he stepped out on to the balcony. Gone was the vacant expression, in came a look of determination. He fished out a pencil and scrap of paper from one pocket and a metal tape measure from the other and measured the dimensions of the balcony roof, and the width and height of the French windows. He made a sketch of the balcony, indicating the direction of north. Then, he stood on the edge of the balcony and slowly surveyed the scene. It took him ten minutes before he was satisfied and re-entered the sitting room. 'Thank you,' said Abu Mujahid to the woman downstairs, his smile reinstated. 'It's perfect. I'll take it, please.'

#

CTOC, St Pancras, London
DI Skeffington was studying his screen intently while talking to three DCs behind him.

'We've had this from Campbell in Bexleyheath, ma'am,' said Skeffington, still looking at the screen. It was CCTV footage from a garage forecourt, timestamped that morning. 'That's Fletcher on the way to use an ATM.' Skeffington pointed to a figure walking across the concrete. He froze the image. 'Looks like he's shaved his head, but it's him.'

Gabriel peered at a figure in grey on the forecourt.

'That's him,' she said. She looked closer, comparing the picture with the photo on his Chilton Park file. 'If he managed to get himself a haircut, then there's no way he was sleeping rough last night.'

'He could have brought a razor with him.'

'Come off it, Neville, look at his clothes, his hair. Hardly look like he's just spent the night in a hedge.'

A second video, from a high-street camera, showed the scene a minute later. Fletcher was walking fast, head still down, towards the camera.

'This is the high street in Bexleyheath,' said Skeffington. 'He goes off camera here and doesn't appear at the next camera four hundred metres down the road. So he's turned off into a residential street.'

Gabriel felt a surge of euphoria. She stood up and considered, but rejected, the idea of a fist-smack into her palm. 'So why Bexleyheath?' She was speaking now mostly to herself. 'We know he lived there as a kid. He must have friends there. Maybe he's visited recently.

'Skeffington, pull Fletcher's financial records, get a team to look for visits to this area, find patterns. And get down on the scene with Campbell – you two make a lovely couple.'

She stormed off, ignoring Skeffington's bewildered expression, and walked over to Bose, who was nibbling at a baguette at her desk.

'I want you to head up the team looking for Fletcher's associates,' said Gabriel. 'And I want his sodding computer. Or at least an internet cafe where he hung out and did whatever people like him do – buy jackboots or browse for Nazi porn. Get the team together in an hour. In the absence of digital devices, we need old-fashioned detective work. I want every right-wing protest video from the last eighteen months – no, make that two years – and I want every pub and cafe in the whole sodding area visited. Get to it.'

Bose left and Gabriel leant back, buzzing with adrenaline. They were close now; she could sense it. Fletcher could be in the cells tonight if this went well and, from what Gabriel knew of him, there was a real chance they would get him to open up about the NRF and the people who recruited him. She closed her weary eyes for a second, and the numbers from the video file spun in her head, rotating like the symbols on the fruit machine she was allowed to play as a kid when her dad took her to the police social club. A underscore C. One underscore three. A of C. And the significance of the numbers dawned on her with a creeping horror. She sat bolt upright. It made sense and she needed Fletcher in the interview room as soon as possible.

#

New Scotland Yard, Victoria Embankment, London
By 7.30pm, the SO15 floor was thinning. Desks were being plunged into pools of darkness as energy-saving lights kept on by the movement of bodies flicked off.

It had been a hell of a day, thought Tennant. Two briefings with the senior team to catch up on progress, another to get an assessment on community tension. There'd been another COBRA, another press briefing at lunchtime and, just now, an update with the commissioner.

It seemed madness to talk about a nation's mood, but Tennant sensed that something had changed in the last twenty-four hours. The latest National Community Tension Report was as pessimistic as he had ever seen it. Protests had sprung up across the country, and a couple had turned nasty. In Bradford, mostly Muslim protestors had thrown stones at police, while in Bristol a peace protest had erupted into a mini riot. Chilton Park seemed to have invigorated the extreme right too and there had been a surge in racist incidents and attacks on Muslims, particularly in white working-class areas.

At least the boss hadn't asked about the press briefing, and he was relieved. Day two of a big story meant news desks were itching for new angles and new leads. They had run the obituaries and the pictures of the victims by lunchtime, and dug up background on Fletcher. The hacks had been door-knocking relatives, tracking down old school friends and dredging up his previous. But by the time of the press briefing outside New Scotland Yard at 3pm, the reporters had become restless. Most of their questions were predictable, but he had been thrown by a shout from the local London paper, 'Is it right to have Sophie Gabriel on the case given her handling of the Isobel Harris shooting?' He had given her fulsome praise, but he knew he had blanched.

The office phoned buzzed. 'The Deputy Prime Minister, sir,' said the switchboard operator.

'Deputy Prime Minister. What can I do for you?'

'I'll tell you what you can do, Mr Tennant,' said Lesley Hogarth. 'You can get those idiots away from my front door. They've been here two hours and do you know what they are shouting? White supremacist. If that's not threatening behaviour, then I don't know what is. Get them removed.'

'Deputy Prime Minister, I appreciate this is a serious annoyance, but the officer at the scene has assessed the protest and says there's no public order threat or other crime. It may be offensive, but not an offence.'

'Don't try to be flippant with me, Mr Tennant. I'm being harassed. That ghastly man Sherif is there too, stirring things up. If they were protesters outside a mosque, you'd be down on them like a ton of shit. I am fed up with these double standards…' She carried on for thirty seconds and slammed down the phone.

So much for the party of law and common decency, thought Tennant. He had some sympathies though. Ishmail Sherif was not a man he would like on his own doorstep.

#

Gabriel picked up the phone to call Tennant, toying with the handset in hesitation. She was certain she was right about the letters in the video file. But would Tennant think she was clutching at straws? She dialled with a sudden determination.

Yet when he answered, she held back from sharing her conviction immediately. Instead, she filled him in on the latest in the manhunt.

'I take it you saw the press conference?' he said when she was done.

'Yep,' said Gabriel hesitantly. 'You reckon the press are going to make this personal?'

'Maybe. You know my motto – feed the monster. Dangle new leads where you can, be honest where you can, and treat them like you would treat toddlers. Distract them, remember they have an attention span of five minutes and try never to take it personally. But that's easier said than done.'

That's an understatement, thought Gabriel. She had experienced a couple of weeks of unwanted media attention over Isobel Harris, but the media's interest in Tennant had lasted years. His crime was not that he was too liberal – there were plenty of other senior officers who fitted that label. What made him stand out, and what had attracted the eye of the *Daily Herald*, was his relationship with Chris, a left-leaning theatre director. It started with an innocuous photograph. Tennant had attended the launch of Chris's play – and reluctantly gone with him afterwards to the after-party at a Soho club. The unlikely appearance of a senior Met officer on the arm of his partner amid the stage glitterati had made the front page of the *Herald* and, sensing it was on to a good thing, the paper began a sniping campaign against Tennant. It was where the 'PC PC' nickname had originated.

Gabriel had been with the Directorate of Professional Standards at the time – and was part of the unit called in when it became clear that the *Herald* had the inside track on Tennant's movements and decisions. The DPS quickly identified the source of the leaks – a disgruntled PA working in Tennant's office. But to Gabriel's astonishment, the deputy commissioner – a shrew-like man with one eye on the top job – instructed the DPS not to tell Tennant in case it jeopardised the investigation. To Gabriel, it seemed an extraordinary decision that put Tennant in a terrible position and she suspected an ulterior motive.

She had met Tennant in person by then, and she had liked him, so she took the decision to contact Tennant, unofficially and discreetly, to warn him that his PA was leaking. Looking back now, it was a foolhardy move that could have ended her career. But at the time, she had simply done what she felt right and fair.

The media campaign did not end, but it calmed down and it had been two or three years since the *Herald* had run a PC PC story. Perhaps they had simply got bored. And the deputy commissioner had himself been forced to resign a year earlier over a tasteless joke about a strip club.

Tennant continued: 'And it's not just the press, Sophie. I had the Deputy PM screaming down the phone earlier.'

'I take it she's not so keen on the current demonstration of free speech outside her kitchen window,' said Gabriel.

'Between you and me, I despair with this current generation of politicians. We've got the rise of the extreme-right terrorism, the continued threat from Islamists, and we're in the middle, supposedly protecting the public. And meanwhile, the political class on every side seems more interested in chucking fuel on the fire. Not just Hogarth and her friends; the Shadow Home Secretary's almost as bad, chumming up to Sherif and his cronies.'

Tennant had never been so indiscreet in front of Gabriel before. She was flattered, but also alarmed at the depth of his bitterness. She tried to laugh it off. 'It's technically what they called at Police College a shitstorm, sir.'

'Indeed.'

Gabriel could hear from his voice that he was smiling. 'Listen, boss, there's another reason I've rung.'

She filled him in on the video filename. 'You know how obsessed these people are with codes. I've been puzzling over part of the name. A underscore C. I think it's a number code – one underscore three. And I think I know what it means. One out of three. I think the NRF planned Chilton Park as the first in three attacks, coming in quick succession, to announce their arrival on the scene.'

'That's a hell of a leap from two letters on a video filename, Sophie,' he said. Gabriel felt the kick of disappointment.

'Not just the filename, boss. The language. The tone. The way that it mimics a suicide video. We thought this wasn't a one-off yesterday – well, this is the proof.'

'Why underscore? Why not one slash three?'

'Computers can't cope with filenames containing slashes, I'm told. But it's not just the name. It's part of a bigger jigsaw. And it means we must widen the scope of the investigation – it's not just about tracking down Fletcher, it's about cracking open the NRF and preventing two more massacres.'

Tennant sighed. 'I don't think it's enough, I'm sorry. I'll talk to the head of Thames, but I'm not convinced she'll share your interpretation. I'm not sure I do.'

#

At New Scotland Yard, Tennant ended the call. Time to go home? Time to appease Chris with an appearance before 10pm? Tennant was gathering his stuff when an email popped up on his screen from the head of operations upstairs. Tennant read it with a sinking heart.

Ops had been given notification of a demo in Westminster Square on Saturday, organised by Friends of Islam and the Socialist People's Party. And to add to what was promising to be a really great day, the right-wing protest group UK First were planning a counterdemonstration close to the route in St James's Street. The chances of the day going off without a major public order incident seemed slim, though thankfully that was not his responsibility. But a messy march could fuel the extremists on both sides and the impact on the deteriorating public mood would be major, he thought. Gabriel's shitstorm had just been updated to a fully fledged shit hurricane.

Bexleyheath, South East London
Whoever had designed the interior of the Castle Inn in Bexleyheath was not overly worried with variety. Keep it brown, was their single thought, and the decorators had not let them down.

The walls were murky brown, the ceilings yellow brown, the furniture was grubby brown, and the bar was brown. Only the sticky, faded carpet wasn't brown. It was green. It stank of wood polish, beer and tedium.

'What a shithole,' said Skeffington to Campbell as they stepped through into the snug. 'Just your kind of place, Campbell.'

It was just after eight and a dozen regulars were hunched at small tables. An orange middle-aged woman with bleached hair was reaching below the bar to pull glasses from a dishwasher to give them a wipe with a dirty tea towel.

The search of Fletcher's bank records had led them here. Once or twice a month, always on a Friday, always after closing time, Fletcher had used his bank card in this neighbourhood – in the chip shop, the takeaway and sometimes the ATM. And the Castle Inn was the closest pub.

'What can I do for you gents?' the woman behind the bar asked, barely looking up.

Skeffington flashed his ID. 'We'd like to see the manager, please, love.'

'That's me. What's up?' She glanced up and down the bar, avoiding eye contact.

'Wondered if you recognised this man,' asked Campbell, producing a photograph of Fletcher.

The woman studied it. 'I know him from the telly. He did the stabbing at Chilton Park, yeah?' Her voice was deliberate and cautious. There was no emotion, no concession.

'Did he drink here?' Campbell asked.

'May have done, but I don't remember him.'

Skeffington interrupted. 'Do you have CCTV in the bar, Mrs…?'

'Moorhouse. Angela. And no, we don't.'

'The car park then?'

Skeffington and Campbell had scouted the pub exterior but seen nothing. That didn't mean there was no CCTV – cameras were sometimes tucked out of sight.

'No. The brewery suggested it, but it's a lot of money and not a lot of benefit for us. Anything else? I've got a lot on.'

'I'm sure you have, Mrs Moorhouse,' said Skeffington, looking up and down the near-empty pub. 'All right if we have a chat with the customers?'

She shrugged, picked up the towel and began to wipe the far end of the bar.

BBC News 24 was playing an interview with the Home Secretary on a TV hanging from the ceiling.

'This attack on innocent Muslims was horrific,' said Ben Thomas. 'What we need now is calm and support for the police from the Muslim community. We don't need this sort of potentially inflammatory reaction from the extremists in our community.'

Tosser, thought Campbell, who personally blamed Thomas for his meagre pay rise last year.

A couple in their sixties were talking quietly over an opened bag of crisps at a table placed on a raised end of the pub. Two men in their forties were laughing in the corner on a table next to the toilets. A handful of solitary drinkers were scattered around the remaining tables.

Skeffington and Campbell approached each table in turn. They had no joy until they spoke to a jowly man on his own, reading the sports pages of the *Herald*.

'Saw him on the telly the other day. Stupid bastard,' the man said in response to a photo of Fletcher slid across the sticky table.

'Did he drink in here then?' said Campbell.

'Not often – couple of times a month, maybe less. Always over there.' He pointed to a corner of the pub alongside the dartboard. 'And always with the same mate. Don't know why he would though. Beer's like piss.' He laughed.

Campbell leaned forward, his face close to the man. 'Could you tell us anything about the man he met up with?'

The man took a sip. 'He's regular. A builder. Goes away most weeks, but he's here Friday and Saturday. Now, what's his name?' He called over to the bar. 'Angela, what's the name of that builder who drinks here? The one who fucks off to the north in the week.'

She came over. 'Peter. Peter McAllister. Why? What's he done?'

#

Outside, Skeffington was on the phone to the counter terrorism ops room.

'Peter McAllister. That's right.' He spelt the name out. There was a pause. 'Give me a pen, Campbell.' Skeffington scribbled down the address and put the phone away.

'DVLA say he's at 14 Hope Avenue. Electoral roll confirms it. Peter McAllister. Lives alone, semi in a quiet street. Surveillance on their way now and the CTSFO team are on standby.'

#

Gabriel sat on the grey Formica-topped desk in the ops room. It was through this room that surveillance operations were monitored, calls handled, live feeds processed and decisions made.

If this was Fletcher – and she believed it was – he was cornered, fragile and dangerous. It was always the goal in an operation like this to go slowly and carefully so as to reduce the risks of a fatal confrontation. This evening, with Gabriel's conviction that the NRF had more up its sleeve, her caution was tempered with a burning impatience.

A man's voice came on the radio from one of the team at the rear of the house. 'In position, clear sight of back windows. Movement upstairs.' The voice paused. 'Repeat, movement upstairs. A male, cannot confirm ID.'

The sergeant sat in front of Gabriel co-ordinating the team on the ground spoke into his headset. 'Are the lights on upstairs?'

The reply was a negative.

The sergeant turned. 'Ma'am – there is enough evidence to suggest this is Fletcher. Do we hold back and observe or crash in now?'

Gabriel tapped her hand on the table rhythmically. Under normal circumstances, the safer call would be to wait for the target to come out. Storming a house with no knowledge of Fletcher's mood or weapons was risky. But they didn't have the luxury of time.

'Get the CTSFOs in position, front and rear,' she said firmly. 'We'll go in,' she looked at the digital clock on the wall, 'in five minutes.'

Bose came over. 'What do you reckon, ma'am? Is this Fletcher?'

'Got to be, Eva. We've linked him to this house, we know he's around here, and someone's acting weirdly inside. I'm not in the habit of wandering around my house at night in the dark with the lights off. But then I don't live in South London. Who knows what constitutes normal behaviour down there? But I'd say we've got him.'

She sounded more confident than she felt. *Just get him in one piece*, she said to herself.

'Two minutes,' said the sergeant. 'All ready?'

There were a series of 'Yes, sarge's from the armed team. Then a woman's voice crackled out urgently. 'Sarge, woman is approaching the house. Long brown hair, grey overcoat and bag. She's outside the front door reaching into her bag. Looks like a key. She's going in. Hall lights now on.'

The sergeant spun around. His voice was calm. 'We

have a potential hostage situation, ma'am. Do we send in CTSFOs now?'

Shit, thought Gabriel. Another deep breath. Weigh it up quickly. Is she known to Fletcher? Possibly. She could be his handler. She could be debriefing him. She could be their way into the NRF. But what if she wasn't? What if she was the house owner – a lodger maybe? Someone who didn't know Britain's most wanted – a man capable of cold-blooded murder – was inside in the dark. She had to make this call in a fraction of a second. Get it wrong and Gabriel wouldn't just be facing an outraged media tomorrow morning, this woman could die.

'Send them in,' she barked and, out of sight of Bose and the team around her, she crossed her fingers.

#

Fletcher was in the sitting room when he heard the click from the front door. He had been upstairs for the last twenty minutes, unable to stem the torrent of diarrhoea. Was this Pete, back early? The light came on in the hall, shining a rectangle of light that stretched across the fawn carpet and rested on the tips of his socks. Fletcher stood and stepped back into the shadows. The footsteps on the hall tiles could belong to a man or woman. He pressed his back against the curtain in front of the bay window. There was the gentle thump of a bag dropping, then steps of someone going upstairs. He moved as silently as he could into the hallway and into the kitchen and grabbed at the largest knife from the block by the bread bin.

He was conscious of the rushing of blood through his ears as his heart raced faster and faster. The kitchen was small, but there was room to hide behind the door. He could stand there and not be seen until the person – Pete or whoever – came in.

'Pete, you in?' It was a woman's voice upstairs, London accent and confident and shrill and puzzled. Fletcher recognised her – it was Pete's girlfriend. He heard a creak above him and the sound of feet on the stairs. But this time they were coming down slowly, tentatively and nervously.

'Pete? You there?' The voice had lost its confidence. 'Are you messing with me? Pete?'

Steps were in the hall. A shadow fell across the open kitchen door and onto the black and white chessboard tiles. Fletcher looked up at the window opposite. He could see a woman's reflection framed in the doorway, almost in silhouette. 'Pete? Stop kidding around, will you?'

Fletcher watched her hand reach into the room for the light switch. As she pressed it, he realised two things. One, his trainers were in the middle of the kitchen floor and, two, the woman would see his reflection if she looked up at the window.

Slowly, as if time was stretching itself so that seconds lasted minutes, and minutes lasted hours, Fletcher stepped out into the room, clutching the knife in his left hand. The woman screamed. Without thinking, he put his hand over her mouth, muffling the cries, and pulled her towards him. He didn't want to hurt her. Just to shut her up. His knife was still in his left hand, five or six inches from her face.

'Shut up. Don't talk.' He moved the knife towards her face, intending to scare her. But his hand was shaking so badly the blade nicked her cheek. And as she gasped, from somewhere in the hallway, or maybe at the front door, came another noise. A sound of air rushing from a balloon or car tyre. But there were no balloons here, thought Fletcher. And no car tyres.

At that moment, the world fell around him...

An explosion filled the house, filled the kitchen, filled his head, ending all other sounds, sending a ringing through this brain that wouldn't stop. And at the same time, a flash so bright and blinding that he no longer knew which way was up and which was down. He stepped back away from the woman, but with his knife pointed at her chest, blood pouring from the gash in her face. There was movement in the hallway and then another explosion, this time more compact, and accompanying it a pain so searing that he felt molten lead was pouring into his chest. And then the feel of the cold kitchen tiles on his face and liquid on his mouth and boots moving in front of him and a woman crying and a radio talking and someone rushing forward and someone bending down and turning him over and then nothing. No darkness. No silence. Just nothing.

#

In the ops room, Gabriel listened to the radio chatter with a burgeoning sense of dismay. The officer in the rear garden had a good view of the kitchen and had raised the alarm the moment that the woman switched on the light and Fletcher advanced on her with a knife.

The voices around her were raised, buzzing with excitement tinged with relief that this two-day manhunt was over, relief that the woman had been saved before Fletcher had a chance to attack her again. But Gabriel felt none of that. She slumped into a chair with a sense of despair at the hollow victory. She had needed Fletcher alive. He was a weak man and she believed his vulnerability had been ripe for exploiting in the interview room. They could have got so much from him – not just the person who had recruited and groomed him for Chilton Park, but insights into the NRF, and crucially, clues into what this shadowy organisation was planning next. But in the confusion and mess of this suburban house, Fletcher's secrets had died with him, and Gabriel was no closer to knowing what was coming next.

DAY 3

Friday

Burgess Hill, West Sussex

The A23 was quiet, and it had been tempting for Abu Mujahid to let the speed build up as he passed Crawley and headed towards the predawn glow of Brighton that lay beyond the wall of the South Downs. But he resisted. The speedometer stayed under sixty-nine and the speed cameras let his van pass unmolested through the winter morning.

He pulled off the dual carriageway at Burgess Hill on to a lane that twisted sharply through dimly glimpsed farmland. Then, ahead in the road, low down and small, an object was caught in his swaying headlights. It was hard to see and for a split second, Abu Mujahid imagined it was an IED, an improvised explosive device, the sort he had set many times in Syria. It moved. Abu Mujahid squinted, and the object took the shape of a pheasant. Twenty metres away, Abu Mujahid slowed and honked the horn. Ten metres, now five. Finally, the pheasant took flight, but moved towards his van, thumping into the windscreen, leaving a greasy smear, before bouncing over the roof. Abu Mujahid glanced in the side mirror to see the bird in the fiery glow of his brake lights, stunned and confused among a cloudburst of feathers.

His destination, the industrial park, was on the edge of the town, and the warehouse was at the rear of the park. A red container lorry was parked by the rolled-down shutters, next to a white Honda Civic. Abu Mujahid pulled into the visitor parking space and walked to the office.

A bearded man, all belly and hair, was slumped in his chair reading the *Herald*.

'You're late,' he said, barely looking up.

'I'm sorry?' said Abu Mujahid in a quiet voice.

'I said you're late. I've been waiting twenty minutes,' said the fat man.

Abu Mujahid moved with a sudden ferocity that took the man by surprise. Within seconds Abu Mujahid was behind him, squeezing the man's neck with just enough force to let him breathe.

'Let me get this straight,' Abu Mujahid spat into the man's ear. 'If you have to wait twenty minutes, twenty hours or twenty years for me, you fucking wait for me and you don't utter a word of complaint. Do you understand?'

The man said nothing. Abu Mujahid squeezed harder. The man nodded and clawed desperately, and Abu Mujahid relaxed his grip.

'Excellent.' He smiled a humourless smile. 'Let's get this over with.'

The fat man stood up shakily, scooped up a set of keys and unlocked the door leading into the warehouse.

'In there,' he croaked, waving at two sealed grey plastic crates on the racks.

'You going to take that one?' said Abu Mujahid. It was not a question. The man grabbed a crate and began to carry it back to the office. Abu Mujahid lifted the second, weighed it in his arms and put it straight down. He looked closer at the seal.

'Have you touched these?'

The man was wide-eyed and pale.

'Course not.'

Abu Mujahid studied him. 'If you have…' He let the threat hang. 'Just get them to the van.'

#

Twenty minutes later, Abu Mujahid was stood at the back of his van in a lay-by. He opened one door, took a knife from his pocket and carefully sliced the tape sealing the crates.

His suspicion was right. Two items were missing. He contemplated returning to the depot, making sure the man there hadn't touched them. But it would be getting busy by now and he was sure the crate had been tampered with en route. Maybe at Greece? Maybe before it left Beirut even. A new source was needed. He pulled a phone and pocket book from his jacket and leafed through the numbers and initials before dialling.

#

CTOC HQ, St Pancras, London
The Bexleyheath shooting had been too late for the first editions or ten o'clock TV news. The comms team had released a brief statement to the Press Association just after 10.30pm followed by a more detailed release at 11.30pm once Fletcher's next of kin had been informed. By the time the last print editions went off stone at 1.30am, most nationals had enough for a front page and a couple inside. Feed the monster, Tennant had said and Gabriel, reluctantly, agreed. Not only did it keep the media on side, it was good for the team's morale to have a victory in the public realm.

The tabloids had not held back. *Got him!* was the splash in the *Herald* over a picture of Fletcher's face in the simulated cross hairs of a rifle sight. There was praise for the police, with some stories giving the wrong impression that the intention had been to bring him in dead.

Gabriel had not got home until after two, and even then,

adrenaline had kept her mind busy until three. She'd stirred Ray to tell him about Fletcher, but he had merely grunted and rolled back to sleep.

She'd been back in the office at 7.30am, dosed up on coffee, to review the crime scene report from the lead SOCO and the operational summary from the surveillance team. She read it again now. The woman who had come to the house last night was the girlfriend of Fletcher's drinking friend Peter McAllister. She was shaken but uninjured and due to go home that morning. She claimed she had never met Fletcher and had gone round to feed McAllister's cat. The North West Counter Terrorism Unit picked up McAllister in a Holiday Inn in Bury just after midnight. He insisted he didn't know Fletcher was staying at his house, a claim corroborated by the scene-of-crime report – Fletcher had broken a kitchen window to get access and vomited over the bathroom – not the traditional behaviour of a welcome house guest, Gabriel thought. McAllister had been interviewed again at 6am, but there was not enough to hold him longer.

The SOCO report was intriguing. Fletcher had used McAllister's computer to search the internet, mostly for news about Chilton Park, but also travel websites. His search history indicated he was planning a trip to Belfast by rail and boat. That fact rankled with Gabriel. Chilton Park had been carefully planned by the NRF and yet Fletcher had been making up his escape strategy as he went along. Again, Gabriel had a sense this was not the original intention. Was Fletcher supposed to have died at the park – and then had he chickened out?

#

Two hours later, Skeffington appeared with an uncharacter-istic beam across his pinched face.

'The gods are smiling on us today, ma'am,' he said. 'Digital forensics have cracked the phone abandoned at Chilton Park by the late, unlamented Gareth Fletcher and we've got his WhatsApp messages. Lots of crap, naturally, but two chats are well worth pursuing. One seems to be an alt-right group – the usual juvenile stuff. Bragging which celebrities they'd kill. Fletcher seems to have joined two years ago. There's about half a dozen in it under fake names – "stormfront", "white rage", "ourcountry". We've got a team chasing down the phone numbers and phone records. May be a link to the NRF there – or may be a bunch of kids pratting around. The second conversation is more interesting.'

Bloody hell, Skeffington. Just get on with it, Gabriel thought.

'Fletcher was talking separately for nine months to someone calling themselves R. Looks like they met on a chat room and moved the conversation to WhatsApp, presumably for privacy. This R is goading Fletcher and encouraging him – which suggests he's an NRF recruiter. Crucially, we've got a message from R three months ago, "Brilliant news mate", to which Fletcher replies, "Ta – couldn't have got it without yr help. Start next week."'

'Fletcher started work at Chilton Park two months ago,' said Gabriel. 'Did R get him the job?'

'Looks like he helped him at least, ma'am. Then two weeks ago, R tells him to get rid of his phone. He says "STOP", in capitals, "STOP using the phone. Dump it now." That was the last time he switched it on. God knows why he decided to stash it in his hidey-hole in the cabin, rather than throw it down a drain.'

'So why did this R character tell Fletcher to get rid of the phone?' said Gabriel.

'The previous text had been from Fletcher, who said, "You can trust me". Then, we were right, "one of three". Signed off with an eight eight.'

'I bloody knew it, Skeffington. Show me.' He handed over the paper. There it was. One of three in black-and-white. There was no time for smugness, no time for an 'I told you so'. She had even ignored Skeffington's 'We were right' comment. And the hollowness and anxiety from yesterday swept across her again. If only they had Fletcher in the cells right now. They could have wheedled something out of him, she was sure. Now they had nothing but this threat.

She waved away Skeffington and called Tennant.

#

'There can't be any doubt, boss,' she said after briefing him. 'Chilton Park is the first of three planned attacks. And it was organised months ago. This R, Fletcher's handler, helped him get a job at the theme park nine weeks ago. The NRF are playing a long game.'

Tennant grunted in agreement. 'Trouble is, we're in a minority here. I've been on to the director general of Thames and JTAC, but their assessment is, and I quote, that Fletcher is an "isolated individual, claiming without substance to be part of a fragmented, disorganised group". They'll be hard to budge on moving the threat level up, even with this.'

'That's crazy, sir, we've got more than enough.'

'Not in their view, Sophie,' said Tennant. 'It would help make a case if we had some indication of what the NRF are planning next.'

'Could be anything,' said Gabriel, not hiding her frustration.

'Then narrow it down, take a step back. What do we know about their intent?'

Gabriel paused for reflection. 'We know Chilton Park was designed to be a shocker – extreme right-wing martyrdom with maximum publicity, maximum terror. But not necessarily maximum death toll. They could have killed far more people with a vehicle or bomb, so this was about targeting their victims while not offending their key supporters. No white people were injured or killed, only those from black and Asian ethnic minorities.'

'And?'

'I dunno,' said Gabriel. 'It was unpredictable, out of the blue, I guess. Whoever planned this has an eye for drama, for the spectacular.'

'And?'

'And it was a calling card – statement of intent from a new group,' said Gabriel. 'All good stuff, but how does that help us?'

Tennant paused. Gabriel could imagine his brain exploring angles, sifting them and discarding them. 'There's no Muslim holidays or festivals in the near future, so we can rule that out. Could be a mosque or a school.' Another pause. 'I reckon we can dismiss music concerts – security is too tight. But what if it's not a location, but an event?' His voice was excited now. 'Sophie, what if the first and second attacks are linked?'

'Another theme park? Doesn't seem likely.'

'No. What about the peace march? Think about it. It'll have all the key community leaders, the major opposition politicians, tens of thousands of Muslims, a similar number of allies – all the people the NRF and their supporters are gunning for.'

An unfortunate phrase, Gabriel thought, *but sadly appropriate*. 'Hang on, sir, Chilton Park has been months in the planning. Are you suggesting the second attack is on a march that was organised thirty-six hours ago?'

'Think about it,' said Tennant. 'What happens after every terrorist atrocity on UK soil? We get a mass protest, we get an obligatory two-minute silence. They're part of the grammar of modern life. So, yes, tomorrow's march was only organised a couple of days ago. But the NRF don't need to be psychic to have predicted there would be a protest march. They won't have known the date, but they'll have been certain one was coming.'

Gabriel considered the idea. There was something in it.

'How many are we expecting for the march?'

'Hundreds of thousands.' He paused. 'Look, I'm tied up for a couple of hours now, but can you pop round later?

Seven-ish. I need to talk to MI5 and JTAC again. And I'm going to speak to the public order team, but I know they won't consider ramping up policing for the march if JTAC and MI5 aren't moving.'

The call ended. Gabriel felt like they were building a tower of playing cards with guess carefully balanced upon guess. That the code in the video meant one in three. That one in three meant two more attacks. That the next attack was the protest tomorrow. And after that?

#

Islington, North London
Asad had seen the NRF video half a dozen times, but its brutality still had the power to reignite his rage.

'This is the face of our enemy – the face of those who wish to destroy Islam and defile the Prophet,' said Mirza. 'This is the face that confirms what we already know – that this country is institutionally and deeply Islamophobic. If you doubt me, look at this. See how the kafirs stand by and do nothing.'

The Group members were silent. Mirza leant forward to the computer. A video filmed on a phone appeared showing Fletcher leaning forward and lunging with a knife. A dark liquid sprayed into the air. The video paused, then repeated the scene, this time much slower. Asad looked away.

#

Asad had joined the Group six months earlier at Mirza's invitation. It took only a couple of meetings, in the flat above the electrical shop, for him to realise the Group was the end point on a road he had been on since he was fourteen. That was when he plucked up the courage to walk into Butetown Youth Club and attend his first Youth of Islam study circle, much to his mum and dad's disapproval. His parents had been born in the city, children of those who had arrived from Somalia to work in the docks in the 1950s. The YOI, in his father's eyes, was run by the 'wrong sort' – men who had too much interest in political Islam and not enough in their spiritual connection with Allah. But to Asad, YOI offered friendship and identity, unlike the gangs of white kids at school, who'd offered hatred or disinterest. The members were the first people he'd come across who talked about the plight of the Muslim Ummah, Sharia law, politics, corrupt Muslim leaders and the enemies of Islam. These were the first people he'd met who didn't apologise for striving to establish a Caliphate and the battle against the Islamophobic West in the Middle East. And the first who talked meaningfully about racism.

There were only a handful of black kids in his year at school – mostly third-generation Somalis like himself – and bigotry had been rife. Incidents, scattered through his school days, were seared on his memory. Like the day after a 9/11 anniversary when he had been punched by a boy two years above him without provocation, yet he had ended up in front of the head of year. Or the time when he had been asked by a teacher to take a note to the head in the middle of lessons, and the caretaker had challenged him in the playground with a mask of sarcasm that barely concealed hatred, not because of who he was, but hatred because of what he represented, a black, strong Muslim teenage boy, whose very existence seemed to threaten the old white man's world. Sometimes he had reacted: with words, with fists. But often, too often, he had let it go unchallenged. 'It's part of life,' his father had said. He had come to accept his parents' disappointment. He considered himself a dutiful son, and let their scolding and rebukes go unanswered. But he struggled to respect their views – he felt they were out of touch and compromised.

He had arrived at university from Cardiff blazing with a desire to break free from his home and find people like the YOI. But the ISoc at Islington was safe and relentlessly worthy and its speakers often warned patronisingly about the dangers of looking outside classical Islam. He had joined the Brothers' football team, attended the Ramadan iftars and been a regular at Friday prayers. But when he had talked politics and prejudice, and shared his experiences as a British Somali, he had felt he was not being taken seriously.

So he had looked elsewhere. The Somali Society had seemed an obvious group, but it was full of first- or second-generation Somalis, the children of refugees who'd arrived in London in the 1990s. They regarded him as an outsider and he realised he knew little about Somalia other than the stories his grandma had told him, and the food his mother sometimes remembered to dish up.

And then he'd been invited by Mirza to the Group. Together, the members read books on jihad and watched sermons by inspirational preachers and discussed the plight of Muslims in the UK and across the world. The study circles empowered and energised Asad. He felt reborn with a confidence and clarity about his identity and his life's purpose that he had never felt before. At Group, Mirza and the brothers talked about fighting back. Asad had listened to that kind of bragging in Cardiff. Most of those people in the YOI had been full of bravado and bullshit, talking the talk about joining the struggle in Syria, or signing up with al-Shabaab and taking the fight to Mogadishu, but unlikely ever to do anything.

But there was something different about Mirza and the others in the Group. Their righteous anger, and their willingness to go further, to commit to direct action, had shocked Asad in those early meetings. But that same clarity of vision had transfixed him too. His own anger was more like a forest fire, leaping from branch to branch, out of control, spreading in every direction, impossible to contain, impossible to predict. Mirza and the others seemed more focused, more determined.

'It's for people like us,' Mirza had told him. 'People who want to change the world for the better. For true Muslims.'

#

The video ended and Mirza stood up. 'Tomorrow we've got a chance to take action. Our brothers will be marching on Westminster and we must join them. But marching isn't enough.'

Mirza paused to swoop his black hair back up against his forehead before his hypnotic voice continued.

'There's a war raging, brothers. They torture us, they detain us, they discriminate against us. And they insult the Prophet. And we do nothing. And their Home Secretary tells us to be calm. A man who supports the ban on the veil and who wants restrictions on migration from Muslim countries.

'So we must show our love for Allah by following his command, establishing truth over falsehood, and upholding the forgotten obligation of jihad and defending our brothers and sisters. Don't be afraid. Show your love by striking down those who want to destroy us.'

After the meeting, as the others were putting on coats, Mirza came over.

'Bro – stay behind a second.'

Asad felt a flush of pride. 'Course, Tanvir.'

When the others had shuffled out of the door, Mirza sat on the floor. Two members, Ahmed Muhid and Waheed Saleem, perched themselves on the edge of the sofa. Asad had known both men since fresher's week and their faith seemed unassailable, their passion for jihad undimmed by uncertainty. Asad admired them, but found it easier to relate to Mirza.

'I've been watching you, Omar,' said Mirza. Asad twisted his fingers around his shirt cuff and said nothing.

'You're intelligent, you see things others don't. But something ain't right.' He tapped his forehead. 'You've got conflicts. Last week, when the others were saying what they'd do to protect themselves, you were quiet. Are you too scared for this fight?'

Asad felt Mirza's dark eyes burning into him. He looked

down at the threadbare carpet, avoiding the gaze of Saleem and Muhid.

'You know I believe we need to fight,' said Asad. He raised his face to Mirza's, staring hard into his eyes. 'But last week – the way some of the others were talking, it was like they were boasting. It wasn't about the fight – it was about grandstanding, carrying knives to make them seem the big men. And that's not what it should be about, man. Jihad isn't about showing off.'

Mirza held his gaze. Asad felt himself getting hot. 'So when is it right?'

'To take up weapons?' Asad asked.

Mirza nodded.

'Like you said, man – for a higher purpose, a higher goal, a just cause,' said Asad. 'But for others. For our brothers and sisters. Not for some ego trip.'

Mirza stood and turned to the window. He yanked back the curtain an inch and peered out at the street. The yellow street light cast half his face into shadow as he talked to the glass.

'There's someone I want you to meet, all three of you to meet. He thinks like you do,' said Mirza. 'He's done amazing things, brothers. He's Sheikh Abu Mujahid al-Britani.'

\#

New Scotland Yard, Victoria Embankment, London
Tennant waited while the Number Ten switchboard put the call through. A guttural Geordie voice broke through the crackling.

'Steven, it's Ben here,' said the Home Secretary. 'Just calling for an update before I see the PM. What've you got?'

The day's Community Tension Report had landed on Tennant's desk three hours earlier. It had made grim reading. In Leicester, a sixty-four-year-old man had been knifed outside the public library while collecting for a charity for injured soldiers. In Hull, a mosque had been set on fire overnight by a gang who daubed racist slogans on the pavement. And there had been street fights yesterday evening in Watford between gangs of young Asian and white men.

'Community relations are deteriorating faster than we might have anticipated, Home Secretary,' said Tennant. 'We've got four times as much activity as normal from social media from the extreme right wing and hard-line Islamists. And that's reflected on the streets. In the last twenty-four hours, we've had a tripling of racially motivated crimes.'

Thomas sighed down the line.

'Aren't you being a little apocalyptic?'

'Wish I was, Home Secretary.'

Another pause. 'We've also got this rabble outside the Deputy Prime Minister's house. No chance you can get them moved on?'

'I realise she's angry, but the assessment is that it's lawful – irritating, perhaps, but not illegal,' said Tennant.

'I wonder if that would be the response if it was the hard right protesting against a Muslim politician. But it's your call.' He rang off.

The protest outside Lesley Hogarth's house had doubled following an interview she had given on the radio. She had made a similar point to the Home Secretary's about double standards, but her language had been inflammatory. 'Yet if it were protests about the Muslims, then the police would no doubt move them on.'

Funny how the foolish addition of a 'the' in a sentence made it so much more offensive, Tennant had thought. Normally, he would have put it down to a foolish slip of the tongue, but Hogarth knew exactly what she was doing.

#

Tennant was leaning back in his chair in full uniform, feet on the desk, phone cupped to his cheek, when Gabriel walked in. She dragged a chair over with her foot, piled her papers on the floor next to her and sat down. He ended the call and pulled out a plastic tray of sushi from a paper bag.

'Not got time to eat – drinks at some ghastly fundraiser tonight. Tuck in if you want.' Gabriel gave the sushi rolls a discerning stare and curled her upper lip.

'No, really, sir, I wouldn't want to deprive you.'

'Don't blame you,' said Tennant. 'I keep reading that fish are consuming plastic. This tastes like it's made of the stuff.' He toyed with the sushi before pushing the tray away. 'How are the team holding up?'

'Stretched, but manageable,' she said. She cut to the point. 'Are we getting the extra resources tomorrow?'

'I've tried, Sophie, I really have. But JTAC don't see an elevated threat and I've not been able to persuade the commissioner. It's too much of a leap from a vague hint. That's the trouble with neo-Nazis. No sense of occasion. Just when we want a big statement, they go quiet.'

'So what happens tomorrow?'

'I'm with you that the risks of a second attack are significant, even if JTAC and the grown-ups don't agree. But my hands are tied. We put a strong counter terrorism team around it and I want you to lead it. Security's already tight, but it's a tinderbox. Get a couple of experienced officers at the UK First counterprotest and I need you in the middle of the action. Run the ops room out of CTOC. If anything kicks off, you can step in. I'll be at Gold Command.'

Tennant's phone buzzed. He mouthed an apology to Gabriel and let her walk away.

#

Pall Mall, London
At 10.30pm, two men walked out of the rain and into the fluorescent-lit lobby of the A-Line hotel in Pall Mall. Doug Glenister was short and stocky, dressed in a grey bomber jacket with a damp baseball hat yanked over his head. Rod

Houghton was taller, dressed in baggy jeans and a green hoodie with a holdall over one shoulder. Houghton carried, rather than rolled along, a hard-plastic wheeled suitcase which left tramlines of water on the polished floor.

Glenister glanced at his companion and then at the CCTV camera in the ceiling before walking to the coffee bar. His companion stood back in the darkest corner, his back against a wall plastered with posters of London.

'A reservation, for one night.'

'Of course, sir,' said the young woman. 'Welcome to the A-Line hotel. We hope you have an amazing stay. Follow me, please.'

Phoney cow, he thought as she led him to one of the automated machines. His heart was pumping too fast. He slowed down his breathing.

'Your name, sir, please?'

'Frazer. Samuel Frazer,' lied Glenister.

She leant over to tap his name into the screen.

'There you go. I've got you a lovely room on the third floor, but it's just got twin beds. Do you want to change it for a double? We can do that no problem.' She glanced meaningfully at Houghton in the corner.

For fuck's sake, Glenister thought, breathing hard to stay calm. 'No.' There was a hint of indignation and the woman looked flustered.

'Sorry, sir, I just thought…'

'You thought wrong.'

The receptionist worked on in silence. The machine deposited a key to room 312, which she took out and handed over.

\#

The men kept silent until they were upstairs in the room. Glenister closed the door behind him, placed the suitcase carefully on the bed nearest the window and then, only then, he let out a breath that felt like it had been building inside him since they'd got off the bus twenty minutes earlier.

'Fucking hell, Rod, did you hear what that bitch asked us? Thought we were queers.'

His companion threw the holdall to the floor and pulled the hoodie away from his face. He didn't grin.

'One CCTV camera in the foyer – one staring right at you,' he said.

'Fuck off. I had the cap over my eyes. We'll be long gone before they think to look at that.'

Glenister turned to the case on the bed and spun the combination lock, clicking the lid open and carefully lifting it up.

'All there?' asked Houghton.

'Yep.' He closed the lid, locked the case and placed it on the floor of the wardrobe.

Glenister moved to the window, pulled apart the net curtain and nudged the catch with his finger. It was stuck at first, but then came free with a squeak.

'We need oil for that,' said Houghton. 'Go and get some first thing.'

They were interrupted by the ringtone of a mobile phone. Houghton pulled it out of his pocket. He waved his companion to be quiet with a hand.

'Hello?'

'Hi.' The voice was quiet. 'Is everything ready?'

'Yes. All in place.'

'What you are doing tomorrow is making history. It will inspire others and you should be very proud. Remember, lads. We fight with the blade, the bullet and the bomb.' The call ended.

DAY 4

Saturday

St James's Street, London
A balding white man with a paunch and crew cut leered at the police. He flicked a St George's flag on a bamboo pole over their helmets as another two men, shoulders draped in Union Jacks, stood by him. Another man, his face concealed by a red scarf, held up a placard: UK First.

'Race traitor, race traitor, race traitor!' he screamed over the police cordon to two white women walking in the throng of peace protestors. The cry was taken up by those around him.

'How many Muslims are shagging your kids?' The yell came from a white middle-aged woman with blue hair and an old-school East End accent.

'More of your cockney friends, I see,' said Skeffington to Campbell as they stood a few metres back from the police cordon that separated the counterprotest from the main demonstration. The peace march was filing past and the air was filled with threats and curses.

'I think they've also got a few bigots in the north, sir,' replied Campbell.

'One or two. But in the north, Campbell, most of our bile isn't aimed at the Muslims, it's reserved for southern wankers.'

Campbell gazed at the twisted, snarling faces of the counterprotest on the other side of the police line. Were any of these really planning something on the scale of Chilton Park? The boss seemed to think so, but it was hard to see how any of this rabble would get very far under the nose of the police and media. He shared his thoughts with Skeffington.

Skeffington raised his eyes. 'Fuck knows. When the boss gets a bee in her fucking bonnet, logic goes out the window, Campbell. Besides, the whole world has gone crazy. If one of these guys had a jetpack on right now and decided to fly out over London shitting radioactive waste from his arse, I wouldn't bat an eyelid.'

Over the yells came the muffled sound of a megaphone. Blue smoke drifted through the bodies from a flare dropped to the pavement. Union Jacks, beer cans, baseball caps, white middle-aged faces contorted in rage, and the smell of urine where at least one had relieved themselves against the wall.

The yell 'Murderers' burst into Campbell's ears. It had come from a young black man walking towards him, ten metres away, part of the main protest. He watched the man for a second before returning his gaze to the counterprotest.

The political chants merged into anti-Semitic football chants.

'Wish they'd make their mind up who they hate. First the Muslims. Now the Jews. They're all mentalists,' muttered Skeffington.

#

Asad had lost sight of the University ISoc banner in the churning mass around him. He'd been on the street for two hours and his feet ached in his market-stall trainers.

He walked along the Regency streets of St James's, home to gentleman's tailors and exclusive hotels. The marchers made an unlikely contrast alongside these grand old Portland stone buildings which looked down on banners proclaiming Freedom for Palestine and Stand up to Racism.

There was a sweet waft of cannabis, and a sickly odour of vaping. A woman with a grey megaphone was chanting 'Nazis out' and a couple of dozen marchers were joining in. On the other side, a harassed white father was holding a screaming toddler while he tried to steer an empty pushchair with one hand.

Up ahead, the shouting was louder – and more aggressive. Something had changed and marchers had stopped on one side and were shouting at a group of mostly white men and women on the pavement. With a shocking clarity and growing rage deep in the pits of his body, Asad realised who they were.

'This is free England, no to Sharia. This is free England, no to Sharia.' The yell came from three women with dyed red, white and blue hair.

'Murderers.' The word left Asad's lips before he'd had time to think what he was saying. Two men – almost certainly plain-clothes police – were in front of him. One was white, tall, moustached and lean; the other, black and stocky. Asad could see the shorter of the two eyeing him up before turning his gaze back to the far-right protesters.

#

CTOC, St Pancras, London
Four miles away, in the SO15 operations room in St Pancras, Gabriel watched the crowds on the video screens. Even through the filter of electronics, she sensed the anticipation.

The police operation for the march was being controlled by Gold Command four miles away in the cavernous special operations room near Lambeth Palace. Gabriel's job was to watch and wait. *Not today*, she said to herself silently. *Please not today.*

Bose came over.

'Ma'am, the NRF have put up a new video. On the screen now.'

At first, Gabriel assumed it was the same video as before, but quickly she noticed most of the crude edits had gone. Gabriel watched open-mouthed at Fletcher's previously unseen faltering performance to camera.

'…which is why I am willing to give my life, to die a martyr on the cross of justice, knowing that my death will bring down the Muslims, the Jews, the blacks and the foreigners who are contaminating our glorious country and tainting the Aryan blood. My sacrifice is the start – we will attack all those who oppose us – the Muslims and the white traitors.'

Gabriel felt the blood draining out of her face. For a second, she was paralysed. Then, the adrenaline surged, her heart began to pump. The timing of this release was not coincidental. It meant only one thing.

'Get me Gold Command, now,' she barked. The face of Gold Command, the chief superintendent running the day's operations, came on the screen. 'Sir, the National Resistance Force have uploaded a new video – it's a version of the Gareth Fletcher video from Chilton Park. He's talking about martyrdom. There's a clear threat that a second attack is imminent – and the timing of this release strongly suggests the march is a target.'

\#

St James's Street, London
'Cavalry's here,' said Skeffington as a police van pulled up and officers emerged to reinforce the cordon.

The shouts from the far-right counterprotesters were angrier now. 'What you going to do?' yelled the woman with blue hair.

'Pigs,' shouted the man in the grey shirt.

'How stupid are they, sir?' Campbell said under his breath to Skeffington.

'How long have you got, Campbell?'

And then, above the yelling and shouting from the anti-fascists and the neo-Nazis and peace protestors and Socialist Workers, there was a sudden movement as an Asian man in his twenties wearing a duffel coat broke away from the main march and walked purposefully towards the counterprotest. The man's face was contorted with rage, and he was holding a grey rucksack in his left hand. It banged and swung around his legs but didn't seem to bother him.

'Bloody hell.' Campbell heard Skeffington's curse. The man was around ten metres away now. He slowed down and stopped, bent double, panting so loud that Campbell could hear him.

Campbell was torn – should he run towards him or keep his distance? An armed response unit was close by and had spotted the man. Two officers began to advance, but a clean shot was impossible.

The world seemed to slow. Campbell momentarily felt himself floating above his body, watching the street. There below him were the far-right demonstrators, on the other side the main march, in between the police. And there was the man, reaching inside his coat, pulling something out.

His mind was filled with the thought that the man had a vest – and that it was about to explode, sending shrapnel towards the protesters and police. Campbell was frozen as the man's hand dug deeper into his coat and then pulled out something white. He threw the white object into the air, and it scattered into tiny pieces of paper. They were leaflets. The guy was throwing leaflets at the far-right protest. *Oh, thank God for that*, thought Campbell. One of the uniformed police approached the man and the armed officers lowered their guns.

His head cleared and he was aware that Skeffington was at his side.

'Fucking hell,' said Skeffington. 'Thought you were going to wet yourself for a second there, cockney.'

Trafalgar Square, London

Not for the first time that morning, Zahra felt a flush of guilt. Her mother and Jawad had been buried less than twenty-four hours, and she should be at home with her father and her uncle, grieving, receiving visitors, not here. But the man from the mosque and the solicitor who had told the family not to trust the police had been adamant her place was here and she had been too numb to argue.

She had never seen so many people, such a wide expanse of faces and arms and banners. And the noise – a clamouring shouting, talking, singing. She wanted to crawl away somewhere and sleep. But she stayed and held Maryam's hand in hers.

She stood on the platform, built from scaffolding poles and wooden planks, facing Ishmail Sherif as he addressed the crowd, microphone in one hand, the other hand waving and clutching at invisible nothings in the air. His voice rumbled from the speakers below her.

'…and you are standing up to those who wish to murder Muslims, spread Islamophobia and drive our communities apart. Three days ago, Nazis murdered eight people, mostly Muslims, at Chilton Park. These victims of the far right included the brother and mother of this brave young woman…' He pointed at Zahra but did not take his eyes off the crowd. '…who stands here, a testament to the brutality meted out time and again against our families, our loved ones, our faith. And just half a mile away, the police are allowing Nazis to stand on the street and hurl their foul abuse at us once again. Muslims are no longer safe anywhere. They bombed us in Syria, now they kill us in Britain. We must stand up. We must fight for our safety. Fight for our families.'

A wave of anger swept through Zahra's body. She shouldn't be here. She was a prop for Sherif to wave in front of the crowd, a freak show to be exploited, just like her mother and brother's memories were being exploited. She desperately wanted to turn away and hide, to lock herself up, to be with her family. What remained of her family.

Sherif finished and she could leave. She turned to clamber down the steps and into the crowd. With luck, she would be home in fifty minutes.

#

Pall Mall, London
Asad put his phone away, too numb from the new NRF video to be angry. Around him, he sensed a change in the mood as people shared the news from social media.

A hand touched his shoulder. It was Mirza. His eyes were shining, his hair dishevelled.

'Omar – you seen what the NRF have said?' Asad nodded dumbly. Behind him, a father was struggling with a truculent toddler who refused to get into a buggy, her back arching and legs thrashing each time he tried to strap her in. Asad could see the metal lions that guarded Nelson's Column above the father's head. The speeches had already begun. It was an unimaginative list, thought Asad, who had seen the line-up on a poster promoting the march. The leader of the opposition, the Shadow Home Secretary, a couple of minor pop singers, the daughter of one of the victims of Chilton Park and Ishmail Sherif.

And then there was a sudden searing heat on the side of his face, as if he'd stepped too close to a bonfire. At the same time came the tinkling of glass on concrete and wailing screams. He was shoved to one side as bodies flung themselves towards him. There were more cries – a baby yelling, a man shouting a name.

Asad looked around wildly. Behind him, about thirty metres away, he could see the lick of a yellow flame and a drift of dirty smoke over the heads of the crowd.

Mirza was beside him, eyes wide open.

'Out of here,' said Mirza. 'Omar. Now.'

Asad didn't argue. The instinct to get away was overwhelming. But the same instinct had run through the crowd and bodies pushed and jostled from all around. It was a struggle to move now, he was being pressed on all sides as panic swept through the protests, his body bobbing around like a buoy in a turbulent sea.

He felt an elbow in his face and he pushed back sharply and looked round into the pale face of a woman, aged in her seventies or eighties. 'I'm sorry,' he mouthed, but she was swept away further to his left. Panic grew in his stomach. And the panic, terrifying, paralysing panic, was spreading through the crowd.

There was another pop, a smashing of glass and a second wall of heat. Asad glanced up – more flames, this time on the other side of the street.

He looked around – he and Mirza were being sucked by the torrent towards Trafalgar Square.

'In here, Tanvir,' yelled Asad and he grabbed Mirza, sending him toward a side passage. The entrance to the passage was obscured by scaffolding and most of the fleeing crowd swept past oblivious. Asad stood in the entrance and peered back into the street as people pushed past them down the passageway. Police in yellow vests were pushing through the crowds, trying to hold some back, steering others away.

Then the screams got louder. And this time, the crowds began to run. Asad heard a repeated cracking sound, like a firework had been thrown into the street.

'That's a gun,' said Mirza. 'The police are shooting at the crowd.' The screams got louder. Sirens started to go off.

'Let's get out of here,' said Asad, and they ran down the passageway away from the chaos and into the relative tranquillity of St James's Park.

#

Inside the entrance hall to Charing Cross Tube station, Zahra heard the muffled bang of the petrol bomb. Maryam turned to her. 'What was that? A firework?'

Zahra shook her head dumbly. Her mind wasn't working. She had just one thought. *Not again, this couldn't be happening again. Not again.* Around her, people stopped and turned to the daylight. The crowd was eerily quiet. And then, outside, the sound of gunfire, echoing against the concrete and stone. The noise was unmistakable, as was the rise in volume of shouting outside. *Not again.*

'Go now.' She woke from the mental paralysis, grabbed Maryam's hand and plunged down towards the ticket barrier, towards the safety of the tunnels far below her feet.

#

CTOC, St Pancras, London
In the CT ops room, Gabriel was sat at the conference table coming to the end of an update when a flustered DS came over.

'Ma'am. There's been an incident.'

Gabriel swivelled towards the SO15 video screens. A helicopter camera showed a street close to Trafalgar Square where dots of churning protesters were crushed together. In the midst of the crowd was a gap, maybe fifty metres across. At its centre were four or five plumes of black smoke.

'What the hell's that?' said Gabriel. 'Flares?'

'Gold Command report petrol bombs, ma'am. Presumably thrown by one of the marchers.'

'What do you mean "presumably"? Are you telling me that someone on that march got out and lit a petrol bomb without being spotted?'

'That's all I've got, ma'am,' said the DS uncomfortably.

The camera zoomed to the source of the smoke – patches of orange flames flickering up from the road. Even from the height of the camera, it was clear the crowd was panicking. Gabriel could see people sprinting from the fire. What idiot would do that on a demo? Anarchists maybe? Unlikely to be terrorists, surely. But with kids around? She imagined the scene in Gold Command right now. It would be calm over there but bloody busy. They'd have to let the crowds disperse and they would be deploying armed teams. But until she heard otherwise, it was their concern, not hers. She waited.

'Ma'am.' It was the DS again. 'Reports of gunfire in the same street. Armed response units are moving in to the source.'

Gabriel looked again at the screen with new eyes. Everything was immediately different. If guns were being used, then this was unquestionably a terror attack. The NRF? An Islamist group? Was this two of three?

She stood up. Speculation later, action now. 'Get a CT team down there now – and get SOCOs,' said Gabriel to the team around her. 'First priority is finding the source of the attack – in the crowd, or an overlooking building. My guess would be the latter. Secure the crime scene once casualties are out. And get me photos.'

The flames had burnt themselves out, but the road surface was smouldering. The road was littered with white placards and abandoned banners. Some were scorched.

'What's that?' said Gabriel. 'Can't they zoom in there?'

She pointed to what looked like a discarded blanket lying in the road. The object moved and a police officer ran over and crouched next to it. It was only then that Gabriel realised it wasn't a discarded blanket at all, but a body.

'Getting reports of seven, no, eight people down now,' said the DS. 'Two more – it's carnage, ma'am.'

#

Pall Mall, London
Rod Houghton and Dougie Glenister, dressed in dark grey hoodies and jeans, emerged from room 312 of the A-Line hotel. They checked the corridor was clear, then the shorter man opened the door and went back into their room. After two seconds, he emerged and shut the door, sending a waft of black smoke curling into the corridor.

'Done. The smoke alarm should have gone off by now,'

Glenister said. Houghton shrugged and walked down the corridor to the emergency stairs.

'Give it a moment. Smoke detectors take a while.'

Immediately, a deafening electronic siren pierced the air. The men waited until doors of the neighbours' rooms began to open, then they blended with the other bewildered evacuees and streamed towards the fire escapes.

#

On the pavement outside, DS Campbell crouched over the blood-soaked body of a woman. Five minutes earlier, he had been walking with the crowd towards Trafalgar Square, watching the protestors.

His radio crackled. 'Suspects may be in a building on Pall Mall,' the voice said.

He waited for the radio to clear and then called in.

'Many people down, request ambulances urgently. I'm with a female aged around thirty. Wounds to the stomach and face, still breathing. In the centre of Pall Mall. Other casualties close by. Over.'

Campbell looked up. He was exposed, kneeling here alongside the discarded placards and banners and smoke, surrounded by fragments of glass. *A petrol bomb*, he thought. And where was Skeffington? He'd been with him moments before.

Forty metres away, two colleagues were kneeling next to another body on the pavement. There was a third close by. A cloud of acrid smoke floated his way. Campbell held his hand up to his mouth and coughed. As the smoke cleared, he saw four paramedics running his way. Two peeled away to the other victim, two bounded towards him with a stretcher.

'We need to shift her now,' he barked at the paramedics. 'Get her out of the road.'

He stood back to let them work on the woman and moved to the pavement. *No point standing here now*, he thought.

A woman with a child came up to the steps of the hotel.

'Sorry, madam, but you can't come in here.'

'But my daughter needs a wee. She's desperate.' The woman had a posh Home Counties accent.

'I'm sorry, madam, you need to move away for your own safety.'

The woman swore and moved on. Then the fire alarm went off, and within seconds, people started to flood out of the front doors.

#

CTOC, St Pancras, London

'Update, please,' said Gabriel.

The DS said: 'It's likely the attackers were in a hotel overlooking the route. The A-Line in Pall Mall. Someone set off the fire alarm – unsure whether it's a genuine fire as of yet. We now have snipers on three roofs overlooking the front and rear of the hotel. They've clear vision of the exits, but there's a lot of people leaving the building.'

'And the crowd?'

'We're struggling to contain the rally inside Trafalgar Square, ma'am. They are getting panicky. Looks like we've got three dead, a dozen injured, maybe more.'

'Get someone in the hotel,' said Gabriel. 'We need a list of residents and we need to look at the CCTV. These places are crawling with cameras.'

#

Pall Mall, London

Outside the hotel, Campbell's radio crackled. 'Suspects believed to be in A-Line hotel. Armed. Armed units make your way to A-Line hotel, Pall Mall, immediately.' He forced his way through the bodies fleeing the hotel and into the reception.

'Sergeant Campbell, antiterrorism.' He waved his pass at the woman stood by the desk, ushering the guests through the door to the street. 'I need to know the source of the alarm.' He spoke with such authority, the hotel woman abandoned the evacuating guests and turned to the computer.

'It's floor three, smoke detectors in room…' she screwed his eyes up at her screen, '…room 312.'

'Who was in that room and when did they check in?' said Campbell.

'Shouldn't I be helping them get out?'

Campbell stared hard and said nothing. She gave a nervous smile and tapped away on her screen. 'Two men, checked in last night at 10.30, just one name, Samuel Frazer.'

'How did they pay?'

'Cash up front.'

'Don't you insist on a credit card? Or ID?'

'Not if they pay up front. We have a lot of customers who value their privacy.'

'Bloody great.' Campbell looked around. 'Is that CCTV operational?'

'Of course,' said the receptionist.

'Do you think you could let me have a look at it. Like now?'

The receptionist led Campbell into the back room. 'We really should be out of here. The fire…'

'I'm guessing you have fire doors, yes?' She nodded. 'Designed to contain a fire?' Again, she nodded. 'Then we've got a few minutes. But better be fast, eh?'

The receptionist set to work. It took just forty seconds for her to pull up the CCTV images from the night before – she sped the file forwards until 10.31.

'That's him,' said the woman. It was a grainy black-and-white shot of two men. One, the taller of the two, had a hoodie pulled over this head and kept his face to the floor. But the other man, a stocky figure in a bomber jacket, was looking up.

'Can you get a copy of this emailed to Scotland Yard?'

'Not really – we can't do screen grabs of this.'

'You're not making this easy for me, are you?' Campbell took out his phone and took a picture of the screen.

#

CTOC, St Pancras, London
Tennant's voice was weary over the video link from Gold Command.

'The mainline stations are covered, but if the gunmen slip into the Tube, we've little chance of stopping them amid the chaos,' he said. 'What now?'

Gabriel felt the pull at her sleeve. A DS she didn't know was urgently trying to get her attention.

'Sorry, ma'am, but we've got an image of one of the suspects,' the woman said. 'DS Campbell was on the scene and grabbed it off the hotel CCTV.'

'Get it distributed,' Gabriel said. She turned back to the screen. 'You hear that, boss?'

'I did,' said Tennant. 'Get it out. And not just the usual channels – send it via the WhatsApp group the armed response units use.'

He ended the call as Bose came over. 'Ma'am.' Her face was stony. 'It's the NRF. They've claimed the attack.'

#

Central London
The art of concealment was not to look disguised, or at least that's what his old sarge had said. But right now, Rod Houghton wished he could hide his face a little more. His baseball cap was pulled down hard, so the brim was wedged into his eyebrows, but he couldn't get away with sunglasses on a miserable day and there was no refuge in his jacket.

Glenister should be walking a few paces behind, but he dared not turn to look. His train ticket was tucked into the back of his trouser pocket, the holdall was swinging against his knees – he could feel the weight of the metal with each step and his heart was clattering in his chest, surging blood around his body so violently he could feel the pulse in his neck.

Houghton crossed the road, narrowly dodging a cab which sounded its horn more out of irritation than anger, and headed towards the station, walking briskly past a busker tunelessly strumming a battered acoustic guitar. Somewhere behind him, in the heart of the capital, bodies were lying in the gutter, yet here, little more than a mile away, unconcerned shoppers and tourists were throwing coins into a busker's dirty hat. Bulldog spirit of the Blitz, he told himself. The station, and their escape from the centre of the city, was now just thirty seconds away.

#

At the foot of the majestic white flight of stone steps that led to the entrance of Waterloo station, two armed police stood in Kevlar vests and helmets, their eyes darting around the crowds, trying to pierce through the scarves and hats and coats for someone resembling the picture that had come through on WhatsApp. They held their rifles pointed down, but were ready to take aim if the suspects posed a threat to them or the milling bodies around them.

The younger of the two men scratched his leg. He had dressed quickly that morning and the strap holding his Glock pistol on his thigh was too tight. Getting more comfortable was out of the question, so he continued to scour the faces around him.

#

Houghton was inside the station, a few yards from the stone archway entrance, propped up against one of the red cast-iron pillars that supported the Victorian glazed roof. The crowd in front parted and for a moment he could see an armed police officer, just twenty metres away. He stopped breathing, wondering whether to run or reach into the bag. Time froze – then the police officer walked away. Houghton breathed again, focusing on the air in his lungs, trying to ignore the buzz of adrenaline in his veins. He was just an ordinary person waiting for a train, he told himself.

#

The armed officer swung his head from left to right. Still nothing. And then, a glimpse of someone in the crowd to his left. He turned his head, and his companion sensed his movement. A man in a baseball cap and grey hoodie. White. About the right build as the photo. And with a rucksack. The pair moved forward earnestly, parting the crowds around them. The entrance to Waterloo was too crowded to challenge him, but once the police were on the concourse, there would be more room.

#

The station seemed busier now in front of Houghton. He didn't dare look around for Glenister, he just kept his head down, kept his back jammed against the iron pillar. Ahead was the platform display board. He checked the train – it was on time and in the station. He would leave it until the last possible moment to run for the train. For now, he just had to wait.

#

The crowd had thinned out and the officer had a clear view now. The suspect was ahead of them on the concourse at Waterloo, his back to them. It was a good enough match for the photograph.

'Stop – armed police, get down on the floor, now,' he yelled, and sprinted towards the figure, keeping his rifle pointing down. The man's hands were clear, and he had no reason to lift the weapon. The man's body froze, and then turned in slow motion, his head raising as he looked behind in bewilderment and terror. The officer focused on his hands – if they moved inside his jacket, he would be ready to raise the barrel.

But the officer's rifle stayed pointing at the floor. The man was Asian – Chinese, possibly – with a shock of scruffy dark hair and a nose piercing. He lifted his hands at his side.

'Sorry, sir,' said the police officer. 'Mistaken identity.'

#

Three miles away, at Marylebone station, Rod Houghton left the shelter of his iron pillar and ran to the train. It was too soon to allow himself the luxury of relief, but his destination was now a step closer. Glenister would be on another train by now, heading for Birmingham. His own would be leaving in two minutes, heading to Aylesbury. He felt the sudden urge to urinate and moved towards the toilets.

#

CTOC, St Pancras, London
There was a stifling silence in the ops room, as if all the air had been sucked out. Gabriel looked around at the concentration on the faces of her team as they waited for an update from Waterloo. The sighting of one of the gunmen offered a glimmer of hope that they could salvage something from this terrible day.

'Come on, come on,' she mouthed to herself. An overwhelming sense of frustration seemed to ooze from every pore of her skin. She had known something like this was coming, but she had been unable to do anything. She had persuaded Tennant, but that had not been enough and now there were bodies in Pall Mall and killers on the loose.

A DC sat at a terminal in front of Gabriel was monitoring the firearms channel. 'Ma'am, the suspect spotted at Waterloo is not, I repeat not, the gunman. Mistaken identity.'

Another wave of disappointment crashed around Gabriel.

'Then where the hell are they?' she said aloud. The attack was more than forty minutes ago. They could have fled more than two miles on foot in that time. Her team were searching through CCTV, she had every officer available on the ground looking, and still they had nothing. *Please don't let them get away*, she told herself. *Not this time.*

The seconds tore by on the red digital display above the screen, but still nothing. Reports of injuries and fatalities were coming in. Six dead now. Fifteen injured by bullets, petrol bombs or in the desperate scramble to flee the scene of the attack.

Ten minutes passed and still nothing. The frustration inside Gabriel's guts was turning to a familiar hollowness. Once again, here in this bloody ops room, in front of the dozens of pairs of eyes and ears monitoring the CT room remotely from Gold Command, in front of the whole world, she was overseeing a failure. They had let down the dead and injured, they had let down the thousands of people whose lives had been put at risk and who were still at risk from these two gunmen, wandering out there somewhere. She had known something was coming, she had guessed it would come today and still she had failed.

Her phone rang. She walked into a side conference room and took a call from Tennant. He had called twice so far, leaving short messages each time.

'Boss, we've lost hot pursuit, they are now long gone.' She could not hide the dejection.

'Shit.' There was a pause. 'And you were right, of course, and we had a warning of sorts – and it was thrown away,' he said. Gabriel could hear him repeatedly muttering 'fuck' under his breath. 'Listen, keep the team energised, keep it positive. We'll get them.'

They sounded like empty words to Gabriel. 'Sure. Boss, I need to get on. We've got the photo, so we can build the manhunt. And maybe with some luck, we'll have forensics from the hotel. But it's shit. It's the only word.' She hung up.

DAY 5

Sunday

Stoke Newington, London

Ray's car was at the garage, so Gabriel offered to give him a lift to the rugby club.

'I'll get the bus, babe, I know you're crazily busy.' But Gabriel knew he didn't mean it. It was a drizzly, shadowy day, a little V-sign from winter, a reminder that while the crocuses may have been out early, spring was still many long weeks away. Even the smattering of snowdrops in their scrappy patch of front garden looked forlorn, heads drooping to the bark mulch, buffeted by an easterly wind.

Ray picked up the stack of Sunday papers that his wife had left on the passenger seat, settled in and leafed through the pages. He read for a minute, then threw the pile on to the rear seat with a grunt of disgust.

'What?' said Gabriel.

'Just the usual hack crap. They've dug up the Isobel Harris stuff again.' He paused, fiddling with the radio, then looked up. 'And there's a lovely mugshot of you. You going to be all right?'

'I saw it. It'll be fine. Tennant's got my back.'

She had bought the papers from the corner shop at six

that morning, and the coverage was merciless. *Police under fire for Pall Mall massacre* screamed the *Chronicle*. *Manhunt* was the splash in *The Eye*. There were acres of speculation about the NRF and acres more on the missed opportunities of the police. *The Globe* was claiming the police knew about a second attack but failed to take action. The story Ray had spotted was in the *Herald*. It was a small article, no more than two hundred words, under the headline: *Questions raised over Met blunders*. It appeared to be based on an interview with the Shadow Home Secretary and comments by Ishmail Sherif on Twitter. It named Gabriel as the officer responsible for letting the killers escape, and reminded their readers that she had been in charge during the Isobel Harris business. Gabriel had read it more with sadness than anger. It was a tiny story, and came across as desperate, rather than dangerous to her career. She was feeling so low after yesterday that another wound made little difference.

Ray fiddled with the radio. Gabriel immediately recognised the voice of Chris Walker, a talk radio presenter famed for his straight-talking mockney.

'...and once again, we not only have the failure by the police to protect people on the streets, we have double standards. I have no problems condemning the white terrorists who killed and maimed on Pall Mall yesterday. But where are the Muslim community leaders condemning attacks by Muslims who commit acts of terror on our streets? Like that one that stabbed a charity collector – a charity collector – in Leicester this week? Instead, we have hate preacher Ishmail Sherif on the British Broadcasting Corporation virtually calling for Muslims to take up arms. We have a prime minister refusing to act – allowing the cancer of terror to grow. But last night, Deputy Prime Minister Lesley Hogarth broke ranks with the PM and called for a Freedom Bill with tougher action against the extremists. And she's joining us on the phone right now.'

Gabriel turned it off. She drove in silence.

Ray spoke quietly above the engine as they drove past a trickle of children in rugby kits heading towards the recreation ground.

'He's a minority view, you know that,' he said.

'Yeah, but he's a loud minority view, Ray. With a radio show. And a column in the *Express*. He may be a minority, but there's a hell of a lot of them now. And he – they – are whipping it all up. This isn't going away, Ray. My dad would have hated this.'

#

Gabriel had been sixteen when her father died. He had been a surveillance motorbike rider with the Met, an extraordinary job she now knew, but which at the time he could talk little about. The young Gabriel had sensed a world of speed and danger, secret meetings, exotic hotels and exotic-sounding towns like Aberdeen, Newcastle or Louth.

Sometimes he went away from home, often with no warning, occasionally for a week. And then he'd return, always bringing Gabriel the same present – a bar of Toblerone chocolate. And he'd tell stories of how he had bought it – once from a newsagent who was really a drugs baron, another from a stall where he'd been working undercover. Gabriel devoured the chocolate within a day every time, but kept the triangular cardboard sleeves in a drawer in her bedside table. Years after, she discovered that he bought them from the garage at the end of their road, a last stop before walking through the door. When she learnt that, she had loved him even more.

Then, one Tuesday evening in April, a policewoman came to the door. Gabriel had answered it; her mother was taking a nap. Gabriel had known from the way that woman stood, from the sombre broken face, from the pain in her eyes, what had happened. Her mother came up behind her and she gasped, knowing the worst – before a word had been uttered. The policewoman had come inside and focused on her mother, with Gabriel watching from the velvet chair by the window.

They had gone that night to the hospital. Her father was in intensive care, he might not make the night, they were told, his back injuries were that severe. He lasted four days.

In the months that followed, her mother had not hidden her anger at the service. Yet Gabriel had been drawn closer to the police. Her father's best friend, Guy Longstock, a DI in counter terrorism, had encouraged her to consider a career in the force, and Gabriel had agreed, more to annoy her mother than honour her father. Longstock had stayed in touch, helping and advising her in her early days. And she had repaid the favour on that day when Jack Pearce fled the country on her watch for his new life in Syria as Abu Mujahid. Longstock was ancient by then, approaching retirement age, and was running an operation in the East End and urgently needed a surveillance unit. She agreed to his request and diverted the unit watching Pearce to help him out. She knew at the time that her decision was based more on loyalty to her father's friend than reasoned judgement. In the inquiry, she had conceded it was a marginal call, but one that was defensible. But in her heart, in the darkest moments when she relived that day in her head, she knew she had made the wrong call.

#

Forty minutes later, Campbell slid the scene-of-crime report from the hotel across the table to Gabriel. Two or three dozen of the team had joined Gabriel and Skeffington in the small conference room. The mood was sombre.

'The two men did a good job wiping the slate clean when they set fire to their hotel room,' said Campbell. 'But we got something all the same.'

'From the room?' said Gabriel.

'Better than that, ma'am. The men threw four petrol bombs made from beer bottles. They were careful, but not careful

124

enough because they didn't use gloves. When you throw a petrol bomb, the glass breaks before the petrol ignites – so you can have quite chunky fragments lying around the place that haven't been exposed to heat.'

'Are you saying they got a fingerprint from a splinter of glass from an exploded petrol bomb?' Skeffington's eyebrows were raised. 'You're taking the mickey, Campbell?'

'No, sir. Not fingerprints. But they did get DNA – most likely from skin or saliva.'

Gabriel whistled. 'Could it be from the shopkeeper who sold them the beer?' said Skeffington. 'Or someone at the bottling plant.'

'That's what I wondered. But the SOCOs also got a sample from the door handle of the hotel room. That's been harder to analyse – but they've found a match among the dozens of samples on the handle. They're pretty confident it's the same man. It's gone through the national DNA database but come back as no trace. They're trying a familial DNA analysis, ma'am. Just begun and should have the first results in twenty-four hours.'

Familial DNA searching was a relatively new field for the Met. Rather than looking for exact matches, a familial search looks for close matches – people with similar DNA who may be family members. Gabriel had used it a handful of times in the last few years. Each time, it had generated hundreds of potential suspects, and traditional police work was needed to whittle the shortlist down to something manageable.

'All right, Campbell. As I see it, in addition to the familial DNA search, we have two other strands. We continue the CCTV search – the Tube, railways, streets. The hotel CCTV gives us one of the men. Not great, but better than nothing. He's short, around five foot seven inches, sturdily built, and white, obviously. His face is obscured throughout.' The image from the hotel reception came on the screen.

'I need the video unit working on this. We need a match with driving licence and passport records. The other man stayed in the shadows. Male, around six foot, and wearing a green hoodie, but no visuals.

'Two, go back through the video records of every far-right demo and march over the last ten years, this time looking for anyone resembling these two men. Clear?'

The meeting ended. *What next*, thought Gabriel as the team dispersed. First Fletcher, now these two men. Then who knows what? It was like a hydra. Each time they cut off a head, another two grew in its place.

Bose was waiting outside the conference room with a clutch of papers.

'Ma'am, quick word.' Her eyes showed concern. 'We've had an interesting report from Sussex Special Branch on a lorry full of illegal immigrants.'

'Can't it wait, Eva?'

'Not really, ma'am. The DS from Sussex thinks one of the immigrants is a match for Abu Mujahid.'

#

Cabinet Office, Whitehall, London
The Home Secretary smacked his palm on the table, sending his pencil rolling to the floor. His aide leaned across and returned the pencil. The Home Secretary glowered at her, before turning to Tennant and the head of MI5.

'Tell me this,' Thomas said with slow emphasis, his voice becoming more Geordie with each word. 'The press are ripping us apart and I don't blame them. Not only does the combined might of SO15 and MI5 fail to stop two armed terrorists checking into a hotel and throwing petrol bombs and opening fire on passers-by, they walk straight out of the hotel, past God knows how many armed police, and vanish. Either of you – please, feel free to fill us all in.'

Tennant breathed in deeply through his nose and ran his tongue inside of his top molars. This was supposed to be a security briefing, not a telling-off from the head boy. *Don't get annoyed*, he thought, *stay calm*. When he was new to the police, he'd once been told by a wise chief inspector: 'Steve, always respect the office, even when it's occupied by a dickhead.' The words were in his ears now.

He drew another slow breath.

'It's correct that both these men were unknown to us and to the security service, Home Secretary,' said Tennant. 'As we've discussed before, intel on the NRF is not as good as it could be.'

'That's a bloody understatement,' muttered Thomas.

COBRA had gone badly up to that point. Tennant had given an update on the manhunt for the two gunmen. He had tried his hardest to react positively to JTAC's decision, announced with unnecessary fanfare at the opening, Tennant thought, to raise the threat level to critical. A junior defence minister had muttered 'A day bloody late' under her breath and Tennant had privately agreed. Tennant had been equally annoyed when the head of JTAC said there was no hard evidence of a third attack, 'just a presumption which we are not one hundred per cent confident in'.

Tennant continued: 'Given that JTAC is now raising the threat level, we will need to step up protective policing measures – more armed officers visible, more foot patrols at crowded locations such as stations, and a review of security for forthcoming major events. May I also say that while I understand the position of JTAC with regards to a third NRF attack, I am sure that another is planned.'

The head of JTAC glowered at him.

Hogarth's treacly voice piped up.

'I wonder, Steven, whether you have the right team on this investigation,' she said. Tennant could sense his body tensing. 'The press are asking very legitimate questions about whether Detective Superintendent Gabriel is the right person to have in charge. I mean, her track record isn't great, is it? She let Abu Mujahid escape from under her nose, after killing that young girl. Is she up to this?'

Tennant was brisk. 'Deputy Prime Minister, the reports

in the media are unfair and inaccurate. This is my call and Gabriel has my full confidence. She's an extremely capable, skilled and resourceful officer.'

'Of course, Steven, you know best,' said Hogarth, her eyes betraying what she really thought.

The Prime Minister broke the silence. 'This is not the time for an inquest into yesterday. We need to be responding to the situation now.'

The Home Secretary was quick to jump in. 'I agree. And I believe this response from the far right is, in part, a reaction to the cancer of Islamist extremism which we have allowed to fester. We've allowed the fundamentalist Islamists too much space – and we've seen that in the violence and riots in the Muslim community of the last few days. We must be tougher and we must be seen to be tougher.'

'What are you proposing exactly, Ben?' The Prime Minister's voice was dangerously quiet.

'What we should have done months ago,' said Thomas. 'A raft of measures to stamp down on extremism. New profiling measures at ports. A ban on burqas. Temporary restrictions on immigration from dangerous countries. Repatriation of non-British citizens – even those with settled status – who break the law. No benefits for new migrants until they've paid taxes for five years. Regulation of mosques to eradicate extremism. We crack down on those who abuse our freedom of speech to preach hatred and we increase the presence of military on the streets to reassure the public. Then we bring this all together in a Freedom Bill.'

Far too loudly came a 'Hear, hear' from Lesley Hogarth.

The Prime Minister shook his head. 'This would be the worst time to take the sort of extremist measures you propose, Home Secretary.'

'Extremist, Prime Minister?' The Home Secretary reddened.

'Slip of the tongue,' the Prime Minister said deliberately. 'Extreme. It'd send a signal that we're scared and that the terrorists are winning. We don't let terrorists sway domestic policy.'

#

The Home Secretary was waiting for Tennant outside the COBRA suite. He sidled over and rested a warm hand on Tennant's arm.

'I didn't want to strong-arm you back there in the meeting, Steven, but it needed saying. This was an almighty cock-up.'

'I can't agree, Home Secretary,' said Tennant, sliding one arm away from Thomas and into his navy woollen coat. 'You'll recall the Treasury didn't accept all of our submissions in the last spending round. And that was after we made clear we had gaps in our capacity to deal with the unprecedented Islamist threat, the risk of returners and the new accelerating extreme right-wing threats.'

The Home Secretary gazed at Tennant silently before moving closer. His forehead was a couple of inches away and the smile had dissolved into a waft of stale coffee breath and aftershave.

'I don't care about fucking budgets.' His voice was soft. 'We need results. We need the perpetrators of this attack rounded up urgently. We need you and your team working all the fucking hours God has given you to find these missing men and deal with them.'

He smiled with dead eyes and walked out with Hogarth.

#

CTOC, St Pancras, London
Bose sat across the table, her laptop open.

'Two nights ago, Sussex Police pulled over a van near Gatwick just after 1am,' she said. 'In the back were six people, barely a word of English between them, and very cold, very dirty and very sick. The driver's story was nonsense, so he and his passengers were held overnight at Crawley, and interviewed yesterday.

'It was the usual story. They'd been trafficked on the

promise of a job and house and were heading for a farm in Lincolnshire. They'd come over in a refrigerated lorry to Newhaven, taken to an industrial park in the middle of the night and transferred to the van. The driver of the lorry is a Vicki Braithwaite, conveniently away on holiday. So far, so run of the mill. What makes it interesting to us is that there was a seventh passenger on the trip over from France, described by one of the group, and these are his words, as "very, very scary". He was white, in his thirties or forties, red-haired and bearded, and said nothing the entire time.'

The hairs on Gabriel's neck were prickling.

'Go on.'

'Sussex grabbed CCTV of the handover at the industrial park. It's poor quality but…' Gabriel snatched the laptop from Bose and pulled it over. Bose was right, the quality was terrible and the lighting poor. The CCTV camera was looking down at the rear end of an articulated lorry with its open doors swinging in the wind. The occupants dropped out of the lorry one by one. Four came out on their own, two more were helped, probably suffering mild hypothermia, thought Gabriel. There was a pause, then a seventh figure slid out and walked in the opposite direction. Gabriel froze the video. It was a man in dark clothes with a baseball cap. She rewound and watched again. She'd spent hours scrutinising footage of Abu Mujahid two years ago and she knew his walk. Was that him? She rewound again, and again.

'I think it's him, Eva,' she said. Bose said nothing, a sign that she was not convinced.

'Seriously. That's his walk. That's his build. And the description from the others… Jesus.'

She played it again. Each time she watched the murky image, she was edging closer and closer to certainty.

'Ma'am, I think it's interesting, and it's something to follow up, which is why I showed you,' said Bose. 'But the chances of that being Abu Mujahid are pretty remote.'

Gabriel snapped. 'Don't you think I know what he looks like,

Bose? He's in here, remember.' She tapped on her forehead. Bose looked hurt and Gabriel softened. 'I've watched hundreds of hours of CCTV of him. And I tell you, that's him. He's back.'

#

University of Islington, North London
A constellation of flickering flames greeted Asad as he stepped through the archway into the quad, a reflection of the clear skies above his head. A hundred, maybe two hundred, candles were dotted around the square, most in glasses to protect them from gusts. They cast splashes of light on students huddling together for warmth, whispering and talking with subdued voices.

He'd come here straight from prayers to pay his respects to the brothers and sisters who had fallen just metres from where he and Mirza had been cowering, and the words shamed him now as he heard them in his head. He had done nothing. He had run like a child.

Asad stood, hands in his jacket pockets, next to the central fountain, the light playing on his face as he gazed down at the water trickling into the drains. He had brought a candle and he placed it next to the water, struggling in the biting wind to bring it to life with a disposable lighter. Sugary incense wafted through the cold night air, contrasting with the sour odour of burning plastic.

'Brother.' Mirza's soft voice was in his ear. For a moment, he wondered if he'd imagined him, but Mirza was standing in the shadows next to him.

'We did nothing. We were cowards, Tanvir.' Asad's voice trembled.

Mirza shushed him. 'We protected ourselves. We stuck together. Don't tear yourself apart over this, bro.'

Asad followed Mirza through a brick arch passage and into a car park shielded on three sides by buildings and on the fourth by iron railings, a gate and the porter's hut.

'Listen, Omar, we saw the real enemy yesterday – the British state. They shoot our brothers in cold blood overseas, and they allowed the Nazis to shoot and petrol bomb our brothers and sisters – and children – in London. They let them stab innocent people at a theme park. That's the value this country puts on Muslims. Ishmail Sherif is right.'

His eyes were wide open as he sat on a low wall, hands rested palm down on his knees.

'We can choose to do nothing, or we can take up arms and defend our brothers and sisters as a team. It's us against them. This is a war, and we are God's soldiers in this war.' He wrenched his arm around and pulled out a copy of that morning's *Herald* from his backpack.

'Have you read this? What Hogarth wants? To stop our sisters covering up in public. She wants to tear off their veils. And stop Muslims coming to Britain. Not Jews. Not Hindus. Not unbelievers. Just Muslims.'

This time there was no dissent, no arguing over nuance. Asad could feel his mind beginning to clear and a fresh sense of purpose emerging. He nodded grimly.

'And I've got a date to meet him.' Mirza did not need to say Abu Mujahid's name. 'Tomorrow evening. I'll tell you where on the day.'

#

Wandsworth Common, South London

Rod Houghton heard the crunch of tyre on gravel outside the house as headlights swept over the curtains. He rose from the sofa and opened the cream curtains a fraction of an inch. He heard laughter as the car door opened and slammed and the young couple from upstairs came towards the porch light, giggling and clutching each other. He returned to the sofa and sat in silence as they made their way noisily through the hall and up the staircase.

Houghton had arrived at the flat twenty-four hours earlier

132

after a circuitous route through Aylesbury and back to London. It had been the NRF safe house for two years, chosen for its seclusion and anonymity. The other flats in the building were occupied by students and youngsters fresh from college, the sort who paid little interest in the comings and goings of neighbours and who rarely stayed more than a few months.

In the darkness, it was easy to lose his thoughts and he drifted back to his twenty-one-year-old self, risking his neck in Helmand on behalf of a country that didn't give a shit, a time when his hair was still black rather than silvery grey. He'd seen everything in black and white at the time – it was a fight between decency and the death cult of the Taliban, between right and wrong. And then, when he came back to Britain, years later, he discovered that the same cult had its fingers around the throat of his homeland and was injecting its venom in the very streets of Bolton that he'd grown up in. Places that had changed beyond recognition – not just with Muslims but with Russians and Poles too. And while there'd always been Poles in Bolton, they were now everywhere. It felt like he was a firefighter coming home to discover his own house burning down.

And the frustration, after all that he'd seen and done, all the times he'd risked his life in special ops, to come home and end up begging for work while the Poles and the Russians and the Muslims took the jobs and the council houses and the appointments at the doctors and the places in the decent schools. He felt he'd fought for another country, only to lose his own. And then, to rub salt into the wounds, he had watched with disbelief and dismay as the politicians washed their hands of Afghanistan and walked away, abandoning his dead comrades' legacy and leaving its people to their miserable fate.

His phone buzzed. The number was withheld. He put it on speaker.

'It's me,' said the quiet voice. 'You secure?'

'All good.'

'And Glenister?'

'In Leeds,' said Houghton. 'Arrived this morning and in the safe house.'

'Good. I need to be quick. Debrief me on Chilton Park. How come the police got hold of Fletcher's phone?'

Houghton was thrown. He bluffed. 'He was supposed to have ditched it,' he said.

'Well, he fucking didn't ditch it, he left it behind at the theme park, hidden in a roof space. And he left incriminating messages on it – from you.'

The first outward hint of anger, thought Houghton. 'It's not a problem. They've got nothing to link him to me.'

He had been careful to ensure that. He'd found Fletcher on an incel forum, devoted to the 'involuntary celibate' community. The overlap between men who love to talk about killing women and those who feel the same about Muslims was conveniently large. Within six weeks they'd spoken on the phone, six weeks later they'd met face to face. They had met half a dozen times since, but always somewhere anonymous, always somewhere different.

Silence down the other end. Footsteps on wood echoed through the ceiling above Houghton, and he could hear muffled voices and the sudden sound of a TV being switched on.

'Okay.' The voice was warmer now. 'It's not been perfect – but not a crock of shit either. How are we for phase three? Everyone in position?'

'Not a problem. I'm getting daily updates from now on – all good so far.'

'Good – we need to keep the momentum going. Stay here another three days. I'll let you know if the police are on to you. But from what I hear, they're clueless. This is the dawn of something big, so let's not fuck it up.'

Houghton gave the NRF's traditional rallying cry. 'To the fight back.'

'To getting our country back, one dead foreigner at a time,' came the reply.

CTOC, St Pancras, London

Gabriel was overwhelmed with exhaustion. She had called GCHQ to learn Abu Mujahid's last confirmed trace was six weeks ago. She had arranged for her team to interview the six migrants, chase up the driver of the refrigerated lorry, and check up on Abu Mujahid's family. Each decision took resources and attention off the NRF manhunt, and she knew that within a day she would get a call from on high, questioning her priorities. But she pushed those doubts deep down.

It was late. The rain had held off, so she left the office and, keen to get some air, walked past her usual bus stop at King's Cross towards Angel, dodging the tourists in their fluorescent colours and Londoners in their drab greys and brown overcoats. *Why did British people dress so miserably in the winter?* thought Gabriel as she trudged towards the station. Maybe it was a form of camouflage, dress like the winter to blend in.

The job was never boring, she reflected, but there were days when things were quieter, when her role was more routine. There were weeks when all the people they had under surveillance were cooped up inside all day, doing little other than watching TV and arguing. But now, there was too much at once. Her head was struggling to contain the information. First Fletcher, then Pall Mall and the DNA hunt for the killer, and now Abu Mujahid. She wondered about her dad. Days upon end of watching the same people, focused always in the now, never having to juggle a dozen operations. She envied his life sometimes.

By the time she was at home in her kitchen, mug of mint tea in hand, trying hard not to wake Ray upstairs, her head was a little clearer, and her conviction that Abu Mujahid was back in the UK a little stronger.

DAY 6

Monday

CTOC, St Pancras, London
Gabriel had once been told at a professional development course on public speaking that the best way to silence a room was to stand still holding her arms out wide, palms down, and then to gradually lower her arms. The most important thing Gabriel had learnt that day was that much of the advice shared at professional development courses was nonsense.

'Shut up, please,' she bellowed. The babble of sixty people squeezed into the ops room simmered down quickly. Gabriel could sense the crackling in the air, but felt numbness where she should be feeling energised. The media was still sniping at her over the Pall Mall fiasco and there was still nothing more on Abu Mujahid. He had made no obvious contact with his family, the lorry had vanished and so had four of the six migrants pulled over by Sussex Police. The remaining two were due to be interviewed that afternoon.

'This week has been like none I can remember,' she said, summoning an enthusiasm she did not feel. 'You've given up your leave, your home lives and shown a level of dedication that I'm not surprised to see, but I am gratified to see, nonetheless. And I'm asking you to continue.

'We are in the firing line, but we're used to that. And the best answer to our critics is to do our job well. So we'll start with Pall Mall and the two missing killers. Facial recognition software has come up with a longlist – some two thousand-odd faces from driver's licences and passports. The video unit's whittling them down now by hand and should have something by first thing tomorrow.

'Even better news is the familial DNA results from the petrol bomb fragments are in. We've got a reasonably close match between the DNA extract and the DNA of a forty-eight-year-old-male called Tony Roberts. We know he wasn't involved in Saturday's attack because he's currently serving time in Wakefield for seven sexual assaults including a serious assault on a child. However, his family tree is large and complex, and we've narrowed our suspect to one of fourteen adult males closely related to Mr Roberts. It's likely to be a sibling, cousin, second cousin, uncle or nephew. The family are spread over South London, Essex, Sussex and Devon. Surnames are likely to be Roberts, Clark, Houghton or Clifton.'

There was whispering at the back at this. The DNA results had not been announced to the team.

'We need covert DNA from all fourteen family members,' Gabriel continued. 'We haven't got the bodies to go after all of them at once, so we go for three or four samples a day.

'At the same time, we use old-fashioned police work on these fourteen suspects – we need to know where the suspects are right now, and where they were Friday night and Saturday morning. We need to know who is too fat, too ill or too much on holiday, or in prison, to have been one of these men.' She waved at the screen, which displayed the CCTV grab from the hotel.

'There's urgency to this, people. We have two dangerous, reckless killers walking free right now.

'Another thing. As you know, it's likely Chilton Park was the first of three planned attacks by the NRF, and that Pall

Mall was the second. These attacks are intended to destabilise Britain and spread terror and mistrust between Muslims and non-Muslims. And just look at the papers and the crime reports – it is working. We don't know what the third attack will be, but it could be soon.'

She walked to her seat as Bose stood up to take over. But she was barely listening, her thoughts still preoccupied with Abu Mujahid.

#

Twenty minutes later, Gabriel clicked on the link sent from the comms team, which opened up a video from *Rise & Shine*, a lightweight TV magazine programme. She instantly recognised the girl sat on the famous beige sofa as Zahra, the teenager from the Chilton Park staff canteen, the one who had asked if she would be safe, the one who reminded her of Isobel Harris. The host, a smiling Welsh woman with a gentle voice and a suspiciously unwrinkled forehead, was famous for her soft interviews, described by Ray once as the velvet hand in a velvet glove.

'So, Zahra,' oozed the host, 'we can't imagine what you've been through, and I know everyone watching just feels so much for you. We'll go back to the tragedy of Chilton Park in a moment if you're up for it, but on Saturday you were at the Pall Mall attack too, weren't you? Were you okay?'

Zahra paused, her head tilted down as she seemed to summon the words. Then, with a confidence and clarity that surprised Gabriel, she gazed directly at her host and spoke.

'Yes – I was okay. I was on the platform at Trafalgar Square, but we got away safely. I didn't see anything, but obviously I've seen it on TV.'

'I mean, you've been extraordinarily unlucky, to be involved in two of these attacks, one after another.'

Zahra nodded.

'And what support have you had?'

'That's been good. I've got a police liaison officer who's been brilliant. Really nice and she's there all the time.' Zahra paused. 'But you know, that's good, of course, but it still doesn't help answer how they let this happen. Again.'

'The police?'

'Yep. How did they let that man do what he did to my family and all those people? And then how did the same people, this NRF, just walk into a hotel and do it again? Why didn't the police stop them? Why are they not watching these people?'

'You were on the platform with Ishmail Sherif, who many people feel is a controversial, divisive figure. He's called for Muslims to stand up and fight, those are his words. Do you agree?'

Zahra shook her head. 'No. Of course I don't agree with everything he says – he's one voice. I don't like the language of fighting and violence, that's not the way. But he's right about the government – they are just doing nothing. They are so obsessed with Islamist terrorists they are missing the neo-Nazis. Is it going to happen again? I keep asking, are we safe?'

Gabriel watched to the end of the video, then shut down the laptop. She couldn't blame Zahra – the girl had gone through so much and lost so much. She was usually immune to complaints about the police, yet today she felt an echo of the girl's frustration. They could have done more. Perhaps they wouldn't have stopped the attack, but if she'd had the resources she and Tennant had asked for, then maybe, just maybe. But this wasn't the time for self-flagellation. She needed to turn her frustration into action.

#

Croydon, South London
Saturday evening was the quietest period of the week in the Croydon leisure centre and the only time Bob Houghton could guarantee a half hour alone in the sauna. The thought of sharing

the confined space with other sweaty male bodies turned his stomach. He glanced at his watch, the only item of clothing he had on. 7.40pm. Another minute. He played listlessly with the strap. Lizzie had given him this Tissot watch for his thirtieth. Two weeks before she'd walked out. He'd been tempted to chuck it away, but he liked the chunkiness of the stainless steel. It was almost inevitably a fake, but he didn't care.

Time up. He nudged open the glass door and padded barefoot to the changing room across the grimy floor, white towel wrapped around his waist. He had laid his clothes neatly on the bench, confident that no one would be interested in his tatty sportswear. But something was missing. Where was his Adidas vest? He loved that vest. It was vintage. Who would steal that?

Bob Houghton looked around the floor. Nothing. Only one other man was in there – a short guy with cropped black hair and a holdall. He was just leaving.

'Excuse me – seen my vest? It's yellow?'

'Sorry, buddy – not seen it.' And the man left.

That was odd. *Really odd*, he thought. He opened the locker and put his leather jacket over his bare chest and stomach, zipped it up tight. *No one will notice*, he thought. But who the hell would want to nick a sweaty shirt?

#

One hour and five minutes later, Bob Houghton's second cousin Joe Clifton was sitting in the snug of the Clarence Arms in Hounslow, with his back to the bar and his eyes on the door. Clifton swigged from his beer bottle and placed it on the beer mat. A young couple sat down at the next table. He looked like a typical East End barrow boy – all muscles, shaved hair and swagger – but she looked quite fit though, he thought.

'Joseph, you old poof, what can I get you?' Jamie from work was stood by the bar. *Bollocks*, thought Clifton, turning round. He was waiting for someone else – the last person he wanted to see right now was Jamie, the dullest man on the planet. But he was left with no choice.

'I'll have another of these – cheers.' He turned around to pick up his half-empty bottle to wave at Jamie. But the table was empty and his bottle was gone.

Bloody hell, someone's nicked it. He looked around angrily but saw no one. The couple were still deep in conversation, he with his hands on the table, she clutching a large handbag tightly to her stomach. He looked at the floor, but no, it hadn't rolled off. Someone was taking the piss.

He stood up and walked to the bar to get a replacement off Jamie.

He didn't see the couple stand up and leave, but by the time he'd returned to his table, they'd cleared off. *Shame*, he thought. That woman clutching the bag had been a bit of a looker.

DAY 7

Tuesday

West Ealing, West London
'Kippy, here girl.' Graham Clifton slapped his leg and Kippy, a lethargic retriever, ambled across the kitchen. He grabbed a parka coat and clipped a lead around the dog's collar.

Kippy had been Cheryl's idea. 'It'll be company for me – and good exercise.' She'd not added 'for you', but the missing words had floated unsaid in the air. Graham Clifton looked down at his belly. One too many takeaways maybe.

He grabbed a packet of Benson & Hedges from the hall table and felt for a lighter in his jeans. If he had to get up at 6.30am, then at least he could have a fag, he thought as he stepped through the front door.

That was better, he thought as he pulled the smoke down into his lungs. The best smoke of the day, that first head rush that lifted the spirits and cleared the heaviness from his chest. It was worth smoking just for that. At the end of his drive, he looked left to where a white Ford Fiesta was parked in the cul-de-sac under the street lamp. It looked like it had been left overnight, only there was someone sitting in the front looking at a map. *Good luck to you, feller*, he thought, *if you're trying to find a house, the numbering on this estate is atrocious.* He threw down the cigarette butt and yanked the lead. Kippy reluctantly followed.

#

The woman in the car watched through the side mirror until the man with the dog had gone around the corner. The door opened and she stepped out. She slipped a plastic glove on her hand and pulled out a clear plastic bag. Bending over quickly, she picked up his still-smouldering cigarette butt and wafted it around until it was cool enough to go in the bag. Then she folded it over and got back in the car.

#

CTOC, St Pancras, London
Gabriel met Skeffington and Campbell outside the cafe on the ground floor as she was taking a mug of coffee back upstairs.

'You look like you've won the lottery, Skeffington,' she said.

'Pretty close, ma'am,' said Skeffington. 'Just come down from the video unit. They've got a decent visual match on one of the Pall Mall gunmen.'

Gabriel perked up.

'He's a Douglas Glenister,' said Skeffington. 'Dougie to his mates, ex-squaddie, thirty-seven, divorced, one kid. Served in Afghanistan, left the army eight years ago and now a school caretaker – sorry, apparently he's a school premises manager, for fuck's sake.'

'Try to restrain your irritation at the twenty-first century, Skeffington,' said Gabriel. 'Where is he now?'

'Unknown. A team's gone over to his house, we've pulled his records and we're fast-tracking his phone and bank details, all the usual.'

'Anything of note?'

'Not a lot, ma'am,' said Skeffington. 'Previous for public

disorder and criminal damage, but sod all to link him to the NRF. But he's got a DNA sample in the files – and it wasn't his dabs on the petrol bomb fragment.'

'That's something at least. It means we've got leads for both Pall Mall attackers. What news on the familial DNA search of the other man?'

'Also promising, ma'am,' said Skeffington. 'As of twenty minutes ago, they'd nabbed four samples from the male suspects. They've been fairly enterprising. One of the suspects was in the gym, so they pilfered his sports top. The rest are the usual – beer bottles, fag ends, spent tissues. Two results back already and both ruled out. Should have another three or four by the end of play today.'

'And surveillance?'

'Slower, ma'am,' said Skeffington. 'We've ruled out one old geezer – he's been in a mobility scooter for the last two years. Officially it's arthritis, but looking at pictures of the fat bastard, it could be laziness.'

Gabriel slurped from the mug. 'We're still left with eleven suspects at least. We need to prioritise them further. I'm assuming that you've looked for military connections in the extended family.'

Skeffington looked uncomfortable.

'Oh, for God's sake, Skeffington, you've just told me that his associate Douglas Glenister was in the army. It's the obvious call. Get on to it now.'

\#

Twenty minutes later, Gabriel, Skeffington and Campbell were stood behind a DC, with the profiles of the DNA targets on the screen.

'So how many are military?' said Gabriel, shooting a withering look at Skeffington.

'Two,' said the DC. 'A sixty-year-old former naval warrant officer, now living in Truro with wife and grown-up daughters. The other's Rod Houghton, ex-SRR in London. A second cousin to the paedo in the nick. His house is under surveillance, but there's no sign of him.'

'SRR?' asked Campbell.

'Special Reconnaissance Regiment, Campbell. Jesus, man, get a grip,' said Skeffington. 'Special Forces. They're the monkey's bollocks – intelligence gathering, surveillance. Think Bravo Zero Zero. This Rod Houghton knows a sod of a lot more about dodging surveillance than you do, cockney.'

Gabriel stroked her chin. 'Get more resources on those two – and a team into Rod Houghton's house. He's the best lead we've got. And Skeffington, sharpen up, man.'

She fumed. Was Skeffington her punishment for some sin in a previous life?

#

Chiswick, West London
Two figures stood in the back garden of Rod Houghton's pebble-dashed house and peered through the kitchen window. The garden was quiet, the only sound the tick-tick alarm call of a robin watching from its perch on the creosoted fence.

The woman pulled out a card and metal pick from her pocket and prodded and teased the lock of the back door until it clicked open. The pair stood in silence for a moment before the woman gently pulled on the handle and stepped over the doorway.

The woman pointed to a silver bin which the man opened while she pulled down the window blind. It was empty, the black bin liner inside unused. He shook his head and then pulled open the fridge door. The rectangle of light dazzled their eyes. Inside was an unopened carton of long-life orange juice and a sealed block of supermarket cheese. No fresh food, no signs that anyone was living here. The owner hadn't left in a hurry either. This place had been tidied up and cleaned. There were no abandoned cups, no dirty plates.

The pair crept into the hallway. The woman's torch cast a narrow beam across the floor and onto a scattering of junk mail addressed to Rodney J. Houghton. They stood in silence, ears straining for any noise upstairs. But there was nothing. The woman opened the door to the tiny cloakroom by the front door and lifted the lavatory seat. She smelt the pine before her eyes registered that the water was green from a squirt of lavatory cleaner around the rim. The house had been abandoned by someone who knew that they would be away for a few days. Someone meticulous who didn't like loose ends. She removed a sealed plastic bag from her pocket and began to take swabs from the toilet seat, toothbrush and towels.

#

CTOC, St Pancras, London
The woman from the Home Office was insistent.

'I'm sorry, Detective Superintendent, but we need the briefing note urgently. The Home Secretary has asked for it personally.'

Gabriel forced herself to be calm. The woman's sing-song voice was intensely grating. 'And as I explained, I don't have the resources right now to prepare a briefing note.'

'And what do I tell the Home Secretary?'

'To be honest, I don't actually care. I'm too busy chasing down real terrorists today to do your paperwork.' She slammed down the phone and clicked open the transcript of the interviews with the two migrants smuggled into the UK in the refrigerated lorry.

The first interview, with a Sudanese young man probably no older than eighteen, was hopeless. He had clammed up and said nothing of value. The second, with an Iranian journalist, was more promising. He had paid traffickers to get him to the UK, where he had cousins, on a convoluted route through Turkey, across the Black Sea through Ukraine and across Europe. He had been picked up by the lorry near Lille, and spent a miserable fourteen hours in the back. Gabriel read through his descriptions of his fellow passengers, stopping at the description of the 'hard white man'. Tanned, possibly American or Australian or, when pressed by the interviewer, possibly English. He was quiet, red-headed and wore 'a long, old man's beard', the Iranian had said. Some of the other passengers had talked about families in broken French, but the white man had been silent throughout.

Gabriel read the description again with a growing excitement and emailed the interviewing team. 'Get an e-fit.'

She was lost in her thoughts when Skeffington walked up to her desk. He grinned down at her. Gabriel thought it looked more like a leer.

'Ma'am, Rod Houghton's our prime suspect. He hasn't been seen for three or four days and his house is deserted. Looks like he knew he would be away for a while.'

'What's his history?' asked Gabriel.

'Top-rate military career. He was involved in a botched rescue op of prisoners held by the Taliban. Left the army three years ago. There was an allegation of bullying against an Asian colleague, but it wasn't substantiated and the allegation was withdrawn. Currently lives alone and works as a part-time security guard. Took his entire four weeks' holiday in one go and isn't due back for another two weeks. No activity on his phone or bank accounts for the last four days. His phone was last used in London on Wednesday, bank card used to withdraw three hundred pounds on Friday from Central London.'

'Have we nothing better? DNA from his house?'

'Forensics are around there now,' said Skeffington, annoyed that the breakthrough had not been received with a pat on the back. 'And we've also been able to rule out three more family members from covert DNA collected last night and this morning – Joe and Graham Clifton and a Robert Houghton. I'm pretty confident this guy's our man, ma'am.'

Gabriel gazed through the window to the pavement below.

Circumstantial, yes, but also plausible. And like his associate, Douglas Glenister, another ex-squaddie.

'Get the team together. Rod Houghton's our man.'

#

Victoria Street, London

The Black Goat was tucked down a side street off Victoria Street, close to the Cinnamon Club, five minutes from Parliament and four from the Home Office. It had a reputation for expensive, mediocre British food and discreet private dining rooms. The paucity of the servings and the suspect wine list put it off the circuit of eateries beloved by MPs, political advisers and lobby journalists, and so made it ideal for Ben Thomas.

Hogarth was late. Her spad Nina O'Brien had agreed 12.30pm, and it was already twenty to one. He'd rather be having lunch with O'Brien, he thought, glancing again at his watch. Maybe it was the red hair or the piercing, but she looked like she'd be good fun. He felt a stirring and allowed his mind to wander.

'Deepest apologies, Ben, so sorry to keep you.' Hogarth's voice broke his reverie. He dropped a napkin into his lap and half-rose as the waiter pulled out her leather high-backed chair. Hogarth was clad in a floral dress that was either cutting-edge fashion, or thirty years out of date. She looked like a pair of Laura Ashley curtains on legs, Thomas thought as he pecked her on each cheek. Old woman's perfume too. Something an aunt would have worn.

'Glass of something, Lesley?' offered the Home Secretary.

'Thank you – white, please. Italian. Are you not…?'

Thomas waved his mineral water with one hand. Hogarth knew perfectly well he was on the wagon. He watched in silence as she bustled and fussed like a cat preparing to settle down.

'Nice piece in *The Post* this morning,' said Hogarth. 'Captured the public mood perfectly.'

Thomas agreed. The column had called for a tougher stance on Islamists and migrants.

'Can't imagine the PM will have been chuffed,' continued Hogarth.

He certainly wasn't, Thomas thought to himself. 'It needed saying, Lesley. These moments come once in a lifetime and we have to grab them.'

They ordered – he a steak and salad, she monkfish – and got the small talk out of the way. Hogarth brought the conversation back to Thomas's opinion piece.

'It's the crime of the age, offending people,' she said. 'We mustn't offend anyone, must we? Not the gays. Or the blacks. Or the Muslims. Or the vegans. And when the public see their leaders so scared of causing offence that they don't speak out against the Islamists arguing for Sharia Britain, you can understand why so many people are angry.'

They were silent as the waiter brought the food and Hogarth arranged the vegetables around her plate.

'One of the things I admire about you, Lesley, is that you value loyalty,' he said. Hogarth continued to eat, but sat ever-so-slightly more upright, her eyes ever-so-slightly more focused.

'It's a trait that seems to have gone out of fashion,' said Thomas. 'Take my dad. Extraordinarily loyal man – to my mother, loyal to his friends and colleagues in the pit and loyal to the union. He hated Arthur Scargill, yet he stayed out all through the miner's strike – right up to the end in March '85. Absolutely futile. But that stubbornness, that loyalty. I loved that about him.'

'As you say, Ben, it's an old-school trait and not many of us have it,' said Hogarth, who, Thomas noted to himself, had knifed the previous head of her own party to grab power.

'And I've always been loyal to the PM,' Thomas continued. 'We've had disagreements before, of course. I'd be lying if I said it had all been easy. But I've stuck with him and he with me. And yet…' He trailed off, waiting for Hogarth to pick up the cue.

She did. '…And at a time when we need firm leadership and the balls to push through the Freedom Bill, we seem to be lacking it?' Hogarth toyed with her glass. 'You know, Ben, the thing about a coalition is that it needs a leader who is prepared to give and take. Every day of a coalition is a negotiation. And there seem to be so many areas of potential common ground between our parties which we are unable to act upon because of the PM's intransigence.'

Thomas chewed the beef. God, it was overcooked. He'd asked for it bloody.

'Difficult times call for difficult decisions, Ben. And sometimes we must put aside our ideals for the greater good.'

'Maybe,' said Thomas. 'But it goes against the grain.'

'Something is changing, we can all sense it out there. People are crying out for change. They want Britain to fight back against all this nonsense. Not just the public. We're seeing it in the press. The *Mail* and the *Express* have turned against the PM. The Telegraph is wavering. There's growing restlessness on your backbenches.' She took a swig of wine. 'And my MPs too. I fear I'm losing them. They want affirmative action, they want strong leadership, they want to end this liberal nonsense that allows Muslims to preach hate in the street and yet which means critics of Islam on Twitter are hounded by the police. They want the pendulum swung back in favour of common sense.'

Thomas put down his knife. 'Are you saying they might withdraw support for the coalition?'

'I'm saying they want change. And I guarantee that they will get behind anyone who offers firm leadership against this insanity.' She waved her fork to the window. 'As I'm sure a significant number of your own party would. As would the *Herald*. And neither of us want a general election right now, do we?'

Job done, thought Thomas. 'Pudding, Lesley?'

Finsbury Park, North London

The entrance to the flat was at the back of a row of shops, up a metal staircase. Asad, his hood up and his face covered with a scarf, nudged the intercom four times with his thumb. The yellow pane of frosted glass blackened as the hallway light was turned off.

'You're late,' said Mirza, who opened the door enough for Asad to squeeze through and led him into the sitting room. The TV was on loud, almost certainly to make it harder for MI5 eavesdroppers, if there were any. Lesley Hogarth was on and her voice dominated the room.

Asad smiled nervously as he panted from the climb. His heart was bursting in his chest, and he wiped his clammy palms on the back of his jeans. The man they were meeting wasn't here yet. Muhid and Saleem were sat awkward and upright. Saleem's tongue was darting out to lick his lips every few seconds and even Muhid, normally so unflustered and determined, was fiddling with his fingers.

There was a knock on the door. Mirza cast his eyes speedily around the room as if to check everything was in place, then he brushed his shirt and went into the hall.

He returned, accompanied by a weasel-faced white man with a red wispy beard. He had a bent nose and a cauliflower ear, but the most striking thing about him was his eyes. Hard, humourless, powerful.

'Brothers, it is my great honour to welcome our Amir Sheikh Abu Mujahid al-Britani.' Abu Mujahid smiled with his mouth – if not his eyes – and held out his hands, clasping each of the men's palms in turn. Asad swallowed and attempted a smile. The man was a legend. He'd escaped twice from under the noses of the British establishment – once by walking free from some jumped-up trial, again by walking away under the eyes of the secret British police. And then the things he'd done in the Caliphate. He was a hero and the bravest man that Asad was ever likely to meet.

Mirza stood by the sitting room door, shuffling his weight from one foot to the other. 'Let me introduce you to our brothers. This is Ahmed Muhid, Waheed Saleem – and this is Omar Asad.'

'Take a seat, please.' Abu Mujahid paused and smiled again. He leant forward, his elbows on his knees, his fingers interlocked. He spoke quietly, so quietly that Asad and the other men had to lean forwards themselves, their faces just a few inches from Abu Mujahid.

'Assalamu-Alaikum,' said Abu Mujahid. 'It's an honour for me to meet you, brothers. We don't know each other yet, but we are part of a noble brotherhood.' He leant back. His voice remained soft, almost hypnotic. His manner reminded Asad of a cat.

'The attacks on Muslims in Syria, and Muslims in England, are attacks on all of us. Allah tells us that our duty is to defend the oppressed and the poor and the vulnerable. Allah is calling you to fight in his war, to defend our brothers and sisters slaughtered at Chilton Park and Pall Mall and to defend the Muslims I've seen with my own eyes, oppressed, beaten, tortured, raped and abused overseas.

'The Deputy Prime Minister,' he pointed at the TV, 'wants to strip our sisters' faces, to force them to bare skin like kafirs. This ban will force our sisters off the streets, out of schools and hospitals and workplaces and into their homes.

'A secret, brothers. I'm back here because of that woman.' He pointed to the screen. 'Because of her and people like her. I'm here to teach this country a lesson that it will never forget. A lesson about the plight of Muslims around the world, and a lesson about those like Lesley Hogarth who want to crush us.

'I could tell you stories of bravery that I saw in the glorious Caliphate. Of our blessed brothers who martyred themselves fighting the enemies who were raping our daughters and killing our mothers. That bravery is in us all. Allah knows when our time will come – and what our roles are. Allah is saving us all for his greater purpose.

'Did you see the interview yesterday with the girl who lost her family at Chilton Park – and who nearly died again at Pall Mall?' The listening men nodded intently. 'Did you see her anger at the police who turn their cheek when the far right attacks innocent brothers and sisters – but who scream and shout when we dare speak up? That girl's anger should ignite your rage.

'And soon, it will be your chance to stand up, to establish Sharia law, to defend the Muslim Ummah, and to strike the infidels and apostates so that they can no longer oppress us without suffering the wrath of Allah.'

The men sat still. Asad barely breathed. His initial excitement had died down, but the energy in the room had changed. It was now intense, quiet and tangible. Outside the window, footsteps echoed on the metal grid of the staircase.

'And if Allah wills it,' Abu Mujahid continued, 'you will have destroyed countless enemies of Islam, and you will live for eternity in Paradise. You are part of a bigger plan – and when you succeed, as you will, you will have contributed to the resurgence of a new Islamic State – greater and stronger than before.'

DAY 8

Wednesday

Gabriel put the phone down with a scowl. The DNA samples taken from Rod Houghton's house had matched the smear of sweat and skin on the petrol bomb debris. Houghton was their missing man, but they were no closer to finding out where he was. His house in West London was under surveillance, his known friends and family were being tailed, but since he had slipped from the Pall Mall hotel four days earlier, he had vanished.

She had resisted the urge to release his picture to the media. Maybe in a day or two, but now she wanted to find him and follow him in the hope he would lead them to the next NRF target.

The photofit from the interview with the Iranian journalist smuggled into the UK had come through. Like many of these images, it was next to useless. She stared at the long face and hard eyes. The red hair was a good match for Abu Mujahid, and the beard fitted the most recent description. 'Is that you?' she asked the picture on the screen. Did she have enough to push this line further – and maybe raise it with Tennant?

By lunchtime, she sensed she was becoming unreasonably

irritable, but lacked the urge to restrain herself. She had snapped at Bose, bitten the head off a DC and felt herself close to thumping Skeffington. This was no good, she thought, she needed to stretch her legs, clear her head.

She emerged into an oppressive winter fog. *There's nothing romantic about city fog*, she thought sourly as she walked towards her favourite sandwich shop opposite St Pancras, unable to see more than a few metres in front of her. It was a bloody nuisance. Her phone rang.

'Ma'am.' It was Skeffington. 'Report from the surveillance team outside Rod Houghton's house. Guess who's just walked through his front door.'

#

New Scotland Yard, Victoria Embankment, London
Gabriel waited in the poky conference room overlooking the Thames and watched the stream of cyclists on Victoria Embankment below. Even on a misty winter day, the cycle lane was congested with rental bikes and Lycra-clad commuters.

Tennant came in and sat opposite. *Do I look that knackered too*, wondered Gabriel as she studied his washed-out complexion and the battleship-grey creases under his eyes.

'Excellent work on Rod Houghton,' said Tennant. 'What now? We've got the DNA match – haul him in or let him run?'

'Think we keep him out, sir,' said Gabriel. 'We've got nothing on the third NRF attack, we've got nothing on the location of Douglas Glenister, his conspirator. If we bring him in, we tip off the NRF and they'll change their plans or bring forward the next attack.'

'But he's canny. He's special ops. There's a risk we'll lose him.'

'We just have to make sure we don't. It's the least imperfect of two imperfect options.'

Tennant mulled it over. 'Do it. Twenty-four hour surveillance, and the full monty – tap his phones, wire up his

155

car. I want a full account of every time he goes to the toilet. What about trigger plans?'

'We'll pull him in if he visits the high-risk locations – ports, airports, the usual,' said Gabriel. 'And if we get wind that he has access to weapons.'

'The Home Secretary's office is constantly on the phone, but I'll keep the politicians out of the loop for a day or two while we work out the strategy,' said Tennant. 'Nothing more on this associate of his, Douglas Glenister?'

Gabriel shook her head. 'Nothing. He's gone to ground. Family haven't seen him, he's not used his bank card, he's not popped up on any CCTV.'

Tennant gathered his papers and half-rose, then noticed Gabriel was still sat, so dropped down again.

'Something else, Sophie?'

Gabriel paused.

'We may have something on Abu Mujahid, sir.' She waited. Tennant's eyes raised a fraction.

'Go on.' His voice was cagey.

She filled him on the last couple of days, played the CCTV video on her laptop and handed him a printout of the photofit. Tennant took it and stood up, sending his papers to the floor. He walked round the table, tucking his shirt back into his trousers as he read. Gabriel waited, holding her breath.

'I know how much finding Abu Mujahid means to you, Sophie. I really do.' His voice was measured, but Gabriel detected a note of annoyance. 'And I commend your efforts to keep tabs on him. One day we will get him back where he belongs. But,' and he paused, as if trying to choose the right words from a menu in his head, 'but I don't believe that's him.'

'With all due respect, sir…' Tennant raised a hand and she stopped.

'Let me finish. You're going on the report from a terrified person smuggled into the country that they were accompanied by a white man who gave them the willies. You know how many people are smuggled into the UK each year? Tens of thousands. I'd bet a fair few of those are terrifying individuals. I'm sorry, there's not enough.'

'But the video – that's him. You can see it.'

'No, you can see it, Sophie. I can just see a grainy figure. You're chasing shadows. I need you to focus on the real threat here.'

'Sir, I can't disagree more. We can't let him get away – he's here.'

Again, he raised his hand, a gesture that infuriated Gabriel.

'Sophie, you need to let it go. Look, I know you're under huge pressure, but I'm already putting my neck on the line for you. I don't want to add to your burden, but you need to know that people are watching you – not just the commissioner and the media either. Lesley Hogarth asked about you in COBRA on Monday.'

'Asked what exactly?'

'Asked if you were up for this. Of course, I put her straight. But I need you focused. You're too close to Abu Mujahid and it's clouding your judgement. Again.'

The word 'again' hung in the air. Tennant looked as if he wished he had chosen his words better. His voice lowered. 'What I need is you to focus on the NRF. Focus on Rod Houghton. Focus on stopping whatever it is the NRF are planning next. Forget Abu Mujahid.'

#

Gabriel was seething. She resisted the urge to do violence to the cheese plant in the corridor, but kicked open the doors to the lift lobby so violently she stubbed her toe. She had been relying on Tennant to back her up – and when it mattered most, he had failed her. Despite everything that had happened between them, despite her risking her neck to save his career, despite a relationship that bordered on friendship. How had she misjudged this? And why couldn't he see what was glaringly obvious to anyone? Abu Mujahid had gone off the grid in the Middle East – and three weeks later, a man matching his description was smuggled into the UK in the most suspicious circumstances imaginable. Unless... and then came a niggling doubt... unless Tennant was right. Was she jumping at ghosts? She jabbed at the lift button again and smouldered inside.

#

Stoke Newington, North London
It had been a dispiriting day for Gabriel. She had come home late to find Ray in an equally bad mood. They had sniped at each other over a late supper before Ray sought refuge with a pile of year eleven coursework in the downstairs bedroom they used as a study, leaving Gabriel to watch the TV.

The news reflected Gabriel's mood. There was more on the PM, who was under attack from his own backbenches for failing to stop the unrest on the streets, and a bombardment of bleak news stories. A teenage boy had been stabbed in a Birmingham park for holding hands with another boy. They had been set upon by a gang of youths. An Asian soldier had been beaten up by three white kids in Grimsby's shopping centre and was fighting for his life in hospital. An ambulance had been pelted with stones during a skirmish between rival gangs in one of the most deprived estates in Bradford.

What the hell was going on? And then, between the splurges of violence and anger, politicians and commentators from the left and right blaming each other, blaming teachers, blaming parents, blaming immigrants, blaming everyone but themselves.

Lesley Hogarth was urging for calm, while insisting that Britain's identity was under threat. Harry Drake, the expelled opposition MP who'd made himself a name and a laughing stock dressed as a cowboy on a TV dancing competition, was stirring it too. The news had a clip of him addressing a rally in Tower Hamlets calling for a general election, calling for a new Muslim political party and demanding the streets to be 'swept clean' of the enemies of Islam. Whatever that meant.

After thirty minutes, Ray came in and Gabriel switched it off. She wanted a shower badly now.

'More shit?' asked Ray.

'Remember when we used to complain the news was boring? God, I almost miss those days.'

'You shouldn't watch it. It brings you down.'

'This,' she waved at the TV, her voice a little too loud, 'doesn't bring me down, Ray. What brings me down is the fact that the entire world seems to have lost the plot. We've gone back to sodding medieval times.'

'Come on, love, you're exaggerating. It's the bubble of your job, it distorts your perspective. You see the worst bits of life, and you focus on the worst people. Step back – it's not that bad. Most people are good people. Most people don't go on Twitter to abuse strangers. Most are just getting on with living their lives shopping, laughing, watching TV. Being boring. Being human.'

Gabriel stared at Ray. 'Don't give me that. It's not me living in a bubble, it's you. I see what's going on every single day. And of course most people aren't evil. I'm not saying they are. But it's worse out there than it was five, ten, twenty years ago. If you can't see it, you're deluding yourself.

'How did this happen – this appeal to the lowest common denominator in politics and this turning of debates about serious issues into shouting matches that means Hogarth and her like turn from rent-a-mouth columnists into supposedly serious political leaders? This rudeness that's seeped through public life? The abuse heaped upon politicians by the voters and the press? The cynicism?'

She stomped upstairs to the shower. Ray followed.

'Look, love, I know I'm not supposed to ask about work.

But you haven't seemed yourself this past week. I know it's been batshit crazy, but it's more than that, isn't it?'

And for an instant, Gabriel wanted to tell him everything. About Abu Mujahid. About Tennant refusing to take her side. About whatever shit was coming next. She stared at him and listened to his heavy breathing after bounding up the stairs after her. But she couldn't.

'It's just work, Ray, I'm fine,' she lied.

DAY 9

Thursday

M1, Luton

'Pack light,' Abu Mujahid had told them, but even so, the Transit was cramped.

Abu Mujahid was in the passenger seat and Mirza was driving. In the back, Asad sat with Saleem and Muhid on the rucksacks and bags, using coats for cushions.

Last night they'd eaten together. Asad had volunteered to cook vegetables and spiced rice using a recipe his mother had taught him. It was one of the few Somali dishes he knew. They'd sat on the floor of the flat eating and listening to Abu Mujahid's stories until midnight.

But this morning, conversation was muted and Asad felt queasy. Was it the swaying of the van, or the enormity of what they were about to do? Every minute they spent in the van, every mile they drove up the M1, felt like a step towards the invisible line he'd created in his head – the line that separated his old life and this new one. Once he crossed that line, he would never be able to go back.

A long canvas bag was wedged in one corner with a scrap of sacking thrown on top. Asad lifted the fabric – underneath was a set of number plates.

'Put the radio on, Tanvir,' said Saleem.

Mirza grunted and idly flicked round the van's radio. '…these air strikes on innocent civilians by the UK and US government are a disgrace. No wonder Muslim communities feel like outsiders in the UK.'

Asad recognised the voice as the Shadow Home Secretary.

The interviewer came on: 'What do you say to those who call you an apologist for Islamist terrorists—'

'That's a ludicrous accusation and doesn't warrant a response,' the Shadow Home Secretary interrupted.

'—and who question your judgement? This weekend, for instance, you are standing on a platform with the extremist Ishmail Sherif, who repeatedly refuses to condemn terrorism and preaches that Sharia law is the only way to save Britain.'

'Look, I'm proud we live in a diverse country with free speech, and I…'

They were turning into the services. 'Turn it off now,' said Abu Mujahid.

He waited until the van had stopped before turning around to Asad and the others in the back.

'Be discreet, keep your heads down and go in separately,' said Abu Mujahid.

'Do you know Ishmail Sherif?' asked Muhid.

Abu Mujahid smiled. 'I do. We go back a long way. Sherif was the man who opened my eyes when I was a kid. I'll tell you the story on the way up. But first grab some food and go to the loo. We've got another four hours.'

#

Waiting in the WHSmith next to the gents, Asad browsed through the papers. The front page of the *Herald* had a cartoon of the Prime Minister playing a violin while London went up in flames behind him with the headline *For God's Sake: It's Time to Go. Pressure Builds on PM to Step Down* was on the front of the *Guardian*.

'Black bastard.' Asad heard the words before he saw the man – a white man in a suit – pass behind him, and shove him in the back. The words were uttered under his breath, but Asad was in no doubt what he'd said. The white man turned and stared momentarily before walking out of the store. Asad started. The rage that had lain dormant for days erupted. He resolved to follow the white man out, tackle him, punch him to the ground – when he felt a hand on his shoulder. He spun around, ready to strike, and saw Abu Mujahid.

Abu Mujahid said quietly: 'Not now.'

#

As they passed the road signs for Lancaster, the landscape either side of the motorway was still gentle, and the fields green and rolling. It was only when they turned off onto the A350 that the land began to rise in the distance. Gaps in the trees lining the dual carriageway revealed snatches of purple and grey mountains. They reminded Asad of the hills of the Brecons where he and his parents spent summer Sundays long ago. The fields changed too; there were grey drystone walls now, and flocks of sheep, some heavily pregnant.

The atmosphere inside the van had changed too. There was silence now. The closer they got to their destination, the more serious the mood. They drove up a bumpy track and stopped.

'Stay in the van till I've got the keys,' said Abu Mujahid. He stepped out, his open door sending a cold blast to the rear of the van. Asad heard muttered voices then Abu Mujahid returned.

'We're here. Pile out.'

They were parked on a gravel drive of a cottage, a battered yellow Volvo Estate was parked alongside them. Abu Mujahid was stood next to a silver-haired woman dressed in a green Barbour. Her face hardened momentarily as she took in the four passengers.

'I'll need a deposit. Cash,' she said.

Abu Mujahid nodded and pulled out his wallet. She counted the notes and gave Asad, Mirza, Muhid and Saleem another hard stare.

'You don't look much like climbers. Do you have your own gear or are you hiring?' she asked Abu Mujahid.

'We've got our own in the van,' said Abu Mujahid, speaking in a soft, almost flirtatious voice that Asad had never heard him use before. 'Thank you so much – it looks fantastic.'

'Call me if you need anything.' She gave another nervous glance at the men before walking to her Volvo and driving off.

'Climbing?' Asad asked Abu Mujahid as they walked into the house.

'It's what we're doing,' he replied. 'We're a mountaineering club from London – students. We're doing the Langdale Pikes and Helvellyn, if anyone asks. Get the stuff inside.'

Asad looked around him as he fetched his bag. The cottage looked down into a valley that had just three houses and a couple of farms. The hills on the opposite side were forested until two-thirds of the way up. Abu Mujahid had chosen well. They were unlikely to be disturbed.

#

Chiswick, West London
The waitress smiled at Rod Houghton.

'What would you like today?' she said, staring unblinking, her pencil tapping her cheek.

'Cup of black coffee, please, love. And a glass of tap water.'
The waitress made a note but didn't move away.

'You from Manchester? I like your accent,' said the waitress.
Jesus, he thought. She wasn't making this easy.

'Yep,' he said, attempting to end the conversation, before turning back to his phone.

The waitress moved off while Houghton switched on the phone, tapped in the Wi-Fi code printed on the greasy menu propped against the ketchup bottle. He gave a fake Gmail address and was online. He opened WhatsApp, typed two messages and turned the phone off.

A middle-aged, plump Asian woman with a magazine was sat by the door. An elderly white couple were at the next table, sat in silent boredom. A black man with a toddler was on the phone in the corner. He'd give it a few minutes then leave. He settled down to drink his coffee as quickly as decency would allow.

#

Thirty seconds after Houghton had left the cafe, the Asian woman with the magazine stood up. She walked through the door and paused in the street. A white man in a grey jacket walked past her – their eyes caught for a second and she gave him an almost imperceptible nod. He continued walking in the same direction as Houghton.

Around the corner, safely out of sight, she checked behind her and spoke out loud. 'I'm at the cafe in Chiswick High Road. The target has used his phone. Repeat, he's just used his phone.'

The reaction from the voice in her ear was ecstatic.

'We've got him,' said her sergeant.

#

Downing Street, London
Thomas had been kept waiting in the foyer for ten minutes and was fuming. He entered the Prime Minister's office and lowered himself onto the leather sofa without being invited. The PM stood with his back to the Home Secretary, staring through the bulletproof glass into the garden.

'Tell me, Ben,' said the PM slowly, without turning. 'How are you finding Lesley Hogarth these days? There was a time when you couldn't stand her. Yet I hear you've been enjoying her company quite a lot recently.'

'Wouldn't go that far,' said Thomas, unflustered. 'I'm

keen to build bridges. She is what she is, we can't do anything about that.'

'Indeed.' The PM sat heavily at his desk rather than moving alongside Thomas. At times like this, he reminded Thomas of their old Cambridge college dean, a pious white-haired don who regarded his students as an unwelcome intrusion into his otherwise well-ordered life. 'I know you well enough, Ben, to be confident that you wouldn't be so unscrupulous to be using Hogarth for your own personal ends.' Thomas said nothing. 'Just as I'm confident that you wouldn't be using the situation out there,' he waved carelessly toward the window, 'to reposition yourself. We go back far enough for me to be confident in your loyalty.'

Again, Thomas said nothing. This was not the time to get angry. He leant back in the sofa and watched his old friend through narrowed eyes.

The PM continued. 'But my worry is perception – it might look to some that you are jockeying, which I know you are not. And this Freedom Bill… Again, some might even see it as the sort of illiberal measure that plays into the hands of extremists and fuels the kind of mindless violence we are seeing so much of out there. So a friendly warning, Ben. Be careful.'

Thomas resisted the urge to snap back at his old friend. It felt like he was being dismissed, so he stood, walked to the door, then half-turned.

'Thank you, Prime Minister,' he said. 'Please be reassured that while we may disagree from time to time, you have my complete support.' And he left.

#

New Scotland Yard, Victoria Embankment, London
Tennant was on the phone when Gabriel walked over. He had a coffee stain down his pale blue tie which looked fresh. Gabriel tried not to look at it. She shifted a pile of newspapers from the spare chair to the floor and sat.

Tennant ended the call. 'Mayor's office,' he said to Gabriel, cautiously, eyeing her carefully to judge her mood. 'Wants to know if we should be worried about next weekend's sports fixtures – we've got an England international, a charity half-marathon and the Calcutta Cup on Sunday.'

Gabriel looked blank.

'Calcutta Cup? Six Nations… England and Scotland… Rugby?' He gave her a mock-withering look, then checked himself when she responded blankly. There was an awkward pause.

'Look, I trust your judgement implicitly, Sophie,' he said eventually. 'But I need you focused on the NRF. I get that you're bothered by Abu Mujahid.' Tennant studied her expressionless face. 'Remember it's not personal, Sophie,' he said carefully.

'Yeah, but it kind of is, isn't it?'

There was another moment's silence before Tennant spoke. 'What have you got?'

'Rod Houghton.' Gabriel's tone was formal, businesslike. 'He used a phone in an internet cafe a couple of hours ago. We've talked to the cafe's internet provider, and we've got the metadata from his phone. He sent two messages via WhatsApp, so we've got the number of his contact too.

'He's been smart, as you'd expect given his special ops background, and he's using a burner phone. But whoever he's been contacting has been less clever. He, or she, kept their phone on for two hours earlier today.'

'Where are they?'

'Leeds. We've had teams up there trying to pin them down but with no success yet. They've stayed in busy areas – shopping streets and the Trinity shopping centre mostly. We're also going through their movements over the last nine months looking for patterns.'

'A potential lead into the NRF then.'

'Think it's more than that,' said Gabriel. 'Houghton has been ultra-careful with this contact. He messaged them only using public Wi-Fi hotspots, he kept his phone on for seconds at a time only. And the frequency of texts has shot up in the last thirty-six hours.'

'The third attack,' said Tennant after a moment's reflection. 'So, we pull him in.'

'I think so, sir. There's a good chance his phone will lead us to whatever the NRF are planning in Leeds. At the very least, it will shed light on his Leeds contact. The question is how to arrest him and ensure his phone stays unlocked. It's a brand-new iPhone, and digital forensics say they will need days to crack it. We can't wait that long. This could be imminent.'

'What are you proposing?'

'We pull in Houghton, and we pull in everyone associated with Houghton,' she said. 'And we get warrants for every address associated with him.'

'That sounds bloody desperate to me,' said Tennant. 'And if it doesn't work we are clueless to stop the next attack.'

'It's worked for us before. If we pull in enough people, we're bound to find something. Everyone gets sloppy at some point.'

'We're not "bound" to get anything. This is dangerously high-risk.'

'I disagree. It's our best option right now.'

Tennant shook his head. 'No.' He almost barked the word. 'I'm sorry, but not this time. Not with Houghton. I don't believe some kind of hit-and-hope operation is going to pull in the results we need. We need the phone unlocked and I'm not gambling on a mistake. I want something better. Find a weakness – anything where he is vulnerable. And exploit it.'

#

An hour later, she was on the phone to Tennant.

'Make this good,' he said.

'I've got an idea – I reckon we can get him to unlock it for us.'

DAY 10

Friday

Cumbria

Asad had been woken just after 6am by footsteps on the wooden floor outside the bedroom he shared with Saleem. Saleem was lying on the bed under the duvet, snuffling through a blocked nose. Asad had slept fitfully on the floor with a cushion propping up his head. He had gone to bed with his mind fizzing and it refused to switch off. He was unable to squeeze in the enormity of what was happening – today, tomorrow and later that week.

The cottage was tired and musty. Red and green floral curtains were pulled against the window, while knick-knacks, coated with dust, littered every surface – white china figures of women holding umbrellas and tiny ceramic jars. But there were bonuses. The nearest farm house was five hundred metres away and the nearest village two miles.

They prayed that morning in the living room, pushing back the sofa to create space. Overnight, Abu Mujahid had lifted the canvas bag from the van and left it against the wall by the TV. Throughout their breakfast of porridge, orange juice and coffee, Asad found his eye being drawn to the bag. He had little appetite and felt desperate to get breakfast out of the way.

They sat in a circle around the living room, some on chairs, others cross-legged. There was electricity in the air. Abu Mujahid dropped the canvas bag in the centre of the room and slid out something long and thin, wrapped in a piece of stained sacking. He picked up a newspaper and spread its pages over the carpet as Asad held his breath.

Abu Mujahid's voice was steady. 'I want to introduce you to your new best friend.' He opened up the sacking and carefully lifted out a rifle. Asad could feel the droplets of sweat on his brow and his heart banging in his chest and ears as he gazed in awe.

'This is an assault rifle,' said Abu Mujahid. 'It's an SA80, the weapon of the British Army, which is kind of appropriate.' He lifted the rifle with one hand and passed it to Saleem, who held it in his palms like an offering. Saleem's face broke into an excited grin.

'It's going be a busy day,' said Abu Mujahid. 'This morning, we'll be working on the rifle. If you were soldiers with me in Syria, you'd spend a day learning how to disassemble it, clean it and put it back together. You'd be so proficient you'd be able to do it blindfolded. But for our purpose, you just need to know how to use it. There's a wood close by and it's the last weekend of the pheasant season, so no one will bat an eyelid at the odd gunshot. Just don't use it on automatic. And I'm giving you these.' He pulled out four mobile phones and new SIM cards still in their plastic packaging. 'They are only for emergencies – I mean that, only emergencies. Keep them with you, but use them only as a last resort.'

They spent the next hour watching Abu Mujahid taking the rifle apart and cleaning the parts before assembling them. Asad was transfixed. He'd never seen a gun close up before, let alone had a chance to handle one. Abu Mujahid went through each part, explaining its function – the receiver cover, the recoil spring and rod, the carrier assembly.

'The rifle will be loaded when you take it out, but you will have a spare magazine. And you may get to use it. The magazine has thirty rounds. The safety catch here,' he pointed to the level on the right side, 'has three positions. Up is safe. When you are ready to fire, push the latch all the way down. The bottom position is semi-automatic. The middle position is fully automatic. If you use it on automatic mode, you'll go through the magazine in seconds.'

Asad was surprised at the lightness of the gun in his hands. He held it up, looking through the sights under Abu Mujahid's guidance.

At 10am, Abu Mujahid took it back. 'I need to go into town now – I'll be back at noon, so be ready for me.'

#

The internet cafe was on the ground floor of a red-brick building off the high street in Kendal. Abu Mujahid sat in the window with a baseball cap pulled down over his forehead and pair of black-rimmed glasses on his nose. It wasn't an ideal seat, but it gave him a clear line of sight into the street.

He logged on using the ID he'd bought at the counter and went to the Amazon site. It took him thirty seconds to find what he wanted and another two minutes to make the order. He chose a collection address in Kendal and paid with Amazon gift cards he had bought with cash at a supermarket the previous Sunday. There was no CCTV in the cafe, although he'd spotted two cameras on his walk from the van. He would take a different route back.

#

Chiswick, West London
Rod Houghton stood on his doorstep, breathing in the tang of cold air of this golden morning through his nostrils, his eyes roving around the street for people who should not be there.

Conditions were perfect today, here and in Leeds, according to the TV forecast. Good weather meant a good turnout. He took another gulp of air. He was not a twitchy man and had seen enough action overseas to have any residual nerves knocked out of him, but even he could sense his adrenaline pulsing through his veins as his mind raced through the day ahead.

Paper first, then the cafe for the final texts. He glanced at his watch. Within nine hours they would have another victory under their belts. Three in ten days. It was incredible. Britain had seen nothing like this – not since the days of the IRA's mainland bombing campaign that he remembered as a child.

He'd spoken to the boss last night. Police were sniffing around DNA traces found at the hotel, but were no closer to identifying him. He had no criminal record, and no DNA stored on a police database. He was fine.

A white van streaked with city grime was parked outside the newsagent at the end of his road. The driver got out as he approached, carrying a parcel and computer tablet, and walked into the shop. Two Asian youths were loitering outside the doorway, one in a red hoodie, the other in an Arsenal top. Houghton gave them the once-over before he walked in.

The shop was owned by a second-generation Greek in his fifties or sixties. He didn't mind Greeks too much, even if the stale spices and overripe foreign fruit in the shop offended his nose. The Greeks hated the Turks for a start, and an enemy of an enemy is a friend. He picked up the *Herald* and a pint of skimmed milk and handed over a fiver.

The front of the *Herald* made him smile inwardly. *Enough is Enough* it screamed in big bold type over a picture of three women in burqas. *It's time to ban the burqa* ran the subhead underneath. Six months ago, the press would have been too scared to run that. But what a difference a few weeks made. He read on. The front-page editorial was calling for tougher immigration laws and for the Prime Minister to stand down.

He was walking towards the open door, his thoughts still on the front page, when he heard a woman's panicked yelp from the pavement outside. He stepped outside to see a white woman in her fifties lying curled on the ground. The two Asian youths were standing over her – one was yanking on her handbag as coins, make-up and receipts tumbled and fluttered over the pavement towards the gutter; the other was lashing at her stomach with his foot. He didn't make contact, but she recoiled, letting go of the bag and allowing the accomplice to snatch the bag. Both pelted down the street into a side alley. Houghton's instinct was to give chase, to catch up with those wankers and give them a pasting they wouldn't forget. But he held back. Not today. Not today of all days.

'Help me,' the woman gasped from the ground. Houghton knelt beside her. Her eyes were red, and she was ashen-faced.

'You all right, love? You hurt?'

'My leg. I can't move my leg. I need my husband.' She started crying. 'I need my husband. I need him. They've got my phone.'

'Here, you okay to stand, love?' He didn't offer to call the police but held out a hand and she grabbed it, scrabbling to stand up. Her grip was surprisingly strong.

'I need to speak to my husband. I need him.' She was babbling now, oblivious to Houghton. He looked up and down the street. There was no one in sight to help.

'Let me take you into the shop, you can sit in there.'

'I need my husband. They've got my phone. I must speak to him. Have you got one? I need to talk to him.'

For a moment, Houghton wavered. But the guilt he felt for not giving chase was strong. 'Okay.' He pulled out his mobile from a trouser pocket.

'Can you dial it for me – my glasses…' She waved in the direction the men had fled.

'Sure.' He pulled out his phone and pressed his finger on the sensor. It was so cold it took a couple of attempts for the phone to register his fingerprint and unlock.

'Thank you.' Her voice had changed. No longer was it croaky or whimpering. There was something almost triumphant there instead and before his brain could process the change, he was unable to move. His hands were pinned to his side from behind. He struggled, taken aback, and the woman reached out to grab the now unlocked phone from his fingers.

Houghton twisted his neck – he was in the grip of two, maybe three, men. He tried to move his head further and swore.

The woman's transformation from vulnerable victim to triumphant victor told him everything he needed to know. She was undercover police and this charade on the streets was not just to arrest him, it was to get the phone, and get the phone unlocked.

Houghton knew enough about phone security to realise the danger he had just put the operation in. He had been careful – this was a burner that he had used only to speak to the boss and the Leeds connection. But if the police had the unlocked phone, they had everything – the location of today's attack, the means, the names. But if he could somehow lock it before he let it slip from his hands, then the operation had a chance.

He clenched his fingers around the phone as the woman tried to prise it from him, and pulled back his arm, towards his body, surprising the man behind him. For a second, he could move his arm. He fought to get his thumb on the off button on the right-hand side of the phone. If he could just press it, the phone would be safe. Or if he could keep it out of their hands, the phone would lock itself automatically in a few seconds.

In the fumbling and jostling, his hand slipped and the phone dropped to the floor. He flinched back and swung at the phone with his foot, sending it scurrying into the gutter. The woman dived, a look of anxiety across her face.

Had he done it? Was it safe?

The woman stood up. She held the phone above her head and her smile told Houghton that he had failed.

'On the floor, you're nicked,' the voice yelled in his ear as he was pushed down, his arms pulled tight behind his back, his face in a gritty puddle. 'You are under arrest for conspiracy to commit a terrorist act.' The officer cautioned him, as he struggled and kicked, and then bent closer to his ear. 'And cheers for the phone. That'll be really handy.'

The woman was standing in front of him now, panting. She held the phone in one hand, pressing the home button from time to time to stop it locking. A police car pulled up and she got in the back. The car, with its extraordinary load, accelerated down the street with lights flashing.

#

CTOC, St Pancras, London
'What have we got?' said Gabriel as she entered the conference room, dropping her coat and bags on the floor.

Skeffington turned to the screen.

'Digital forensics have downloaded the data image from Houghton's phone and they're still working on it. For now, we've got his text messages and WhatsApp,' said Skeffington. 'It's a burner, only used to reach one number, the contact in Leeds. It's obvious that Houghton was planning an attack, although the details are not clear. This message was sent a week ago.'

The message appeared on the screen: *Package received. Will collect remaining goods tomorrow. Vehicle D confirmed as suitable.*

Skeffington continued: 'And then this a day later.'

Another text message came on the screen. *Pitch confirmed.*

Gabriel stood up to look at the messages more closely. 'Pitch? What kind of pitch? Business pitch? Sports event?' She mulled over the word.

Skeffington interrupted her thoughts. 'Finally this, from earlier in the week.'

A third text appeared. *On rota as passenger. Will bring driver to house and swap there.*

Skeffington's phone went off. He spoke briefly before

ending the call. 'That was forensics, ma'am, with an update. They've just gone through the web browser. They reckoned they've identified the target. If forensics are right, the attack is today. We've got four hours.'

#

This time there was no need for Gabriel to subdue the babble of voices as she stood up. Word of Houghton's arrest had gone around the building and there was silence in the largest conference room as she walked to the front.

'You'll have heard that Rod Houghton is enjoying the hospitality of Bow Street and that we've got his phone unlocked. Congratulations to the team who pulled that off.' She nodded in the direction of the undercover team to the left of the room. There was a ripple of applause and a 'Sheer fucking luck' from the back.

She flashed up a map of Leeds city centre with a park outlined in red.

'This is the target. Muslims in the Park. It's a council sponsored, so-called community cohesion event at Roundhay with talks, food stalls and prayers. One of the guests is Ishmail Sherif and he's on at 3pm. The shadow home secretary's speaking too. It's a relatively small event – no more than one thousand people and mostly under canvas.

'We're confident this is the target. The browser history on Houghton's phone shows he's searched for this event a dozen times over the last few weeks. And we believe they are planning something within hours.

'We know it involves a vehicle – discussion of the suitability of a vehicle comes up several times. And there's also clearly something important about the type of vehicle and its driver. The texts talk about bringing the driver to the house and swapping there.

'So far we've been dealing with fact. Now I'm having to enter the realms of speculation. From the context of the texts, the vehicle is crucial to this operation. I think it's likely that Houghton is planning a car bomb.'

'Why not a vehicle ramming?' The voice came from the back.

'Possible, but less likely. There are no significant crowds in a place with vehicular access at this event. It's not like a Christmas market or busy city centre. And any vehicle could do that. This needs to be a particular vehicle with a replacement driver.

'We're not proposing to cancel – it's far too late. We have a thousand people expected and they will be more exposed milling around the streets. West Yorkshire Police have a massive operation underway to protect the venue – that obviously needs to step up a notch now. As an additional precaution, we're not letting vehicles within five hundred metres of the venue.

'That's the target. DI Skeffington will now brief you on what we need today.'

#

Gabriel had moved to the ops room. Around her, the seats were filling up and the screens flickering into life.

She'd briefed Tennant on the phone and spoken at length to the Gold Command at Leeds policing the Muslims in the Park event. Now she had to wait as the teams around her did their work. 'Ma'am.' Campbell came over, sweaty and urgent. 'We've got the triangulation report for Houghton's associate in Leeds. It's taken a while to process the data, but we've got an address. It's a terraced house on an estate in Armley. The target has been in and out of the house dozens of times. It's almost certainly where they're based – maybe an NRF safe house.'

'Fantastic,' said Gabriel. 'Get me North East on the line. Now.'

#

Armley, Leeds

The Stevenson Estate had been dubbed the 'ghost estate' by the local media. The two hundred low-rise flats had been earmarked by the council for demolition, but the developers supposed to be turning these red-brick modern-day slums into designer flats had gone bust and the plans to usher in young media types and internet entrepreneurs were on hold. For the moment, this corner of Armley was in limbo. Most residents had moved out, leaving behind rows of boarded-up houses and rubbish-strewn gardens. Just a dozen residents remained, mostly elderly, mostly poor and mostly complaining bitterly to the council and local paper that they had been abandoned.

Shortly after 11.30am, a white van with darkened windows turned into the estate. It drove past the terraces, most now with their windows covered with grilles, pulling to one side to let a St John ambulance pass on the other side of the narrow street. The van came to a stop in an alleyway and five armed police emerged, crouching in the gap between the wall and the vehicle. They shuffled forward, rifles pointed at the ground, visors down, and waited by the gate leading into the backyard of 4 Foster Street. Another team, who had entered the estate from the rear, had the front entrance of the house in their sights.

#

CTOC, St Pancras, London

Two hundred miles away, the counter terrorism ops room in St Pancras was equally focused.

'Surveillance teams are in place,' said Campbell to Gabriel, who was prowling like a restless cat through the desks and chairs. 'The curtains of the house are drawn. No movement inside.'

The next sixty seconds dragged interminably. Gabriel looked at her watch every few seconds. 'Right, lads – time to go,' she said to herself.

#

Armley, Leeds

'Go, go, go.' The unit stood up as one and ran forward. The officer at the front fixed in place the hydraulic door opener, a black rod-like device that clamped to the door frame, and stood back. There was a swish of air and the crackling of splintering wood as the door came off its hinges and banged to the ground. He stepped back and two colleagues barged through the doorway, turning their faces away as their flash grenades bleached the hallway with light and sent a tremendous crash echoing through the house. The first door on the right was open and the officers pushed through. Within seconds they were in a sitting room, decorated with striped scarlet wallpaper and clashing green sofas. Cardboard boxes and newspapers littered the floor, but the room was empty.

Upstairs, two officers were on the landing. There were three doors, all open, one to a milkshake-pink bathroom, two to bedrooms. The pair pushed into the bathroom and pulled back the floral shower curtain. In the bath, face down, his hands tied behind his back, lay a shirtless man, blood oozing from his temples and trickling into the plug-hole.

#

CTOC, St Pancras, London

'What have we got?' said Gabriel moments later.

'One man, injured, ma'am, dumped in the upstairs bathroom and tied up,' said a DS from the front of the ops room. 'He's barely conscious. Had a wallet on him. Only occupant, although the house was recently occupied.'

'Who is he?' asked Gabriel.

'John Clarence, mid-fifties. Looks like he was coshed and stripped.'

'What?' said Gabriel. 'Stripped of his clothes?'

'Yes, ma'am. He was topless. Not a pretty sight, apparently.'

'Anything else in the wallet?' said Gabriel.

'Driving licence, Tesco Clubcard, membership card for St John Ambulance and a library card.'

There was a clattering noise on the line and muffled voices.

'What's happening?' said Gabriel.

'Ma'am,' said the DS. 'The second unit have just reported that an ambulance was driving away from the house when they approached. About five minutes ago. We believe that the suspects may have been inside.'

That's it, thought Gabriel. It made perfect sense. How do you get a vehicle through the security cordon of a high-security event outdoors and then abandon the vehicle and walk away without raising suspicion? Impossible if it's a car or ordinary van. But what if it's supposed to be there? What if it was a St John ambulance? And the words of the texts that Rod Houghton sent to his NRF operative in Leeds came back to her. *Pitch confirmed.* And what was the other one? *On rota as passenger. Will bring driver to house and swap there.*

So that was the plan, Gabriel thought. Get someone to infiltrate St John Ambulance, posing as an ordinary volunteer, do the training, put in the hours, then get on the rota as an assistant for today, somehow lure the driver down to this house, then cosh him and replace him with the second person. They'd need the uniform and ID – so that's why they removed the poor sod's top.

But they had the licence plate of the ambulance. And that meant they could use the network of Automatic Number Plate Recognition cameras to trace its path through the city.

#

New Scotland Yard, Victoria Embankment, London
'What's the plan?' said Tennant down the phone line.

'The unit passed the ambulance minutes before they arrived at the house and caught its licence plate on the dashcam,' said Gabriel. She had moved to a quiet, windowless side office off the control room. 'ANPR has picked up the ambulance heading north-east towards Roundhay Park. It's normally a twenty-minute drive, but the traffic is bad today, so it's more like forty minutes. The goal is to stop the ambulance half a mile from the park. Forensics are at the house in Armley, and early indications from some of the packaging and residues they've found in the kitchen suggest an old-school fertiliser bomb.'

'Any indication if it's a suicide bomb or a conventional car bomb?' said Tennant.

'Could be either, sir.'

'And could they detonate the explosive en route if they detect they are being followed?'

'We can't rule it out. A surveillance car is in position behind the ambulance and a firearms team should be joining the pursuit any moment. Right now, all we can do is keep our fingers crossed.'

#

Leeds
Sergeant Sameer Rehmann weaved his way down the dual carriageway in the direction of Roundhay Park. The blue light, normally hidden in the grille of the anonymous SUV, was on, and he made good progress. His three passengers were silent and Rehman knew what they were thinking. In a speedily arranged operation like this, there were so many uncertainties. They did not know how the target was armed, if the van was booby-trapped, how the explosives were rigged to go off. In these nervy moments, the desire to ring home or leave a message on their partner's mobile was overwhelming.

He'd done it a couple of times himself in the early days, but had stopped when he realised the messages caused more alarm than comfort.

Within four minutes they were at the junction and pulled into a petrol station forecourt. Rehman switched the blue light off and waited. The vehicle was new and the plastic smell of a new car hung in his nostrils.

'Target is now on the A58 heading east, approximately three minutes from your location,' the voice from CT ops told him.

He stared at the vehicles coming past the forecourt from the right and rehearsed the manoeuvre in his mind. He would need to time this perfectly. The surveillance car – a black BMW – had got into position behind the ambulance a few minutes earlier. If, as expected, the ambulance continued on its route, it would pass the petrol station and Rehman was in the ideal spot to pull out into the road and get himself one or two vehicles behind it.

He looked at the dashboard clock. Less than a minute. Now thirty seconds. And there it was, in his wing mirror, a few seconds away. 'Couldn't be easier to spot if they'd stuck a flag on top,' Rehman said, half to himself, half to the passengers.

As the ambulance passed the forecourt, he got a glimpse of the driver, a stocky man with a shock of dark hair. A black unmarked BMW – which Rehman recognised as the surveillance car – was driving two vehicles behind the ambulance. It slowed as it approached the forecourt, allowing Rehman to pull out aggressively and squeeze into the gap. *Cheers, mate,* he said silently to the surveillance car, now behind him.

He spoke to the ops room. 'We're in position. Two vehicles behind the target.'

They were driving slowly, stopping and starting along a residential street, square red-brick houses set back from the road behind tall railings on one side, mobile-phone shops and takeaways breaking up the houses.

Rehman knew that a few hundred metres ahead, a pair of unmarked police cars would be pulling into the road and blocking the traffic. He imagined, rather than heard, the honking of irritated drivers somewhere in front of him as the traffic slowed and came to a halt. That jam would now be rippling backwards down the road. Any second now. And yes. There, the brake lights on the ambulance came on. They were all slowing down. And stopping. *Good work*, he thought.

#

Glenister had driven ambulances before, but never anything as flash as this. He fiddled with the radio, trying to get a signal, then gave up in frustration. The sweatshirt they had pulled off the driver in the bathroom was a size too small and the material was pulling across his shoulders.

But at least he was outside. It was his first trip out since he'd arrived in Leeds five days earlier. After fleeing the scene of the Pall Mall attack, he had first made his way to Birmingham, then caught a slow train to Leeds. The last five nights had been spent in the NRF's safe house in the ghost estate in the company of a man who called himself Roger, a portly man who spoke little and who was now in the passenger seat chewing his moustache.

He had never met this Roger before, and he doubted it was his real name. The leadership of the NRF had run this operation on a strict need-to-know basis. Glenister's job had been simply to get from London to the Armley safe house and stay put, ready for the third phase. It had only been this morning, over toast and coffee, that his companion had outlined today's operation, concocted by the leadership in London months ago. Roger told him he had infiltrated the St John Ambulance months earlier, was on the rota for today's Muslim festival and that the ambulance driver was expecting to pick him up en route. Glenister's job was to cosh the driver and take his place.

The two men had barely talked since they had loaded the drum into the rear of the ambulance back at the flat. He was confident it couldn't go off without the detonator, which was currently in the passenger footwell, but that hadn't stopped his palms from sweating. The rifle was stowed away in a green bag behind him, the same bag he had carried it in since Pall Mall a week ago.

What was this jam? The lights at the pedestrian crossing ahead had changed from red to green twice now and still they weren't moving. He glanced in the side mirrors at the line of stationary cars behind him. A green Volvo with a solitary woman driver and behind that a dark grey SUV. He couldn't see the driver or passengers.

His companion Roger was an odd one, Glenister thought, and wondered where Rod Houghton had recruited him. Not the army, that was for sure. Maybe he was one of those internet types. There were a lot of those nowadays, bedroom warriors rather than squaddies with experience.

The traffic was still not moving. He wished he could check on Google Maps to see how far they were from the hold-up, but using a phone was out of the question. He drummed his fingers on the steering wheel and peered ahead.

#

Two cars back, the voice in Rehman's ear was clear and urgent. 'Firearm team, you are clear to proceed with the interception. Good luck, lads.'

Rehman heard the doors behind him open as the two officers stepped out into the road, rifles pointing down. The man in the passenger seat next to him joined them. The men darted ahead, keeping their heads down, tucking in behind the car in front before moving forward again. They crouched behind the ambulance, out of sight of the wing mirrors. Rehman imagined the look of astonishment on the driver ahead as the gunmen ducked down in front of their bonnet.

Rehman said a silent prayer as he sat behind the wheel watching his colleagues wait for the final signal to advance.

#

There was still no movement in the road ahead and Glenister was getting impatient. He needed to get the ambulance into position in Roundhay Park by 12.30pm. He ran through the procedure in his head again and again.

'Something's up. We've not moved for five minutes,' said his companion in the passenger seat. 'Can we put the lights on and jump the queue?'

'Maybe,' said Glenister. The siren would draw attention to them – and could attract a police car or bike. The last thing they wanted was their own police escort taking them to the park, but it might get them out of this hole.

The siren was operated by pressing the vehicle's horn. A toggle switch turned it from the normal 'blues and twos' two-note wail to the more urgent 'woop-woop'. But was it worth the gamble? Sod it. He flicked on the blue light and the siren and checked the right-hand side mirror. What the hell was that? For a second, the mirror had flickered dark, as if something had temporarily blocked the view. And then the mirror and door swung open as he heard a yell above the wail of the siren.

'Police! Hands on your head. Now. Get out of the seat.'

A strong hand on his shoulder twisted him down and out of the ambulance. Glenister fell a couple feet onto the tarmac, the impact sending a jarring pain through his left leg.

His head was pressed against the road, and he could see three men in uniform around him. Where the hell had they come from? Outside the cab, the siren scream was blocking out all other sounds. The road surface was cold on his cheek. Looking underneath the ambulance, he could see a body lying on the road outside the passenger door.

Glenister felt the metal of the cuffs on his wrists and then his body being lifted round. He stared up at the face of a young officer, whose eyes widened. The policeman reached for his radio. Another officer reached into the cab and pressed the horn to turn off the siren. There was a brief parp of the horn and then silence, apart from the Barnsley accent of the young officer, who spoke into his radio.

'Driver and ambulance are secure, scene is secure, repeat secure,' he spoke urgently. He looked down again at the handcuffed man on the ground beneath him. 'And, sarge, you're going to like this. The driver has been identified as the suspect wanted in the Pall Mall bombings. He's Douglas Glenister.'

#

CTOC, St Pancras, London
Tennant cleared his throat and loosened his tie, a crimson paisley design, which Gabriel reckoned must have been fashionable a decade ago. He had come from COBRA, and judging from his buoyant mood, it had gone well.

'First up, bloody well done, the lot of you,' he said to the officers stood around the conference room. 'I know you've had a crazy ten days, and you've had no sleep, no rest and no showers by the look of some of you.' There was a ripple of laughter. 'Forensics played a blinder with the DNA from the petrol bomb fragments, as did the teams who found Houghton.'

He banged the desk with his palm, triggering raucous applause. Gabriel forced a smile.

'That's the congratulations dealt with. Loose ends. Sophie?'

Gabriel took over. She could see the smiles and sense the relief in her colleagues, but still she had that niggling sense they had missed something.

'First, we've got enough to link Douglas Glenister, the driver of the ambulance, to Pall Mall. We've matched him with DNA found at the hotel room, and he's a good fit with the CCTV in the hotel reception. So yesterday, we didn't just stop the Leeds atrocity, we also found our missing man. That's a major result. We've also got Glenister's accomplice, who calls himself Roger Smith and inveigled himself into the St John Ambulance several months ago. He was the man who Rod Houghton was contacting by phone in Leeds over the last few days. He's not speaking, but we'll have an ID on him within the hour.

'I know the temptation now is to take the foot off the gas, but there is much to do. We cannot afford to slack now – as much as we all need a rest. We've stopped Leeds's attack, but we've not stopped the NRF. We've got a list of lines of inquiry as long as my arm. Have we got the whole cell, or is there anyone else left and are there other NRF cells off the radar? And what's the organisational structure? Was Rod Houghton the leader or a senior planner? If not, who is the leader? Somewhere in history, there will be a crack and we need to find it and prise it open. The NRF trusted him with not one but three attacks in two weeks and that means he is trusted implicitly. And there will be a trail to them in his comms, in his finances, in his history. These are urgent questions – and if we don't get them answered, we can expect another Chilton Park, maybe soon.'

Her earnest tone had sapped the levity out of the room. The officers watched in silence.

'Second, weaponry and ammo in the ambulance. The bomb was home-made – sourced from over-the-counter chemicals. However, the rifle is more interesting.' She held up the report from the National Ballistics Intelligence Service. 'According to NABIS, it is standard army issue. It's almost certainly the weapon used by Glenister in Pall Mall – we'll have that confirmed overnight. But I want to know where it came from. DI Bose's team will chase that up, starting with the Ministry of Defence. I repeat, I need you to put everything into this. Time is against us.'

As the meeting broke up, Gabriel watched Bose standing at the edge of a group of officers hanging around Skeffington, laughing at a joke in the corner. She strode over and steered her away.

'Sorry to interrupt the festivities, Eva, but anything new on Abu Mujahid?' she asked. Again, she felt irritated with the cheerfulness of the men and women around her.

Bose was flustered. 'No, ma'am. Nothing more in the last few days. But I've not been pushing. We've not had time.'

'We need to make time, Eva,' said Gabriel, 'you know how much this matters.' She paused, relenting slightly. 'Look, I'm not having a go, we've all been tied up, but this isn't the time to take our eyes off the ball.' She looked pointedly at the laughing officers surrounding Skeffington.

'Sorry, ma'am, I'll get on to it first thing.'

'Thanks.' Gabriel softened. 'Maybe we need to approach this differently – go off-piste to unofficial sources.'

'Are you still in contact with that woman from the Israeli embassy?' said Bose.

'Rachel Isaacs?' said Gabriel. Isaacs was an old friend from her student days at Nottingham. Nominally, she was a cultural attaché at the Israeli embassy. In reality, she was a liaison officer for Mossad.

'You know what, that's a bloody stroke of genius, Eva. I'm overdue a lunch. I'll see if she's free tomorrow.'

Bose nodded and walked back to the laughter in the corner. Gabriel turned around to see Tennant standing behind.

'I thought you were giving that line of inquiry a rest, Sophie,' he said quietly.

'I was, boss. But now we've got a bit of capacity, won't do any harm to chase it up.'

Tennant shook his head softly. 'And give them a bit of leeway.' He nodded towards the officers scattered around the room. 'They deserve a chance to celebrate. This has been a big win.' He walked out.

#

Gabriel gazed out of the window. Even through the double glazing, Gabriel could hear the relentless thudding as the sleet smashed into the pane before sliding out of sight. How did Abu Mujahid manage to do this – to get into her head on the day she should be celebrating with the others? Through the window, she could see the street lights coming on as dusk fell over the wet streets. Gabriel looked out at the horizon, as if trying to find a glimmer in the darkening skies.

DAY 11

Saturday

CTOC, St Pancras, London
Campbell was smouldering with indignation.

Gabriel started. 'He said what?'

'They said they didn't have the manpower on a Saturday morning and we should call back after the weekend,' said Campbell. 'I pointed out that this was an urgent inquiry, and he said everything was, and I quote, "fucking urgent with you lot" and hung up. Rang back and no answer. Tempted to go over there and knock on a door, ma'am.'

'Unbelievable,' said Gabriel. 'We're in the middle of a major investigation and some idiot at the MOD doesn't want to work weekends? I'll sort this out.'

She ushered Campbell away and scrolled through the contacts book, muttering under her breath. What was the matter with these people? It was the same with the media – anyone looking at the news would be forgiven for thinking the whole NRF gang had been banged up and the case done and dusted. Had they no idea how much more there was to do?

She found the name. Lieutenant General Peter Holsworthy, head of Home Command, based in Aldershot. She'd met him at a counter terrorism exercise in Wiltshire four months ago and he was a nice guy, if a bit awkward with women in positions of authority. When in doubt, go to the top.

She rang his office and left details with his duty PA, stressing that it was urgent and linked to recent terror attacks. Eight minutes later, her phone rang.

'Peter Holsworthy here.'

'Thank you, General. One of my team has been attempting to identify a rifle found at the scene of yesterday's terrorist attack in Leeds – which we believe is army issue – and has just been fobbed off by one of the junior weekend team at the Ministry of Defence.'

'I'm sorry, but I'm not sure what this has to…'

'Please let me finish. I'm sure this wasn't the intention, but it did feel rather like the army obstructing the police investigating a major terrorism incident, which would be embarrassing if it became public, which neither of us want.'

There was a bristling silence at the other end. 'Go on.'

'What I need now is your best man, or woman, available for my team first thing to look into the source of this firearm. Would you be able to sort that out? Please.'

The second she dropped the handset onto the cradle, it chirruped again.

'Sophie Gabriel?' It was a man's voice. 'It's Tom Crowther from the *Herald*. Sorry to bother you, but I wondered if I could have a quick word? Just two minutes.'

She swore in her head. That was stupid – answering without checking who it was. She knew Tom. A languid, floppy man with a public-school haircut and a taste for expensive, ill-fitting suits.

'Sorry, Tom, you'll need to speak to the press office.'

'Actually, it's something that you might want to deal with yourself, Sophie. We're working on a story that your team had strong evidence of a second attack by the NRF after Chilton Park, but despite that, failed to put out more police to protect the marches. Any truth in that, and was it Steven Tennant's decision?'

And for a whirling moment, she was half-tempted to go

off the record and tell Crowther to fuck right off. It was a tiny, half-glimpsed moment of recklessness that would never come to pass.

'Sorry, Tom, press office.' She put down the phone. Where had they got that from? It was half-true – distorted, of course, but with a grain of reality. Her instinct was to ring Tennant and warn him that the *Herald* were sniffing around, but she held back, fearful of showing weakness to him. If they ran with the story, she would need to deal with it herself. And not for the first time since Tennant's refusal to take her warning about Abu Mujahid, she felt terribly alone.

#

Kendal, Cumbria
Abu Mujahid found a space in a car park five hundred metres from the shop. It was an unlikely venue for an Amazon pickup. One half of the store was a grocers and newsagents, the other was devoted to souvenirs. On the wooden shelves, lopsided china panthers stood guard among the crystal skulls, flimsy selfie sticks and boxes of fudge made in Birmingham with postcards of the Lake District stuck crookedly to the front. A stack of papers by the till were plastered with headlines about yesterday's terror plot in Leeds. Abu Mujahid picked up a copy of the *Guardian* and asked for his package, handing his fake ID to the cheery woman behind the counter.

'You're lucky, love, your order only came in twenty minutes ago. Three boxes, was it?'

'That's right,' said Abu Mujahid, pretending to examine a postcard while he looked out for a CCTV camera in the shop.

'I'll get the Useless One to give me a hand. Just be a second.' She pointed to a heavily moustached white-haired man serving a customer. She called out: 'Oi, lard arse. Give this customer a hand.' She turned to Abu Mujahid conspiratorially. 'My husband. The parcels are bulky, so you'd best get your van out front, but take care. The wardens are sharp-eyed round here.'

Ten minutes later, the van was in front of the shop.

'What you've got in here then?' said the white-haired shop owner.

'Photography equipment,' said Abu Mujahid coldly. 'Birdwatching.'

'Oh,' said the white-haired man, looking surprised. He handed the second of the boxes over to Abu Mujahid, who stacked it in the rear, shut the doors and clambered into the driver's seat.

#

Ministry of Defence, Whitehall, London

Tony Metcalfe of Defence Equipment and Support was a jowly man in his mid-fifties with greying hair plastered greasily over his forehead. His double-breasted jacket and floral tie looked like a relic from the early 1990s. He ushered Bose and Campbell into a conference room on the second floor of the Ministry of Defence offices.

'Sorry we can't do coffee – the machine's broken and we can't get the parts,' he said in an Etonian drawl. 'I understand that your boss has been ruffling some feathers. Best way to get things done round here. What do you need?'

Bose nodded to Campbell.

'We're tracing an assault rifle found at the scene of yesterday's terror attack in Leeds and which we believe was also used at the Pall Mall murders,' said Campbell, sliding over a photo. 'It's army issue, an SA80 A3. The number's been filed off and it's not been used in any other known criminal activity.'

'Hmm. That's going to be a tall order,' said Metcalfe, rubbing his face as he eyed the picture. 'This looks like an A3 all right, the most recent upgrade. There's a lot of these in circulation now – sourcing this baby is a bit like looking for the proverbial needle.'

'I understand the army has upgraded thousands of these over the last few years from the old A2s,' said Campbell, who had spent the morning reading up on the weapon. 'Could this have been nicked during the refurbishment programme – say from the factory or in transit?'

'Anything's possible, but it's unlikely,' said Metcalfe. 'The procedure for collection, refurbishment and delivery is extremely tight. Every rifle's serial number is logged and traced from the moment it leaves an armoury to be taken to the factory for the upgrade, to the moment it arrives back at the armouries. The records are checked, double-checked, tripled-checked. It'd be easier smuggling the Crown Jewels out of the Tower than getting hold of one of these. If you're looking for the source of this weapon, I'm confident it wasn't during the refurbishment process. If I had to put money down, I'd say it went walkabout after it was delivered back to the army.'

'Could someone have snuck it out of a base?' said Bose.

'It's possible, but not easy, inspector. But there are other ways to get round the system. Weapons malfunction, for instance. These rifles are pretty reliable, but things always go wrong. So they get returned to the armoury, they get cannibalised, some go missing. Of course, the records are supposed to be tight, but mistakes happen and things get taken. And the army has had considerable inventory issues in the last few years.

'If this rifle was stolen as a one-off, then there's little chance I'll be able to find the source. But if it was part of something bigger, say a systematic theft of weapons, then we may have a chance. Let me look through the system – see if I can spot any irregularities.'

'How long will that take, sir?' said Bose.

'A day maybe, maybe more.'

'Tell you what, Mr Metcalfe, how about three hours?'

#

King's Cross, London
Stepping into La Traviata was like stepping back four decades, Gabriel thought as her eyes became accustomed to the gloom.

It was like a pastiche of an Italian restaurant, designed by someone who'd watched too many 1970s sitcoms, and was littered with red-checked tablecloths, plastic flowers and heavy maroon wallpaper. The terrifying Neapolitan owner welcomed Gabriel like an old friend and escorted her to the table with more flourishes than were strictly necessary. Gabriel had eaten here four or five times and she no longer bothered giving her order. The owner was convinced Gabriel only wanted spaghetti al pomodoro and refused to be persuaded otherwise.

Gabriel rarely had time for lunches like this, but Rachel Isaacs, with her Mossad connections, was worth pursuing. Isaacs had been surprised to take the call last night, but had agreed to meet today. Gabriel and Isaacs had lived in the same halls of residence in their first year at Nottingham and had met during an uncomfortable 1960s-themed fresher's disco. They found solace in each other's awkwardness at the enforced jollity of the event, and the bond formed by social embarrassment turned quickly into friendship. They had stayed in touch after graduating and had met three or four times since Isaacs had returned to the UK a few years earlier, nominally working in the Israel embassy's cultural department.

She was already waiting at the table and seemed ageless, thought Gabriel, as Isaacs rose to kiss her, the same straight black hair, cut shoulder-length, the same clear and clever brown eyes and quizzical half-smile. They chatted, passing on office gossip and discussing politics until the food arrived.

'I had a look this morning and we've got nothing on your old pal Abu Mujahid, sadly,' said Isaacs. 'He was last seen in Syria six months ago and has gone off the radar.'

'That's what I keep being told,' said Gabriel.

'But we've got something on an associate of his. Have you come across the Global Islamic Defence? They're fairly new players.'

'I've heard of them,' said Gabriel. Jihadist splinter groups were emerging from the ruins of the so-called Caliphate all the time, all with new names – even when the faces, slogans and goals usually remained the same. Some went by half a dozen different names, which made tracking them hellish.

Gabriel continued: 'I thought they were more into organised crime than anything else.'

'That was our view until the last couple of months,' said Isaacs. 'But some interesting names have become associated with them – individuals who played a major role in ISIS – and we're starting to take them more seriously. One of them is Mohammed Huzaifa.'

Gabriel put down her glass of water too hard and a splash hit the tablecloth. 'Nasty piece of work.'

'Yep. He was involved in the Druze massacre, alongside Abu Mujahid. He's now running the GID and has been for the best part of six months. And since he took over, the organisation has been busy. Since December, we've been concerned that they were moving weapons out of Syria into neighbouring countries. A kind of logistics service for jihadists in need of an anti-tank missile or an additional few thousand rounds, that kind of thing. We've been regularly keeping an eye on their shipments, but nothing substantial has come up. Until this. It's got Mohammed Huzaifa written all over it.'

She pushed a folder across the table.

'We're going to pass this to MI5, but no harm you seeing it first.'

Gabriel put her fingers on the buff folder. The intel would be going into Thames House shortly and would be landing in her lap following further analysis from MI5, but Isaacs was doing her a big favour by giving her an early look.

'We've identified two shipments which we believe originated from GID,' said Isaacs as Gabriel leafed through the folder. 'Both are linked to the same commercial shipping office in Beirut and all went via Greece – one to Canada, one to the UK.'

Each shipment was dated alongside a list of contents. Gabriel's eyes widened as she read.

'You certain?' she said.

Isaacs nodded. 'Source is good,' she said.

Gabriel read again. Explosives, assault rifles, ammo. What alarmed her was not the quantity but the quality. AK-74s, Uzi submachine guns, and M4 Carbines.

'When did this ship?' said Gabriel.

'Around six weeks ago, Sophie. It would have arrived in the UK within the last two weeks.'

This cannot be a coincidence, Gabriel told herself as she walked back to the office. Two weeks ago, a terrorist arms shipment – of the like not seen since the peak of the IRA decades ago – arrives in the UK, sent from a terror group with links to Abu Mujahid. And within days, a man resembling Abu Mujahid smuggles himself into the country.

She pulled out her phone to call Tennant, then stopped and returned the mobile to her pocket. No reason to tell the boss yet, particularly when he was being such an arse.

#

CTOC, St Pancras, London
Bose took the call at her desk.

'Tony Metcalfe from DE&S.' The accent was even posher on the phone. 'I've pulled the records for the SA80 refurbishment as requested and there's nothing untoward on paper. But there is one thing that came out in conversation with colleagues at Bristol…'

'Go on, sir,' said Bose.

'Well, the whole bloody point of remodelling the rifle was to improve its reliability. You'll recall that the first model, the A1, used in the Gulf, had significant flaws. They were ironed out in the first major upgrade to the A2. The latest upgrade to the A3 has raised the game even further. Since it was phased in, they've not needed anything like the same level of aftercare. Orders for spare parts are down in every armoury in the country. Except one, I should say. The Royal Electrical and Mechanical Engineers armoury attached to

197

Hedingly Barracks in Hampshire has seen a fairly hefty hike in orders for SA80 spare parts over the last two years. It's possible – and it's only a theory – that these spare parts being ordered by the armoury at Hedingly were not for repairing faulty rifles at all but were being used to create new ones. It's theoretically possible that someone could order enough spare bolts, firing pins, barrels, stocks, grips and so forth – to produce rifles virtually from scratch.

'It sounds fanciful, I know, and of course you couldn't create an entire rifle that way, but you could go a long way, particularly if you were an armourer holding on to useful parts from older models supposedly intended to be decommissioned...

'Another thing. I showed the pictures to our guys at the factory and your weapon analysis was nearly right. But this isn't quite an SA80 A3. It's a hybrid. Some parts are from the newest A3 modifications, but others are from the earlier A2. It's been cobbled together, which fits the theory that it's being done by someone with access to parts.'

'If someone in the armoury was creating SA80s from spares and selling them on the black market, how come no one's noticed?' said Bose.

Metcalfe hesitated. 'To be honest, Sergeant, bits and pieces have gone missing from armouries since the dawn of time. You know the sort of thing – rounds that are signed out and never accounted for. A high-ranking NCO would have no problem getting them off base. And the army's always overstocked. It's engrained in the military mind. The fear isn't running out of storage space, it's running out of stores. Inventory control has been terrible for years. It's perfectly plausible that a certain number of weapons are being assembled and smuggled out.'

'You say weapons? Based on the excess parts orders, how many military-grade rifles could we be talking about?'

'I don't know,' said Metcalfe. 'Certainly no more than twenty or thirty from this source in the last couple of years.'

'Thirty?' Bose was incredulous. 'Are you telling me that

it's possible thirty high-performance assault weapons have gone walkabouts from Hedingly and no one has even noticed?'

'As I say, inventory has been a bit of a problem in recent years. But yes, it's possible.'

#

Stoke Newington, North London
Gabriel was brushing her teeth when the phone rang. She cursed, spat out the toothpaste and dabbed her mouth with a flannel.

'Sorry to call late, ma'am, but I've an update on the NRF rifle,' said Bose.

Gabriel was half-expecting the call. Bose had been liaising with the Ministry of Defence Police earlier that evening. The MDP were a tiny force, with no more than two thousand five hundred staff, based at a former US Air Force base in Essex with responsibility for protecting military sites.

'The MDP has identified a prime suspect, the head armourer at Hedingly Barracks,' said Bose. 'He's a Sergeant Christopher Jones. We've got more than enough on him, so I've arranged a team to go down at dawn to bring him in and pull his flat apart. MDP will provide support.'

'Good work, Eva,' said Gabriel. 'Bring him up to St Pancras – I'd quite like to listen in to the interview myself.'

She hung up with a smile. A slightly smug smile, she conceded as she studied her face in the bathroom mirror. But deservedly so. Interviews with their two Leeds terrorists – Rod Houghton and Doug Glenister – had gone nowhere. And the search of both men's homes had yet to yield anything of significance. But this Sergeant Jones could be the break they needed to crack into the NRF – and maybe even start to unravel the leadership.

DAY 12

Sunday

King's Cross Police Station, North London

The constable from the Military Defence Police fiddled with his wispy moustache as Gabriel and Campbell approached the door to interview room two. Gabriel avoided looking at the moustache, worried her face might crack into a smile.

'I'm going to watch,' she said, handing over a file to Campbell. She walked into the next-door room and settled down behind the two-way mirror. She knew these rooms well, with their drab, stark interiors and stench of sweat and coffee.

Staff Sergeant Christopher Jones, the armourer from Hedingly Barracks, sat facing her through the glass, his hands folded on the battleship-grey table. His shrew-like solicitor, with narrow eyes and a tongue that seemed to be forever licking his lips, sat to his right.

Campbell started the digital recorder and gave the introductory legalese.

'Staff Sergeant Christopher Jones, you have been arrested for the unlawful supply of Section One firearms,' he continued. 'The details of which are an unregistered SA80 assault rifle discovered at the scene of a major terrorist incident in

200

Leeds yesterday afternoon. Can you confirm that you're the armourer at the Hedingly Barracks, Hampshire? Correct?'

Jones gave a curt yes.

'How long have you worked at Hedingly?'

'Four years.'

'And your job is what exactly?'

'Armourer. Repairing, maintaining and modifying weapons as needed. I check them out for training and check them back in.'

'And it's also your role to order spares, is that right?' he said.

'That's right.'

'Could you have a look at this document, please? It's a summary of the spares requisitions for the last three years. For the record, I'm passing Sergeant Jones a document marked as exhibit AM/7. Notice anything unusual?'

Jones studied the papers and shook his head. 'Nope.'

'And now have a look at this. This is the spares requisition for the battalion in Bigby. For the record, I'm passing Sergeant Jones exhibit AM/4. Notice anything now?'

'I'm not sure what you're getting at,' said Jones.

'Do you agree that you appear to be ordering six times as many spare parts as your colleague at Bigby forty miles down the road, even though yours is a significantly smaller base? Particularly, spare parts for the SA80s.'

Jones said nothing.

'Why is that, do you think?' said Campbell.

'I don't know,' said Jones. 'Rifles break. I order stuff when we need it.'

'Do you ever take your work home with you, Sergeant?'

'Of course not.' Jones was indignant.

Campbell studied him before continuing. 'Do you know a Douglas Glenister, Sergeant?'

At the name, did Jones flinch? thought Gabriel.

'Never heard of him.'

Campbell handed over another sheet. 'Have a look at this, exhibit JT/1, Sergeant,' he said, pointing to the top of the sheet of data. 'Is this your mobile phone number?'

'Yeah, you took it off me.'

Campbell continued. 'It's the GPS records from your mobile phone provider, Sergeant Jones. We've run an analysis of your movements over the last twelve months and it's come up with some strange patterns of behaviour. For instance, you visited the large out-of-town Sainsbury's in Allington six times in the last year after work. Allington is forty miles from your barracks, and sixty miles from your home. Why were you there?'

'I don't know. I need to shop, don't I?'

'Indeed you do, Sergeant. But it's an odd choice of supermarket. It's a long way out of your way – you'd driven past half a dozen Tescos and Aldis and at least two other Sainsbury's to go there. Or perhaps you're keen on that particular Sainsbury's. I hear their fresh deli counter's excellent.'

Jones was silent.

'And you were never there for more than ten minutes – doesn't sound like a very thorough shop to me.'

Jones remained silent.

'You visited the Allington Sainsbury's most recently last Sunday at around 12.30pm. Who did you meet then?'

'No one.'

'Ever been interested in politics at all?'

'Not my cup of tea,' said Jones.

'Now I've got a bit of a dilemma, Sergeant,' said Campbell. 'It's possible you've been ordering significant spare rifle parts just because your lads are particularly clumsy. Seems a bit unlikely considering they're using them on firing grounds in leafy Hampshire, rather than using them in a hellhole in the Middle East, but it's possible. It's also possible that you have been ordering too many spares because you are incompetent, of course. But your records suggest otherwise.'

Campbell paused. He wasn't doing this too badly, conceded Gabriel.

'It's also possible that you made six visits to Sainsbury's

more than an hour away from your home for legitimate reasons. Although right now I can't think of any. Or perhaps you made the visits to meet someone? To make a delivery?'

Silence.

'Sergeant Jones. I have listened to your explanations and I am now arresting you under Section Forty-One of the Terrorism Act of 2002 for being concerned in the commission, preparation or instigation of acts of terrorism. You are still under caution. Is there anything further you want to say?'

#

Outside the interview room, Gabriel waited for Campbell.

'Good work,' she said. 'Pull the video from the supermarket CCTV. Jones is supplying the NRF, I'm sure of it. How long will it take?'

Campbell looked at his watch. 'May take an hour or two to rouse the right person at the company HQ on a Sunday. But with luck, we should have something late afternoon.'

One step closer to the NRF, thought Gabriel as she walked away. And for the first time in days, the excitement and anticipation drove the worries about Abu Mujahid from her mind. Her first instinct had been to tell Tennant, who had parked himself upstairs in a conference room for the day, one of his weekly visits to the factory floor. But not today, not now.

#

County Durham

The forecast was for snow, which suited Ben Thomas's mood and made the likelihood of getting back to London tonight remote. He glanced through the window of his study across a scrubby back garden, through to the grey fields and moors of Long Bank beyond. He'd bought this cottage in his County Durham constituency two years ago, and while it made a welcome escape for spring and summer weekends, he had to drag himself here in January.

A dark object moved across the field. Thomas squinted his eyes to bring it into better focus. It was a fox, as brazen as anything, strolling across the grass in broad daylight, with a dead bird in its mouth. Thomas watched it cross to the stone wall then vanish into a hole.

Thomas threw himself back in the leather office chair and rubbed his eyes. The morning papers were scattered around the wooden table and the PM had pushed the Leeds terror attack off the front pages.

He picked up the *Mail on Sunday*. *The PM, The Prince and the Payoff*. The *Sunday Telegraph* had *PM in Saudi bribe row*. *The Sun* had the PM's face superimposed over a pig alongside: *The PM's Porky-Pies*. And the *Herald*, which had broken the story the evening before, an emphatic: *Time to Stand Down*.

The story was simple enough. Six years ago, while the PM was still Foreign Secretary, he'd received a payment of nineteen thousand pounds from an investment bank owned by a Saudi prince. The payment had been declared on his income tax form, which the *Herald* had got hold of. It was an unambiguous conflict of interest.

Number Ten had been on the phone last night, asking Thomas to shore up the PM on the Sunday morning shows. He'd declined. Instead, he'd tweeted a line giving full support to the PM.

The phone went. It was Hogarth.

'Ben. Are you alone?'

'Couldn't be more alone right now. In the bloody constituency. Nothing but the missus and a flock of sheep for one hundred miles.'

'Well, don't get snowed in. Listen, I wanted to touch base about the PM. Terrible business.'

'Terrible,' echoed Thomas with as much sincerity as he could bother to muster.

'Goodness knows where the press dig these things up, of course.'

'Indeed. Almost certainly from the Saudis, I imagine. Someone probably had the evidence sat in a safe in Riyadh for six years ready to use at the right moment.'

Which is nearly true, thought Thomas. Only the evidence hadn't been sat in a safe in Riyadh for the last six years, but the private safe in Thomas's own London flat. One of the perks of being a former chief whip was that it allowed the accumulation of useful data on friends and colleagues. He wished now he'd waited a few days for maximum impact in the media – but he was not to know the NRF were planning to blow up Leeds on Friday.

'Is he going to step down?' said Hogarth.

'Not immediately, Lesley, not his style. That would be taken as an admission of impropriety, particularly at a time of national crisis. He'll want to wait, get the feelers from the backbenchers and constituency chair.'

'And then?'

'And then he'll almost certainly step down in a few weeks in the interest of national unity.'

'What we don't want, Ben, is a lame duck at a time of national crisis. Look at the mess out there. Muslims picketing primary schools. Soldiers getting attacked in the street. Gangs of youths holding their communities to ransom. We need strong leadership now.'

'I'm in no position to persuade him to do anything right now, Lesley.'

Hogarth paused. *Here it comes*, thought Thomas. *Here comes the threat.*

'I agree that you are not in any position to do anything more,' she said. 'And yes, the PM is unlikely to step down off his own back. But the party might be persuaded to force his hand if they thought the stability of the coalition was at stake.'

'You'd do that? You'd threaten to pull it all down?'

'If he doesn't go, then yes, damn it, Ben, I would.'

Thomas tried to keep the smile out of his voice. 'And then what?'

'Well, constitutionally, the post goes to the next most senior member of the cabinet. Which is you.'

'And would that particular line of succession be enough to keep the coalition in place, Lesley?'

'Of course it would.'

'Without any conditions?'

There was a pause. 'One. The Freedom Bill. I want it introduced in three months. The public are angry, and they want leaders willing to stand up and protect our way of life. No compromises. That's the deal-breaker for my members.'

Thomas looked out of the window overlooking the lane. An elderly couple, faces muffled with grey scarves, were being dragged along the path by a chocolate Labrador. The woman spotted the Home Secretary and waved through the reinforced glass. He raised an arm in salute. He didn't recognise them – maybe they'd taken the holiday cottage by the stream for the weekend. Poor sods.

'I'm back in town tomorrow,' he said. 'Come to the office at four. But use the back entrance.'

'Of course. In the meantime, you know where to find me.' She rang off.

Under a stone probably, thought Thomas. He placed the receiver back on the cradle. The couple were out of sight now, probably drudging across the footpath to the top of Long Bank. The first few flakes of snow were settling on the lane. The view from the study of the lane and barn was still familiar and faintly tedious. And in a few hours, the landscape would be unrecognisable.

#

CTOC, St Pancras, London
Skeffington and Campbell were huddled over a screen when Gabriel walked in from lunch.

'Catching up on *Love Island*?' she said.

Campbell spun around to face her. 'It's the CCTV from the Sainsbury's. It's taken us all day to get hold of it, but we've now got footage from the six occasions where Jones's phone data suggests he was in the car park.'

He's anxious, thought Gabriel. Skeffington, in contrast, was almost grinning. He sat on the desk, swinging his legs, unable to sit still, watching and waiting for Gabriel's reaction to whatever they were about to show.

'He's definitely making an exchange each time,' said Campbell. 'He follows the same routine – he gets there first, parks as far from the CCTV camera as possible and waits for his rendezvous. His customer's car pulls up in the bay behind him, boot to boot, and the deal is concluded in a couple of minutes. This one is typical. It's the first visit. And you may recognise his buyer.'

He fast-forwarded the footage.

'It's not easy to spot, but there's Jones,' he said. He touched the screen, causing a bubble of distortion. A dark car – it was impossible to identify the colour – was parked at the left of the supermarket car park alongside a border of shrubs. The time and date stamp in the bottom left-hand corner showed it was 8.48pm on a Saturday, eleven months earlier. Another vehicle pulled up behind. It was dark – possibly black or grey. The driver and Jones got out of their cars and met by the boots. They spoke briefly, exchanged a package, then returned to their cars. Campbell rewound the video and froze. It was Douglas Glenister.

'ANPR shows Glenister's car was in the area at this time,' said Campbell.

'Good work, Campbell,' said Gabriel. 'So who else was he selling to?'

'It seems he was happy to sell to pretty much anyone in the market,' said Skeffington. 'Turns out he has an ex-wife, two mortgages and ten thousand pounds gambling debts.'

Again, there was something in his voice, something almost mischievous, thought Gabriel.

Campbell clicked on the next file. 'This is rendezvous number two – a few days later. The VRN of his customer isn't visible this time. But again, he's exchanging something. And then this is visit number three, which is more interesting.'

This time, the car visiting Jones turned into the beams of an oncoming car's headlights. Campbell froze the image. The VRN, or vehicle registration number, was sharp.

'This one was five months ago. The VRN is linked to a London crime gang, the Millwall Boys. We're a long way from their stamping ground but obviously they were happy with their purchase because the same vehicle makes another trip a few weeks later.

'I'll skip four and five. The VRN is out of shot and the pattern is just the same as the first three encounters. But number six is clear. It's the most recent exchange from last Friday.'

Jones's car was parked in its usual spot. A van pulled up in the bay behind it, the door opened, and a figure got out. The new driver was male but he was too far away and too badly lit to make out clearly.

'Can we enhance the image?' said Gabriel.

'Yes – but it doesn't help. But stay with it.'

The driver of the black car, presumably Sergeant Jones, got out and joined the other man. The boot flew up and the new arrival leant in, pulled out a bag and took it to his car. Then Jones got back in and drove off. The second man shut his boot, but instead of driving off, left the car and walked towards the camera. Within a few seconds, Gabriel was able to make out his clothes – a blue jacket over black jeans. He was bearded, but more than that was hard to see.

'Is that all we've got?' said Gabriel, frustrated.

'Course not, ma'am,' said Skeffington. 'We went back and asked for the CCTV from inside the supermarket.' Campbell clicked on a new file icon. The brightly lit interior of the supermarket appeared.

'The light's much better and we get a good look at him,' said Campbell.

The camera was angled towards three checkouts. The bottom half of the entrance was visible in the top right.

'Now look.' He slowed the video as a pair of black jeans and the bottom half of a blue jacket entered.

'He's gone to get a sandwich,' said Campbell. 'But he's about to come into view.'

She clicked again, and the camera switched to an aisle view – *sandwiches and drinks*, thought Gabriel. The man in the blue jacket was walking down the aisle with his back to the camera. He was red-headed, and the hair was close-cropped.

'Turn around,' said Gabriel to the screen.

He did. For a second, he turned towards the camera, his pasty face, narrow eyes and straggly beard clear in the white light from the display shelves around him. Campbell clicked on the pause.

The world stopped. 'Jesus Christ,' said Gabriel.

'Not quite, ma'am,' said Skeffington with a grin. 'Abu Mujahid.'

#

Cumbria
Abu Mujahid left the cottage early in the afternoon.

'Stay here and practise assembling and disassembling the rifle,' he told them. 'I need to test these. Waheed – you're with me.'

Saleem looked delighted to have been singled out. He carried the two Amazon boxes that Abu Mujahid had collected yesterday to the van. Abu Mujahid dropped a briefcase which Asad knew contained a laptop in the front seat. Asad heard the van scattering stones along the gravel pathway as it accelerated away.

After the adrenaline of the day before, today was a comedown for Asad. The three spent an hour with the rifle, removing the components, cleaning them, putting it back together. Mirza was particularly quiet.

'What's up, mate?' asked Asad when they were alone in the sitting room later. Muhid was in his bedroom, reading another of his books on jihad. He had brought a dozen or so, and to Asad, they were mostly impenetrable. It was getting dark and the crows were calling to each other in their raspy, guttural voices as they settled in the ash tree outside the back door.

Mirza sucked his teeth. 'Nothing, bro. Just tired.'

'Go on, something's up.'

Mirza looked around before lowering his voice. 'It's Abu Mujahid, man. I'm just wondering about him.'

Asad looked at Mirza's trembling hands. 'What do you mean?'

'He's not, you know, like us. There's something about him. Do you trust him? I mean properly? Is he going to be a martyr too? At the end?'

Asad said nothing. Abu Mujahid had never made it explicit whether he too would be entering martyrdom. He rubbed his chin with the back of his hand. His beard was getting too long – he liked it trimmed close.

Mirza continued. 'I mean, it would be better if he was, bro. It would feel like he was one of us. But sometimes he acts like he's a general – you know what I mean. Like we're just shit. Him telling us we can't speak to families or nothing.'

'You know why we can't,' said Asad.

'Yeah, but isn't it more suspicious that we've just vanished into thin air? Isn't it better to talk to people? To hide in plain sight rather than be up here away from people?'

Muhid re-entered the room and looked quizzically at him.

'What you talking about?' said Muhid.

'Nothing much.' Asad watched Mirza again.

'Time for Maghrib prayer,' said Muhid austerely. He walked to the bathroom to perform ablution.

Mirza didn't look Asad in the eye as he put away the rifle. One hand was still trembling.

#

CTOC, St Pancras, London
Through the window of the conference room, Gabriel could see the gothic spires of the old Midland Grand Hotel outside St Pancras station, cast in an orange glow of floodlights against the darkening purple sky. The hotel was an extraordinary building, a Victorian fantasy in red brick and gold leaf, with grand fireplaces and palatial staircases designed to rest weary passengers after their journeys from Birmingham, Manchester and Carlisle. The station had been converted into the Eurostar terminal, and the spires reminded Gabriel of a beacon, a signal that a more tantalisingly exotic life could be accessed from just a street away.

She turned back to face Bose, sitting at the desk. Abu Mujahid. She needed to focus on Abu Mujahid.

'We know nothing about Abu Mujahid – where he is, what he's doing, when he came home,' said Gabriel grimly. 'I've just spoken to MI5 and they are equally in the dark. They'll be taking the lead on him for now.'

That was the nature of the relationship between SO15 and MI5. In the early days of a case, Thames led the joint operation, supported by police. If arrests were needed, or an attack was looming, Thames handed the lead to the police but continued their support.

'MI5 are calling this investigation Operation Hippocampus,' said Gabriel. 'Terrible name, but there you go. You've done some amazing work over the last few years on returners, so I want you to focus full-time on Abu Mujahid – be our liaison with MI5. Liaise with Thames and get some feelers out via the CTPLO network.'

Counter Terrorism Police Liaison Officers were the Met's global eyes and ears. There were currently forty-eight experienced counter terrorism detectives working in partner nations and source countries, usually based in British embassies and often operating closely with MI6 officers.

'And we need more on the Global Islamic Defence,' Gabriel continued. 'If the intel from Rachel Isaacs is reliable, there's a strong chance Abu Mujahid is involved in whatever the GID are planning. We know there is an arms and explosives shipment coming from Greece and it's safe to assume it's heading to him.'

Bose left Gabriel alone in the conference room. She opened up the Abu Mujahid file and began to flick through it once more.

She struggled to focus. Her mind kept drifting back to the supermarket CCTV. There was something obscene about the image of Abu Mujahid wandering through the aisles of baked beans and spaghetti, as if he was just another ordinary shopper. It was like opening a fridge door and coming face to face with an alligator. *Focus, woman*, she told herself, and read again.

Born Jack Stephen Pearce, in Haringey. Aged twenty-seven. Parents divorced aged five – father in sales, mostly absent, mother died six years ago. One older brother in the north, selling cars. *Brother isn't close to his family*, thought Gabriel, *but should be watched*.

Bright, ruthless, geeky. Grade A student until fifteen, then he went off the rails. Predictably, got into dealing – coke, LSD, methadone. Aged eighteen, he was stealing pushbikes and mopeds. Picked up by police aged nineteen, convicted and given a suspended sentence and community service. A year later, he was picked up again. This time he got two years in Wandsworth.

Until then, Jack Pearce had shown no interest in religion. But in prison, everything changed. He fell in with Ishmail Sherif, then an up-and-coming preacher doing time for fraud, and within six months Jack Pearce had converted to Islam. By the time he left prison, he had a mission and new friends.

On the outside, Pearce worked at the North London Mosque for a few months as a volunteer. Once off licence, and free to travel, he went to Pakistan for four months. And there he got intensive training in explosives, basic terrorism craft and handling weapons, along with some impressive leadership training. He left Britain an awkward twenty-two-year-old, and returned eight months later a charming, charismatic manipulator. God knows how they did it, but it was an extraordinary transformation, according to those who knew him.

On his return from Pakistan, he was stopped and interviewed at the border. Nothing could be proven, but Pearce had the attention of MI5. He was rated initially as a high threat on the ladder of risk used by Thames and SO15. There were some four and a half thousand suspects of interest at the time he came back from Pakistan and within four months of his return to the UK he was in the top thirty.

Within six months, he had a cell preparing for an attack on a music festival in Cornwall using spiked drugs. An uneasy part of his drugs supply chain tipped off police and he was arrested. He went on trial for conspiracy to commit murder with two associates, but while they went down, Jack Pearce was cleared on a technicality.

And then Gabriel got involved. The facts of that next year were engraved on her head. She hadn't needed to review them last night. The Home Secretary put a control order on him. And then, after Gabriel diverted a surveillance team to a live emergency, he slipped away, killing Isobel Harris as he fled the country.

In Syria, he popped up five months later, working his way up the ISIS hierarchy, under his kunya, Abu Mujahid al-Britani. He was implicated in the beheadings of two Canadian aid workers, and the massacre of twenty-five government supporters. He rounded them up from their cell, crammed them into a cage and set fire to them. Two were children.

He took part in an attack on a Druze community in Jabal al-Druze which left ten dead, and was suspected to have been part of a beheading of a US journalist. His last sighting was in Aleppo three months ago. And then he went off the radar.

And I let him go. Those deaths – Isobel, the Canadians, the children, they are on my head.

The thought was there before Gabriel could put it back inside the box where it belonged. She knew with the rational part of her head that it was nonsense. She knew she had been cleared. That the choice she had made that had led to Abu Mujahid slipping away had been a reasonable one. In fact, it had been the best one available to her. But it wasn't the right one. How could it have been? And the other voice, the one that spoke to her from her guts, told her she was to blame. She had failed those anonymous victims in Syria. She had failed Isobel Harris, and her parents. She'd failed her own dad. And, Jesus, it was coming back to haunt her.

And she had been right. That was the galling thing. For the last seven days, she had known he was back in the UK – and for seven days, she had taken her eye off the ball. No, she corrected herself, she had been forced to take her eye off the ball. What damage had that week done? How far behind were they, when they could have been snapping at his heels?

The resentment that had been growing since she had come in here to read the file was growing. Sod it. She needed to talk to Tennant. He was still upstairs – she'd passed him in the cafe earlier.

#

'Sophie?' He looked up from his laptop.

'Abu Mujahid.' Her face was blank, her voice calm.

'For God's sake, don't start this again,' said Tennant.

'He's back.'

'So you've told me. And I thought I'd made it abundantly clear, I didn't want you chasing ghosts.'

'No, sir. He's back.'

Her voice calm and steady, she updated him on the Sergeant

Jones interview and Sainsbury's video. Tennant leant back and sucked his top teeth, studying her face. His face was icy, defensive. 'And what? You've come to tell me you told me so?'

'We knew he was here a week ago. We could have done something. We've thrown away seven days.'

Tennant stood up. 'You had a hunch – a guess that turned out to be lucky with the benefit of hindsight. There was no way of knowing it was him.'

'That's bollocks, sir, utter bollocks. We had plenty of evidence – you chose not to see it, you chose not to take my professional judgement on board.'

'Your judgement about Abu Mujahid is anything but professional, Detective Superintendent,' snapped Tennant.

'With all due respect, sir, I know him better than anyone.' She was shouting now. 'And if I tell you that he's in the country, then surely you take that seriously.'

'Lower your voice, Detective Superintendent.' Tennant's face was flushed. He took a breath. 'Listen, Sophie, I get that you're frustrated—'

'No, you don't get it. You are missing the point here.'

'I get that you're frustrated. But the call I made last week was the right one.'

'How can you stand there and say that? We've given him a week to do God knows what.'

'The call I made was the right one based on the data we had at the time. Come on, Sophie. You've been doing this job long enough to know there are no right and wrong decisions in this shit, you know that more than most. There are just decisions. You take them, you do the best and you move on. Sometimes there are no choices. Hindsight doesn't change that.'

'And sometimes those choices are still wrong, sir.'

She turned on her heels and marched out. She was too angry to regret the words. That would come later. Now, she needed some fresh air.

She ignored the lifts and bounded down the fire stairs to the lobby and to the street.

DAY 13

Monday

University of Islington, North London

'Mrs Asad, please speak more slowly.' The Islington university welfare officer pushed the handset harder into her ear.

'My son. Omar. He should have come home on Thursday, but he didn't. He's not answered his phone in days. We're very worried about him.'

The woman sighed inwardly. It sounded like another pushy parent trying to run their kid's life on remote control. 'Okay, Mrs Asad, please let me have your son's name.'

'It's Omar Asad. He's a second-year student and he's studying engineering. He's in halls.' She gave the hall and number.

'I'm afraid we're not allowed to pass on information about students. But we can get a message to him asking him to contact you. How long has he been out of touch?'

There was a muffled noise at the other end, then a man's voice spoke.

'Hello? This is Omar's father. What do you mean, you can't tell us how he is?'

'I'm sorry, but we can't pass on confidential information

about students. Your son is an adult. But we will of course do our best to help. When did you last contact him?'

'A week last Saturday.'

'That's not very long for students to be out of touch, Mr Asad.'

'No, but he's not been himself recently. It was his mother's fiftieth birthday at the weekend – he should have come down on Thursday. His sisters were all here. But we've heard nothing and he's not answering his phone, his WhatsApp or his emails. I asked my cousin to pop in and see him yesterday morning and again today and he's not in his room. We're at our wits' end.'

The welfare officer promised to look into it, took their details and rang off. Normally, she would email the hall warden and let her deal with it, but the name was familiar. She pulled out her Prevent Duty referrals file and, yes, there it was. Three months earlier, a student had raised a concern about Omar Asad with his personal tutor. He had been concerned Asad was hanging around with a hard-line faction on campus. The complaint had been forwarded to a local Prevent Duty adviser – in this case, a Medieval specialist in the Faculty of History, one of a dozen academics given responsibility for assessing whether students were at risk of radicalisation. The tutor had found evidence Asad was spending time on the extremist fringes but none that he had intention to use violence or the determination to do so. The review had been inconclusive – there was insufficient evidence for the college to offer Asad support or forward concerns to outside agencies – and his case had been put on file.

#

Three hours later, the director of student services had her Marks & Spencer sandwich lunch interrupted.

'When was Omar last seen?' she asked.

'Tuesday,' said the welfare officer as she stood in her

doorway. 'He went to a lecture in the morning. No attendance since. He's in Buckingham Hall – we got the warden to look in on him earlier. He didn't answer, so he used the master key. No sign of him and there's post from Thursday onwards in his pigeonhole.'

'That's not long. Surely he's most likely to be away with friends.'

'Possibly,' said the welfare officer. 'But the warden was alarmed by some of the literature in his room. Some was pretty far out.'

The director of student services groaned and put the sandwich down. 'In normal times, my instinct would be to wait for him to show up. He's probably gone off to spend a week with his girlfriend. But I guess these aren't normal times. Leave it with me.'

A red box file marked University Contacts was sat under the window ledge covered with a thin layer of dust. She leafed through the papers and pulled out the file labelled Prevent. The police contact details were on the front. She walked back to the phone and dialled the number.

#

Stoke Newington, London
Gabriel had woken at six and forced herself to go for a run – her first since Chilton Park. Dawn was still two hours away and, although the sky was starting to lighten, the stars were as clear as she had seen them in London's light-polluted skies. She headed for the park, illegally jumped over the padlocked gate and began her first circuit. She ran for thirty minutes, up and down the park, and by the time she returned to the bedroom, where Ray was stirring, some of yesterday's anger had been swept out of her head.

In the office, Gabriel threw herself into the massive paperwork that had accumulated over the last two weeks. Was it nearly two weeks since Chilton Park, she wondered as she sat down with a wad of files. The team working on the file for the Chilton and Pall Mall inquests were bombarding her with queries, and Tennant's office wanted details to feed the ever-hungry media. She recalled her dad moaning about paperwork when she was a teenager. *He can't have had much then,* she thought. *Wonder what he'd think of all this?*

Tennant called at eleven. She tensed when his number came up and contemplated letting it go to voicemail. Another slap down for her or an apology? It could go either way. She snatched at the handset.

'Listen, Sophie,' he said, before she could speak. 'Yesterday. I don't want to leave it like that. I know that Abu Mujahid is the last person you need to be dealing with right now.'

'With all respect, sir, the fact that I have history with Abu Mujahid is irrelevant.'

'Let me say my piece. Yesterday was out of character for you. And I hear you slammed the phone down on one of Ben Thomas's people at the Home Office the other day.'

'I've got more important things to do than write their sodding reports, sir.'

'Don't we all? But let me finish. MI5 tells me you've given short shrift to the team working on Abu Mujahid at Thames. That's not like you. And I've picked up things from within SO15. Even the commissioner has asked if you're up for this.' Gabriel waited for the ticking off. But instead, Tennant's tone softened. 'Look, I've not called to give you a bollocking. I've called to give you a friendly warning…'

Gabriel bristled.

'…and to apologise. You were right about Abu Mujahid. You are entitled to be angry that your view wasn't taken seriously, by me in particular. Yes, I needed you focused – and the fact you were focused on the NRF meant we got the job done. But I'm sorry.'

'That week could have made the difference, sir,' said Gabriel.

'It could also have meant that we missed Leeds.'

Silence. Gabriel picked up a phone cable left on the desk and twirled it around her fingers.

'Take it from me, I know what's it's like when it gets personal,' he said. 'When the press were going for me and Chris, it was the shittiest time of my working career. And I also know that no one, not even you, can perform at the top of their game when they are distracted by personal issues.'

'Seriously, I'm fine, sir. We're making progress. I'm sorry if I've pissed off some snowflakes in Whitehall, but their feelings shouldn't be anyone's priority.'

They ended the call. She welcomed the distraction from her thoughts when Bose came in.

'Had something from the Canada CTPLO, ma'am. Two days ago, a customs official at Montreal opened up a container from Athens, supposedly full of olive oil, but actually containing two crates of firearms and explosives. The paperwork was Greek and there were anomalies in the details, which was one of the reasons that it drew the attention of the port authorities in the first place. They've checked with Athens and it's a proxy address.'

'And the contents?' said Gabriel.

'They match perfectly the list you got from your Mossad friend,' said Bose. 'Looks like it's one of the GID shipments. It left Athens twenty days ago. I've contacted the Greek authorities to see if we can get a trace of the shipment sent here – should hear back today.'

#

Bose spent the next four hours on the phone and firing off emails. The Greeks had raided the shipping office that lunchtime and were sifting through the paperwork. It would be another twenty-four hours before they had anything.

It was after 4pm when she got an email from a local Prevent officer based at Shoreditch. A missing student, suspected hardliner, parents worried. There were no active cells at his university – no clues as to where he might be. Bose put the email in her To Do file. Probably just overanxious parents. Certainly not a priority for now – she forwarded it to a DC to look into it.

#

Cumbria

Abu Mujahid stood by the open van doors. The rifle was in the back, hidden under blankets and backpacks, and the Amazon boxes were stacked in the doorway.

'Well done, brothers, you've trained hard this weekend,' said Abu Mujahid as he led them to the kitchen where a box of unopened lager, bought that morning, sat on the table. He took each can in turn, ripping open the tabs and sending the contents gurgling and glugging into the sink.

'Leave the cans in the recycling box,' he said. 'Make sure the old dear sees them. Omar – you come with me. We need to change the plates on the van.'

The beers were Asad's idea. What better way to mask their devotion and their activities than by leaving behind the detritus of a boozy weekend? Mirza had suggested leaving a pornographic magazine behind too, but Abu Mujahid had drawn the line at that.

They stepped into the yard where the owner, wearing a well-padded quilt jacket and accompanied by a well-padded Labrador, was stood.

'You boys ready to go now?' Abu Mujahid put down the Amazon box he was about to slide into the back of the van and stood in front of it. He smiled at the woman.

'We're nearly done – just got to get the rest of the gear in the van.'

'Of course. I'm in no hurry – I only popped round on the off-chance you'd gone early. I know it's a long drive back. Bristol, wasn't it, and it'll be getting dark soon.'

Abu Mujahid and Asad nodded.

'Everything okay with the cottage?' she asked.

'It was perfect, thank you. It's a lovely place. And thank you for letting us stay so late – we were able to get a few hours climbing done this morning, which was hugely appreciated,' said Abu Mujahid.

She looked pleased as she turned and walked back down the lane.

#

Half an hour later, the owner was back, rooting around in her handbag for the key. She opened the door and stepped in. *Not too messy*, she thought. She'd had concerns when she'd taken the booking – five boys on a climbing expedition sounded like trouble. When her husband was alive, he'd have said no. And she'd had even more concerns when she saw them face to face. But she couldn't be picky now, and in the end, they'd been okay, nice even, she thought. Considering.

In the kitchen, she smiled when she saw the empty cans teetering out of the recycling box. Typical of students to drink cheap, nasty beer. Students and tramps. But reassuring that they drank beer. They couldn't be too extreme, not like those angry Muslims she saw all the time on the telly. No. They were nice boys. Considering.

#

Kensington, West London
'It's absolutely ridiculous, Nina,' said Lesley Hogarth, throwing the ticket onto the coffee table. It slid across the polished granite and came to a rest alongside a pristine copy of *Country Life*.

Strange choice for the house, thought O'Brien. A magazine that no one reads, that's left out for show in dentist waiting rooms. Was her boss even on show at home?

'Sorry, Lesley, but it's a no-no,' she said. 'Imagine the

222

headlines in tomorrow's papers – particularly if the PM resigns tonight. Imagine the fun the cartoonists would have.'

'But I paid two hundred pounds – right in the centre of the stalls. And it's Matt Smith. Matt sodding Smith, for Chrissakes. I love Matt Smith. And Bertie's away with the dog. I've got it all sorted.'

'It's *Macbeth*, Lesley. You cannot possibly go. It's a play about regicide. Come on.'

'Bollocks. You take it then. Have a night off…'

'Not really into Shakespeare, but thanks. Listen, stay in tonight, work on your red lines for the meeting with Ben Thomas. Get a good night's sleep.' She stood up, grabbing her duffel coat and satchel. 'And stay away from *Macbeth*.'

#

Hogarth swore under her breath and returned to the sitting room. O'Brien was right, of course, but that didn't make it any easier. She loved the theatre and she'd not had a chance to go for weeks. She phoned her school friend Valerie to say she'd not be going with her, but it went to voicemail.

She padded in her fake fur slippers across the grey carpet into the grey hallway and to the front door. Which was grey, she thought. Everything was sodding grey. Her fault for buying a show home.

The protection officer, Bob Brake, was lurking on the doorstep. Good-looking young man but a bit grumpy. She preferred Ollie – a beaming Ulsterman with a quick tongue and joyful eyes who'd been on duty earlier.

She leant out of the door. 'Listen, PC Brake, I'm staying in tonight. I've got a friend, Valerie, due to pop round in twenty minutes – apart from that, not expecting anyone.'

'Thank you, ma'am.' *Not a hint of a smile*, thought Hogarth as she shut the door.

The protesters had packed up two days ago. Nothing to do with the police – they'd simply got bored. But her conversations with the Met over their failure to remove them rankled still. A bunch of wet blankets. And Tennant? The worst sort of wishy-washy liberal. Part of the pseudo-intellectual woke elite that had ruined the police, just like they'd mucked up the BBC.

She poured herself a Winchester Gin – no tonic – and flicked on *Sky News*. It was the usual roll call of grief, the ticker tape running along the bottom of the screen like a shopping list of aggravation, the symptom of a world gone mad and perhaps a world finally fighting back. 'Thirty-two-year-old Basingstoke Mosque bomber arrested... Muslim rioters clash with police in Glasgow... Two youths charged with dropping bricks on M6... Asian woman filmed being punched on crowded Tube...' So much news, so little joy.

Her attention was distracted by the sound of a soft thump on the front door. Why the hell didn't Valerie use the doorbell? That woman. Hogarth turned off the TV and walked into the hallway. Her hand was on the door handle, when she pulled back. Why wouldn't Valerie ring the doorbell? She usually did. Somewhere in the back of her mind, behind all the anxieties and excitement of the last twenty-four hours, amid the frustration at missing her play and the loneliness of being stuck here for a night, a small mental alarm bell was ringing.

Silently, she locked the security chain in place across the door and turned to the tiny TV screen the police had insisted on installing when she'd become Deputy PM. Fiddling for the switch at the back of the box, she got a picture. For a moment, the image made no sense. A black object like a bag of laundry looked like it had been thrown on her doorstep. Dirty clothes? She looked closer and, with rising horror, recognised the shape of a body, slumped back against the door. Its face was obscured, but Hogarth knew it was Brake.

For a moment, her mind drifted high above her body. She saw herself standing panicked in the hallway, small, insignificant and all alone. And then she heard the crash of glass from somewhere in the house and a crack of breaking wood. Her home had four bedrooms and the noise was from her left, from the spare bedroom that overlooked the garden. Had someone come up the fire escape? The building was on a slope – the back garden dropped away and so the fire escape led from the spare bedroom to the patch of neglected grass outside. That was the only other way in.

For a moment, she was paralysed. Then a surge of hot blood swept away the fear. She slammed her hand on the red panic button by the front door, slid the chain back and opened the door, which flew towards her under the weight of PC Brake's body. She didn't have time or the presence of mind to check if he was alive, so she stepped over his body and into the street.

Her front door was raised by five stone steps off the pavement and she flew down them in a second. Turning to look, she saw the figure of an intruder, his head hidden by a hoodie and a scarf, framed in the doorway. He held something in his hand which glinted in the street light.

Hogarth sensed she couldn't outrun him, but she could get to a public space. Her house was in a mews off Kensington High Street and a crowded pavement with late-night shops and office workers and pub drinkers was close by. She willed her legs to move faster, but despite knowing that she would be quicker if she kept going, she turned around. At the same moment, there was a burning red stab in her left leg. She tripped and as she fell, she heard the crack of a firework, or maybe a car backfiring. But cars didn't back fire nowadays, did they? Their engines were more finely tuned than that. She once had a lovely Rover. Or rather she hadn't. Her father had. Leather seats. She once spilled ice cream on them. He was furious. But what a smell.

Hogarth slipped into blackness.

DAY 14

Tuesday

CTOC, St Pancras, London
Gabriel slammed down the phone. Skeffington and Bose looked up expectantly.

'Still alive?' asked Skeffington.

'You'd need an elephant gun to take down Lesley Hogarth,' said Gabriel. 'She's bloody lucky. Her assailant fired four times from a distance of ten metres, but only one bullet hit her and that was in the leg. She's expected to make a full recovery.'

'Got to be the shittiest marksman in London,' said Skeffington. 'What about the officer on duty outside her house?'

'Less lucky,' said Gabriel. 'Took a heavy blow to his head and neck – concussion, broken skull and possible vertebrae damage. He's in an induced coma.'

Bose shook her head. 'Poor sod. And definitely an assassination?'

'That's how it's being treated,' said Gabriel. 'The leading hypothesis is an Islamist retaliation.'

'Abu Mujahid?' said Skeffington.

'Who knows?' said Gabriel. 'He's in the UK, so it's possible.'

'Fucking hell, ma'am, it's not as if we've got enough on our plates as it is,' said Skeffington.

Gabriel snapped. 'Sorry to ruin your busy day, Skeffington, I'm sure you've got more interesting things to do. As it is, it's not our baby – DSU Clifton's team upstairs are taking it on. Still, we need to feed him anything we get on Abu Mujahid that links him to this shooting.'

Bose stepped in. 'What's the CCTV like?'

'Hopeless,' said Gabriel. 'Shows a male at some distance. Ballistics haven't turned up anything yet. If it is him, then he's branching out – he's never been one for this type of precision assassination before. Bombs, yes. Beatings, yes. Shoving children and women in a cage and setting fire to them, yes. But not this.

'Also, we know he's been sent a shipment of weapons and arms by the GID. Whatever he's planning, it wasn't just an assassination with a lone gunman. If it was him, then he's up to something else – something far bigger.'

Skeffington snorted. 'If it's not Abu Mujahid, don't need to look too far for motive, ma'am. Imagine trying to compile the list of suspects for shooting that cow. You'd need to bring in sixty million people for questioning.'

'That "cow" is our democratically elected deputy prime minister, DI Skeffington, and I'd ask you to show some respect.' Gabriel glowered at him.

'Joke, ma'am,' said Skeffington, staring hard back. 'I know you feel under the cosh, but it's called having a sense of humour.'

'Tell you what, DI Skeffington, when I want someone with a sense of humour, I'll hire a proper clown.'

Skeffington fumed silently.

Fifteen minutes later, Bose was back at Gabriel's desk, her eyes bright with excitement.

'Confirmation from Greece about the shipment from GID, ma'am,' she said in response to Gabriel's raised eyebrow. 'The Greeks have sifted through the files at the Athens shipping office and they've got the destination in the UK. It came in via Southampton and on to an electrical goods warehouse in Burgess Hill, West Sussex. A family firm – nothing on the file, no links to terrorism or organised crime groups. It's on an industrial estate on the edge of town.'

'Burgess Hill?' said Gabriel. 'Not your traditional hotbed for Islamist terrorism. Not really a hotbed for anything, come to think of it.' She called to Skeffington. 'Get down to Burgess Hill. Take DS Campbell too. Pull their paperwork, the CCTV and the names of anyone who might have picked up a shipment from Greece. Abu Mujahid arrived in the UK two weeks ago – so focus on the last fortnight. How long to get there?'

'Sixty minutes, maybe? Quicker to get them to send it over, ma'am,' he said.

Gabriel ignored him. 'Contact Sussex Police – get the warehouse shut down immediately. Keep everyone there until you arrive.'

#

Chelsea, London
Hogarth held the vanity mirror aloft and dabbed at her face with concealer. Her shin ached despite the painkillers, as did the bruises on her back and shoulders from the fall. Her left hand was grazed and she'd scraped her cheek on the pavement.

'What on earth are you doing, Lesley?' O'Brien was in the doorway to the private room.

'Putting on some warpaint, of course. I'm not going to face them looking like I've been slapped round the face with a brick.' Hogarth continued, sticking out the tip of her tongue in concentration.

'Lesley, that's a bad idea,' said O'Brien. 'Surely we want people to see how much you've been hurt.'

Hogarth put the make-up down on the bedside table. 'It's only a little concealer, Nina.'

O'Brien reached over and took it off her. 'But right now, we want to be sending a clear message. If anything, you should be accentuating your injuries.'

'Nina, that's cynical even for you.'

'Maybe, but this is a golden opportunity – use it to our advantage. And the police are saying it's an Islamist attack, so use that.'

Hogarth looked troubled. 'Hang on, Nina, they're saying that's a possibility, among many.'

'Sod that, Lesley,' said O'Brien. 'This isn't time for nuance. Do you think Ishmail Sherif held back after the failed attack on him in Leeds? No, he exploited that attack, he drained every drop of blood from it. Sod the warpaint. Just declare war.'

#

Hogarth allowed herself to be pushed to the hospital entrance, but then wrestled aside the nurse's hands on her wheelchair to do the last bit herself. The automatic doors swished open and for a moment she was blinded by the eruption of camera flashes.

She eased on the brakes and waited while reporters pushed microphones and smartphones into her face.

She needed no megaphone.

'Ladies and gentlemen, first may I say thank you to the doctors, nurses and other staff of St James's for their tireless work. They are, quite simply, the best in the world and we should celebrate them.'

She paused. Three key messages, O'Brien had said. Just three then back to bed.

'I have information that last night I was the victim of an assassination attempt by an Islamist terrorist. This man broke into my home, knocked unconscious PC Bob Brake, who works tirelessly to protect me, and then shot me in the leg from some distance. PC Brake is badly injured, but he is expected to make a full recovery. Our best wishes and prayers go to him and his family. I speak with Bob almost every day, a proud father and a dependable officer. That he nearly lost his life protecting me is the most upsetting aspect of this brutal assassination attempt.

'As one of the few politicians who have stood up for our communities, I am not surprised that Islamists have come after me… it will not diminish my determination but rather strengthen it. Unless they put me in a coffin, you can rely on me.' *That seemed to go down well*, Hogarth thought. Another cracking line from O'Brien. The woman really was extraordinarily good at this sort of thing.

Her voice changed, hardened, deepened. She stared around at the cameras, catching each one in turn for a moment.

'Let me say this – and this is a message to you, the Islamists and those politicians in the opposition who sympathise with the thugs and bullies.

'You are not welcome here. To the terrorists who bring violence to the streets, and to the Islamists who seek to destroy our way of life, I say this – go home, go back to your parents' homes, go back to your grandparents' homes. If you try to destroy us with violence, we will rise and destroy you. For too long, Britain has been a place of tolerance, where foreign cultures have been allowed to set up stall alongside traditional British culture. But no longer. We have had enough. And that starts here. We need tougher laws to protect our own – and that is why I am determined to see a Freedom Bill introduced into law to protect traditional British values of decency, fair play and justice. I've talked before about the need for a Second Battle of Britain. That battle starts here, and it starts now.'

#

Burgess Hill, West Sussex
The warehouse resembled an outsized Meccano to Skeffington's eyes. It stood in an industrial park alongside a row of willows, which dipped their branches into a stream lined with tin cans and plastic bags.

Three cars from Sussex Police had arrived to support SO15. No vehicles had left or entered the site in the last two hours and seven employees were being kept in the staff restroom. An articulated lorry was parked on the slip road outside the complex, its driver sat angrily in his cab on the phone, unable to drop off the load or drive to his next destination.

Skeffington was sat in the manager's office with Campbell. The manager – a sweating, red-faced man with a flop of thinning hair – was fiddling with his thumbs. His assistant stood behind her boss, unsmiling and severe.

'Have another look, sir, go on, a really good one,' said Skeffington.

The manager held the photograph of Abu Mujahid in his clammy fingers. His forehead inched forward to bring it closer to his eyes, but he shook his head.

'Sorry, inspector, I don't know him.' He pushed the photograph back across the desktop.

'Who works nights?' asked Skeffington.

'Any one of four or five – we rotate the night shift. We can get deliveries pretty much any time, so we always need someone about.'

'We'll need your work rota for the last three weeks then – and I'll need access to your CCTV, of course.'

The manager blinked. 'That's a bit irregular – don't you need a warrant for that?'

'You could insist we get a warrant, that's true. But that could take a couple of hours to sort out while we all sit around here doing sod all. And unless you've got a bottle of Scotch and a good movie, we might just get a bit bored. On the other hand, you could just volunteer to show us now. Which, if you think about it, would be the more normal thing for someone to do, considering you've got nothing to hide.'

The man blanched. 'Of course. It's on the hard drive – I can get a copy.'

'Thank you – but one of our officers will do that, if that's okay.' He nodded to Campbell, who left with the office assistant. 'And I also want your deliveries logbook.'

Flustered and uncertain, the manager pulled up the record and printed a copy.

'Many deliveries here at night, sir?' Skeffington asked as he flicked through the list.

'One or two a week – usually early morning when a container comes off Newhaven. The overnight ferry gets in at 5am and we're usually their first delivery. It's about 6am.'

'What about sending goods onward? Anything at night?'

'No. That's all done in the day. We have a security guard on overnight and the first colleague usually arrives by 5.30am. The office staff are all here by 8.30am and last to leave is 4.30pm,' said the manager.

Campbell entered the room with the office assistant.

'Got it, sir.' He waggled a portable hard drive.

'Excellent. That was easy, wasn't it? Tell you what, let's have a quick look while we're here. I'd like to see from 5.15am to 7.30am – each day, starting two weeks ago,' said Skeffington. 'If nothing comes up then, we'll go back a week at a time.'

'That'll take ages, inspector,' protested the manager.

'But think of the fun we'll have, sir. Better make yourself comfortable,' said Skeffington.

#

The office assistant showed Campbell how to operate the system.

'Go back to fast forward,' said Skeffington when Campbell took over. Under his breath, he added: 'Although the chances of us finding anything are zero. Yet another wild goose chase because the boss has got her knickers in a twist.'

Campbell ignored him. The CCTV started on the Monday, two weeks ago. Four images were displayed on the screen, one showing the front of the office, another the loading bay, the third the car park and the last a wide-angle shot of the gate.

The footage showed the arrival of the first person shortly after 5.30am. It was a large, bearded man. Skeffington didn't recognise him from the staff waiting in the break room – must be the early-morning shift. No one else arrived until 6.15am. Campbell slowed down the video and took a note of the number plates. It took five minutes to speed through Monday, another five for Tuesday. By Thursday, the pattern of early-morning arrivals was becoming clear. The first car came at 5.30am, the second at 6.30am and then a flurry of drivers parking up between 7am and 8am.

'Focus on that first hour when there's only one person on duty from now on,' said Skeffington. 'If I was Abu Mujahid collecting a package, that's when I'd do it.'

Friday's footage came up. The first car arrived at 5.30am, according to the timestamp. The driver got out and opened up the office.

'Stop,' said Skeffington, moments later. The headlights of a vehicle had appeared. It drove up to the car park and halted. No one got out. It was a van, parked sideways to the camera, so its number plate was out of shot.

'Who's that?' asked Campbell.

Skeffington looked at the list of collections and deliveries. 'Nothing was picked up that Friday till 8am.'

The van was stationary for another thirty seconds, and then a figure emerged. Their back was to the camera as they walked to the office.

Moments later, the figure re-emerged with the bearded member of staff. Both people were carrying boxes the size of old-fashioned tea chests.

'Who is the staff member?' said Skeffington.

'Dave Johnson, early shift,' said the manager. 'His shift finishes at noon, so he's at home now.'

Campbell wrote down the name, paused the image then enlarged it. It was still dark and the light from the car park wasn't good enough to make out their features clearly. Campbell pressed play and the men walked on to the van. They were still in semi-darkness as they opened the back and loaded up. The driver got in and pulled away.

'Can we get a sharper image?' asked Skeffington, barely masking his irritation.

'Not here. Video forensics should be able to get something clearer, sir.'

'Is that Abu Mujahid?' Skeffington wondered aloud. The driver had the right build, but his back was turned. 'Go back to the start – I want to see the van arrive.'

Campbell rewound. 'Stop,' said Skeffington. 'Now forward a frame or two. There. Gotcha.' And he pointed at the screen.

For a second, as the van turned into the car park, its front was facing the camera. And for a second, its number plate and the driver, Abu Mujahid, were visible in the street light.

'That's the bugger,' said Skeffington. 'Bloody hell, the boss was right.'

#

Downing Street, London
Rupert, the Prime Minister's Cocker Spaniel, was dozing on the carpet in front of the desk, his feet flexing as his sleeping mind enjoyed a fantasy dog paradise, chasing rabbits, or teasing cats. Thomas crouched down to tickle his ears.

'Take a seat, Ben.' The Prime Minister was alone. Thomas could not recall the last time the pair of them had sat face to face without a civil servant eavesdropping. The PM waved towards the sofa. Thomas selected the end furthest from the window and leant back, cross-legged, his fingers resting on his trouser pocket, his expression neutral and his mind racing faster than the sleeping dog's.

'A while since we talked, just the two of us. Like the old days, eh?' said the Prime Minister from an armchair diagonally opposite Thomas.

He looks ancient, thought Thomas, and he wondered whether people said the same about him. 'There's no time, is there?' he said.

'Perhaps we should have made time, Ben. Perhaps we wouldn't be in the mess we are now.'

'Listen, you know I'll back you one hundred per cent. Whatever you say, however you decide to play this. It's chip paper – no one will care in a week.'

'You know that's bollocks. You know they've got my head in a sodding noose and all they're waiting for is the final kick of the stool,' the Prime Minister said softly.

'I don't know that. I do know that you're not a quitter.'

'Forget it, Ben. I've made up my mind.' There was a moment's silence as the Prime Minister scrutinised Thomas's face. 'I was hoping to announce my departure date in March, give the party time to hold an election. But I can't now. The party has made it clear. Hogarth has made it clear. She'll withdraw from the coalition if I remain and we can't survive as a minority government. And we can't afford a general election either. No, I need to go in the next twenty-four hours. And it means you stepping up as acting PM.'

Outside the window, the band of the Horse Guards struck up a jaunty sea-shanty tune.

The PM continued: 'We're releasing a press statement at eleven tomorrow morning followed by a presser outside. Then I'm at Buckingham Palace at 11.45, then on the phone to Pickfords to book a removals van.'

'Where are you going to live? The Sussex place?'

'For the time being. Let the dust settle and work out what to do. A job in finance is probably out of the question now. The wife wants to travel.'

Thomas laughed. The Prime Minister continued. 'And the leadership campaign that will follow. You ready to win it?'

'Is it me, then? Are you sure?' said Thomas.

'Of course. We've had our moments in the last few years, but it's always been you.'

'I'm not sure I want it,' said Thomas.

'And that's how it should be. If you want it unquestioningly, without doubts, without anxiety, you're not fit for the job. Every day you've got to look in the mirror and ask yourself why you're doing it. The day that you don't ask that question is the day to step down.

'One thing. Hogarth. Watch her, keep her at a distance. We're three years away from an election and we need clear blue water between us and the People's Party. Shelve the Freedom Bill, or water it down.'

Thomas said nothing.

The Prime Minister moved to the drinks cabinet. 'Ben, I have one favour to ask. We need someone to bring the country together. Find a way. These are crazy times – we've never had as much civil unrest and we've never had so many leaders fuelling the violence, turning neighbour against neighbour. You know who I mean. The Shadow Home Secretary. Ishmail Sherif. Lesley Hogarth.' The PM poured from a bottle. 'I've been saving something special for a moment like this.' He handed Thomas a glass of single malt. 'To the future.'

And drawing on every reserve, every ounce of self-control, Thomas continued to look sombre in front of his old, and closest, friend.

#

Stonebridge, North West London

There was no parking in the street outside the flat and Saleem had to make two trips around the block looking for a space. Eventually, he pulled into a gap in front of a garage emblazoned with a No Parking sign, five houses from their destination.

'Going to have to unload from here, bros,' said Abu Mujahid from the passenger seat. He leapt out of the van and pulled open the rear doors.

'Up here,' he said, leading them into the entrance of the

flats and up the stairway. On the fourth floor, he opened the door with a flourish. 'Dump the gear in the living room – we'll sort out sleeping quarters later.'

It took two trips to unload the van before Saleem could drive off into the darkness in search of parking. He was back in twenty minutes.

Upstairs, Mirza complained of a sick stomach and shut himself in the toilet while the others settled in.

'Welcome to your new home for the next few days,' said Abu Mujahid once they had sorted out their rooms and made coffee. 'From now on, you stay here – you don't leave without my permission, understood? And you keep silent to the outside world. Where's Tanvir?'

'Taking a shit,' said Muhid.

'He's been a long time.' There was steel in Abu Mujahid's voice. He rose and strode to the bathroom door, opening it without knocking.

'What are you doing, Tanvir?' He spoke quietly, barely more than a whisper. It set the hairs on Asad's neck tingling.

'Nothing, man,' Mirza said from inside the bathroom.

'Give me that.' Asad craned his neck to see into the hallway. Abu Mujahid was holding the phone he had given them in Cumbria. 'What is this, Tanvir?' Again, his voice was subdued.

'I was just checking on the scores, you know. Arsenal's playing tonight.'

'You lump of useless shit,' said Abu Mujahid. He deliberately dropped the phone on the linoleum and raised his left foot.

'Brother, no. I'm sorry.'

Abu Mujahid's heel came down hard on the screen, which cracked. He ground his foot down again and again, kicking and kicking, fragments of glass and plastic whizzing across the hallway. Then he bent over and pulled out the SIM card and thrust it into Mirza's face.

Still, Abu Mujahid didn't raise his voice, but he oozed

237

anger. His eyes were ablaze, and he towered over Mirza, who was still sat on the toilet. 'You're a disgrace. Are you going to betray us all? Are you trying to get us all killed?'

He took the SIM card, pulled up Mirza's hair off his forehead, then dragged the card along his hairline. The edge broke the skin. Abu Mujahid withdrew his hand and plastered Mirza's hair back over the bleeding graze. 'Get out of my sight.' His voice was pure fury.

Asad wondered if he would hit Mirza, but he simply walked back to the living room.

#

Wandsworth Common, South London
The pigeon was perched on the back of the sofa, its one visible eye darting around the room as the two men entered the living room of the NRF safe house.

'Fucking hell, what a mess,' said the first man. The acrid odour of bird droppings filled the room. The pigeon had left mess on the sofa, and carpet, but mostly on a wooden occasional table pushed back against the wall. 'How did it get in?'

'Chimney?' said the second man, arms outstretched as he shuffled slowly towards the bird. 'Get a towel or something.'

The first man returned from the bedroom with a duvet.

'What fucking use is that?' said his companion.

'Just chuck it over him.'

'For fuck's sake.' He pulled the cover off the duvet and, holding it over his hands, dived at the pigeon. 'Open the window.'

'Don't be so gay. Break its neck,' said the first man.

'I'm not killing a fucking pigeon. Open the window.'

The first man yanked at the wooden sash, which gave way and crashed down on the sill. The second man held the duvet cover to the window. The pigeon flopped outside and sat on the ground in a patch of light streaming from the window.

'Fucking stupid creature. I hate pigeons,' said the first man.

They set about tidying up the mess, wiping off bird mess from the table with a stale cloth, smelling faintly of drains, which they'd found under the sink. The first man washed his hands.

'Have you spoken to the boss since Houghton was nicked?' said the first man.

'Have I fuck,' said the second. 'Don't want to get my head bitten off. It was a cock-up. Houghton virtually handed over his fucking phone to the filth. What a fucking idiot.'

'Has he talked?' said the first man.

'No. Not Houghton. He's military. They're hard.'

The sound of a key in the front door halted the conversation. A figure was silhouetted in the sitting room doorway by the hallway light. The pair breathed again.

'For fuck's sake – I could hear you halfway down the street. Why not just email the police a full confession and be done with it? Sit down and act like fucking grown-ups for just one second.'

Brushing a loose strand of her red dyed hair behind an ear, Nina O'Brien stepped into the room.

DAY 15

Wednesday

What a difference a week makes, thought Gabriel as she stood at the front of the ops room. A few days ago, the prevailing mood of her team had been exhaustion mingled with desperation. A week on, they were still tired, but the success in Leeds had bolstered their confidence and there was now the glimmer of something around the corner, like the smell of the air just before a snowstorm. The call from Skeffington in Burgess Hill yesterday had been the break she desperately needed. They were no longer a week behind Abu Mujahid, they were just a few days behind. And that gap was narrowing.

Tennant had been on the phone earlier. The inquiry into the attempt on Hogarth's life had stalled and he was desperate for a break. Gabriel could only imagine the pressure he was under from the top on that one. But there was still nothing to link Abu Mujahid with the shooting, other than the timing of his arrival in the UK. Last night she'd attended the Joint Operational Team meeting at Thames House during which it was confirmed that the hunt for Abu Mujahid should be handed back from MI5 to SO15. The objective was now to arrest him as quickly as possible and she had left the meeting relieved but acutely aware of the burden pressing down on her shoulders. If she let Abu Mujahid go again, if he took yet more lives, nothing would save her career, nothing would ever lift the guilt.

'Quiet, please.' She clicked on the keyboard and a map of London came on the screen, with an area south of the Thames hatched out in red.

'As many of you know, we had a breakthrough last night on Operation Hippocampus.' She could say the name now without a hint of a smile. 'We now know from CCTV at the Burgess Hill warehouse that Abu Mujahid used a grey Ford Transit to collect two boxes a week last Friday morning. We believe the boxes contained weapons and explosives shipped from Beirut via Greece by the GID.

'ANPR cameras show Abu Mujahid drove back to London after collecting the weapons and took a convoluted route clockwise around the M25 to enter London from the west, here.' She pointed to the screen.

'And at this point, he entered a black hole with no ANPR coverage. He was last seen at 8.11am here in Hammersmith – and he emerged from the black hole ninety-five minutes later here in Highgate.

'So question number one is this – where was he during these missing ninety-five minutes twelve days ago? The journey from Hammersmith to Highgate should have taken him no more than forty-five minutes. So he was doing something. Meeting someone? Dropping off the weapons cache?

'Once he emerged from the ANPR black hole, he drove across North London to Islington. There's no trace of his van on ANPR for nearly a week from that point, so we can assume it was parked in a garage or street. The van reappears again on the morning of last Thursday – six days ago – when Abu Mujahid made several stops, driving in and out of areas with good ANPR coverage.

'We're pulling in the local CCTV now, and we hope to have a better idea of where he was at the time within the next few hours. Around 10am, he drove the van north – up the M1 and M6 towards the Lake District.

'Crucially, he stopped on his way north at these services,' the map changed to show the whole of England, 'around 1pm. CCTV from the service station shows Abu Mujahid was travelling with four young men – three Asian, one black. We can safely assume he had picked them up earlier that morning in locations in North London. So question two is who are these men? How does Abu Mujahid know them? What connects them?'

Gabriel looked around the room. The team were making notes or staring at the map.

'After a toilet break, they drove off. They turned off the M6 onto the A590 and were last IDed three miles south of Kendal in the Lake District, two hundred and seventy miles and five hours from London. And that's it. Question number three is where did they go, and what were they up to?'

Gabriel paused quite deliberately.

'CCTV and ANPR are sketchy in the Lakes, and we have only four sightings of the van from this point on. The day after they arrived – last Friday – Abu Mujahid was picked up by ANPR driving into Kendal at 8am, and then back out at 10am. The van made an almost identical journey the following day. And then nothing for the last three days – which means one of two things. Either Abu Mujahid and his friends are still enjoying their little break in the Lake District, or they've moved elsewhere and changed the van's plates.

'All of that leaves us with some good lines of inquiry and a mountain of work. Priorities are as follows. One – find out where Abu Mujahid went in this missing ninety-five minutes in West London. Two – identify the four young men. And three – we scour the Lake District for signs of Abu Mujahid, whether he's there now, or whether he's back in London. It seems hard to believe that a cell is launching a major terror attack in the Lake District in the middle of winter, unless they're really pissed off about sheep. Are they training? Are they plotting? We are working closely with North West CTU on this and they are taking the lead here.

'And in addition to all of that, we will continue to chase down the international links, and work with Thames on looking for phones for these guys. Listen. It's taken some time, but we are finally on his tail. We now know where Abu Mujahid was four days ago – and I'm confident by the end of the day, we'll have pinned him down further, that we'll know the identity of those four men. Each hour we catch up with him means we are an hour closer to stopping whatever he is planning.'

#

Three hours later, Bose was at Gabriel's desk.

'We've got a breakthrough on Abu Mujahid's associates,' she said, breathing a little too hard.

'Explain?'

'We had the CCTV of the four young men with Abu Mujahid at the service station. We put it through facial recognition overnight, but nothing's come up.'

That didn't surprise Gabriel. Despite the hype, facial recognition software was largely hopeless. It worked well enough if pictures were lit and the face was staring at the camera. But with screen grabs from grainy CCTV, it failed to deliver more often than it worked.

Bose continued: 'This morning we've had the team looking through CCTV footage of Abu Mujahid and his van six days ago, driving around North London. Pretty quickly, it's become apparent he was picking up his group, mostly from Islington and Hackney. We've found CCTV of two pickups – both in public areas. Two men got in the van around 9am, a third ten minutes later. We've not found the fourth pickup yet, but it won't be long.

'The next job was to ID the four men. And that's when the penny dropped. Because I think we know one already.

Two days ago, the University of Islington got a call from the parents of an engineering student – second year, Islamist supporter, from Cardiff. The family are third-generation Somali, all very respectable, and worried that their son – Omar Asad – had vanished off the face of the earth. Asad was on the university radar because he was hanging around with some potential unsavouries – but there was insufficient evidence for an intervention under Prevent. This time the university passed it on and it's been sitting on my computer for forty-eight hours along with a picture of Asad. It's the same man from the motorway service-station CCTV.'

'Bloody hell. What about the other three? Also students?'

'The university has IDed one – Waheed Saleem – a maths graduate. Doesn't appear to be a friend or acquaintance of Asad. Still waiting to hear on the other two.'

'Do they have any previous?' asked Gabriel.

'None. They're clean skins. Nothing on any of our systems. Thames has Saleem in the system from old intel as an Islamist extremist, but he was assessed not to be a threat.'

'Get down there,' said Gabriel. 'Interview the student Islamic Society leading lights, find out everything we can about this Asad and Saleem. I want to know where they prayed, what clubs they joined, who recruited them and which toilet they liked to piss into.'

Once Bose had left, Gabriel called Tennant.

'It's doing my head in,' said Tennant, after Gabriel had updated him. 'Imagine the impact of another successful Islamist attack right now. And meanwhile, we've got the country ripping itself to pieces while the likes of Hogarth and Thomas and the Shadow Home Secretary and Sherif whip up the hatred, pile on the rhetoric and make the job a million times harder. We'll have riots before the end of the year.

'Listen, Sophie, we need one more thing. I want the behavioural science team to identify potential targets for Abu Mujahid's attack. High profile, spectacular, imaginative – everything that fits his profile. Get inside his head.'

I don't need a psychologist to do that, thought Gabriel as she carefully replaced the handset.

#

Chelsea, London
Hogarth sat on the bed, the hospital TV screen hanging from its cradle in front of her. O'Brien watched from the plastic chair next to Hogarth's pillow as the Prime Minister clutched the wooden pedestal with both hands.

'...and so, with reluctance, I have decided it is in the best interests of the country and our party to stand down and make way for my successor. In the meantime, my good friend, the Home Secretary Ben Thomas, will serve as acting prime minister.' There was a stuttering of camera flashes as he looked briefly at his script.

'It has been a privilege and honour to serve the people of this country over the last two years. I say this – that our country is the finest, and our people the greatest. We will get through the current troubles, and we will emerge a better, more unified, more diverse and more tolerant society. Thank you.'

He stepped down from the pedestal and walked to the black limo as the reporters began their futile barrage of questions.

'Nicely done,' said Hogarth, turning down the volume. 'I think he nicked a line from Blair, but still, nicely done. I do like a good resignation speech.' She beamed at O'Brien.

'Are you ready to meet the Home Secretary, Lesley? Are you fit enough?'

'Oh, stop fussing, girl, I'm tip-top. I've had worse injuries gardening. But get the car to pick me up at the back entrance. I don't want a media scrum.'

'Indeed,' said O'Brien. 'I've got the new red lines for the Freedom Bill discussions with Thomas. They're pretty much what he's expecting, with one or two surprises. A media ban on hate preachers and former convicted terrorists for one. A crackdown on health tourists – no free NHS hospital treatment, not even in A&E, without proof of citizenship. And a ban on head coverings in state schools. Always negotiate with something new up your sleeve.'

'Excellent. I'm sure they're excellent. Lead on, O'Brien.' The pair exited slowly from the room, towards the hospital kitchens.

#

New Scotland Yard, Victoria Embankment, London
Tennant shut down the file. Since the Israelis had shared their intel on the Global Islamic Defence and the links with Abu Mujahid, he had been pushing the intelligence agencies for anything on the organisation. What he had found confirmed his fears.

Until six weeks ago, the group had appeared dormant. Then, for no obvious reason, the GID had raised its profile with a burst of propaganda. The content was predictable and vitriolic – it was the usual railing at Western decadence, calls for a Caliphate and a recruitment drive aimed at disaffected European Muslims. Most featured the GID leader Mohammed Huzaifa, who was clearly attempting to make a name for himself. And there was also a call for supporters to take up arms at home. It was a new line for the GID which had previously focused its efforts on Syria and Iraq.

Tennant was deep in thought when the phone rang.

'The Deputy Prime Minister on the line.' The voice from the switchboard was expressionless as ever.

'Thank you,' said Tennant. There was a click and then the familiar accent.

'Assistant Commissioner, apologies for ringing so late,' she said.

'No problem at all, ma'am,' said Tennant. Was there something in her voice? Even more confidence, if such a thing was possible, and she'd called him Assistant Commissioner rather than Steven.

'Wanted to give you an early heads-up,' she said. 'There'll

246

be more detail in the morning, but our new acting prime minister has asked me to take on the role of Home Secretary, a huge honour, as I'm sure you realise. Obviously, I'll be joining the National Security Council in addition to attending pre-COBRA briefings at Number Ten. In the light of that, I want a full update from you and MI5 on current threats and investigations. Fairly urgently, if you please.'

For a moment, Tennant was lost for words. Of all the people to assign to national security, Hogarth was the least qualified, and most unreliable. What was Ben Thomas thinking? *Tread carefully*, he told himself.

'Nothing substantially new to add, ma'am,' he said. 'We're getting intel in all the time, of course, but filtering out the good from bad is time-consuming. We believe we have identified a possible new cell, managed by the returner Abu Mujahid. Goals and location currently unknown.' That was a bit of a fudge, but close enough, he thought.

'I'm sure you realise that the regime and expectations of the police will be very different under Ben and me, and for the better, I'm sure you'll agree,' said Hogarth. 'These are difficult times and we need our security and police to step up to the mark.' She paused. 'Have you still got Sophie Gabriel on the case?'

Tennant felt his body tensing. 'She's doing well, thank you. Her actions during the Leeds attack largely led to the successful outcome and the arrest of one of the two Pall Mall killers. She also raised concerns about Abu Mujahid's return long before we had confirmation. There's no one I'm more confident in.'

Tennant could tell that Hogarth was smiling. 'Just be careful. It never does to tie one's own reputation to one's juniors, Steven. As for identifying Abu Mujahid earlier, it's a shame Gabriel wasn't able to do anything about that before he tried to kill me. Could have avoided a lot of unpleasantness.'

'I should point out, Home Secretary, that we have no evidence Abu Mujahid was involved with the attack on you.'

Hogarth snorted and ended the call. Tennant swore under his breath as he returned to his screen. Hogarth had a way of getting under his skin.

#

Stonebridge, North West London

Sometimes Asad thought he was losing his grip in the confines of the flat. He was tired and crazily awake at the same time, and unable to sleep properly. He sought comfort in the Quran, reading and rereading the same passages. The words from the Verse of the Sword. The instructions to obey Allah and to obey the Messenger.

They were a group now. It felt like they knew each other better than they knew their own families. Asad knew their foibles, their likes, their pressure points. They were no longer five strangers – they were brothers, bonded together in the care of Abu Mujahid. Saleem and Muhid were more devout and more excited each day, and followed Abu Mujahid's every move like two puppies, desperate for love from the great man. And Mirza seemed to have got over his anxiety.

Abu Mujahid sat with them every couple of hours. Sometimes to run through the plans or to read the Quran together. Always, Asad's thoughts would turn to the weekend. He avoided counting down the hours – Abu Mujahid had warned them against that. 'Brothers, stay in the present, not the future or past. Focus on the moment. Pray. Reflect on the honour and victory that is coming. Read. And prepare yourself for the greatest journey of them all. Make yourself pure and clean to enter Paradise.' But he couldn't help it.

He remembered when he was a child, aged seven or eight, being taken by his father to his first football match. In the crowd outside, amid the bustle of fans, and jeers of opponents, his father had held his hand tightly. And then he'd let go for a second and Asad had felt himself swept away. He could see no friendly faces, just angry white men stinking of beer and cigarettes and body odour. During the eternity that it took for his father to push back through the bodies to find him, he had imagined that he was about to die and would never see him again. That same feeling washed over him from time to time now. He knew the only sensible way to contemplate death was to not think about it. But right now, he could think of nothing else.

They spent the afternoon huddled around Abu Mujahid's laptop. He connected it to a pay-as-you-go mobile phone and opened up the Street View map application, and he talked each of them through the routes they would be taking and the vantage points he had chosen for them.

Each of the men spent half an hour tracing their routes, familiarising themselves with the locations where they would be standing. By the end, Asad could plot the route with his eyes closed.

That evening, they gathered after prayers. Abu Mujahid sat in the centre, his face lit from below by flickering candlelight. The others watched, their eyes shining, basking in the glow of their leader.

'The Quran is clear that jihad is justified to defend ourselves, to protect the freedom of our brothers, to protect our brothers from oppression and to make our faith stronger,' Abu Mujahid told them. 'Do not let the unbelievers fool you. They have declared war. To those against whom war is made, permission is given, because they are wronged.'

Asad went to bed early that night. The others were talking in the sitting room, listening to Abu Mujahid's war stories, discussing the attack. Saleem's voice was the loudest. He seemed to have no doubts, no uncertainties, just adrenaline-fuelled excitement.

Asad lay in the semi-blackness, a patch of light from the hallway shining through the glass panel over his door. Could he go through with this in three days? Did he have the strength that Muhid and Saleem shared? He prayed silently, lying on his front, eyes closed. He missed his family, his younger sister

Aisha. What was his mother doing right now? Her life would never be the same. And when he opened his eyes, tears fell down his cheeks and splashed onto his pillow and he knew he loved Allah and would submit to Allah's will. He would sacrifice his family, his friends and his life for Allah's noble cause. For Paradise.

DAY 16

Thursday

Stonebridge, North West London

Asad was lying on his bed reading a densely written book on martyrdom and struggling to concentrate, and mostly thinking about Saturday, when Mirza entered.

'What's up, Tanvir?' asked Asad, resting the book gently on the bedside table.

'I need to go out for a bit, Omar.' Mirza's voice was quiet.

Asad sat up. 'What you talking about, bro? You know what Abu Mujahid said. You mad?'

'I need some fresh air. It's too crowded…'

'You're not serious? You know you can't.'

'We've been cooped up for days. I'm going crazy, man.'

'You know you can't,' Asad repeated. 'Go out on the balcony if you need air.'

Mirza shook his head and pulled at his beard with his left hand. 'Abu Mujahid won't know. He's gone out. I'll just be a few minutes. I'll knock quietly and you let me in.'

He walked out. Asad heard the front door to the flat open and close. He tried to read again, but gave up and turned on the TV. He flicked through the stations, and ended up on the news channel. The lead story was a new call from the Met's head of counter terrorism for public vigilance.

The report cut to the face of Steven Tennant, speaking to MPs in the Home Affairs Committee.

'…which is why it's vital we don't take our eye off the ball. Yes, the extreme right wing remains a threat, but the far greater threat in terms of numbers comes from Islamist terrorism. We have a record number of cases on our books right now and we have a terrorism threat level at critical. It's vital that the public are vigilant – and report anything suspicious. The message is, don't worry about wasting police time, just call us straight away…'

Asad swore and turned off the TV. The Islamophobic police were the reason he rarely watched the mainstream media, he thought, before returning to his books.

#

One hour later, Asad heard the key in the front door.

'Tanvir?' he called out.

'Me,' said Abu Mujahid, walking into the bedroom holding a bulging grey canvas rucksack. 'Where's Tanvir?' he said suspiciously.

'He's…' Asad didn't know how to answer. 'He just… He needed some fresh air.'

Asad had expected Abu Mujahid to erupt. But he didn't. He just nodded and went into the kitchen. Asad followed him.

'He's okay, but it was getting to him, being stuck in here,' said Asad. 'He wasn't going far. He just needed some fresh air.'

Abu Mujahid didn't look up. He continued to stare at his hands, his face expressionless.

'I tried to stop him, but he said he was going to be a few minutes,' said Asad.

Again, silence. Asad walked back to his bedroom. Next door he could hear Abu Mujahid moving around, opening cupboards and drawers. Then he heard the rustling of plastic. What was he doing?

Unnerved, Asad went into the small living room. Saleem and Muhid were talking loudly at the table next to the open window leading out on to the balcony.

'What's he doing?' Muhid looked up.

Asad shrugged. 'Tanvir's gone out.'

'What?' Muhid looked aghast. Saleem shook his head piously.

Five minutes later, there was a faint knock on the front door. The three men stood up at once and edged to the living room door. Abu Mujahid was stood in the hallway. The only natural light came through the living room behind the three men. Abu Mujahid opened the door slowly and stood back as Mirza stepped into the dimness.

Abu Mujahid slammed the door behind him, causing Mirza to start.

Abu Mujahid's voice was calm and cold. 'Where have you been?'

'Nowhere, Akhi. Just out. To the park to clear my head. No one saw me. I had a hoodie on, and I kept my head down.'

'What were you doing in the park?'

'Nothing, bro. I swear. I needed some fresh air. I've been feeling claustrophobic. But I'm fine now. Honest. I just needed some space. But I'm okay. I really am.'

'Did you meet anyone?'

'Sheikh, no! Of course not. I wouldn't jeopardise the mission, man. I wouldn't do that. I just wanted some air.'

'Did you call anyone?'

'Look – you smashed my phone, man. I haven't got one.' There was a rising panic in Mirza's voice.

'Turn out your pockets. Now.' Abu Mujahid was barely speaking above a whisper.

Mirza pulled his jogging-bottom pockets inside out. A crumpled tissue fell to the floor. 'Honest, Sheikh, all I did was go for a walk.'

'I believe you.' And Abu Mujahid put his right arm out to Mirza's. For a fraction of a second, Asad wondered if Abu Mujahid was going to embrace him. Mirza's confused expression showed he felt the same. But then Asad saw a glint of silver in Abu Mujahid's hand as his thumb hit a switch. A blade, three or four inches, shot out from the handle in his clenched fist.

Slowly, far too slowly, Abu Mujahid dragged his hand around Mirza's throat, slicing deep into the flesh from right to left. Mirza opened his mouth in shock, but no words came from him, just a jet of blood that arced across the hallway and landed with a gentle splatter on the carpet. Mirza's body crumpled immediately as the blood left him, and he fell to his knees, one arm outstretched, fingers touching the floor. Abu Mujahid wiped the blade on Mirza's shoulder and slid it back into its case before dropping it on the floor.

Mirza's throat was gurgling as the blood drained through the gash and his chest heaved. He slumped again to the floor, face down, and was still. Abu Mujahid went into the bathroom and returned with two towels which he draped over Mirza's motionless head. The blood soaked up into them.

The three men stood in silence. What could they say, thought Asad. What words were appropriate now?

'I'm going out to get some bags,' Abu Mujahid said. 'I guess I don't need to tell you to stay here this time.' And he smiled a toothless smile.

#

Wandsworth Common, South London
This time there was no pigeon mess, but the room still stank. They'd not been at the house in the daylight before and were surprised to see in the weak winter sunlight that the grand rooms were shabby, that the wallpaper was stained and peeling, and that the plaster roses and cornices in the downstairs rooms were crumbling.

'Could do with a makeover,' said the older of the pair.

'Who do you think you are? Kevin McCloud? Fuck off, you queer,' said the other.

They were interrupted by the click of a key in the lock. Nina O'Brien walked into the room.

'I hope the smell in here isn't you?' She grinned, her eyes flashing. 'I brought something – thought we deserved a little celebration.' She rummaged in a red leather rucksack and pulled out a half-bottle of whisky and three plastic beakers. 'Was going to bring single malt, but it's too fucking expensive on the salary Hogarth pays me.' She laughed and unscrewed the bottle, splashing whisky on the carpet as she poured three cups.

'Here's to our new prime minister.' She raised a glass in mock celebration. 'And here's to the Freedom Bill. And here's to Dougie Glenister and Rod Houghton. Fucking good men. They won't let us down and they'll carry on the work in the nick.'

For a moment, they stood in silent tribute.

'Look, I know you were pissed off that I couldn't protect Houghton,' said O'Brien. 'But Hogarth wasn't in the briefings from police about the hunt for him – I only knew they were on to him after he'd been nicked. But now Hogarth's Home Sec, we'll be in the loop in the future.'

'And she's no idea about any of this?' The older of the men waved around the room.

'Not a fucking clue. She trusts me and that means we'll have the inside track for the next campaign. So here's to Chilton Park and Pall Mall. And, yes, Leeds was unlucky, but we were close. Two out of three isn't bad. Fourteen words! We must secure the existence of our people and a future for white children!'

They repeated the phrase and raised their glasses.

'What next?' asked the older man.

'We make noise. The Home Secretary's been told there's a major Muslim terror attack imminent. Could be this weekend, could be early next week. The police have no clue what the target is, but we want to be ready. Our people are champing at the bit, so when those wankers hit us, we are ready to hit back. I want to prime our people. Get them so fucking cross that when the Muslims murder again, they'll be ready. Get leafleteers out at the gay march, in Oxford Street, at the marathon and at Wembley for the football match.

'Every time the Muslims kill one person, they sign up another one thousand to our cause. And each thousand supporters bring us ten more soldiers – that's enough for another cell. I want to build an army. And Hogarth's on the rise thanks to the attack at her house, so well done for that one, mate.' She raised a glass in mock toast to the younger of the men. He grinned.

'It was a piece of piss, like shooting a fish in a barrel,' he said.

'More like missing a fish in a barrel, but don't do yourself down,' said O'Brien. 'It took a lot of guts, and you did a good job. It's easy to kill someone at ten feet, but a lot harder to maim them, so good marksmanship. You turned her into a martyr. The police, and Hogarth, are convinced it was the Muslims and it means Hogarth's influence – and our influence – is all the greater. Remember the slogan – the Armalite and the ballot box. It bought power for those IRA cunts, it will work the same for us.'

She raised a glass to the two men. 'To England. Fourteen words.'

#

Cumbria
Jennifer Hall rarely watched the news. In fact, she rarely put on the TV until *Emmerdale* at seven. But she'd been feeling headachy all day and she found herself at a loose end with a cup of tea on her knee and the remote control in hand an hour earlier than usual.

It was all so depressing. It was shocking what these people were doing. It didn't feel like Britain any more, more like America or one of those violent Arab countries. But still, better than nothing right now, and she watched the opening story.

Twenty minutes later, Hall was stood by the kitchen telephone, breathing more quickly than usual and with a fluttering in her stomach. She'd made a note of the number that had flashed up on the screen after that podgy policeman had been on.

'Oh, hello. Yes. I wanted to report something suspicious. I've just seen the item on the news calling for people to contact the police if they've seen anything funny... That's right. Yes. Well, I've got a holiday cottage in the Lakes. Near Windermere. And I had a group of young men up here for a few days. Thursday last week, late, and they left Monday. Five of them. Looked like students. Three were Indian gentlemen, and there was a black feller with them. And a white man too who was a bit older... What?... Ginger. Pasty. With a beard. I thought they were a bit odd. And the policeman said to report anything unusual or suspicious – particularly people with holiday lets like me... Well, we don't get many of their sort staying, if you know what I mean...'

#

An hour and a quarter later, two officers from the North West Counter Terrorism Unit were sat on Jennifer Hall's blue velvet sofa. They'd arrived five minutes into *Emmerdale* – and it looked like they could be here through to the end of *Corrie*, thought Hall.

'Was there anything unusual about them, Mrs Hall, other than they weren't all white?' The woman did most of the questioning, which surprised her. She was a sergeant. Not in uniform, but quite smart. Nice bobbed hair, which was unusual these days. So many girls had their hair long. The man was silent and made notes in a tiny pad. She wondered how he could write small enough to fit the pad. Brown suit. A bit shabby. And a scuff on his shoes. Needed a woman's touch.

'Not really,' she said. 'They left a lot of beer cans – but thinking back, they didn't look like the sort who'd drink beer, if you get my drift. What with, you know...' She mimed a beard.

The woman police officer smiled patiently. 'And what did they drive?'

'Oh, a big van. A grey van. They were loading it up when I left. The ginger man was putting in some big boxes – big cardboard boxes, big brown ones with a smiley face on them.'

'Sorry, a smiley face?' the woman asked.

'That's right. Some writing – I couldn't see – and a smiley face. A sort of smile with an arrow.'

The man pulled out a mobile and pressed a few times on the screen.

'Like this? The Amazon logo?' he said, putting it in front of her face.

'That's it. Yes – a smiley face.'

The man pulled out a file from his bag. 'I've got some pictures here, Mrs Hall. Do you recognise any of these men?'

He handed over a sheaf of large colour photos. Mrs Hall studied each one in turn before placing them on the coffee table. She pulled a face and went through them a second time.

'Well, it's hard. But no. Him. He was one of them.' She pointed to a white man with a ginger beard. 'And maybe him.' She pulled out a picture of a black man with cropped hair. 'Yes, I think he was with them.'

#

CTOC, St Pancras, London
Skeffington slammed down the phone and briskly walked to Gabriel's desk.

'Ma'am – just heard from North West CTU. A landlady from Cumbria had a group of five men staying at her holiday cottage from Thursday to Monday driving a grey van. She's IDed two of them – Omar Asad and Abu Mujahid. Forensics are on the way now from Manchester. They should have the cottage searched by the morning.'

Gabriel's face lit up. 'Did she see the van's plates?'

'No, ma'am. Says they left around four in the afternoon on Monday, so I've got Campbell pulling CCTV on major roads around the cottage. But it's a long shot. It's a remote spot and there's a dozen routes or more they could have taken to get back to London, if that's where they were heading. We'll have to look at hundreds of thousands of vehicles.'

It took a second for the significance of the dates to settle in Gabriel's head.

'If they left late afternoon on Monday, it means Abu Mujahid can't have got to London in time to take a potshot at Lesley Hogarth,' said Gabriel.

'Not unless he flew down on a private jet, ma'am, no.'

'Anything else useful?'

'Possibly, ma'am,' said Skeffington. 'Abu Mujahid's cell had at least two large Amazon boxes with them. They were loading them into the van. Doesn't sound much to me, but the North West team seem very excited.'

Gabriel sat upright. She ran her finger through her fringe. 'What were they doing with an Amazon delivery in the middle of Cumbria?'

'Maybe they fancied a night in binge watching *Game of Thrones*, ma'am,' Skeffington. 'Or maybe, more likely, they were simply reusing a load of old, empty boxes.'

'Maybe,' said Gabriel thoughtfully. 'Get on to Amazon HQ anyway. Find out if they ordered anything. Anything on Abu Mujahid's missing hour in London two weeks ago?'

'Nothing yet, ma'am. We're going through local council CCTV footage, but it's a massive area to comb. We've got about two hundred cameras to look through. And grey vans are common.'

Monday. They had left Cumbria just three days ago. But

to go where? Could be anywhere – but most likely to head back to London, thought Gabriel. It's where Abu Mujahid had been based for the last two weeks, it's where he recruited his cell, it's where he returned to after collecting his package from Burgess Hill.

So why had they been in Cumbria? Training? Shooting practice? It made sense. But wouldn't they attract attention firing off guns in the middle of the Lake District? Unless... She googled the shooting season for pheasant and grouse. Yes – they were still in season. Just. Gunfire in a remote Cumbria wood this time of year wouldn't draw any undue attention.

They were just three days behind them now. Gabriel had the sense they were catching up on them, getting closer each hour. But would they catch up in time?

DAY 17

Friday

CTOC, St Pancras, London

The woman from Amazon was adamant. 'Sorry, Sergeant, we've triple-checked and there's been no delivery to that address in the last six months,' she said firmly.

'What about a subsidiary company – someone using Amazon Marketplace say?' said Campbell.

'That's not possible. It would be logged on the database. I'm sorry, but there's been nothing to that address.'

Campbell rang off. He'd seen Skeffington in the canteen, so went down a floor to look for him. The DI was slumped in the corner tucking into a plate of eggs, bacon and toast.

'All right, cockney?' said Skeffington. 'Come to nick some food?'

'No thanks, sir, I'm trying to avoid a heart attack before I'm at least forty,' said Campbell. 'Just heard from Amazon. They've delivered sod all to the Cumbria cottage.'

'Perhaps the old biddy got it wrong then,' said Skeffington, shovelling in a forkful of runny egg as some dripped down his chin. 'Or they were just old boxes they brought with them.'

'Maybe,' said Campbell. 'But why bring old Amazon boxes to the Lake District?'

'I don't know. I'm not a homicidal Islamist terrorist. Fuck knows what goes on in their heads. Now, if you've nothing useful to tell me, bugger off and let me have breakfast in peace.'

Campbell returned to his desk. If Abu Mujahid had ordered something online, where would he get it delivered? He knew from the search over the last few days that Abu Mujahid had no Cumbrian associates. So what about an Amazon locker, or a collection point? He went to the Amazon website and searched for pickup locations near Kendal, where Abu Mujahid's van had been spotted by ANPR on the previous Saturday morning.

Twelve addresses came up. Five were Amazon lockers in public places or shops where customers could collect packages using a code. The rest were post offices, newsagents or supermarkets where packages were handed over the counter. The boxes described by the Cumbrian landlady were large – so a pickup was more likely than a locker.

By 9.30am, Campbell had sent a list of possible pickup points in Kendal and a set of photos of the known cell members to Cumbria CID. He'd also been on the phone to Amazon again for a list of deliveries to Kendal pickup points on the Friday and Saturday of the previous week.

#

'I remember him,' said the white-haired man behind the counter of the souvenir shop in the centre of Kendal. He studied the picture again. 'Ginger fellow. Birdwatcher or something.'

The DC from Kendal made a note in her book. This was the fourth shop she'd been in, and she'd been convinced she was on a wild goose chase. 'What can you tell me about him, sir? And do you remember what he was driving?'

'Aye. As I said, he said it was birdwatching equipment. Parked on the double yellow lines. Told him he'd get a ticket there, but he didn't heed me. They're crafty, the traffic wardens though – don't matter if they're loading here, they'll just stick a ticket on you… Sorry, love, what was the question again?'

The DC smiled patiently and gritted her teeth. 'His vehicle?'

'Oh, yes. He had a van – Transit, I think. Grey or white, I can't remember. I helped load the boxes.'

'Do you have details of the delivery still, sir?' she asked.

'Aye. Hang on a second.' He went over to a file by the till. 'I keep a printout – don't trust these machines to be honest not to lose stuff.' He pulled out a sheet with an order number and name and address. 'Here you go. Ordinary enough bloke. But funny-looking. Scruffy, long beard.'

#

'Ma'am.' Campbell came across Gabriel, who was talking to Skeffington and Bose. 'Something in from the university. They've identified the two other cell members – both students, both went missing at the same time as Mirza and Asad.' He checked his notepad. 'Ahmed Muhid and Waheed Saleem. I've got the family addresses and full university records.'

'So we've got the whole cell. About bloody time,' said Gabriel. 'Get the phone records, bank records, everything. I want to know their sodding shoe size if it helps.'

Each hour, it felt they were getting closer and closer to Abu Mujahid. But had they left themselves enough time? Once again, she bitterly wished they had started looking hard for him a few days earlier, when she had that conviction he was back in the UK. They could have found him by now. Now they were closer, but still scrabbling in the dark.

#

Stonebridge, North West London
When Asad closed his eyes, he could see Mirza's face. When he opened them, he saw his face. He lay in the darkness, the

263

echoes of Mirza's gurgling blood pulsing through his ears, drowning out the sirens and shouts outside the flat. He should have stopped Mirza going out. He should have stopped Abu Mujahid from attacking him. He should have kept quiet. He should have done something. But he knew, deep down in his core, that he would have changed nothing.

Abu Mujahid had returned later that evening with black plastic sheeting. Together, they had wrapped Mirza's body, tightly binding the plastic with tape, making a seal to keep in the blood and stench of death. It had taken three of them to lift his body and push it into a walk-in cupboard in the hall, squeezed up alongside a vacuum cleaner and a mop. Muhid and Saleem appeared to relish the work, taking turns to denounce him as a traitor.

'Leave it there,' said Abu Mujahid. 'The police can find it in a few days. We'll be long gone.'

Abu Mujahid had been in and out of the flat all morning. He'd left at 8am and returned with a full rucksack, emptying the contents into a crate in the bathroom. He made the trip almost immediately again and returned with another bulging rucksack.

In the afternoon, Abu Mujahid called them to the sitting room. He opened up a duffel bag, pulled out a video camera and tabletop tripod. 'Take this,' he handed the black standard of Global Islamic Defence to Muhid, 'and find something to pin it against the wall.'

Muhid took the flag eagerly. Saleem handed over a box of nails and a frying pan to hammer the flag to the plasterboard wall. Abu Mujahid placed the camera on a coffee table and pushed the sofa out of the way. He pulled out four balaclavas from his bag and opened up the crate, taking out three assault rifles.

Muhid pulled the balaclava over his head and laughed. Asad put on his. The fibres scratched his chin. He felt hot, uncomfortable. His mind was wandering now – it was hard to concentrate on what Abu Mujahid was saying.

'You are speaking to the world,' said Abu Mujahid. 'Tell

the world that you are becoming a martyr with your eyes open, and your heart full. Let them see your courage and your faith. Let yourself become an inspiration to brothers and sisters around the world.'

The three men stood awkwardly in front of the flag, clutching their rifles. It was chilly in the flat, but the balaclava made Asad's face oppressively hot.

'Go,' said Abu Mujahid, and he pressed record.

Muhid spoke clearly and loudly. Asad was impressed with his performance and his conviction. 'People of Britain and the world, I speak on behalf of Global Islamic Defence. You have brought this war upon yourselves.

'You have been warned what will happen to those who fight the GID. And yet you've killed and maimed and destroyed Muslims all over the world. You have got blood on your hands and you will pay for everything you have done, for every bullet fired on innocent children, for every bomb dropped on innocent women.

'What we do, we do in the name of Allah and the name of the Prophet. In the name of the Global Islamic Defence, in the name of our brothers around the world.' There was more. Much more. Lines from the Quran. Warnings about retribution.

Abu Mujahid leant forward and switched off the camera.

'That'll do. Now we pray for tomorrow.'

#

CTOC, St Pancras, London

There are an estimated five hundred thousand CCTV cameras dotted around London in addition to the two thousand or so ANPR cameras, and the typical commuter is caught on camera hundreds of times a day. But a Londoner determined to dodge CCTV cameras can still successfully avoid being captured on video. And, Bose conceded as she reviewed the latest report, Abu Mujahid appeared to have done just that.

Bose's team had been trawling for three days for his van.

First, they had searched through video collected by three local authorities, as well as the cameras owned by Transport for London at Tube stations, railway stations and bus stops.

The team had started by tracking Abu Mujahid's route from the point his van – freshly laden with whatever weapons, ammo and explosives he'd picked up in Burgess Hill – was last seen, driving through a bustling junction in Hammersmith at the start of his missing hour a week last Friday.

The next local authority CCTV camera on that road was a quarter of a mile further on, and a trawl of the footage had shown he hadn't gone that way. That meant he had turned off the main road. So then the team began the careful screening of CCTV camera footage of all the side roads he might have taken. And the side roads that led off those.

It quickly became clear that the team needed more coverage than the local councils and Transport for London could offer. Officers had been sent out on foot to trace the route, find shops, petrol stations and offices whose cameras covered the road, and grab the footage to send back to HQ.

The team had then viewed hundreds and hundreds of hours of those camera feeds over the missing hour, replaying each video twice, looking for Abu Mujahid's grey van. Even when they ran the videos at high speed, it had taken twenty officers and civilians forty staff-hours so far. It was a mammoth, tedious job. And so far, there had been no sign of the elusive van.

#

'Ma'am, sir, I've got the details of Abu Mujahid's order.' Campbell jogged over to Skeffington and Gabriel. 'And you were right, ma'am. Amazon confirmed they were delivered to a newsagent in Kendal on Friday evening – a week ago – and were picked up on Saturday at 9am. The timing of the collection matches Abu Mujahid driving in and out of Kendal.'

Gabriel snatched at the sheet.

Campbell continued: 'Abu Mujahid made the order under a false name – H. Townsend – using Amazon gift cards he bought or stole. He probably used an internet cafe to place the order and he had them delivered to a newsagent in Kendal.'

'What did he order?' said Gabriel.

'Two drones,' said Campbell. 'Worth about five hundred pounds each – not top of the range but not kids' toys either.'

Drones? That wasn't what Gabriel had been expecting. Chemicals, perhaps, or fertiliser, or something to make a bomb.

'What does he want drones for? For snooping?' said Skeffington, mirroring Gabriel's train of thought.

'Maybe, maybe,' said Gabriel. 'Okay, guys, get the whole team together in ten minutes. This changes everything. I want to know our options and the potential targets. Pull together a list of possible targets for a drone attack.'

#

Tennant walked into the conference room as Campbell was mid-sentence. He gave an almost imperceptible nod for the DS to continue as he slumped into his seat.

'The drones are quadcopters,' said Campbell. 'Thirty minutes flying time, and a range of three or four miles. Fitted with GPS and a bloody good HD camera. The remote control can work with a smartphone, which displays the live video feed. And they can be preprogrammed for independent flight.'

Gabriel took over. 'In summary, we know that Abu Mujahid picked up four recruits from London, drove them to a remote retreat in the Lake District, ordered and collected two drones from Amazon, and has now left the Lakes.

'We know he has additionally collected a cache of weapons and explosives at a warehouse in Burgess Hill – we presume similar to those uncovered in Canada – and an army rifle from our army sergeant in Hedingly.

'In the last forty-eight hours, we have gone from being

largely in the dark about Abu Mujahid's objectives to having a much clearer idea of his potential threat. Ladies and gentlemen, we need to continue our progress and find the target.' That last line was mostly for Tennant's benefit. No harm boosting the team in front of the boss.

'Maybe the drones are to disrupt or attack an airport?' said Campbell. 'Remember the chaos that drone caused at Heathrow a few years back.'

'Not convinced that's his style,' said Gabriel. 'He will want to maximise impact, kill as many as he can, and do it in a spectacular way.'

'Could he fly them into a plane then?' said Skeffington. 'A bird can rip apart an engine on its own. What would a chunk of metal and plastic do?'

'I think the impact is too unpredictable,' said Tennant, speaking for the first time. 'You might take out an engine if you were lucky, but there's no guarantee of bringing a plane down.'

'Agreed,' said Gabriel. 'And he's got explosives – we know that. He can use them as flying bombs. We've seen ISIS do that already in Syria with similar drones. He could get them over any security line he wanted.'

'Surely that kind of drone wouldn't have the power to lift explosives?' said Skeffington.

Campbell shook his head. 'These would. And you wouldn't need much explosive to cause havoc.'

'It's a theory, and it's something to work on,' said Gabriel. 'Eva – have you got the list?'

'Yes, ma'am,' said Bose, who had walked into the room a minute earlier and was hovering on the edge of the conversation. 'The drones narrow down the potential targets considerably. Abu Mujahid would need an open-air event – or at least a large crowd gathered outside.'

Gabriel took the paper. 'Jesus – there's a hell of a lot on over the next few days.' She read from the list. 'A marathon in South London tomorrow morning. A Pride march at noon in

East London. An England football international at Wembley against Hungary, kick-off at 3pm. And the Calcutta Cup on Sunday at Twickenham.

'Another thing, if Abu Mujahid is using drones, then he'll be operating from a secure base, with access to the outdoors. And not overlooked. Somewhere relatively close to the attack scene. We've got two jobs – find the target, find Abu Mujahid.'

#

Later, Gabriel spoke with Tennant alone. 'I've brought in more bodies to go through the CCTV overnight,' she said.

'Good. All leave has been cancelled for the next three days, and I've ordered a security review of every major event in the capital – and elsewhere. We've no proof this is going to be a London attack. What's your judgement on the timing of this? Over the weekend?'

'Soon,' she said.

They paused. Down below, commuters were scurrying home for the weekend.

'It would be Abu Mujahid, wouldn't it?' said Gabriel, more to herself than Tennant. 'Of all the possible people to be running this, it would be Abu Mujahid.'

'At the risk of sounding like some ghastly self-help guru, that's not necessarily such a bad thing, Sophie. It's personal – I get that. But that's meant you've pushed yourself, pushed your team, even harder.'

'Maybe. But I feel like I've been running on instinct for the last week.'

'Don't underestimate the value of instinct. The brain isn't a computer. You don't shove in data and get data out the other end. A gut instinct isn't some random feeling – it's what you get when you feed your brain facts, emotions, experience, life. So far, those instincts have been largely right. Instinct – a kind of reasoned, intelligent instinct based on knowledge and experience – is what makes the difference between an okay cop and a brilliant one. Skeffington is okay. You're much better. You're brilliant.'

Gabriel said nothing.

Tennant continued: 'Look, your instinct is good. I could have listened to you earlier about Abu Mujahid. Perhaps I should have done. And I'm sorry for that. We rarely get a second chance in this game. Abu Mujahid has walked back into this shitstorm and this is our chance to nail the bastard. He could have died in a ditch in Syria and you'd be none the wiser. This way, we've got a chance to put him inside permanently.'

And that would be sweet, conceded Gabriel as she returned to her desk. For herself and for Isobel Harris.

DAY 18

Saturday Morning

Stoke Newington, North London
The green figures of Gabriel's bedside alarm were too
blurry to make out, so she blinked repeatedly to shake the
sleep from her eyes. It was 2.50am. Had she only been
asleep for twenty minutes? Ray was snoring beside her, so
she pressed her finger gently against his nose. He grunted,
turned over and stopped. Drones. Abu Mujahid. Assault
rifles. Explosives. Fireworks. The images were revolving
in her head. What would Abu Mujahid do? What would
have most impact?

She dreamt of drones flying over crowds, coming to a
stop before falling with a flash and boom. She dreamt of
Abu Mujahid standing in a high street in front of Marks &
Spencer, a little girl holding his hand. Isobel Harris. Her blue
eyes were gazing up at him lovingly and he raised his fingers
to his lips. A river of humanity flowed around them, yet Abu
Mujahid was rooted to the pavement, a remote control in his
hand. It was London. Gabriel was frozen on the other side of
the street, unable to move. Isobel smiled and waved. Gabriel
opened her mouth to shout, but no noise came. She waved
desperately at the girl, and Isobel waved back before turning

and walking away with Abu Mujahid. Gabriel screamed but, again, no sound came from her mouth. And then Abu Mujahid was back in the street, his mouth open, but instead of speech, out came a buzzing noise. A samba band passed, and a float. And on the float was Skeffington in a sparkling gold dress singing. The noise continued in her ear and with a creeping awareness, she realised that the sound she could hear was her phone.

Gabriel sat up, banging Ray's shoulder with the back of her wrist. He grunted and rolled over. She struggled for her glasses on the bedside table.

'Yes.' She slammed the phone, too hard, into her ear.

'Boss, you okay to speak?'

Gabriel straightened the collar of her pyjama top and yanked her pillow from under Ray's arm. He moaned but went back to sleep. Gabriel looked at the alarm clock. It was 4.49am.

'Sure. Hang on.' She wriggled up more, shoving another pillow behind her back.

'Sorry to call, ma'am, but we've got the analysis from the phone records of Tanvir Mirza's family.'

Gabriel was suddenly fully awake. 'Go on.'

'They live in West London – Hounslow. Mother, father and younger sister. We were looking for unusual activity. His parents' home number was called on Sunday this week, late at night, from a mobile phone. The call lasted fifteen minutes. It appears to have been a burner – the SIM card was bought from a store in North London two weeks ago. It's only been used once, to make a single call from a mobile phone in Cumbria – almost certainly from the holiday cottage where they were staying or nearby.'

'That's Mirza. Listen, Eva, I know it's early, but I need you round at his parents'. Get them up. How long will it take?'

'Twenty minutes this time of morning, ma'am.'

There was no chance of sleep now, so Gabriel rose and dressed. She would drive to the office and be there when Bose reported in.

#

The Mirzas lived in a 1930s red-brick end-of-terrace house. The front garden had been paved over to create a parking space, and the entrance was around the side. Bose rang the doorbell twice and waited, ensuring her face was lit from the street lamps. The lights came on in the hallway and a chain rattled before the door opened. The silhouette of a rotund, short man, possibly in his fifties, stood in the doorway and Eva held her police ID card in front of his nose. The sudden roar of a plane heading into Heathrow just a few hundred yards above Bose's head made her jump.

'Sorry to wake you, Mr Mirza. It is Mr Mirza, isn't it? I'm with the Metropolitan Police. May I come in? It's very urgent.' She put on her calmest voice.

The man nodded and opened the door. He looked terrified. Inside, Mrs Mirza stood on the stairs in a cream dressing gown.

'What is it?'

'I was explaining to your husband, Mrs Mirza, I'm with the police. No one is hurt – nothing like that. I just need to talk to you about an extremely urgent investigation. Shall we sit?'

They moved into a sitting room. Bose perched on a floral sofa. 'This is a lovely room, Mrs Mirza.'

Mr Mirza stared. 'It's Tanvir. Isn't it?'

'Yes, Mr Mirza, it is. Do you know where your son is?'

The mother got in first. 'He's at university, Islington. What's happened? Is he okay?'

'We don't know, Mrs Mirza. We have reason to believe that he may be involved in something serious and we're keen to find him before anything happens that might put him, or others, at risk.'

Silence. The parents glanced quickly at each other. The glance told Bose everything she needed.

'He's been in contact, hasn't he? Recently?'

Mr Mirza stared again, then appeared to give up. He nodded, and his head drooped.

'When did you last speak to him?'

'Monday, no, Sunday,' said Mrs Mirza. 'He called here. Late. Ten o'clock. What is he involved in?'

Bose took a gamble. 'I think you know, Mrs Mirza. I think you have suspicions. Am I right?'

The mother nodded, her eyes brimming with tears, her hands shaking.

Bose continued. 'What did he say to you?'

'He told us not to worry,' said Mr Mirza. 'He said not to ring him, but that he was okay. He said he… he said he loved us and he loved Allah.'

'He's a very devout boy,' said Mrs Mirza. 'He's a good boy.'

'How was he on the phone? His normal self?'

Again, the parents glanced at each other.

'Not really,' said his mother. 'He seemed funny. He doesn't drink, but it was like he had.'

'Did you ask him where he was?'

'Yes,' the father said. His face was now more confident, almost defiant. 'He said he couldn't tell us what he was doing, but that we'd know soon.'

'What did he mean by that?' Bose asked Mrs Mirza, who shook her head.

'I thought he had some good news – like a job, or a scholarship,' said Mr Mirza. 'He was such a bright boy at school – had got all As at A level. Could have gone to Cambridge. But he wanted to stay in London.'

'What else, Mr Mirza? Did he say when you'd know what he was doing?'

'Yes. He said we'd know at the weekend. On Saturday. Today.'

CTOC, St Pancras, London

Tennant, unshaven and his silver hair unbrushed, was nursing a coffee when Gabriel, Skeffington and Bose walked in. A senior case officer from MI5 was sat opposite Tennant, her elbows on the table. Around them sat and stood a dozen senior counter terrorism officers.

Tennant looked up. Gabriel nodded. 'DI Bose will give the latest update, sir.'

Bose took over. 'Tanvir Mirza rang his parents on Sunday night. He was evasive, incoherent at times, and upset. He repeatedly told them he loved them, he quoted scripture throughout and crucially he told them they would find out exactly what he was doing today.'

Tennant shook his head. 'No indication of where he might be?'

'Nothing, sir,' said Bose.

Gabriel took over. 'This is our clearest indication yet – I don't think there can be any doubt that whatever Abu Mujahid is planning, it is due to happen today. So we have two issues on the table. How do we catch up with Abu Mujahid and his four associates? And how do we identify their target?

'On Abu Mujahid, our best lead is still the missing hour when his van went off the radar in London two weeks ago. He was either visiting his base, or storing some, or all, of the weapons he'd picked up earlier that day in Burgess Hill. Either way, we need CCTV of him during that hour. DI Bose's team has ploughed through CCTV footage cameras across the black hole with no success yet. I want more resources on that search.

'And his van is somewhere. It may be in a lock-up, it may be on the streets with new plates. I want every grey Ford Transit in a public space checked and double-checked.

'So far he's not approached his family or any known associates. We've had them under surveillance, but it's time to bring them in and squeeze them dry. Now, on to possible targets.'

A map of London, with three red circles, appeared on the screen.

'We've narrowed it down to three,' said Gabriel. 'All involve large crowds, all outside, and with potentially high impact. The marathon, the England match at Wembley, and the Pride march in East London.'

Tennant signalled with a finger to the MI5 case officer sat opposite.

'I think we can help on that,' she said. 'As you know, the GID has been increasing its propaganda online over the last couple of months and we've been running a content-analysis study. We've found a disproportionate emphasis on Western hedonism compared to similar propaganda from similar ISIS splinter groups. The GID are pushing hard on Western sexual immorality and, in particular, homosexuality. It's a significant difference which is likely to reflect nothing more than the personal bugbear of the GID leader Mohammed Huzaifa. But if this attack by Abu Mujahid is designed by Huzaifa to put the GID on the map and serve as a declaration of intent, it's plausible that they would target Pride. There is no clear intel, but that is our best judgement.'

'I think it's got to be Pride, ma'am,' said Skeffington.

That was quick off the mark, thought Gabriel. I*s he trying to impress Tennant?*

He continued: 'Not just for the ideological reasons, ma'am. It'll be chaos down there and our officers will be hard-pressed to monitor the crowd. Abu Mujahid could get a drone over the crowd without anyone spotting it or hearing it over the din.'

Tennant sat back, scratching his armpit. 'I tend to side with our colleague from MI5 here too. Pride is outdoors, it's vulnerable, it's contrary to conservative Islamic teaching. GID want impact, but they also want to reduce the risk of a backlash from their potential supporters overseas.'

Gabriel hated to do this in front of junior officers, but there was no time for protocols today.

'I'm sorry, sir, but I disagree. I know Abu Mujahid. He'll want something spectacular, in front of the world. The Wembley match is going to be on live TV. The impact is far greater. Can you imagine a drone exploding above the spectators?

'Also, his van went missing in the west of London. That's not far from Wembley. If he's storing weapons there, it makes sense that the target is nearby.'

'I'm not so sure, Sophie,' said Tennant. 'He's also recruited from the University of Islington – these four men live within half a mile of Hackney where the Pride march is ending up. You could equally argue that his movements point to Pride. That's where I'm going to focus most assets.'

Gabriel fumed inside. She was certain Tennant was wrong, but she didn't want to challenge him in public a second time.

'Do we warn the public? Do we allow these events to go ahead?' said Bose.

That was the big question, thought Gabriel. It was now 7.45am. There was time to cancel all these events, to turn the football fans back at the mainland stations and airports, to disperse the LGBT protestors, to scrap the marathon. But that was one hell of a call. She looked to Tennant.

'If we cancel all three events, we are telling the world London is closed,' he said. 'That's a political call ultimately. And we are still working on assumptions here – that today is the day, that Abu Mujahid is in London. Given that, then I can't see how we can realistically persuade them to cancel. But we remind the public about risk, that we ask for vigilance, and we get as many officers out there today as we can. And we focus resources on the Pride march.'

'Well, this is it then,' said Gabriel. 'We have work to do. The clock is ticking.'

#

Bose had stopped at the coffee machine to grab some liquid breakfast when Gabriel caught up with her.

'Listen, Eva, my neck is on the line here if this goes belly up. I need the CCTV to focus on cameras on the west side of the ANPR black hole.'

'The side closest to Wembley, ma'am?' said Bose.

'That's right.' Gabriel said nothing more.

'I thought the boss had gone with the Pride theory.'

Gabriel gave her a steely look. 'He has. And that's where uniform resources are being focused. But I want the CCTV search focused on the Wembley side of the black hole. Look, I trust my judgement on this. I'm not ruling out Pride, but we'd be mad to neglect Wembley. Okay?'

Bose nodded and left.

#

For the last two hours, Bose's team had concentrated on ten major junctions between Hammersmith and Wembley. Hundreds more hours of footage had come in overnight from shops, petrol stations and security firms. The team of thirty-five had been working in long shifts, fourteen hours at a time, watching, rewatching, filing, recording, and they looked exhausted this morning.

'Ma'am,' said a young civilian woman who had just come on shift. 'Think I've got something. It's from a Network Rail 360 camera…'

Bose looked at the screen. The date stamp was 08.34, some thirty-three minutes after Abu Mujahid had entered the ANPR black hole. It was a frozen image, showing a grey van on a minor road in an industrial park next to a railway siding. The woman replayed the previous ten seconds. Bose felt a rush of euphoria.

'That's him,' said Bose. 'Fast-forward.'

The clip sped up. At 9.04am, the van appeared at the bottom of the screen, driving away from the camera.

'Get the address up now and send the details and the address to me ASAP,' said Bose.

She picked up the phone to call Gabriel. 'We've got Abu Mujahid's movements in the missing hour, ma'am. He was,' she looked at the screen where a map had suddenly appeared, 'driving along West Link Road, Willesden, at 8.34 and then he left around half an hour later. Looks like an industrial estate. We're pulling up the map and list of properties and businesses. I'll send it over. We need a team in the area ASAP.'

#

Kilburn, North London
Campbell switched off the morning news.

He'd rung up the office earlier and been told to stay at home. If Abu Mujahid was in North London, as the boss seemed to suspect, then Campbell's Kilburn flat was close by.

The phone buzzed. It was Bose. 'Jorell – we need you over at Willesden. We've found Abu Mujahid on CCTV driving to and from an industrial park yesterday. There's a storage unit on the park and he may well have been keeping the explosives and weapons there. I've got a dog unit, PolSA and forensics on the way too, but you'll be there before then. Sending over details now.'

#

Stonebridge, North West London
Today was the day of jihad, the day of purification, the day of victory. Around him, the cell members were in a state bordering delirium. They spoke too quickly, their laughter was too loud. Muhid and Saleem seemed to be competing to see who could be most enthusiastic. And yet, as Asad had knelt in prayer with the others in the living room, his mind had returned to the hallway cupboard. Abu Mujahid had told

them to spend an hour alone, reading the Quran, preparing mentally for the journey ahead, yet every few minutes his mind would drift from his bed and into the darkness where Mirza's body was cocooned in plastic. Where was Mirza now? Had his soul been extracted painfully because he had not properly committed to the struggle? And what journey had his soul taken? Would Asad be with him soon?

Asad walked into the living room. He was too nervous to speak to Abu Mujahid, who had laid his laptop on the table in the corner and was assembling the drones. The boxes he'd brought to the flat the day before were sat on the floor beside the table. Two empty rucksacks, each long enough for a rifle, were piled by the door.

Abu Mujahid greeted Asad and called the others for prayers one last time. Afterwards, he sat on the floor cross-legged.

'You're lucky,' he said. 'Many of our brothers and sisters have no time to prepare themselves for martyrdom. They are snatched from this world with debts, with anger and with work unfinished. You have the blessing to be beginning this journey in full knowledge of where you are going. You will have eternal peace and honour in the gardens of Paradise. And now it's time to go.'

Asad stood. He had gathered his things the night before and stuffed them into his coat pockets. He grabbed the coat and he and Muhid trudged out of the front door clutching the rucksacks, now heavy with the weapons. Saleem hugged them both, too tight, his face grinning, his heart clearly bursting. Muhid slapped him violently on the back.

'See you in Paradise, bro,' said Muhid, and hugged him again. They climbed down the stairs together and then separated at the main entrance to the block. They were going alone from here on to reduce the risks. Asad was going on the Jubilee line, Muhid on the bus. They hugged briefly and wished each other luck. They would meet again soon, Muhid told him, his eyes wide and his smile broad.

Willesden, North West London

West Link was a soulless street, lined with identical vast metal sheds and empty car parks. Campbell pulled up outside the Black Box Storage Company. Normally, it would be better to go in with support, but with the clock racing, he decided to go in alone. Skeffington would be there in fifteen minutes, forensics, PolSA and the dog team soon after.

A bored woman with a nose stud sat behind the orange desk. Behind her was a bank of TV screens relaying CCTV images from around the site. Campbell flashed his ID card and asked for the duty manager, and a minute later, a thin-faced man with a shiny tight suit ushered him into a glass-fronted office.

'We're investigating the movements of an individual two weeks ago yesterday who we believe may have visited here,' said Campbell after making his introduction. 'I'll need access to the log – along with the CCTV.'

'Of course,' said the manager, flustered. 'Give me a sec.' He fiddled with his keyboard and mouse. 'There – here's the record of everything in and out that morning.'

He twisted the screen around. Eighteen people had been in that morning.

'Could you print that off, sir? We're also going to need to look at the CCTV for that morning,' said Campbell.

'That'll take some time to sort out, I'm afraid. You know. GDPR. I'll need clearance from head office. Can you come back this afternoon?'

Campbell leaned forward, conspiratorially.

'The thing is, we don't have any time. This guy we're looking for is planning something nasty, possibly in the next few hours. Is it okay to have a look now anyway and do the paperwork later?'

The manager hesitated and rubbed his nose between thumb and forefinger. Then bit his bottom lip and nodded.

He led Campbell into an even smaller room on the other side of the reception.

'We keep the CCTV video for twenty-eight days, so it'll still be here on the hard drive. Give me a second.'

A shadow fell across them. Campbell looked around. Skeffington was standing in the doorway.

'Morning, Sergeant Campbell. Getting everything you need?'

'Yes, sir. The manager is being exceptionally helpful,' said Campbell, emphasising the word 'helpful' so that Skeffington wouldn't start getting pushy.

'That's nice. Any chance of a cup of tea, love?' Skeffington called out to the woman behind reception, who decided to ignore him.

The screen showed four images from CCTV cameras, arranged in a rectangle. Two outside, two inside the building.

'This is from 5am two weeks ago yesterday when we open up – I'll fast-forward till 8.30am,' said the manager.

The first visitor, a middle-aged Asian man in a blue Ford Focus, arrived at 8.31am. He walked into reception and picked up a trolley. The cameras followed him pushing the trolley through the wide, brightly lit corridors to a row of lockers. He pulled out a piece of paper and tapped the number pad. The door swung open and he pulled out three large boxes, placed them on the trolley and then wheeled it out.

'Not our guy,' said Skeffington. 'Next.'

A grey van pulled up. The timestamp was 08:39. Skeffington and Campbell sat up straight.

The door opened, and a white man in a baseball cap got out.

'Is that him?' asked Skeffington.

'Think so,' said Campbell, barely able to breathe. 'Wait till he gets into reception – the angle is better.'

The reception camera was pointed over the shoulder of the woman on the desk – the same woman working there now by the looks of it, thought Campbell – as the man walked in. For the briefest split second, the figure looked up at the camera.

'Yes,' said Skeffington, so loudly that the manager started.

Campbell grabbed the sheet of paper that the manager had printed. 'Which one is it?' he asked.

'There.' The manager pointed. 'One large locker. Three weeks' rental. Customer reference number 56232H99. He's calling himself Simon Gabriel.'

'Gabriel? He's got a nerve,' said Skeffington. 'Can we get in there now?'

'Hang on a moment,' said the manager as he typed on the keyboard. 'You can, but the locker's empty. He cleared it… yesterday. Came in at 10.14am and at 11.02am.'

'Can you show us the CCTV from those times yesterday, please?' said Campbell.

'It's on a different file. Hang on. It'll take a sec to load. Got it,' said the manager, and started the video. Again, four images – two from outside, one from the corridor and one in the reception – appeared on the screen.

'Get ready to take his plate down,' said Skeffington to Campbell, who scribbled the registration in his notebook. 'Oh, bugger it. He's walking there. There's no van, no car, nothing.'

Abu Mujahid, this time without a baseball cap, had strolled purposefully through the car park and into the storage unit lobby. He had a rucksack on his back.

He walked past reception and appeared as a distant figure on a shot of a corridor.

'Can't you get the image any bigger?' muttered Skeffington.

'That's as good as it gets,' said the manager.

Skeffington swore. Abu Mujahid was too distant to see clearly, but he appeared to be removing something from the locker and putting it into his rucksack. 'Show us the later visit,' said Skeffington.

The video fast-forwarded. Again, Abu Mujahid arrived on foot, collected a box and left.

'Is that it?' said Skeffington, disappointed.

'Yep,' said the manager.

'We're going to need to get a team in that locker with

sniffer dogs,' said Skeffington. 'In the meantime – Sergeant Campbell, call HQ.'

#

CTOC, St Pancras, London
'And you're sure he was walking?' said Gabriel.

'Yes, ma'am,' came Campbell's voice. 'He arrived on foot twice. Each time he was in the unit about four minutes.'

'Hang on, Jorell.' She put her hand over the phone. 'Eva – get a look at CCTV from West Link Road, yesterday around 10.10 and 11.00.' She took her hand away from the phone. 'Jorell, the timing here is significant. If he was walking the entire time, then he was carrying this stuff – which we assume are explosives and weapons – to a location within twenty minutes. A safe house? A flat? A vehicle?'

'Why walk? Why not drive?' said Campbell.

'ANPR?' said Gabriel. 'Maybe he wanted to keep off the radar. Maybe he doesn't like buses? He'll have had a reason. But what was in the locker? Have forensic swabbed?'

'Yes. Waiting for results. But the dog team picked up traces of explosives. The handler is pretty confident and I have got EOD on their way with their kit to double-check.'

Explosive Ordnance Disposal would be able to generate an immediate result.

'That's our answer,' said Gabriel. 'He's collected the explosives and rifles from Burgess Hill then dropped them off at the storage unit. Or the explosives at least. And then he picked them up yesterday.' There was a moment's silence. 'Yes, Eva?'

Bose had appeared, flushed and breathless.

'Got the CCTV of West Link Road and, yes, he was walking, ma'am – both times with a rucksack,' she said. 'He vanishes soon after, no sign of a car.'

'Right – get a map up on the screen. We can start to narrow down the location of his destination. Campbell, stay up there for the moment. It's likely you're near the cell. I'll send armed response up there immediately.'

#

Tennant looked at the map on the video conference screen. 'What if he wasn't walking there and back?' he said. 'Who's to say he didn't use a vehicle?'

Gabriel shook her head. 'Don't think so, sir. He arrives at the storage unit at 10.14 and leaves four minutes later with rucksack laden with God knows what. He's back at the depot with an empty rucksack at 11.02. That means he was away for forty-four minutes. We can assume he will have taken a few minutes to get into his house, or warehouse, or shed, or whatever hole he's using as his base, unpack the explosives and stash them safely, and then come out. Let's assume that's taken him four or five minutes. So that leaves him twenty minutes to get to his destination, and another twenty to get back. We know he walked into the depot and walked out – there's no sign of a car or van. Explosive Ordnance Disposal have confirmed that there were explosives in the storage locker and I can't accept that he'd have risked hopping on a bus.'

'Even if you're right, Sophie, you've made a hell of a lot of assumptions here,' said Tennant. 'He could be dumping the explosives in a hiding place to pick up later.'

'Sir, with all due respect, that makes no sense. He needs to get the explosives to the drones and he needs to attach them somehow. That needs space and privacy. He's also got four men to hide. So he needs a place that's big enough for five people, plus a shedload of drones, guns and ammo. And it's within a twenty-minute walk, a mile at best.' She sounded more confident than she felt.

'Put up the map,' said Tennant. A map of North West London appeared with a yellow dot at the location of the storage unit.

'This is the storage unit,' said Gabriel. 'And this blue circle is everywhere within a one-mile radius.'

The blue circle stretched up to the North Circular in the north-west, and down to the A40 and Wormwood Scrubs in the south. Just to the north-west of the circle – maybe half a mile from the circumference – was a tiny circle of green.

Gabriel let the significance of the green circle sink in for a moment. 'And just outside it is Wembley Stadium. I know, sir, that Pride seemed the most obvious target this morning. But the evidence surely points to Wembley now. And the biggest, most exposed, more vulnerable, most contained crowd today. Ninety thousand men, women and children sat down to watch a football match.'

'You've sold me it, I agree,' said Tennant. 'It's the priority. But only the priority – not our sole focus. It's 1pm now. It's too late to cancel or evacuate Wembley even if we were one hundred per cent sure it was the target.'

'Some of us are,' muttered Gabriel under her breath.

Tennant continued. 'We'll move the extra resources away from Pride to Wembley. I'm going to move to Gold Command – I'm sure they'll be thrilled to see me there today. Sophie, you use whatever you need today, you do whatever you need to do to prevent this clusterfuck. Keep me updated and if anyone gets in your way, use my name and take no crap.'

DAY 18

Saturday Afternoon

Special Operations Room, Lambeth, London
It took Tennant nineteen minutes to get to the special ops room, south of the river. The SOR was quieter than the last time he'd been here, on the day of the peace march ten days earlier. Ten days? More like ten years. He walked through the pods of the cavernous operations room into the smaller Gold Command suite. The team rose as he entered, but he waved them down.

The Gold Commander, an old-school chief superintendent with a beer belly and white moustache whom Tennant liked immensely, rolled his eyes. 'Fucking hell, boss. It must be bad if you're here,' he said in a Glaswegian wheeze.

'Sorry to ruin your day, Tom. Where are we?'

'I've mobilised the specialist assets to the stadium – the sniper teams will be up there shortly, the armed response vehicles and CTSFOs are in place. Officers are under instruction to be visible – be chatty and engage the crowd as much as possible. And I've pulled in additional BDOs.'

Behavioural detection officers were plain-clothes officers skilled at spotting unusual behaviour in crowds. They looked out for groups who were deliberately keeping themselves apart, for people paying too much attention to their surroundings and for those whose body language suggested a criminal intent.

'One more thing, sir,' said the Gold Commander as Tennant sat down at an empty terminal and began to log in. 'It seems the NRF have been busy.'

Tennant looked up. 'In what way, Tom?'

'Officers have picked up leaflets on the ground, claiming to have been published by the National Resistance Force. It's the first time they've been leafleting at Wembley to our knowledge. We've got eyes on the crowd and not seen anyone distributing them. It's the usual stuff – war against Muslims, blah, blah, blah. What's a bit more out of the blue is they're claiming Islamists are planning an attack on London within days. Lucky guess, I suppose.'

A bloody lucky guess, thought Tennant as he settled back down at the computer.

His mobile rang. 'Excuse me,' he said, rising to walk to one of the smaller offices.

'This is the Downing Street switchboard, I have the Home Secretary for you,' announced a prickly voice.

There was a pause and a click before Hogarth came on the line. 'Assistant Commissioner. Why the hell are you allowing Wembley to go ahead?'

'With all due respect, ma'am, cancelling the match would be the worst thing to do right now,' said Tennant, failing to hide his exasperation. 'Cancel Wembley and we've got ninety thousand people on the streets, buses and Tube, all heading to the perimeter of a closed-off stadium and exposed to any terrorist. Keep them in the stadium and they're behind a security wall – everyone entering the stadium is searched for weapons.'

'What about the marathon? And this gay march?'

'The same argument applies, ma'am. We have marchers assembling – and we have marathon runners assembling.'

'It's your call, Assistant Commissioner. I have no desire to interfere with operational matters. But I want regular updates. And is DSU Gabriel still handling the investigation?' There was no attempt to disguise Hogarth's contempt.

'Yes, Home Secretary,' said Tennant. 'As I've said many times before, she has my complete confidence.'

'I see.' Her voice made it clear that she didn't. 'Feel free to speak to Nina O'Brien – my spad – if I am unavailable. I expect to be kept informed and I expect the public to be protected. No more cock-ups.' She hung up.

#

Stonebridge, North West London
DC Kathryn Jenson had been door-knocking for twenty minutes. Bose had taken the one-mile-radius circle surrounding the Black Box Storage Company and split it into eight and Jenson had been allocated to the northwesternmost sector closest to Wembley. It was traditional, tedious legwork – knocking on the doors of shops, pubs and community centres, starting at the circumference and working inwards.

Jenson was using an iPad to mark her route along the row of dirty grey 1920s semis that sat within coughing distance of the dual carriageway, plastic window frames blackened with a layer of exhaust and dust. The Islamic Cultural Centre was her next stop. It had been created in a converted car showroom set back from the road behind a row of bollards. The sign above the door was painted in yellow – it looked more like a carpet warehouse, thought Jenson. The mosque was in a conversion to the rear; at the front was a cafe.

The woman at the desk didn't recognise the pictures.

'Sorry. And I'd remember him.' She pointed to Abu Mujahid's face. 'Try the Spar over the road? Mr Gill is a real curtain-twitcher. He sees everything and doesn't mind telling you about it.'

Mr Gill sounds a real pain in the arse, thought Jenson as she thanked the woman and crossed over the road, where they were greeted by a chubby elderly man with a grey beard and tiny round glasses.

Jenson introduced herself and showed the pictures. Mr Gill scrutinised them.

'Not seen him – or them,' he said flicking through them. He stopped at the image of Abu Mujahid. 'Ah. I know him. He moved in a few days ago – always in and out, in and out, like he can never make up his bloody mind.'

Jenson could barely repress her excitement. She'd done enough door-to-door inquiries to know how rare it was to get a result. 'Where have you seen him, Mr Gill? This is really important.'

'Over there – that block of flats on the corner. The yellow-brick one. I was working in the office, up there.' He pointed to the ceiling. 'My wife was running the till. I say running, she was on the bloody phone the whole time. Out he comes – then twenty minutes later, he goes back in. In and out all day. Can't have a proper job. I thought he dressed odd – like a white guy pretending to be Asian, if you know what I mean. You don't see so much of that.'

That's him, thought Jenson. *That's Abu sodding Mujahid.* She was desperate to radio in, but needed to keep Mr Gill talking for a moment longer. 'Do you know how long he's been there, Mr Gill?' she said. Her heart felt like it was bursting in her chest.

'Only a few days. Maybe since Monday or Tuesday. But he's in that block. I'd swear on my mother's grave.'

#

Special Operations Room, Lambeth, London
The command team were assembled around the conference room. A woman Tennant didn't know introduced herself as the Met's tactical adviser on drones, Amanda Elliott. 'Let's keep this brief,' said Tennant. 'Options for stopping a drone attack. What have we got?'

Elliott pulled out a file.

'Over the years we've tried a number of approaches on drones, sir, both kinetic and electronic,' she said. Tennant suppressed his amusement at the use of military euphemisms.

'All work to some extent, but nothing is universal. If a drone is on a preprogrammed course, there may be no signal to jam, although you can sometimes take electronic control. If it's being flown by remote radio control, then we have a greater chance of electronic intervention, but jamming the signal is not always successful.

'We've got a jamming kit on its way to Wembley. We know the model of drone that the cell is using and that gives us a good head start. But they may well have adapted the radio control units. My assessment is only a fifty per cent chance of success.'

'Military options?' Tennant asked.

'The MOD have their own team working with specialist kit. We're in touch with them, but that's more aimed at fully armed military drones in theatre, not these sorts of consumer models.'

'What about physically stopping them?'

'We've experimented with drone vs drone tech with mixed success. The Dutch tried birds of prey trained to swoop on these, but again with variable success and the risk of injury to the bird. I regret to say that if the electronic options don't work, then the only kinetic option we can fall back on is snipers.'

'Christ,' said Tennant, 'that's a desperate tactic.'

'Yes, sir, but the small tactical advantage the sniper option gives us is that the drone may not explode, and if it does, at least it's over an area of our choice, not the terrorists'.'

'Thank you,' said Tennant. He'd hoped for more reassurance than this. He turned to the firearms commander sat alongside her. 'Your take?'

The commander looked at the picture of the drone on the video wall. 'A sniper certainly could take one of these out, but these drones can be fast – the model they're using can reach thirty to forty miles per hour. The odds of hitting a target like that are better if it's coming towards you – so we'd need a team high up on the roof at Wembley.

'Two things. If these are packed with explosives, and possibly shrapnel, shooting them down over civilians could have serious implications. Even if the drone doesn't explode, we're talking about a three-kilo object dropping one hundred and fifty feet into a crowd. Additionally, there's collateral risk from stray rounds. A round could travel up to eight thousand feet if fired upwards and it could land anywhere or on anyone within two miles.'

'Let's keep our options open,' said Tennant. 'Get the kit for jamming the signal ready at Wembley ASAP, and brief the snipers. And I want to see the risks of collateral damage against the risks of exploding something above Wembley.'

#

Wembley, North West London
A toddler scooped up the chunk of bread and crammed it into her mouth with a fist. She chewed three or four times, then wrinkled up her nose in disgust and stuck out her tongue, globs of sticky dough dropping to the floor. Her mother tutted, bent over to pick them up with a tissue and lifted the girl. The toddler's face was now level with Asad, and she stared at him from the next table over her mother's shoulder, her brown eyes alive and wide. She gave a full-throated laugh.

Asad was sat at a two-person table in the corner of the cafe, as far from the door as he could, his rucksack on the chair opposite. The German waiter brought over his mint tea with an obsequious smile. Asad took a sip but couldn't drink it. He felt sick again, his mouth was dry and a wave of panic swept over him. Was the mother of the toddler watching him?

Mirza would be making a joke right now if he was here. He'd be making faces at the toddler. He'd be cheering Asad up. But he wasn't here. He was wrapped in plastic in a cupboard in a flat. The blood around his slashed throat would have dried by now – it would be crusty and blackened, like the gunk in your nose after a nosebleed.

What if that toddler was there in the crowd later? What if she was a Muslim? Could he do it then? He tried to picture the girl's body on the concrete, her eyes open and her face dusted with ash. He tried to imagine the crowds screaming around her, her mother crying out. He couldn't. Instead of the girl's face, he could only see Mirza. Instead of the crowds, he could only hear the gurgling of blood as the knife slit Mirza's throat.

He thought of his father, always so severe and critical. What would he be feeling tonight when he heard what Asad had done? Pity or anger? His father had never understood the passion that Asad felt. He was a small man in every way, happy in a little world in Cardiff, content with his lot. And his mother? What would she be feeling tonight? Would she understand why her son had to do this – to make the world safer for her, better for them?

He thought of Abu Mujahid's words that morning.

'We are part of a small noble group of true Muslims who will sacrifice our lives in order to raise the banner and establish the Deen. We will not reach glory except by traversing the path of this blessed jihad. Allah will raise us and make us victorious. You will be bestowed with great honour in Paradise with your beautiful maidens. Soon you will be in the highest part of Paradise with the Prophets, the truthful and the martyrs.'

The memory strengthened Asad's resolve. These anxieties, these worries about his family, and the child in the cafe, they were sent to test him. And he would not fail. How many toddlers had died in Western attacks in Iraq? How many children had died of starvation or thirst or illness because Western governments and citizens let them die? This was war. And with war came difficult decisions and sacrifices. And this was no sacrifice for him. He was following Allah's command and soon he would be in Paradise.

Abu Mujahid had told him exactly where to wait and when to open fire on that first evening in the Lake District, sat around the table in the cottage with the chintz curtains. His words came back to Asad now.

'Make each bullet count, brothers. Once you start, they will try to run back. But they won't be able to fight back against the tide of people behind them. Some will fall, some will be trampled, some will put others in the way of your bullets. But their deaths are justified. This is a just war and you are a soldier at the gates of Paradise.'

He reached into his pockets for change and found six pound coins and a twenty-pence piece. He left it all in his saucer and walked out.

#

CTOC, St Pancras, London
The low murmur of activity in the CT ops room at St Pancras had subtly moved up a gear with news that Abu Mujahid had been sighted. The map of the street showing the block of flats was already up on the video screen while officers around Gabriel frantically scrambled for support.

'A CTSFO team is on their way – will be with you in less than ten minutes,' said Bose down the phone. 'Keep eyes on the building and the exits covered.'

'Yes, ma'am,' said DC Jenson. 'Looks like three entrances – two at the back, one at the front. I've had a recce of the main entrance – there are eighteen flats spread over five floors. Those at the rear, facing north, have substantial balconies – those on the opposite side, overlooking the road, don't.'

'Have you got a list of names on the buzzers?' said Bose.

'Yes, ma'am. I'll send it over now. We'll hold back till the CTSFOs are here.'

Gabriel bounded over and sat on Bose's desk, her legs swinging urgently. 'What have we got?'

'Eighteen flats, ma'am, five floors,' said Bose.

'That's too many. Anything from the helicopter?'

'Nothing. We've got the rooftops covered,' she pointed to the live video feed from the helicopter, 'but nothing out of the ordinary, ma'am.'

'What about the occupants?' asked Gabriel.

'The flats are owned by leaseholders – freehold is owned by a third-party company, LB Properties, based in Clapham. The electoral roll is of limited use. A lot of these may be sublet unofficially. LB Properties should have a more accurate list, but no reply to calls to the office or the home addresses of the directors.'

'Probably watching the football,' muttered Gabriel. 'What we need is a foot in the door, someone who can give us intel, someone who likes twitching the net curtains.'

'How about her?' said Bose, looking at the electoral roll. 'She may do. Rebecca Gladstone, lives at number three. Been there,' she looked again, 'since 1999 and she's over eighty.'

'Perfect,' said Gabriel. 'Send Jenson in – she's got a good head on her.'

#

Stonebridge, North West London
Rebecca Gladstone stroked her lank, nicotine-stained white hair and eyed DC Jenson.

'Mind if I smoke, officer?' she asked.

'Not at all,' lied Jenson. She eyed Gladstone as she fiddled in her handbag, pulled out a cigarette and lit it with trembling, elegant fingers. She was a gaunt woman, her skin – stretched and blotched – evidence of a life in the sun. The cigarettes hadn't helped, thought Jenson. Her flat smelt of lavender and stale Benson & Hedges.

'As I said, we're doing investigations in the area and wondered if anyone had moved into the flats in the last few weeks. Have you seen anything out of the ordinary?'

Gladstone gave Jenson a penetrating look. 'People are always coming and going, young lady. They don't stay long here.'

Jenson didn't have time for this. She needed to get her on her side, to find a connection. Jenson looked around the room. A picture of a couple on their wedding day stood on the sideboard. The bride, maybe aged twenty, was recognisably the old woman.

'Is that your husband, Mrs Gladstone?' Jenson nodded towards the picture.

'My late husband, yes. I've been a widow for fifteen years.'

'He's very good-looking. What did he do?'

'A scientist. Nuclear physicist. He worked in the Middle East a lot.'

That explains the weather-beaten skin, thought Jenson. 'I studied chemistry. At Bristol,' said Jenson. 'I considered a career in sciences but then was lulled into police work.'

And then Jenson knew she had her. The woman's face softened.

'I was a chemist too – that's how we met.' She nodded towards the wedding picture. 'What do you need from me?'

'I'll get to the point. We've reason to believe that one of the flats has been taken by a person of interest to us. I can't tell you more than that, but please believe me, I wouldn't be here if it wasn't extremely important.'

She pulled out her stash of photographs and laid them on the granite coffee table. 'Do you recognise any of these faces?'

Mrs Gladstone puckered her face and lifted her left hand, finger outstretched. 'It's hard.'

'But do you recognise any?'

She moved her long finger, wavering, over one picture. 'I think I've seen him. Or someone like him. He was waiting outside the other day. But it's hard to be sure.'

'Thanks, Mrs Gladstone, that's been really helpful. Do you mind if I call my boss from the kitchen?'

CTOC, St Pancras, London

'I'm at the Gladstone flat.' Jenson's voice came over the speakerphone in the CT ops room. 'The lady reckons she saw Tanvir Mirza here on Wednesday or Thursday. She's also helped us narrow down the search – she's given us a list of six flats where she knows the residents.'

'Okay,' said Bose. 'Get back outside and watch the exits from the flat. CTSFO are a few minutes away.'

Bose looked up at Gabriel. 'Still too many possible flats,' said Gabriel. 'That leaves twelve. We need to narrow it down. Any news from the freehold company?'

'No, ma'am.'

Gabriel sat in her chair, hand running through her bobbed hair.

'Okay, Eva. If you were Abu Mujahid and you wanted a safe space for a few weeks and you wanted to avoid a paper trail, what would you do?'

'Local estate agent? Lettings agency? *Time Out*?'

'Maybe. What if you were looking from overseas though? What if you were planning this from say, I don't know, the Middle East? Surely it would have to be an online search.'

'Agreed.'

'So where would you go? We'll start with the biggest. Pull up Airbnb.'

Bose opened up the browser.

'Search for flats, Wembley area, at least two bedrooms, available at any time in the next few months,' said Gabriel. Bose typed in the details and a map of North West London popped up. Eighteen bubbles, each containing a rental, came up.

'Zoom in... there, that one,' said Gabriel, pointing at a flat costing seventy-one pounds a night. Bose zoomed in closer. The flat was in the block of flats in Stonebridge Park.

'Got him,' said Gabriel.

The flat's host was called Helen, who described herself

as a bubbly lady always happy to help. 'Sounds like a dating app,' muttered Gabriel. 'Have we got a number?'

'Just an email address, ma'am. I'll get someone on to Airbnb now.'

Gabriel looked up. One of the screens was showing the live match from Wembley. Kick-off was in twenty-four minutes.

#

Special Operations Room, Lambeth, London
Tennant turned to the team sitting alongside him.

'Give me an update on anti-drone tech.'

'MOD say they've nothing suitable within London right now,' said the drone expert, Amanda Elliott. 'Our electronic jamming gear is now in Wembley.'

'And snipers?'

The Gold Commander pulled up a satellite image of Wembley on the video screen. 'We've got them in position on the roof here and here, and on strategic rooftops along the routes of the march and marathon. But they're spread thin. As a last resort, the procedure is to try to shoot down the drone before it reaches a crowd. Frankly, boss, it's a desperate tactic, but any location away from the crowd is better – over the car park or top of the building would be best.'

'Understood,' said Tennant. 'A drone falling into a crowd is preferable to one exploding into it. Let's just pray that's not a choice they have to make.'

#

Stonebridge, North West London
The buzz of a police helicopter scanning the streets and rooftops had been a constant background noise for Abu Mujahid for the last half hour, but his two drones were hidden out of sight from above under a patio table. He recalled that first visit to the flat when he'd measured the door frame of

the French windows and the space on the balcony to ensure they would fit. Little details, his trainer had told him years before. Little details – they'll make you or break you.

Semtex, the bag of nails and the radio control relay were firmly taped to the drones. Saleem was giving them the final check over. The two smartphones he'd bought were connected to the remote-control units on the kitchen table.

The original plan, devised in Syria in those long evening talks with the GID leaders months ago, was for the drones to follow a preprogrammed course. They could be released and sent on their way with no human involvement, leaving Abu Mujahid to get out of the flat and into a safe house.

But the tests of the software in the Lake District had not gone well. The software was unreliable. And besides, he and Saleem wanted to be part of the day, not spectators. So last night they'd made the decision to launch the drones on a preprogrammed course, but then take over the controls for the final descent into the stadium. They would each have one drone. Saleem would take the first, and detonate it immediately after kick-off at 3pm. Abu Mujahid's would follow. He would wait for the perfect moment – when the crowds were densely packed at the exits – before flying in the second drone from a holding position above wasteland near the stadium, and creating the largest death toll.

The cameras on the drones would relay their pictures back to Abu Mujahid and Saleem's phones in real time. The explosives would be set off by a separate radio signal using a small relay, built into a box the size of a pack of cards. The two relays had been assembled in Syria and sent to Burgess Hill in the cache of weapons and Semtex. Having two controllers each – one for the drone, the other for the explosive – was clunky, but it was the simplest and most foolproof way.

Abu Mujahid went onto the balcony and stared again at the helicopters. Something was not right. One was not just circling the area, it was staying close to the flat – up one side of the street, around to the kids' park and back again in a loop.

A coincidence? Unlikely. Had Mirza betrayed them? Again unlikely. The boy was an idiot, not a traitor. Maybe the block was under surveillance. He watched the helicopter for a few seconds longer. If the flat was being watched, then police could be here any second. *Change of plan*, he thought.

'Stay here, Waheed,' he called out. 'I'm going to check out the street. I'll find somewhere secure outside and run my drone from there. Move the drones clear of the table in five minutes ready for the launch. Watch your camera feed and detonate at the right moment.'

Saleem looked surprised but said nothing as Abu Mujahid grabbed his phone and one of the grey relay boxes and stepped into the hallway. He opened the cupboard door, reaching behind Mirza's wrapped body to yank out a motorcycle helmet from the shelf, out of sight of Saleem, then slipped out of the flat's front door into the communal hallway.

#

CTOC, St Pancras, London
It took five minutes to get the owner's details from Airbnb.

Bose gave the news to Gabriel. 'It's flat seventeen, ma'am, top floor, facing north with a large balcony. It's currently being rented – for four weeks, starting two weeks ago.'

'And the host?' said Gabriel.

'Turns out to be an estate agent herself. Forty-two, no previous, not on our radar. Has multiple properties and has been with them for three years. Lives in West London. According to Airbnb, she hands over the keys in person to the renter. Do we send someone round to her, ma'am?'

Gabriel hesitated. Normally she'd say yes. This woman could be in on the plot. But there was simply not enough time to be cautious. She would have to gamble. 'Given her profile – and the fact she's got a few flats – we've got to assume she's not involved in whatever Abu Mujahid is planning. Get her on the phone ASAP and get a description of the person renting.'

'They've spoken to the owner of the flat on the phone, ma'am,' said Bose. 'And it's the right flat. It seems Abu Mujahid booked it initially for a week from overseas, but then asked if he could extend the rental for another three weeks once he'd seen it in person. He came to meet the owner a couple of weeks ago to collect the keys. We texted the owner a picture of Abu Mujahid and she's ninety per cent sure it's him.'

Yes, shouted Gabriel, but only in her head. *Stay professional*, she thought.

For the last few minutes, Gabriel had been setting the strategic parameters for the raid. The armed team were under instructions to detain anyone in the flat on suspicion of preparing acts of terrorism. She'd ensured they were briefed on the likelihood that Abu Mujahid and his associates were armed.

She didn't like being this unprepared. Normally, they'd have had time to get hold of the plans of a flat they were raiding. But there was nothing on the rental website to help, other than some photos of the rooms, and today there simply wasn't time.

'Ma'am,' Bose was almost shouting. 'Report from air support – two drones have just launched from the balcony. Heading north towards Wembley Stadium.'

'Shit,' said Gabriel. 'How far away are the firearms team?'

'Just arriving, ma'am. Ready to go on your order in one minute.'

'Give them my authority to enter the flat as soon as they are in position.'

Stonebridge, North West London
Outside the closed front door of flat seventeen on the fourth floor, six CTSFOs clad in Kevlar body armour, with visors down over their helmets and assault rifles in their hands,

waited silently for the signal. Three more officers were in the hallway, including the unit's medic.

The lead officer waved her hand – the signal to begin. The team had been doing this long enough not to feel nerves. Drill after drill, exercise after exercise, scenario after scenario – the most intensive training of any armed police in the UK – had taught them how to keep calm under this extraordinary pressure.

Two more officers emerged from the stairwell, carrying the hydraulic door opener. They stood back and activated it with the press of a button. The unit hissed and pushed the door open and downwards. Before the door had hit the floor, a third officer threw a flash grenade through the opening. A fraction of a second later, an overpowering explosion boomed through the flat, shaking the floor and his stomach.

No one in the hallway, no signs of explosive devices.

'Clear,' shouted the team leader and, one by one, the team shuffled into the hallway, their rifles raised.

'Hallway clear.' There were three doors off the hallway to the right – and one straight ahead. The first door was slightly ajar.

The team leader kicked it open and threw in another grenade. The flat lit up and the room shook with the bang. Empty. She put her hand to the second door, twisted the knob slowly and then kicked hard. It was a bedroom, recently used with a mess of dishevelled sheets on the two single beds. She entered the room. It looked clear, but could someone be under the bed? She ran in, a colleague behind, and checked under the beds and in the wardrobe. 'Clear,' she called, then returned to the hallway.

The team's nostrils were filling with grenade smoke. The third door looked like a cupboard. The team leader pulled the door open towards her, releasing the smell of excrement and rot.

'Sarge,' she shouted. 'There's a body in here.'

The man behind flashed a torch into the darkened space. Something man-sized was wrapped in black plastic. It was smeared with red and brown – and an arm was sticking out from under the covers. The medics in the team pushed forward, with kit bags already open.

'He's dead, ma'am,' said the medic.

\#

Special Operations Room, Lambeth, London
'Boss,' said Gold Commander to Tennant. 'Air support reports the drones are heading in different directions – the helicopter wasn't able to track them, it needed to keep sights on the flat. But one's approaching Wembley. On screen now.'

Buggeration, said Tennant to himself. They'd missed them. Had Abu Mujahid launched them early because he knew he was about to be raided?

Tennant looked up. The top screen showed a handheld video of the skyline above West London. The video zoomed in to a black dot which came in and out of focus.

'How far is that from the stadium?' said Tennant.

'About a quarter of a mile away.' The dot didn't seem to be getting any closer, but Tennant knew that was a trick of the camera.

'How long until it arrives?' he said.

'Thirty seconds,' said a junior officer around the table.

'Is the electronic jammer active?'

'Yes, sir, but it appears to have made no difference.'

Tennant thought quickly, weighing up the limited options. 'Delay kick-off. Get the teams back inside. We may need to shoot the drone down over the pitch.'

\#

Wembley Stadium, North West London
Sulaiman Khan was impatient to get to his seat as he waited in the concrete corridor for his brother to get his coffee.

'How much longer?' he mouthed, leaning over toward the queue.

'You go – join you in a minute. Sure you don't want nothing?' said his brother.

'I'm fine. Catch you later.' Khan headed towards the stairs leading to his seat, his seven-year-old boy's hand gripped in his. But when he emerged from the grey fluorescence into daylight, the scoreboard was still *England 0 Hungary 0* and the players appeared to be walking off the pitch back to their dressing rooms. *What's happening?* thought Khan.

He began the vertiginous descent with his son, nudging the fat man on the end to let him through. As he shuffled along the row doing the walk of shame – apologising and grimacing as he forced eleven people to stand up while he passed – something caught his eye in the skies.

Earlier he'd been watching the two helicopters buzzing above the stadium. One was TV maybe, the other for police. But the new object in his eye was smaller. It looked like his son Darren's video drone – the one he'd had for Christmas and used for a week before smashing it into a tree. It was hovering over the stadium roof, higher than the arch of Wembley, like it was on a wire hung from the clouds.

There was a sudden popping sound, like a firework going off outside the stadium. And another. And a third. *What the hell?* Khan looked around – he wasn't the only one who'd heard the noise.

#

Stonebridge, North West London
One more door. It was locked and the hydraulic opener was needed again. Another hiss, another clatter as the door fell, another flash grenade, and the team was inside a yellow sitting room.

A man was stood by the French windows leading on to a balcony. His face was blank, his mouth open.

'On the floor,' screamed the team leader. She moved into the room, his rifle aimed at the man's chest. The man was Asian, aged in his twenties and wearing a T-shirt and thin jumper. There were no bulges, no wires, no obvious signs of a bomb. The man was holding a phone. And a grey box.

The man froze – he seemed unable to move. His brown eyes met the barrel of three rifles.

'Praise be to Allah,' he said quietly.

The team leader squeezed the rifle trigger. Those hundreds of scenarios in the crumbling concrete training houses, the simulation on videos, the fitness regime and drills, all came together in this moment of split-second decision-making. Some highly focused part of her brain instinctively weighed up the situation, judged the threat, noted the man's refusal to surrender and assessed the box in his hand.

The impact of the three bullets threw the man's body back against the glass of the French windows, where he slumped, a smear of crimson on the pane behind him. The ripped gash in his shirt oozed with red and his hands fell beside his body. He was still clutching the grey box and his thumb was pressing hard on its button. Whatever the grey box was for, whatever device it was connected to, the man had activated it with his final movement.

#

Wembley Stadium, North West London
Sulaiman Khan was standing now. He pulled his son close to him and watched, transfixed by the drone, now above the partial stadium roof that protected the spectators from the rain. It was almost exactly over his head. A few of the other supporters around him had spotted it too and were also on their feet, pointing. Was it the BBC or police? It dipped away from the pitch towards the stadium roof above him. Were they trying to land it up there?

And then there was a flash followed by a bang, like a

lightning bolt had struck the roof. But before Khan had time to put his arms out to shield his boy, the clattering of metal was all around him.

#

Special Operations Room, Lambeth, London
The flash above the stadium was caught on one of the screens in Gold Command. There was a stunned silence for a fraction of a second.

'The drone?' Tennant said, keeping calm, but only just. 'Did we hit it?'

'No,' said a DS. 'Two, no, three shots, all missed. It looks like it's detonated over the stadium roof. That will have absorbed some of the shock wave and shrapnel if it had any.'

Jesus, thought Tennant. They'd know soon enough if anyone was dead. One down. The Wembley Police operations room would take over the scene and get casualties down to ambulances on the pitch. But what about the other drone? Where the hell was it?

#

Stonebridge, North West London
The flash grenades had sent waves of thunder again and again through the five floors of the block. Abu Mujahid, stood in the kitchen of a ground-floor flat, could hear doors slamming and voices raised. Saleem would be dead by now, he thought. Abu Mujahid had no way of knowing if he had been able to detonate the drone before he died.

He listened intently to the noises in the hallway outside, feeling for the remote-control relay box for the drone's explosive payload in his jacket pocket and studying the video feed on the phone, held firmly in place in the cradle of the remote-control unit in his hand.

He had been right not to go out into the street after he

left Saleem. It was obvious now the flat was being watched. Instead, he had knocked on the ground-floor flat and charmed his way past that hard-nosed old bitch. The woman was now slumped on the sofa, her pastel-blue cardigan stained with a puddle of blood from her neck, her eyes rolled back in their sockets, her hair strewn over her face. And the smell. Why did they always shit themselves when they died?

He had been worried whether the radio signal from the remote control would get through to the drone from down here on the ground floor, but he had been able to launch it as planned, seconds after hearing Saleem's taking off. And while the signal to his own drone – now a mile away and hovering over waste ground – wasn't as strong as he would have liked, it was good enough.

He glanced down at his phone again, ready to send it on its final leg of the journey to Wembley. Shit. The radio signal to the drone had dropped out and the video feed was black. He moved around the flat, holding the remote control up against different windows, but still no signal.

Without a signal, he had no way to control the drone. He knew what would happen – and he had perhaps a minute to act. Net curtains hung over the open kitchen window. He reckoned his chances of getting out through the doors were zero, but the kitchen window overlooked a storage area for bins. The yard was fenced off, but he could clamber over easily enough and drop down to the road on the other side. He just needed to pick his time.

#

Special Operations Room, Lambeth, London
Tennant watched and listened as reports came in to Gold Command. The spectators were trying to get out of the stadium and there was still a missing drone. It was galling to have lost one in broad daylight. Two more helicopters had been scrambled to search for it, but so far, no sign.

Tennant's phone buzzed. The number indicated the Downing Street switchboard. 'The Home Secretary for you,' said the voice. There was a pause.

'I need a scale of the injuries,' called Tennant to the team.

'Ambulance service say four serious, and sixteen walking wounded. No fatalities yet.'

Tennant breathed a sigh of relief. The TV footage was avoiding close-ups. He could see that stewards and police were trying to keep the pitch clear for the injured, but crowds were spilling on to the grass from all sides.

There was a click on the phone. A familiar voice launched into a tirade.

'Tennant – what the hell is going on? I warned you to abandon the match. How many have died?' Hogarth was ranting now. Tennant held the phone away from his ear.

'Twenty injuries, Home Secretary, and no deaths. As I explained, cancelling the match would have made no difference.'

'It would have prevented twenty people from being injured watching a football match, that's the difference it would have made.'

'Home Secretary, I do need to be brief, but may I point out that police action today, including the decision to focus on Wembley, has prevented many more injuries. We raided the flat at the point the terror cell was about to detonate the drone in the crowd – and that could have killed dozens. As a result, the injuries are relatively light.'

'Have you got them all yet?' she said.

'No, ma'am. We've neutralised one of the cell members. Another was found murdered at the scene. That leaves three missing.'

'For God's sake, Tennant.' And she hung up.

Tennant swore under his breath. Of all the times to get a call from that woman. Every time he spoke to her, she made it personal. It was intolerable.

And there was still a missing drone. Why hadn't it been

spotted yet? He had three helicopters circling Wembley and still no sign.

#

CTOC, St Pancras, London
Aside from the body in the cupboard, there had been no other nasty surprises, no booby traps and no other people.

'If it's clear, I'm sending in forensics,' Gabriel told the CTSFO team leader before turning to the counter terrorism ops room. 'Put me through to Gold.'

Tennant's face appeared on the screen.

'Sir, the flat is empty. From what we can see, the explosives were operated by a handheld radio relay and we believe the drones themselves were controlled by a smartphone. The phone that the terrorist was using was smashed in the raid, so we've no idea what software they used – and whether the drones were on automatic or being controlled live.'

'Okay, Sophie. There's still no sign of the missing drone, but we know it's out there. We've got snipers and observation teams scanning, and we've now got three helicopters scouring. We've alerted the Pride command team and the marathon team too in case they were targeting two events. But we're spreading ourselves thinner and thinner. Any signs of Abu Mujahid?'

'Nothing, boss.'

'Stay in touch.'

It made no sense. Two drones had taken off from the balcony. Was the second one heading somewhere else?

#

Special Operations Room, Lambeth, London
'Drone spotted, sir.' Tennant turned to the young officer in headphones, one of a team acting as a liaison between the pods outside and Gold Command.

'Where?'

'It was about a kilometre to the east of the flat. It was hovering over waste ground near a railway. Hard to spot when it's not moving. But it's now travelling back south.'

'Not towards Wembley?' said Tennant.

'No, sir. Seems to be flying at full speed south.'

'Sir.' It was Amanda Elliott, the drone expert. 'I've had a thought – and not a pleasant one. Consumer drones like this tend to come with a fail-safe. If they are under manual remote control and the signal fails, or if the battery is running low, they automatically return to their base – the launch point – for safety.'

Tennant froze. 'Are you sure?'

'Not sure, sir, but it's a very real possibility that the drone – carrying its explosives – might be heading back to the block of flats.'

'Oh, Jesus. Get the entire building evacuated now. How long?'

'They've got about two minutes, I reckon, sir,' said Elliott.

#

Stonebridge, North West London
The rising and falling wail was overwhelming and seemed to emanate from within Abu Mujahid's head. It took a second for him to realise what it was. The fire alarm. They were evacuating the building.

In the old woman's bedroom that smelled of lavender and talcum powder, he grabbed a sheet from the bed and pulled it to the sitting room, laying it out on a rug on the floor.

He picked up the old woman's frail body and placed it on the sheet, then wrapped the sheet and rug around her. He found it easy to carry the body – she must have weighed less than eight stone – to the bathroom and drop it in the bath. The bathroom door had a lock that could be opened from the outside with a screwdriver. He dived into a kitchen

310

drawer and pulled out a knife. That would do. He locked the bathroom from the outside and returned to the kitchen to wash his hands and face. It wouldn't take anyone long to knock down the bathroom door and find the body, but those extra seconds could be the difference between life and death for him. He was wearing an anorak over his jacket, so pulled the hood over his face and put on a pair of dark glasses. He felt inside the jacket pocket for the relay box – and his handgun – and stood by the kitchen window.

#

Special Operations Room, Lambeth, London
The new injury estimates were better than Tennant could have hoped for. Two serious injuries now, twenty-five walking wounded, no fatalities. But the spectators were building up at the turnstiles. The commander on the ground at Wembley sent through a request to open the doors.

The Gold Commander swore. 'If they're in the stadium, at least they're within the security cordon. Let them out and we have no control over their safety.'

'I accept that, sir, but there's a serious risk of crushing.'

The Gold Commander cursed again and gave the order to evacuate the stadium.

Tennant called Gabriel.

'Sophie – we're letting the crowd out of the stadium, but encouraging as many to stay,' he said. 'Nothing else is practical right now – without the risk of the poor sods getting trampled in the panic.'

'I have to say I'm uneasy about this, sir. We've still got three cell members unaccounted for and armed with semis.'

'I know. But there's no alternative. What's happening at the flat?'

'We're evacuating, sir, and containing residents in the street. If the drone is returning here, Abu Mujahid may choose to sterilise the crime scene.'

#

Stonebridge, North West London

Campbell had pulled up on the road outside the Islamic Centre, opposite the flats. The street had been closed off at both ends and the first residents were tumbling, scared and bewildered, onto the pavement.

At first, Campbell could barely make out the sound of the drone over the police helicopters and rumble of traffic on the North Circular. But within seconds, its distinctive high-pitched whirring was audible to all those outside the flat.

'Keep them moving back,' shouted Campbell to the constables controlling the residents. 'Get back as far as you can – get on the road. Get as far away as you can.'

The residents of the flats huddled together. They'd been joined by occupants of the neighbouring block.

The whirring grew louder – and the drone appeared at the top of the block of flats. It hovered for a moment, then descended, as if it was being let down on a fishing wire. It went out of sight behind the building and the noise began to quieten down.

#

Inside Gladstone's flat, Abu Mujahid listened as the drone's blades came to a stop. He felt for the grey relay box again. What he needed was a distraction while he got out of here and maybe a last V-sign to the police. His thumb found the switch. He shielded his face with the crook of his elbow, crouched behind the wall and pressed the switch.

For a second, he wondered if the relay box had broken, or if its radio signal – like the signal from the drone controller – was also too weak to get through the walls and floors of the flat. But then came a tremendous boom, which echoed off the buildings and walls around him. A man outside shouted; a toddler cried.

Calmly, slowly and with the arrogance of victory, Abu Mujahid slid open the kitchen window, thrust his hand through the visor of the motorcycle helmet so he could carry it on his arm and keep his hands free, slithered out of the flat, crept across the yard and shimmied up the fence, dropping into the street on the other side. His right ankle gave way awkwardly as he fell. He could walk on it, but it hurt badly, he thought, before limping away.

#

Wembley Stadium, North West London
Sulaiman Khan held his son in his arms. All he could think about was the boy slipping and vanishing beneath the crushing, trampling feet around him.

A trickle of blood had splashed on to his shirt, but it was just a scratch. The prospect of walking down to the exposed pitch to summon a paramedic had filled him with terror. He wanted out; he wanted his son out. He had joined the bodies pushing towards the exits at the top of the concrete steps and allowed himself to be washed along the corridors of the stadium.

A couple of hours ago, this same crowd were singing and chanting. Now there was a dour grimness about their purpose as they hurried, not running but walking steadily, towards the exits, towards Wembley Way and towards the Tube station.

#

CTOC, St Pancras, London
Gabriel watched the flow of bodies on the screens with unease. She knew things could turn quickly. A shot. A bang. A scream. They might all be enough to make someone push or trip and, once someone in a panicking crowd is on the floor, there's little that can be done to help them. It's impossible to wade against the flow. Often, someone will

only know a fellow human being has fallen over when they feel their bones underfoot.

And a shot or a bang was what she feared. This was already Abu Mujahid's work. He had sent these people fleeing, he had activated the drone, injuring dozens, turning a day that was supposed to be a celebration into a day of grieving and anger once more.

Abu Mujahid was in her thoughts now, as he had been two years ago – and for much of those intervening weeks and months. Was it about to happen again on her watch? She felt like Abu Mujahid was a spirit sometimes, sent to test her. Did he know she was leading this inquiry? She felt they were so close – yet she had never spoken to him. She had only seen him in the flesh three times – twice at court and once in the high-security cell after his arrest. But she had seen him in her sleep pretty much every week for the last two years.

Was he watching this too? Had he been in the block of flats when that man had been shot, and when that drone had exploded?

As if reading her thoughts, Campbell called her.

'Ma'am, looks like we got everyone out before the drone went off. It was on the balcony when it detonated and the shrapnel damage was mostly contained. The floor below was damaged but nothing structural. Looks like it was packed with nails and nuts and bolts, like the Wembley one. No sign of Abu Mujahid or the others – we're starting a search of the flats.'

'Okay, Jorell.' He hung up. Her eyes turned back to the screens. The camera was pointed at the faces of the spectators walking towards her. There was an Asian man with a bleeding head, carrying his son in his arms.

'Oh, people, I need ideas,' she said to the DCs and DSs around her. 'What's Abu Mujahid planning? Where's he gone? Where are the other two cell members?'

'Pride, ma'am?' said Bose. 'Split the targets, divide our resources?'

'Maybe. Come on. What else?'

'Maybe they weren't needed, ma'am,' said a young sergeant. 'Maybe he recruited four, saw who was good, picked the best and then dumped the others – killing one along the way.'

'He's a terrorist, Sergeant, not running an episode of *The Apprentice*,' said Gabriel. 'Come on. Better.'

'The marathon?' said a DC from the back of the room.

Gabriel shook her head. 'It's possible, I suppose. The plan could be to hit the stadium hard, and then when our attention is focused on Wembley, strike at the marathon. But my assessment tells me no. Everything we've uncovered points to the drones strike, to this flat, and to Wembley.'

But what was his next move? she asked herself. Had Abu Mujahid been at the flat? She knew he was no suicide bomber. He was the sort of man to groom others, but when it came to martyrdom, he'd be long out of the door before the bombs went off. She turned again to the screens. The people looked so vulnerable. And then a shiver of ice ran through her guts. What if the drones were part one? She knew Abu Mujahid. He liked setting up complex plots, multi-part plots, like his behaviour since returning: hiring a flat, going to the Lakes, all that complicated business with Amazon. It was good, but it wasn't simple. He didn't do simple. And what about the rifles? He'd gone to huge trouble to get rifles not just from the cache sent to him from Beirut, but he'd found a contact in the army and got one off him face to face. Abu Mujahid wouldn't have taken that risk without a good reason.

And then she knew what he was planning. Her insides screamed out the answer and the horror of what was about to unfold hit her.

'Get me Gold now.'

The radio came on. The face of the Gold Commander came on the screen.

'I think I've got it, sir. What Abu Mujahid is planning. I need to talk to all the officers at the stadium. Now.'

'Hang on, Gabriel – that's a bit irregular. There are channels.'

'I'm sorry, sir, but there is literally no time for your channels. We have seconds. Please. Now.'

Tennant came on. He spoke decisively, in a tone that no one would challenge. 'Do it. Put her through.'

There was a crackle. 'You're through, ma'am.'

She spoke clearly, steadily and with more confidence than she felt.

'This is Detective Superintendent Sophie Gabriel from SO15. I am leading the hunt for the cell of five terrorists planning today's attack. We have shot and killed one of the drone controllers, another – the cell leader Abu Mujahid – is on the run. But I now have evidence…' That technically wasn't true, but there was no time for semantics, '…I have evidence that the other two are waiting with assault rifles to fire upon the fleeing crowds. I repeat, I have evidence that there are two men armed with assault rifles preparing to fire upon the spectators leaving Wembley. One is an IC4, the other an IC3, and you will get the photos on your devices immediately. The more quickly we can identify and neutralise them, the more lives we will save today. Thank you and good luck.'

IC3 was the radio code for a black person; IC4 for sub-continental Asian.

She turned around to see Bose staring, a mixture of admiration and concern on her face.

'You said there's evidence that they're in the crowd, ma'am?' she said.

'If I'm right, no one will care. If I'm wrong, they can hang me out to dry later.'

Feeds from a dozen or so CCTV cameras filled the main screen in CT ops. Gabriel's team were transfixed by the screens, looking for a glimpse of Asad or Muhid or even Abu Mujahid among the bobbing heads.

The spectators were moving quickly, but still not running. Any second she expected to see people falling and tripping, and the people behind them stumbling over the bodies, only to feel the piercing pain of a hail of bullets. And as they fell, more and more bullets until the concrete walkway was blocked with the screaming, clawing, bloodied hands and arms and the crying of children and the sobbing of adults.

Come on, she willed the armed patrols and the spotters on the ground. *Come on.*

#

Wembley Stadium, North West London

Sulaiman Khan's arms ached. His son was asking to walk and perhaps it would be okay, particularly if he held the boy's hand tightly. He'd lost his brother in the crowd, but his son was safe, so that was all that mattered. His forehead was stinging from the graze. He'd get his wife to look at that when he got home.

The crowd seemed to be more restless now. There was more pressure on his back and it took more of an effort to keep walking. And they were going slower, if that was possible.

He let his son slide down in front of him and he grabbed his arm tightly. He could see very little – he was a short man, only five foot six inches – and the only things in his sights were the heads and shoulders of the other fans, fleeing the ground. Perhaps he should try to get to one side of the path. It might be easier for the boy.

'Oi. Paki.' The shout came from his left. Khan looked around, shocked more than angry. The voice came again. A group of ten men – white and drunk – were standing on the railings of the walkway down to Wembley Way, Union Jacks over their shoulders, beer cans in hands. The ringleader, a man with closely cropped hair and a face tattoo, was staring him in the eyes.

'Go home, you terrorist cunt. England for the English. Remember Pall Mall?'

The voice carried over the crowd. Voices around Khan were subdued. His son looked up, big-eyed and anxious.

Another voice, somewhere to the left and behind, shouted out: 'Fuck off, you racist shit.' Another voice uttered an incomprehensible yell of agreement.

'You're fucking dead,' shouted the skinhead, and jumped into the crowd, his fists flailing.

Around Khan, the mood had evolved into panic. The drunk men were pushing through the crowd, lashing out indiscriminately, and Khan saw with a mounting horror that he and his son were in the way. Where were the police? Khan scooped up his son and tried to push through the crowd in the direction of the Tube station.

#

CTOC, St Pancras, London
'Ma'am, we've got a disturbance just outside the stadium,' the young DC called back to Gabriel.

'Gunfire?' said Gabriel, looking at the screens, desperately trying to spot the trouble.

'Fighting,' said the DC. 'Officers are moving in. Looks like far right.' One of the cameras zoomed into a section of the crowd. Four skinheads were standing on the railings alongside the walkway jeering into the mass of bodies. Gabriel could see arms and fists, waving above heads below them. Ripples from the fighting were running through the surrounding crowd. Two police officers were trying to push their way through to the scene but were struggling against the oncoming mass.

'Reports of at least one person down. Wembley Command is moving horses into the area,' said the DC.

'Jesus Christ, just what we don't need,' said Gabriel.

It was harder now to see what was going on as the speed of the evacuating spectators increased. And if the gunmen opened fire now, the chances of getting an armed officer within a clear shot was receding fast. *Sod it*, thought Gabriel.

Wembley Stadium Car Park, North West London
The echoes from the drone explosion had ricocheted around the glass and concrete offices surrounding Wembley Stadium. Diners sat at the outdoor tables around Ahmed Muhid had twisted their heads to find the source; some had stood up. He had remained seated, his coffee and salad – props to allow him to remain at the restaurant – untouched. His heart was battering his ribs and sweat was dribbling down his back. He struggled to remain unruffled.

'Stay calm on the outside,' Abu Mujahid had told them that morning. 'Give no signs.'

It had taken only minutes from the dull boom of the drone exploding for word to reach his fellow diners via their phones that an attack was underway. The exodus had been immediate. Within thirty seconds, most diners outside had flown, putting wads of cash on the tables, or moving inside to settle their bills or take shelter.

Abu Mujahid had chosen Muhid's location well. It had a clear view of one of the raised walkways leading from the stadium. The walkway was wide enough for twenty people perhaps, enough to provide a good target, but not too wide to allow any of the spectators to flee.

In the Lake District, Abu Mujahid had been adamant. 'Fire on those advancing to you, take out the front line, then the second line and keep going. But wait till they are close – fifty metres. Be patient.'

Muhid could see the first fleeing spectators now on the walkway, in England and Hungary shirts, spewing out of the nearest exit and into the concrete concourses like mince from a grinder.

Two hundred metres now. Muhid thought of Paradise. He thought of children gassed by the West in Syria. And those thoughts burned deep inside of him. He felt nothing but hatred for the cowards fleeing the stadium. These were the same people who had willingly supported the wars in Iraq, and who had watched without question or doubt while their soldiers murdered Muslim brothers and sisters in Afghanistan and Syria. These were the same people, sub-people whose lives were mired in sin, sexual corruption, deviancy, perversion, delinquency.

Muhid stood, groped inside his rucksack for his wallet, and left a ten-pound note on the table. He must die with no debts, not even for a meal he hadn't touched.

Time to move. He stood and walked purposefully to the concrete anti-vehicle block he'd seen a dozen times on their practice runs using Google Street View. The block was intended to stop terrorists driving cars from the car park into the walkways. Today it would give him some shelter from the rear.

He placed the rucksack at his feet and faced the unbelievers. He couldn't kneel here, that would stand out in this crowd of scum, but he could pray silently in his head.

He imagined the next few minutes. Standing there in the oncoming storm of people, letting loose bursts of bullets, spraying the advancing crowd, watching them fall like the British soldiers emerging from the trenches in the First World War.

That man – the fat man with the beard – he would go. And that woman in the miniskirt, flashing her flesh at everyone. And that woman with short hair. His aim would be true, his bullets would find the people who were not worthy. The rifle seemed lighter in Muhid's hands now. He half-expected a scream or shout, but no one was looking at him, no one had noticed the functional slab of metal and plastic in his hands.

The advancing spectators were a hundred metres away now. Close enough. He slipped the catch to the automatic mode and looked up again.

And then he saw the lone policeman. A tall, red-haired man in blue shirt, bulletproof vest and navy trousers, moving towards him, his rifle slung over his shoulder, his face pale and puffy. The policeman was watching the faces – swinging his head from right to left. He hadn't seen Muhid yet. A knot of poison solidified in Muhid's stomach. This was the moment of choice – the moment of damnation, or the moment of martyrdom. He had a few seconds now. When they were fifty metres away, he would lift the weapon.

And then came the shout.

'Drop the weapon.' The policeman, now running towards him, his own rifle pointing at him.

This was it. This was the moment Muhid had been preparing for – not just for months, but for his entire life. This was the moment of crystal certainty, his test. And a test that he was going to pass.

He had to fight, not surrender. He moved quickly, determined to start firing before the policeman stopped him. He didn't have time to aim properly. His eyes centred on an overweight man in an England shirt in the middle of the crowd as he lifted the weapon in front of his body. No time to lift the sights to eye level.

His finger touched the trigger, but before he could squeeze it to unleash death on these kafirs, he felt the kick in his stomach and he lost his balance. It was hot and wet, but there was no pain, not yet. Muhid's feet were yanked out from under him and he fell sprawling onto the concrete.

Still no pain, just the heat and damp. He was still holding the rifle; his finger was still on the trigger. And as his hand sliced into the floor, scraping off the flesh on his knuckles, his finger slipped. The gun skidded over the paving slabs, kicking back into Muhid's arm, skittering around as a burst of bullets arced along the floor and a flight of spent cartridges were scattered around his body. The burst lasted a second, maybe two, before his hand lost its grip. And then the pain and the burning and the smell of the concrete and more banging, this time into his own body. And more burning. And then darkness as the policeman's bullet entered under his chin and tore up through his brain.

#

CTOC, St Pancras, London

'Ma'am, reports of a shooting. It's…' There was a pause. 'Yes, confirmed one of the suspects is down. Taken out by firearms. Believed to be Muhid.'

Gabriel breathed. It felt like the first time in hours. 'Civilians?'

'Thought to be one dead, ma'am.' The sergeant's voice was concerned. 'Another dozen injured, mostly in the legs. He was shot but released a burst of gunfire on the ground before he died.'

A mix of emotions swept over Gabriel. She'd been right. Her instincts, her knowledge of Abu Mujahid, hadn't let her down. But at what cost. One dead? A dozen injured. And there was another one out there. Asad. The Somali student whose parents had rung the university because they were worried about their poor little boy. The poor little boy that was about to let a rifle loose on thousands of innocent people.

She returned to the screens, staring at, evaluating, every face.

#

Wembley Stadium, North West London

Asad clutched the rucksack to his chest as he stared at the river of supporters flowing from the stadium and down the concrete path of Wembley Way towards him.

Inside, right now, he felt nothing. A sense of calm had descended after the first boom echoed around the buildings, and had remained through the burst of gunfire that told him Muhid had begun.

That sense of destiny, that feeling that nothing mattered, that he was on a roller coaster, or a runaway train, had grown stronger. He no longer felt nerves, just a stillness.

Abu Mujahid had told him to stand in clear ground, to fire upon the approaching masses fleeing the stadium, to rake the lines with bullets, showing no mercy to these enemies of Islam. Each body was a step towards Paradise.

But when the moment came, he froze. The moment he opened fire was the moment everything would end for him, and start again in Paradise. He could wait a few seconds longer, experience the living world just a few moments more. Now they were seventy-five metres away, but still he could pause. Fifty metres. Twenty. Then ten and now they were on top of him, pushing him along towards the Tube station and he had missed his opportunity. He was now part of this terrified, grimly determined funnel of humanity. The press of the bodies shook him out of his paralysis. He had messed up.

He pushed himself out of the stream of bodies, flailing an arm to break through the crowd. He came to a stop on a slight rise. From here he could see the heads of thousands of people walking, stumbling, running towards him from the direction of the stadium to his right. There were no uniformed police nearby. There might be spotters hidden in the crowd. But they had nothing to see. Just a black kid in an England shirt taking a break. He clutched the bag more tightly to his stomach, feeling the hardness of the rifle barrel pushing against his ribs.

A middle-aged woman flung herself out of the spectators and came to rest, panting, sweating, florid and scared alongside Asad. 'Jack,' she screamed out. Her voice was lost in the hubbub of voices and the rumble of helicopters. 'Jack.'

She clutched at Asad. 'My boy – I've lost him. He's only ten. Jack! Jack!'

She climbed up onto the wire-mesh gate. 'Jack!' Her cries were pitiful. 'Jack.'

Then the tone changed from desperation to urgency. 'There he is. Jack – over here.' She pointed and Asad saw in the gaps between faces a terrified little white boy in an England shirt turning towards the voice. He was just five metres away, but he was being swept down the avenue, away from his mother.

Asad, still clutching the bag, forced himself into the crowd and reached out, grabbing the boy's arm, dragging him back to the safe space by the gates.

His mother screamed. 'Jack. Thank God, you're safe.' She hugged him. 'Thank you. Thank you.' Asad dumbly shrugged, as if to say it was nothing. She held her son's hand tightly and Asad watched them dive back into the torrent.

Asad's breathing was slow, his heart calm. He thought of Mirza's blood, dribbling down his frightened and vulnerable throat. And of the day he had hidden from the gunman in London on that peace march, the day he had run away rather than stand up for his brothers and sisters. And Lesley Hogarth and her desire to crush Muslims in Britain. And he thought of the Chilton Park attack, of the video he'd been shown again and again of the murder of his innocent brothers and sisters. What he was about to do was justice. It was right. It was not sinful. It was a necessary fight in the war against Christian Western oppression.

He reached into the bag. The plastic was warm, but the metal was cold under his hand. He pulled out the rifle and held it to one side, its barrel pointing to the ground.

And he thought of Jack. Ten-year-old Jack, frightened and alone in the crowd. And of his helping arm, pulling Jack from safety and restoring him to his mother's arms.

#

Sulaiman Khan's arms were aching with the weight of his son, but he didn't dare put him down. His heart was pounding after the encounter with the skinheads and he wanted him safe.

'Sulaiman.' A yell came from his right. His brother was next to him. 'Thank God you're okay.' Then he looked at his shirt. 'You hurt?'

'I'm okay – I got a scratch from something, but it's okay. Listen, can you take the boy for a moment?'

'Of course.' His brother scooped him into his arms and kissed the child on the forehead. 'Stay close though – it's a miracle I found you. Did you see what happened? Did you hear the gunfire?'

Khan shook his head. The people around them were quiet. There was no shouting, no screaming. Just a flow of bodies moving relentlessly onward.

They were to one side of Wembley Way now. Ahead, a young black man was stood watching their faces, facing the wrong way. Something metal – it looked like a camera and tripod – was hanging down from his right hand.

Khan was closer now, no more than ten metres from the man. Their eyes met and Khan knew immediately that something was badly wrong. The man didn't look scared like the faces around him, but impassive, uncaring, unbothered.

The man glanced down at his right arm and Khan followed his gaze. It took a moment for his brain to register what his eyes were seeing. The metal object was a gun – olive green, functional and incongruous in this crowd. Khan barked at his brother, 'Get away. Now,' before turning back to the man. Their eyes met again.

Afterwards, Khan couldn't explain to the police, his brother or his wife why he behaved like he did. And even as he started forward to the man, he knew the sane response was to run, to hide, to shout. But instead, part of his brain told him to challenge the man.

'Put it down,' he yelled. 'You. Put it down.'

The man was expressionless. He stared blankly as Khan advanced towards him, now just a few feet away. And then he raised the rifle butt in his left hand and swung it up sharply into Khan's cheek. Khan staggered back, blood dribbling onto his shirt from the graze. The man lifted the rifle again and jabbed the butt into Khan's chest. With an exhalation of breath, Khan collapsed.

The crowd parted around Asad, moving back, creating a circle of space in the packed avenue. The Asian man was still lying on the floor, clutching at his chest.

And in that moment, as he stood over the writhing body, the boy Jack's face came back into Asad's head. And Asad knew he could not go on with this. The tsunami he had been riding wasn't unstoppable. He had a choice. And his choice was to walk away now.

He turned, clutching the rifle in his arms like an infant.

'Drop the bag.'

The shout came from behind. A woman police officer was pointing a rifle at him. Another man in uniform, but with no gun, was stood next to her.

'I said, drop the bag.' The woman was Northern Irish. She stared at him with expressionless eyes. Asad could sense the crowd moving away from him. From the corner of his eye, he saw men and women in fluorescent jackets pushing and diverting the crowd, creating an arena for him and these two police officers.

'Last warning. Drop the bag,' screamed the woman. He had a choice. He could stop this now. He could give up. He could find peace. And he would spend an eternity in jail. He knew he couldn't cope with that. No. Once again he thought of Abu Mujahid and his mother. And himself holding his father's hand in the crowd at that football match all those years ago. And letting it go. He clutched the rifle more closely.

A searing heat in his chest and a stumble. There was no pain, just confusion. And then a stabbing sensation like a knife in his heart, twisting and pulling, cutting out chunks and throwing them to the floor. *There is no white tunnel*, he thought as the burning spread through his body. *There is no gateway. No garden. No welcome. Just pain and doubt and tears and suffering.*

CTOC, St Pancras, North London

It was like the first desperate gasp of a swimmer who has dived too deep and too long. Gabriel stood in the ops room, face blazing in the video screen glare, clutched at the desk top and sucked air deep into her body. Four members of the cell – Muhid, Saleem, Mirza and Asad – were accounted for, all dead. The twisting anxiety that one of the cell would emerge from the jostling Wembley crowds and open fire had ebbed away and in its place flowed a soothing wave of relief. Gabriel noticed her shirt was sopping wet.

Campbell was still at the flat, overseeing the clean-up. The drone had done little damage to the building, aside from broken glass and roof tiles – its payload was designed to maim people, not demolish walls – but residents had been evacuated and they would be out of their homes for a few days.

He came on the phone, breathless. 'Ma'am. The bodies are piling up down here. We've got three now. The body in the cupboard has been positively identified as the cell member Tanvir Mirza, as we suspected, and he had been dead some time – a couple of days, by the state of him. His throat was slit and he was bundled into a cupboard.'

'Sounds like Abu Mujahid's work,' said Gabriel. Why kill Mirza? Did Abu Mujahid think he was a mole? Or had he found out about Mirza's phone call to his parents?

Campbell continued. 'The man who was shot when we raided the flat has been IDed as the cell member Waheed Saleem. Bullet to the chest and died within a couple of minutes of internal injuries.'

'And the third?' asked Gabriel.

'She was a Rebecca Gladstone, aged eighty-one. Lived in a ground-floor flat. Her throat was slit. Whoever did it got out by the kitchen window and into the street. She was killed within the last half hour. Looks like the killer was in the flat when we raided, and got out under cover of the fire alarm and evacuation. We found a second relay box by her body – it's likely that the killer detonated the second drone from there as it returned to the flat.'

'Abu Mujahid.' It wasn't a question. What better way to tidy up a crime scene than detonate an explosive?

For a giddying moment, Gabriel imagined him standing in the crowds outside Wembley, gun in hand, aiming at the oncoming crowds. But she shoved away the thought. That wasn't his style. He wasn't one for martyrdom. So where was he? A memory leapt out of the darkest corner of her head. Something she'd seen when the CTSFO team swept through the flat earlier.

Bose, who was listening in, seemed to have sensed her initial anxiety.

'Shall I get on to Gold, ma'am, and warn them that he could be heading for Wembley?' She looked up almost eagerly for approval.

'Come on, Eva, use your head,' Gabriel said. 'He's a coward. He sets up others to die for the great cause and he has no interest in being a martyr. He has an escape plan, and he's had it since before he moved back to London. Pull up the video of the CTSFOs raiding Abu Mujahid's flat,' she called out to one of the duty DCs in the ops room. 'Start when they were in the hallway.'

Moments later, the shaking image of the bodycam of the lead CTSFO filled the main screen. The image swayed and spun as the officer began the careful yet urgent sweep of the flat, room by room, wall by wall.

Bose came over to stand next to Gabriel, who was sat at a desk, her sharp elbows on the surface, her hands clamped around her cheeks and her eyes bright and alert.

'What are you hoping to see, ma'am?' asked Bose.

'If I knew, I wouldn't need to watch this again.'

Gabriel continued to focus on the screen. The camera was now in the hallway, approaching the cupboard where Tanvir Mirza's body had been dumped. A gloved hand opened the door, and the camera hovered over the fold of grey plastic taped tightly around Mirza's body. *Another person robbed of life by Abu Mujahid, another disposable corpse to add to his collection*, thought Gabriel. Had Mirza's parents been told yet, she wondered. Did they know that their beloved son, the young man they had been so worried about, had been involved in this – and was now lying wrapped in plastic bin bags like a piece of household waste?

The camera moved around the cupboard to an ironing board, and across shelves of washing powder and cleaning products.

'What's that?' Gabriel said. 'Go back and freeze it.'

The video paused and rewound, freezing again on an empty white cardboard box, its top ripped off, its contents removed. The writing was illegible, but the image on the packaging was clear. A red motorbike helmet with visor.

Gabriel's eyes glittered. 'That's it,' said Gabriel. 'That's Abu Mujahid's.'

'How can you be sure?' said Bose.

'Because Abu Mujahid's life history is locked away in here, Eva.' She tapped her forehead. 'When he was a teenager, when he was still just plain Jack Pearce, he was nicked for stealing mopeds. And he had his own bike until he went to prison first time round. A blue Honda. I could even tell you its registration number, if you like. That's his helmet. And that means he had a bike nearby. Think about it, Eva, what better way for him to get away from the flat, anonymously? Get CCTV now – close to the flat, and covering the fifteen minutes after the drone exploded. Double-check with the flat owner – see if she had a helmet in the cupboard. But I bet she didn't. And get the CCTV team searching the streets – get them to look in the fifteen-minute window after the drone exploded at the flat.'

\#

Eight minutes later, the video screen in the ops room was filled with wide-angle CCTV footage of a shopping street, two hundred metres from the flat. The frame was paused as a moped, ridden by a man wearing a red helmet, waited at a pedestrian crossing. The timestamp showed it was captured four minutes after the drone was detonated at the flat.

Bose came over. 'The flat owner doesn't have a motorbike and says there was no helmet in the cupboard,' she said, then added: 'Is that him?'

Gabriel peered at the screen. The rider's build was about right, the helmet was a good match and the timing fitted. But was it him? 'I bloody hope so, Eva. Anything from ANPR?'

'Just in. The moped was last spotted on the Westway heading east into the centre of town. He'll be on Marylebone Road by now, given the traffic. We should have a bike with him in three minutes.'

Three minutes? It didn't seem real. Was it possible that her two-year-long search for Abu Mujahid was going to end here and now? All those lives he had taken, all those hours she had spent tracing up false leads and spurious rumours? She searched for a trace of excitement, a gut feeling that she was finally on his trail after these two weeks of searching, after these two years of frustration. But there was nothing. No prickling of the hairs on her neck, no twisting in the gut, no adrenaline rush to let her know she was on the right track, nothing visceral.

Her phone buzzed in her pocket. It was Tennant. She answered in a side office on her earpiece.

'Bloody good call on Wembley, Sophie,' said Tennant. 'The Gold Commander's face was something else when I told him to let you take over the radio. Clearly thought I'd lost it. But bloody glad I did.'

She hadn't the heart or the time to tell him that her fantastic evidence that Asad and Muhid were outside Wembley had been little more than an intelligent hunch. Perhaps she would just quietly forget that.

'Sir,' she interrupted him. 'We've got CCTV on Abu Mujahid. Or at least we're pretty sure we have. On a moped fleeing the scene. ANPR shows he's heading south-west, to the centre of town. Bose tells me we're minutes away from him.'

'You don't sound so sure,' said Tennant.

'I'm not going to celebrate until he's banged up, boss.'

'So what was his great plan? Another attack? A last hurrah?'

'That's just not his style, boss,' said Gabriel. 'He's a schemer, not a martyr. In the three or four years he's been on our radar, he's not once put his own neck on the line. No. He was either going to lay low or get out.'

'If he was planning to lay low, he was going about it a funny way, Sophie. If I were him, I'd be heading for the suburbs, looking for some quiet backwater. But look at him. He's heading into the centre of London, the CCTV hotspot of the entire country. He must know there's a chance we're on to him by now.'

'Maybe.' She glanced through the glass wall to the ops room. Five minutes were up. They should have him by now.

'Listen, boss, right now he's not certain we're on to him. He knows we were at the flat, but that's all. So assume for a minute that he thinks he's in the clear. What's he going to do? He knows that we'll find his DNA all over the flat and he will assume that it'll take us more than a few hours to confirm that the DNA belongs to him. That means he's got a small window to get out of the country. And I know Abu Mujahid. He's a glory hunter – he wants to bask in the limelight from all this, he wants to be back with his acolytes.'

She looked out again. There was a bustle of activity around one of the terminals. Bose was talking expressively at the DCs.

Tennant was speaking. 'So assume he's trying to flee. He's been here a few weeks, he's had time to fix up an escape route. He'll have access to a fake passport. We can rule out a plane, too risky. Same for a boat. Last time, two years ago, he escaped out in a van from Portsmouth? Right?'

'A lorry taking a consignment of toilet rolls to France, sir,' said Gabriel.

'I remember. Headline writers had a field day when that came out. But didn't he have a backup plan?'

Gabriel paused. Tennant was right. There was something in his file she'd seen during the inquiry into his escape. What was it? She glanced out of the door again. Still no sign of an arrest.

'Can I call you back later, sir?' She walked to the door and shouted to Bose over the hubbub. 'What's happening?'

Bose rushed over. 'Sorry, ma'am, just heard from the riders again. They've missed him.'

'What do you mean "missed him"? How the hell could they miss him?'

'He's gone off the grid. He was last picked up by ANPR on Marylebone Road near Baker Street six minutes ago heading east. The traffic's terrible down there, ma'am, hard even for a moped to get through. He should have popped up on ANPR a few hundred yards later near Regent's Park. But still no sign of him. The riders have swept up and down the road, but nothing. They're double-checking and searching side roads now.'

Surely not again, thought Gabriel. Surely he hadn't done it again.

The main screen was showing live CCTV of Marylebone Road. On smaller screens, shots of side roads appeared and disappeared. Dusk was falling and visibility was poor. Somewhere in that grid of white Portland-stone houses and offices, Abu Mujahid was scurrying through the shadows.

The ops room was silent. Street after street appeared on the screen and vanished, but still there was no moped, no figure resembling their killer.

'Shit, shit, shit,' said Gabriel under her breath. He must have dumped the moped and be going on foot. So where the hell was he going? She thought back to her conversation with Tennant.

'Bose, pull up the records from two years ago. I want

to see his phone and internet activity from the moment the surveillance team left him.'

Two years ago, it had taken two days to piece together his escape route using CCTV. The surveillance team trailing Abu Mujahid had been called off at noon and it had taken him less than forty-five minutes to become aware that he was no longer being tailed as he walked around the centre of Basingstoke. At 1pm, he decided to test his hunch by flaunting his bail conditions and walking to the station to buy a single rail ticket to London. He knew that if the police were watching, that was the moment they would have swooped. But they did not. Abu Mujahid waited at the ticket booth for five minutes before turning around and walking back into the centre of town. First stop was a phone shop where he bought a cheap mobile and pay-as-you-go SIM card and made a call. Soon after that, he was picked up by a white van which took him to Winchester, down the M3. There he was met by the driver of a red Mazda who handed over the car. Abu Mujahid took over the wheel and drove to Portsmouth where he was stopped in a random check and where he shot Isobel Harris.

In the days after he vanished, every step in his journey had been forensically examined. The phone shop provided the SIM card details and, after a day, SO15 had his phone and internet records. And it was these that Gabriel was now frantically searching.

She pulled up the report into his phone activity. There it was on the screen in front of her. Why the hell had it taken her so long? She'd bragged to Bose earlier that she carried every detail of his life in her head, and yet here she'd missed a glaring possibility.

Two years ago, while he waited in Basingstoke to be picked up by the white van, he had searched the Eurostar timetable. He had even opened the booking page for an evening train to Brussels before abandoning the attempt. It was clearly his backup plan in case the van could not get him out of the town.

'He's going to St Pancras, Eva, he's getting the Eurostar,' said Gabriel. This time, there was no uncertainty, just the euphoria of knowing she was right. It made perfect sense. He could be out of the country within the hour on a fake passport.

She called for the map on the main screen. If he had abandoned his moped near Regent's Park, then St Pancras was a mile and a half away. If he had set off five minutes ago, he would be there within twenty-five minutes.

'Eva, get two surveillance teams to the station now,' she said. 'Prioritise them – the closest non-urgent operations. And get a DI down there to brief them.'

Again, for a moment she was back in this room two years ago, making a similar call. That time she'd taken a unit off Abu Mujahid and diverted them to her father's old friend's operation. And that decision, that split-second call, had haunted her every day. A tiny decision, made out of some loyalty to her dad's memory, had set off the chain of events that led to Abu Mujahid's escape, Isobel Harris's death and countless other bloody atrocities – a blood-smeared chain that linked her to the death of Rebecca Gladstone less than an hour ago in her ground-floor flat. Was she right this time? Her gut told her yes. She knew Abu Mujahid inside out, better than anyone. She had studied every file, read every report, chased every lead. But a tiny voice of reason urged caution. The evidence was circumstantial, patchy even. He could have one hundred other plans, or none at all. And what if she was wrong again? Could she live with the humiliation that would follow for her, and for Tennant? And could her career survive another cock-up with Abu Mujahid if he appeared in some Islamist video online in days to come, boasting that he had defeated the Met one more time? She went over to a monitor to study the map of Abu Mujahid's likely journey.

A minute later, a DC in the CCTV team called out. 'Think we've got him.' The main image on the video screen flashed to a CCTV camera pointing along Devonshire Street, a broad but quiet road lined with red-brick office blocks, clad at street level with bleached Portland stone. A man scurried along with a small rucksack slung over his shoulder, and an anorak hood pulled over his head.

'He's heading east, ma'am, in the direction of St Pancras,' said the young DC. Again, Gabriel felt a swell of euphoria. Was this how riders felt in the old days of legal fox hunting, when the scent of their quarry was in the nostrils of the hounds? They watched further. The figure stopped and for a moment his profile was frozen on the screen. It was a teenager, aged sixteen or seventeen.

'False alarm,' said the DC, unnecessarily. Gabriel felt a pang of frustration.

'He'll be at the station in fifteen minutes. Who's gone down there to brief the spotters?'

'DI Skeffington, ma'am,' said Bose.

Gabriel failed to mask her dismay. 'And whose idea was that?'

'He volunteered, ma'am.'

'Shit.' She took a deep breath. Skeffington was the worst choice. He'd barely hidden his contempt for Gabriel since the start of the hunt for Abu Mujahid. She could not think of a less suitable candidate for this job.

She made up her mind in an instant. 'Listen, Eva, I'm going down there to join him.'

'Ma'am?' Bose was incredulous. She followed Gabriel, one step behind her as she grabbed her coat, swung her bag over her shoulder and made for the stairs.

'Sod it, Eva, you know it makes sense.' They'd reached the first floor by now, the clattering of their feet echoing up the stairwell, Bose panting as she struggled to keep up. 'I don't have to tell you what I think of Skeffington. And no one, absolutely no one, knows Abu Mujahid better than me. I want the spotters energised – not sent off half-cocked because the briefing officer would rather be in the bar.'

They had reached the basement floor by now and were

heading across the concrete floor towards the revolving door into the staff car park.

'But… ma'am, stop and think for a minute. You're not being objective.'

Gabriel stopped in front of the door. This kind of dissent was alien to Bose, and the challenge unsettled Gabriel momentarily.

'Sorry, Eva, but fuck objectivity. Abu Mujahid screwed me over once. He's not doing that a second time. Grab the car keys and stop arguing.'

#

St Pancras Station, London

Bose said nothing on the two-minute journey, but Gabriel was too lost in the bubbling mess of thoughts to notice she was sulking. Abu Mujahid was out there, somewhere in the cold and dark, pushing his way through the back streets and alleyways, getting closer with every step, believing he had escaped justice once more and his heart set on escape. And this time Gabriel would not let him succeed. She knew that she had been driven by her failure two years ago, but until the last few moments in CT ops, she had not realised just how far she would go. Her outburst at Bose had surprised her. So had her determination to get to St Pancras in person. But so what? She deserved it. And she couldn't let that idiot Skeffington mess this up, not now, when the goal was so close she could almost sense it. She knew she was being not just unconventional but unreasonable and even obsessive. But the thought of letting Abu Mujahid go again – and the prospect of all that pain and the guilt and the self-recrimination – was unbearable.

The car pulled over into the taxi drop-off lane outside St Pancras and the pair jumped out. Access to the police station briefing room was from inside the terminus. Two pairs of armed police were walking casually past the chemists and stationery shops. They nodded to two soldiers, carrying their rifles pointing down. Lesley Hogarth would be pleased to see them on the beat, she thought.

Gabriel walked into the police station, waved her badge in front of the desk sergeant and was let through into a corridor reeking with disinfectant – the smell of primary school toilets and interview cells. The briefing was in the first door on the right. She put her nose against the frosted glass panel and pushed open the door.

Skeffington was facing away from her as he addressed two dozen plain-clothes spotters scattered around the room, some sitting on plastic chairs and desks, others resting against the wall, arms crossed. A silver-haired man in his fifties slouched in a chair at the front recognised Gabriel as she walked in and self-consciously sat more upright.

Skeffington was finishing. '…to be honest, we're chasing shadows here, guys, and the chances that Abu Mujahid is out there is close to a big fat zero. But you know what the boss is like when it comes to her pet subject: we have to show willing. Questions?'

The man at the front raised his hand.

'DS Carter,' said Skeffington.

'Just wanted to know if Detective Superintendent Gabriel wanted to add anything, sir?'

Skeffington spun round, his mouth open and, for a moment, surprise, then anger in his eyes. 'Ma'am,' he said, controlling his voice too calmly. 'I'd no idea you were planning to pop in.' The voice was quiet; Gabriel's reply was quieter – designed for Skeffington's ears only.

'So much for your detective skills, Inspector Skeffington.' She faced the smirking group. 'Listen, DI Skeffington has given you a full briefing, I'm sure. I just wanted to add something from my own personal experience with Abu Mujahid. Firstly, I'm convinced that Abu Mujahid – a man who has killed dozens of people, a man responsible for a string of atrocities against innocent men, women and children including, you'll remember, the little girl Isobel Harris – is somewhere out there.' She waved at the door. 'Second, he is dangerous. He is ruthless, ice-cold and he will stop at nothing to get what he wants, which right now is to get out of the country. And failing that, to leave this world, bringing as many other people – innocent people – with him. But most of all, I believe he wants to get out alive. So be vigilant, be thorough, and be the extraordinary professionals I know you are. Bear in mind he's organised a terror attack with automatic weapons and explosives and may be armed with either. I know you fully understand the limitations of your weapons and training and that the advanced firearms officers on patrol are better equipped to intervene unless it's an emergency.' Of course, they knew all this, but too many years of being second-guessed by courts and public inquiries meant she needed that on the record, even today.

As the officers left, she walked over to Skeffington.

'Sorry to surprise you like that, Neville,' she said coldly. 'But this needs to be done professionally.'

Skeffington was flushed, his breathing heavy. Again, he controlled his voice. 'Understand, ma'am. Abu Mujahid is an itch – it's clear you want to scratch it.'

Gabriel stared up at him. 'Don't compound your arrogance and unprofessionalism just now by patronising me, DI Skeffington.' Skeffington's face winced for a half-second before he could stop himself.

'Think I'll accompany one of the spotters, if that's okay with you, Skeffington. Shall we take a little walk, DI Bose?'

#

The shopping arcades inside the station were busy with people filling the minutes before their departures in boutiques stuffed with overpriced clothes and gifts. Other passengers were briskly weaving their way through the dawdlers, late for their trains or at least determined not to be. A rogue pigeon watched the shoppers with a bemused eye from the railings, seeking out crumbs of sandwich or crisps.

I shouldn't be here, thought Gabriel, *certainly not with Bose*. She had met Abu Mujahid three times before and there was a chance he would recognise her. But it was a small chance, and one worth taking.

She saw DS Carter, the silver-haired man who had sat at the briefing, walking down the steps from the pedestrian bridge above, chatting with well-rehearsed ease to a much younger woman whose ebony hair was tied in a pony tail. A slim white man in a baseball cap, blue jacket and carrying a red holdall stepped in front of Gabriel and Bose, compelling them to slow down. They walked behind the man, Gabriel forcing herself to look disinterested and bored as she took in every detail of every face in the crowd around her.

Gabriel had been to St Pancras station only three or four times since it had been turned into London's rail link to mainland Europe, and each time she was amazed how much this tatty old station had been transformed. Gone were the tired platforms, grimy Victorian arches and the decades of neglect – in their place was clean red brick, wooden floors and steel walkways. There was a cockiness about the place, an echo of the swagger of the Victorian engineers who put up this vast cathedral to the industrial age in iron, brick and glass.

The man in the baseball cap drew her eyes. There was something about his walk that dragged her thoughts back into the moment. He was limping, but that wasn't it. Was it one of her team maybe? And then he half-turned to the display boards above their head that indicated platforms for the next few trains. Gabriel watched as if in slow motion as his profile came into focus just five or six feet away. A sharp nose poking out from the dark glasses. A length of red beard. A haggard cheek.

And then, two years of anger, of frustration, of disbelief swept through her. Abu Mujahid? Her hand reached for her pocket and pulled out her phone. He hadn't seen her. He didn't know she was there. Maybe he wouldn't recognise her. She needed to attract the attention of the spotter with them, who had stepped into an organic snack bar to their right and was out of sight. She stopped, suddenly, and Bose collided into her.

'Sorry, ma'am,' Bose said, too loud and far too much like a police officer. The man turned and stared. And as he did, there was no doubt. It was Abu Mujahid. His cool eyes looked straight at Gabriel – boring through her skull into her brain. For a moment, for the tiniest fraction of a second, as a flicker of recognition passed across his face, the universe came to a stop. There was no sound. No movement. No people. No air. Just the two of them. Gabriel felt she could hear his heartbeat, the sound of his blinking and the rustle of his shirt.

'Shit,' said Bose, breaking the spell. The world turned back to normal and the sounds of the station filled Gabriel's ears once more. Abu Mujahid flicked his head around and launched himself into a limping run away from them and towards a row of shops in the centre of the station.

'Bose – call for backup. Those two.' She pointed to DS Carter and his colleague, who were still on the pedestrian bridge. They would both be armed and while they were not trained to the same level as a CT special firearms team, they were permitted to use their weapons in extreme circumstances. Abu Mujahid was twenty or thirty metres ahead. She started after him. 'Stop. Police,' she screamed, waving her badge as she ran. Pedestrians around her stopped and gawped but did nothing.

#

Gabriel knew she wasn't as fit as she should be, but she was in better shape than Bose, who seemed to be one hundred miles behind her. Abu Mujahid wasn't in great form either – his right leg seemed to be injured and he was making slow progress. What a great police chase this was turning out to be,

Gabriel thought as she began to lose her breath. Two middle-aged women and an invalid. It was hardly *Starsky & Hutch*.

He had staggered past the departure hall and was heading towards the exit on the King's Cross side of the station. Panic swelled up in her chest. Was he about to get away? Where the hell was the support?

The sight of a middle-aged woman pelting through the station in pursuit of a limping man was turning heads. A family stopped and pointed, and their small child laughed. *Oh, sod off*, she thought, panting louder.

Her phone rang. It was Bose. Gabriel slammed the set against her ear where it rubbed awkwardly as she ran.

'Where are you?' she panted into the receiver.

'Coming round the other side. I've alerted the surveillance team – they should be with you soon.'

'Thank Christ.' She hung up. Abu Mujahid was just a few metres from the exit – a dark window of night that seemed to be peering into this brightly lit world of brick, wood and glass. And then she spotted DS Carter and the officer with the pony tail sprinting towards him along the same arcade, pinning him off. Abu Mujahid saw them then sidestepped into a sushi restaurant.

Gabriel reached the doors of the shop at the same time as the two officers and panted: '…in here.'

The three of them paused at the doorway to catch their breath and get their bearings.

The DS introduced himself. '…and this is DC Barker.' His colleague nodded a hello at Gabriel.

The restaurant was part of a chain offering a pseudo-Japanese eating experience. Diners sat in cheerful booths alongside a conveyor belt with garish plates stacked with rice, sushi and suspicious large balls that could be desserts, but which always reminded Gabriel of testicles.

'Have you had sight of a weapon, ma'am?' asked Carter.

'No, but assume he's armed,' Gabriel wheezed.

The few customers in the restaurant moved to the entrance,

their faces bewildered, startled and scared. Gabriel beckoned them to get out.

Carter stayed by the door and spoke quietly into his radio while Barker crept forward, looking into the booths. The walls of each booth were high enough to hide a crouching man.

The second booth was clear. Then the third. Barker signalled back to Carter, who advanced, handgun raised.

Barker walked towards the next booth; Gabriel followed a couple of metres in her wake. She knew that was against protocol. She knew she should give Barker space to do her job. But right now, she didn't care.

Barker paused for a second, glanced around the restaurant to locate Carter and then stepped in front of the fourth booth. Abu Mujahid was crouched in the corner, his knife held against the neck of a young man – aged maybe seventeen – whose pointed face was too pale and whose eyes were wide with terror. Two boys, perhaps a little younger, were frozen in their seats opposite. *More innocents*, thought Gabriel.

'Drop the knife. Now.' Barker's voice was clear and commanding.

Gabriel moved closer. Abu Mujahid wore a tight white T-shirt under his anorak and blue jacket – tight enough to show he was not wearing an explosive vest.

'Jack – put the knife down.' The words left Gabriel's mouth before she realised she had spoken. Abu Mujahid stared at her, but this time there was no moment of stillness. He was shaking, breathing hard, and his face was flushed.

'Final warning. Put down the knife,' said Barker as she levelled her gun at Abu Mujahid's expressionless face, two metres away.

At that, Abu Mujahid turned his face to look at Gabriel. Was it her imagination or was there a flicker of amusement on his face?

'Let me walk out of here, or the kid dies.' Abu Mujahid's voice was unwavering. 'Or do you want another life on your hands?'

Gabriel looked again at the young man's eyes. They were brown. Like Isobel Harris's eyes.

Carter was standing behind her to her left, Barker was in front to her right. Neither had a clear shot, no chance of avoiding the young man.

'Another kid in the firing line then, Jack?' said Gabriel, struggling to keep her voice steady. 'That's usually your style, isn't it? Sacrificing children to save your own life? The ones who can't fight back? Or old ladies maybe.'

Abu Mujahid's grey eyes glittered coldly across the booth. He didn't move.

'I wondered how you live with yourself, Jack? I mean, I'm sure you've come up with some justification for murdering Isobel Harris. And the Muslims in Syria who did not support your cause, and the women and girls you used as sexual slaves and who you raped. I'm sure you've come up with a way that helps you to sleep at night. But I notice you're still alive, Jack? You've not opted for martyrdom? Are you a coward, Jack? It kind of looks like it from here.'

Again, no movement. *What are you doing, Sophie?* The voice in her head was panicky and fast. The teenager in Abu Mujahid's grip was staring at her, unbelieving.

'Does it annoy you, Jack, that you've been caught by a copper? And a woman at that? You're not so keen on women, are you, Jack? Not so keen on me? Tell you something for nothing. The feeling's mutual, Jack.'

She stepped closer. She was now four feet from him. Just out of reach of his knife. She sensed Carter moving to the left to get a better line of sight. She needed to keep Abu Mujahid distracted and busy.

'Do you actually still believe in anything, Jack? After what you've done? Do you still believe in a god or the Prophet? You don't seem keen to join him.' And then, before Gabriel had time to react, Abu Mujahid flung himself forward, one hand pushing the face of the young boy to one side, the other – still grasping the sushi knife he'd grabbed from the chef's table – stretching out towards her. Gabriel flinched back, the knife jabbing now just inches from her cheek.

'You fucking bitch.' It was more of a snarl than a yell. And before Gabriel had time to absorb the words, to register that finally he'd spoken to her, the thunder of gunfire was in her ears and her head and her guts. Abu Mujahid dropped like a puppet, his head falling on the conveyor belt amid the red, yellow and grey ringed plates of food, his blood trickling from the wound in his stomach onto the moving dishes of rice and fish. Gabriel looked down. Abu Mujahid's blood was splattered over her shirt and hands.

Barker pushed Gabriel out of the way and grabbed the boy.

Abu Mujahid was moaning and twitching, his flailing arms trying to staunch the flow of blood from his stomach.

'Good shot,' said Gabriel.

'Not really, ma'am,' said Carter. 'I was aiming for his chest.'

Gabriel stared, then walked away, out of the restaurant, and back into the concourse where her colleagues were shepherding curious passers-by from the restaurant entrance.

Bose ran up, panting. 'Ma'am, did they get him?'

Gabriel stared at Bose's dark, concerned eyes, conscious of the sweat pouring off her own body, and for the first time in hours, or was it days, she allowed herself to smile. The smile came from deep within her. 'We got him, Eva, we got him.'

DAY 22

Wednesday

Westminster, London

The silence swept through the stone pillars and wooden chairs like a wind. Gabriel sat in her freshly pressed dress uniform towards the back of the small congregation, away from the gaze of politicians and the TV cameras. Ahead, she could see the new prime minister's grey head bowed in conspicuous prayer, close to him the plum jacket of Lesley Hogarth, whose bobbed hair flicked from side to side as she looked around the Abbey. Next to her was a woman with dyed red hair whom Gabriel did not recognise.

Tennant was there too, sat in full uniform with the commissioner, a few places from the mayor of London, the Leader of the Opposition and the Shadow Home Secretary. All had come up for the public display of grief and reconciliation. Around her were the families of the victims of the last two weeks, some with dead, numb eyes, many sobbing.

The service was billed as multi-faith and they had been addressed by Muslim, Jewish and Sikh leaders as well as the Dean of Westminster. The colourless voice of the Dean echoed through the Abbey to mark the end of the two-minute silence. There were more prayers, then they rose and trudged out into the drizzle.

Gabriel kept to the back while the PM laid the first wreath at the Abbey's Innocent Victims' memorial: a circular slab of stone set in the ground outside the west door, inscribed with a line from Lamentations – *Is it nothing to you all you who pass by*. The line had puzzled Gabriel when she passed the memorial on the way in. It seemed bitter, challenging and angry – a strange choice, but perhaps more honest than the platitudes found on many memorials, Gabriel thought as she watched the wreaths being placed around the stone.

She caught Tennant's eye, who smiled thinly and continued talking to the Home Secretary. A quiet voice made her turn.

It was the girl who had lost her family at Chilton Park, Zahra. Gabriel froze inside. The last time she had seen her on that television interview, she had appeared to be still suffering from shock. Gabriel knew enough of the grieving process to foresee that shock would have turned to rage.

'It's Zahra, isn't it?'

The girl nodded.

'Once again, I'm sorry for your loss.'

The girl nodded again. She looked like she was struggling for words. Gabriel steeled herself for an onslaught. But instead, the voice was quiet and calm. 'That day, I asked you a question. Do you remember?'

Once again, the image of Isobel Harris came to Gabriel's mind. Something in her eyes maybe. 'I remember.'

The girl continued. 'The liaison woman who came round. She was good. She told me what had happened to the man who killed my father and brother. I wanted to be pleased he was dead. But it didn't work out like that.'

The blast of a siren made Gabriel jump. An ambulance flew past, lights flashing, and barged its way through the cars queuing at the lights in Parliament Square.

'They just kept on coming. The man who murdered them, he was killed. But they came back. At Trafalgar Square. And

346

Leeds. And Wembley. They don't seem to stop. Each time it doesn't get better, it gets worse. And you people, the police, the authorities, the politicians,' she waved a hand towards the group surrounding the mayor, 'don't seem to be able to stop them. Maybe you can't. But they're feeding off each other, whipping each other into greater evil. And people like her don't help.'

She nodded in the direction of Lesley Hogarth, who stood next to the red-haired woman, earnestly engaged in conversation with a thin man wearing a turban.

The girl went on. 'She – and her kind – they feed all this.' She waved towards the memorial. 'For their own ends. They encourage it. Sometimes subtle, sometimes so in your face that you don't believe it. But always for their own ends. So this, the same question. Will we be safe?'

Gabriel could think of nothing meaningful to say, nothing to offer comfort to this angry, terrified, devastated child.

'We're trying. We're trying really hard, Zahra. There's a sickness out there. It's rare, we know that. It doesn't affect many. Most people stand up to it. Most people fight it. And when it gets hold, we do everything we can to stop it, to neutralise and, yes, to make it safe. As safe as we can. Look, let's meet, let's talk. I'll get your details from the liaison officer – we've a lot to talk about.'

Zahra nodded and walked off to a man who Gabriel assumed was her father.

Her phone vibrated. It was a message from Tennant. It said simply: *Pub?*

#

Westminster, London
It was the first time in two years that Tennant had bought Gabriel a drink – the last time had been during the Isobel Harris inquiry. They sat at a round wooden table in the corner of a Sparrow and Goat wine bar.

'Bloody stupid name for a bar,' said Gabriel as Tennant handed over a pint of lager. 'It's a vegan beer, apparently.'

'Thanks, boss.' She paused. 'What the hell is a vegan beer?'

'Chris has just become vegan, so sadly I could answer that in full. But I won't. It's a bloody pain though. Cheers.'

They clinked their glasses and spent a moment sipping. Gabriel flicked her eyes at the TV on the wall. A news presenter was standing outside Downing Street. The PM's press conference was already overdue.

'God, that tastes like badger piss,' said Tennant. 'What did you make of the service?'

'About as good as you'd expect. A nice show of solidarity for the families, a nice photo shoot for the politicians.'

'They're not as bad as that, Sophie.' They drank in silence. Then, 'How is Abu Mujahid?'

'Conscious and sulky,' said Gabriel. 'Doctors say he will make a full recovery, but he's not well enough for a full interview yet. Can't imagine he'll be that forthcoming once he's on his feet. But we've got enough on him. DNA traces in Rebecca Gladstone's flat put him at the scene of her murder. His DNA is all over Tanvir Mirza's dead body. We've got him buying and taking ownership of the two drones, the explosives, the flat…'

'We thought that last time. Don't get overconfident.'

'It's different, boss,' said Gabriel.

'Maybe.' He took another sip and winced. 'I'm putting you up for something for this, you know. Every sodding medal and commendation I can think of.'

Gabriel reddened.

Tennant said: 'I was watching the video of the two gunmen outside Wembley. The first, Muhid, was clear-cut. He had the rifle out; he was seconds away from opening fire. But Asad – I'm not so sure.'

'What do you mean?' said Gabriel.

'Watch it again. He had an opportunity to fire. He didn't. He waited. For about five seconds. He only put his hand in the bag after he'd been cornered and warned. And he wasn't in any hurry about that either.'

'Second thoughts? And then suicide by cop?' said Gabriel.

'Maybe,' said Tennant. 'If he was hell-bent on martyrdom, maybe it was easier just to let events run their course. But I struggle, even after all this time, to understand what makes these people tick, what makes them accept death so willingly, and value human life so little.'

'Boss, I think you're overanalysing things. Normal, well-adjusted people don't do this kind of thing. You can't get into the heads of these people.'

'You did.' They drank on. The TV behind the bar was showing the build-up to the Downing Street press conference. A lectern was waiting in the street.

Gabriel watched the screen in silence. 'What do you make of Ben Thomas's appointment?' she said eventually.

'He was in the right place at the right time. He's in tune with the mood music out there. The days of moderation and compromise seem a long time ago. Just look at the opposition. And who'd want to be prime minister right now?'

'She would, for a starter,' said Gabriel. The TV was showing archive footage of Lesley Hogarth's own press conference from a week ago.

A cry of 'Wanker' from the corner of the pub made both turn around. A heckler was shouting at the TV. Ben Thomas began to speak and the barman turned up the volume.

'…and the violence and riots of the last few weeks have shown us that the old British values of trust, of honesty and fair play can be so easily exploited by those determined to bring terror to our streets. We must send a message to those who would destroy us. No more. Not here. Yes, we are merciful, and generous, but if you bring war, then you will be met by steel, by closed door and by hardened hearts. We will be resolute in protecting our own – and in drawing a line against attacks on our nation, our culture, our children. This is why our first priority will be to pass the Freedom Bill…

'We promise strength and stability and a tough line against extremists. And I say to the opposition who are cosying up to terrorist sympathisers like Ishmail Sherif and others, it's time to decide which side you are on. Britain's? Or would you rather surrender to those who would seek to destroy us…'

Tennant looked at Gabriel and shook his head sorrowfully. Gabriel pretended to stick her fingers down her throat.

'What did I say? Whipping it up again,' said Tennant.

Gabriel said nothing and the pair drank on in silence.

#

In a bar just four hundred metres away, Nina O'Brien was watching the same press conference. The Freedom Bill was a start, a great start, as was leveraging Hogarth into the Home Office. Now she needed to make the most of her. But the work had only just begun. She raised a glass to the TV and silently toasted the new prime minister.

ACKNOWLEDGEMENTS

We are hugely grateful to everyone who was so generous with their time and support during the writing of *The Sleep of Reason*. In particular, a massive thank you to Sabin Khan for her perceptive insights and counsel, Celia Hayley for sharpening up the story, Rebecca Levene for her wisdom, Ross Dickinson for his forensic eye for detail, and Colin Freeman and Josh Rowley for feedback on early drafts.

All the characters in this book, good and bad, are fictional. However, Mark is grateful for the inspiration from outstanding senior counter terrorism colleagues Lucy D'Orsi, Terri Nicholson, Theresa Breen.

If you want to find out more about the causes of hate crime and extremism, the campaign group Hope Not Hate's research is essential reading.

Naturally, all errors of fact and omission in this book are our own.

We are most deeply indebted to our agent Elly James from hhb agency for her encouragement and sage advice, and to our editor Cari Rosen and her colleagues at Legend Press for helping us to take our manuscript from draft through to publication with such skill and enthusiasm.

Most of all though we want to thank Helena and Ali for their love, support, patience, insight and inspiration.